"Did you go to bed with Adam?" Nick had asked.

And Fern had wept silent tears that she knew had betrayed her.

"He doesn't want you, you know," he had told her, softly, gently almost, kinder to her now than he had ever been. If he had shown her such compassion . . . would things have been any different?

Adam was her brother-in-law; that was all, she had reminded herself fiercely. Her stepbrother-in-law. Nothing more. Not now, not once . . . not ever.

And she was Nick's wife . . . FOR BETTER FOR WORSE

PENNY JORDAN

was born in Lancashire, England, and now lives with her husband in a beautiful fourteenth-century house in rural Cheshire. Hers is a success almost as breathtaking as the exploits of the characters she so skillfully and knowingly portrays. Penny's novels have been translated into more than twenty languages and have sold over fifty million copies worldwide.

Some of Penny's previous novels include:
LOVE'S CHOICES
STRONGER THAN YEARNING
POWER PLAY
SILVER
THE HIDDEN YEARS
LINGERING SHADOWS

PENNY JORDAN

FOR BETTER FOR WORSE

Harlequin Books

TORONTO • NEW YORK • LONDON
AMSTERDAM • PARIS • SYDNEY • HAMBURG
STOCKHOLM • ATHENS • TOKYO • MILAN
MADRID • WARSAW • BUDAPEST • AUCKLAND

PROLOGUE

As FERN saw Nick walk into the kitchen, her stomach muscles tensed.

She had heard him arrive from upstairs, had witnessed the impatience with which he had slewed the car to a halt and climbed out, slamming the door, and then glancing up at the house.

She had stepped back from the window then, an automatic and very betraying gesture, pausing as she caught sight of herself in her dressing-table mirror. She looked strained and tired, her eyes empty and lifeless...as empty and lifeless as her marriage to Nick?

Abruptly she had turned away from the mirror and hurried downstairs.

It was her own fault that Nick was in a bad mood, of course. She should not have raised the subject of how much time he was spending working last night. He had always hated her 'interfering in his life', as he called it. She had learned early on in her marriage that Nick loathed any form of restraint, even the mildest hint of criticism.

What was wrong with her? he had demanded to know last night. Didn't she realise how fortunate she was, how many women would gladly change places with her?

'You're my wife,' he had told her. 'Nothing can change that.'

A promise, or a threat?

She tensed now, guiltily trying to suppress her rebellious thoughts. Nick was right. She *was* lucky to be married to him, especially after...

As he came towards her, her tension increased, her muscles locking. Automatically she looked away from him, pain a hard-edged lump in her throat. Nick was a very handsome man, and yet these days she found that sometimes she could hardly bear to look at him.

'I love you...I need you, and I'm never, ever going to let you go,' he had told her when he'd proposed to her, and she, swept off her feet, totally overwhelmed by his intensity, his insistence, dizzy and bemused by the speed with which he had taken over her life, had been unable to resist the pressure he had put on her.

Then she had been flattered; reassured; filled with gratitude and joy by his words.

Then ...

Now, even with the width of the kitchen between them, she could smell the scent of another woman's sex on him.

Fastidiously she increased the distance between them.

Was Nick having another affair? Last night he had denied it. And she had wanted him to deny it.

5

She had invested so much in this marriage, given so much to it. Too much?

How could she stay with him if he was having another affair, and yet how could she leave? Marriage was a lifetime commitment, and when problems arose within it they had to be worked at...or ignored? Her heart lurched. Was she really such a coward?

'What's wrong with you?' Nick demanded sourly. 'Not still sulking, are you?'

Protectively Fern turned to one side, reaching for the kettle, letting the straight swath of her hair swing across her face, obscuring her expression.

'I've got a bit of news for you,' Nick told her.

The surliness had gone from his voice now. It was lighter, tri-umphant...gloating almost. Her tension increased, but Fern suppressed it, concealing her reaction from him as instinctively as she had concealed her face. Inwardly her soul ached at what she was doing; for what their relationship had become.

'It seems my saintly stepbrother is planning to buy Broughton House.'

Fern's fingers tensed on the kettle-handle. She was glad she had her back to Nick.

'Now I wonder what *he* wants with a place that size. All those bed-rooms. A real *family* place...'

Fern could hear the ugly note of triumph quite clearly in his voice now. 'Pity he hasn't got a *real* family to put in it, isn't it? Or maybe he's thinking of acquiring one.

'What is it, Fern? I haven't said something to upset you, have I? Oh, I forgot—you've always been pretty keen on Broughton House yourself, haven't you? You were always up there at one time...or so you claimed...'

'I visited old Mrs Broughton occasionally, that's all,' Fern told him quietly.

Why did he insist on doing this to her? He knew as well as she did that there was no need...no point... He knew how bitterly she regretted what she had done.

'Did you go to bed with him, Fern?' he had asked her. 'Did you?' And she had wept silent tears which she knew had betrayed her.

'He doesn't want you, you know,' he had told her, softly, gently almost, kinder to her now when he had the least reason to be than he had ever been. If he had shown her that kindness before, that com-passion...would things have been any different?

How many men would still have wanted to remain married to her after that? Not many. A husband's infidelity was one thing; a wife's was some-thing very different.

'You're my wife,' he had told her when she had broken down and asked him why he wanted her to stay. 'Marriage is forever, Fern. Isn't that what your parents have always told you?'

She was his wife. He wanted their marriage...wanted her...needed her, so why was there this emptiness between them, this lack of harmony...this ugliness which eroded her pride and her self-respect?

'I'm going up to have a shower,' Nick told her.

To wash another woman's scent off his body? Didn't he realise that it was too late?

The kettle boiled and switched itself off.

So Adam was thinking of buying Broughton House...and of getting married.

Even though she was prepared for it—her body tensed against it—the pain was still sharp enough to make her catch her breath.

Adam was her brother-in-law; that was all, she reminded herself fiercely. Her *stepbrother-in-law*. Nothing more. Not now, not once...not *ever*.

Eleanor saw the advertisement while she was sitting in her dentist's waiting-room flicking through a surprisingly current copy of *Country Life*.

It was the photograph that first caught her eye; the front of the house faced south and it had been photographed on a sunny day so that the stone walls were washed to a soft warm gold, the light glinting on the uneven leaded panes of the dormer attic windows.

The house looked settled, solid, permanent, safe and reassuring, offering a refuge from life's turbulence...offering comfort.

She stared at the photograph for so long that at first she didn't hear the receptionist call out her name.

Later, when she got home and discovered that in her haste to respond to the girl's second clipped summons she had stuffed the magazine into her bag, she stifled her feelings of guilt and put the magazine down on her desk, intending to throw it away. But for some reason she didn't... For some reason, later on in the day, taking a break from a particularly difficult translation of some Spanish documents for one of her clients, as she drank her cup of tea she found herself flicking through the magazine again, stopping when she reached the half-page ad featuring the house, reading the written details below the photograph briefly, her real at-tention focused on the photograph itself, on the warmth the house seemed to give off, the security...the sanctuary...

Sanctuary... The word dug into her conscience like a sharp thorn. What need did she have of any sanctuary? A happy second marriage, a successful career...two well-adjusted sons. She was one of the luckiest people she knew; everyone said so...

Everyone...

'They want us...they want us... *They want us*!' Zoe exulted, breaking free of Ben's arm to perform a brief pirouette of triumph, laughing up at him as he caught hold of her, restraining her and shaking his head.

'Don't get too excited,' he warned her. 'This is only the first step. Now we've got to keep our fingers crossed that they can find the right place.'

He was frowning now with the seriousness which had initially attracted her to him and which sometimes she found heartachingly hard to fathom.

Why did he always seem to fear that life was waiting to deliver a blow? Why couldn't he simply share her exultation? But she was being unfair; she knew that in his own way he did, and that, although he would die rather than admit it, this first step down the road they had plotted out for themselves was intensely important to him.

'Benedict Fraser, Restaurateur of the Year,' Zoe crowed, refusing to allow him to suppress her exhilaration. 'I can see it now. "Benedict Fraser, ably aided by his ravishingly attractive and capable business manager, Ms Zoe Clinton, at their country house restaurant... quite definitely *the* success story of the year..."'

'Hang on. We still have to find our country house,' Benedict warned her. 'Or at least our backer has to...'

'Our backer... I still can't believe it's all happening. And all through you stepping in at the last minute and doing the catering for the Hargreaveses' wedding.'

'I'd never have done it if you hadn't pushed me into it. Wedding breakfasts aren't really my thing, and having to step in at the last minute like that... It's all down to you.'

'It's not down to either of us,' Zoe corrected him firmly. 'We did it together. Both of us. We make a good team, Ben.' She darted him a brief look and added softly, 'In bed and out of it...'

As she had known it would, her reference to the sexual aspect of their relationship made him slightly embarrassed. For a man who was such a skilled and sensitive lover, he was oddly shy and uneasy about discussing sex. His upbringing, perhaps?

She shook her head, pushing the thought aside, not wanting it to spoil her own pleasure in their day.

'How long do you think it will take Clive Hargreaves to find a suitable property?'

'I don't know. But he's obviously already looking. I saw a pile of brochures on his desk when we were signing the contract.'

Zoe gave an ecstatic sigh. 'We're finally on our way. Nothing can stop us now...nothing. It's all there waiting for us...everything we've wanted. Our own restaurant and the option of developing it into a small country hotel. You as the chef—*the chef*—and me managing the administration side of things. Just the way we dreamed.'

'The way *you* dreamed. I would never have let myself imagine...' He broke off, shaking his head. 'I still can't believe it's all actually happening. This chance means so much to me, Zoe.' He stopped walking and looked at her. 'I don't think you realise...'

'Yes, I do,' she interrupted him softly. 'I know just what it means to you to have your own place, Ben. I know how important it is to you.'

'Providing nothing goes wrong...'

'Nothing will go wrong. What *could* go wrong? The contracts are signed, and we're on our way. Stop worrying... *Nothing* will go wrong—I promise you.'

CHAPTER ONE

ELEANOR suppressed a small exclamation of impatience, glancing at her watch as the traffic came to another halt. London was impossible at this time in the morning. Especially when the streets were still grey and wet, the sky sullenly threatening and what blossom there was beginning to show on the trees battered by the sharp east wind.

The traffic moved—inches rather than yards, and she counted slowly to ten, trying to relax her tense muscles. She was going to be late arriving at her office, and she had an appointment at nine-thirty. A potential new client. She gnawed anxiously at her bottom lip, recalling the interview she had had recently with her accountant.

They were still making a profit, he had told her, but their costs were rising; the rent on their offices had doubled in the last eighteen months and was set to rise again. All over the city, peripheral businesses such as theirs were beginning to suffer from the cutbacks made by the conglomerates and multinationals which used them.

The tidal flood of extra and extremely profitable business she and Louise had seen in the last years of the Eighties was now ebbing away very fast and the anticipated upsurge in business they had expected from the new ties with Europe had been a trickle rather than a flood.

The office, which had been so convenient when she still lived in the flat, before she and Marcus had married and she and the boys had moved into his elegant Chelsea house, was now an increasingly tension-inducing drive across London.

Why was it that wet weather always made the traffic slower? she wondered irritably, frowning. She had intended to make an early start this morning, but then Tom had overslept and come down late to breakfast and Gavin had 'lost' his football kit, so that by the time she had actually managed to chivvy them plus their belongings into the car she had already been running behind schedule.

Marcus had already had his breakfast and started work in his study. He had frowned up at her as she opened the door, putting down the brief he had been working on. Even now, after three years of being together plus almost a year of marriage, her heart still turned over when she saw him. A ridiculous reaction in a woman of thirty-eight going on thirty-nine, surely? And to think that until she had met him she had been a woman who prided herself on her common-sense approach to life, on her awareness of the errors of judgements and the misplaced romantic ideals which had led to the break-up of her first marriage.

Until she had seen the brief in Marcus's hand, she had almost been tempted to ask him if he could run the boys to school; the school was closer to his chambers in Lincoln's Inn than it was to her office. But, despite the intensity of their love, a part of her remained brittly conscious that Tom and Gavin were *her* responsibility, just as Vanessa was his.

Vanessa ... She could feel her stomach muscles tensing as she thought about Marcus's daughter.

It troubled her that she was finding it so difficult to establish a good relationship with her. She was after all Marcus's child ... his daughter. Vanessa's parents had been divorced for several years before she, Eleanor, had become involved in Marcus's life. But whenever Vanessa came to stay with them Eleanor felt uncomfortable and on edge. She had even begun to feel ill-at-ease when she and Marcus made love when Vanessa was there.

Part of the trouble was that the Chelsea house had never been designed for two adults and three children. Marcus had bought it after his first marriage broke down; for a single or even a married couple without children it was the ideal London home, small but elegant with its downstairs kitchen-cum-living-room and Marcus's study plus the dining-room, its first-floor drawing-room, which was spacious enough for the kind of parties a highly successful barrister might need to give. There was nothing wrong either with the two good-sized bedrooms, each with its own private bathroom, unless of course you happened to have three children to squash into that one spare double bedroom.

The bedroom which, Vanessa had told Eleanor coolly but very challengingly, had always been hers when she visited her father.

Which meant that her sons had to share the double room next to theirs and then be squashed up together in the small stuffy attic bedroom, which had never ever been intended to be anything other than a temporary emergency bedroom, whenever Vanessa came to stay.

She loved Marcus so much and she knew he loved her, but he had lived on his own for almost seven years before they met; he had been used to a quiet, well-ordered way of life, without the kind of tensions which now seemed to be disrupting their lives.

The obvious answer was to move, to find a larger house which would accommodate them all comfortably, give them all room to breathe...give all three children their all-important personal space.

The trouble was that, in London, the size of house they needed would be so exorbitantly expensive that it was pointless even thinking about moving.

Her business made a reasonable profit, and as a leading litigation barrister, a Q.C., Marcus earned good fees, but living in London was expensive. Her ex-husband had remarried almost immediately after their divorce and had a second young family, and was simply not in a position to continue to contribute to Gavin and Tom's education—at eleven and thirteen respectively both of them still had several years of education ahead of them, especially if, as she hoped, they both went on to university.

Her tension eased as the traffic suddenly started to move.

It was just the miserable weather that was making her feel so on edge, she reassured herself. At this time of the year, everyone had had enough of cold and damp and was looking forward to some sun.

She and Marcus had hoped to spend a week with friends in Italy in May, but one of Marcus's court cases had been brought forward and now it looked as though their week in Tuscany would have to be cancelled.

As she turned into the underground car park beneath the block that housed her office, the sleet started.

It was just gone half-past nine, she noted as she locked the car and headed quickly for the lift.

The office block was a modern one, centrally situated in the heart of the city and a good catchment area for their business. Eleanor and Louise had agonised for weeks on whether or not to take the lease. It had been expensive even then, and in those days neither of them had been sure of what volume of work they could expect.

That they had met at all had been pure chance. They had literally bumped into each other when Eleanor had been delivering some translations she had just completed for a large firm of importers.

Louise had been there on a similar errand and, once they had discovered that their language skills complemented rather than competed with one another, it hadn't taken long for them to decide to pool those skills and set up business as a formal partnership.

It had been a decision which had paid off well; their reputation had spread by word of mouth and within four years of becoming partners they were successful and well known enough to feature in a rash of magazine and newspaper articles about the emergence of the successful businesswoman of the Eighties.

In those days both of them had been single, Eleanor with a bad marriage and an even worse divorce behind her and only too thankful to fling herself head-first into the demands of establishing a new career, not just because she needed the money, but because it also offered her a much needed solace for her wounded pride and battered self-esteem; and Louise, eight years her junior, just emerging from the trauma of ending an intense and destructive relationship with a married man.

Physically so very opposite—she tall and fair, quiet and restrained in both her thoughts and her actions, Louise small, brunette and impulsively vivacious—they had shared a common need to heal the wounds life had inflicted on them, which had bonded them together in their determination to make their partnership work.

And it had worked... *Had* worked? Eleanor frowned as the lift reached her floor, and then shrugged as the doors opened. Had worked and was *still* working, she assured herself firmly.

The office block had originally appealed to both of them because of the brightness of its new design. Built around an atrium, it had a spacious, open feel to it which was emphasised by the atrium itself.

Today, though, the marble and chrome seemed to give off a chilly air that made Eleanor shiver slightly.

They had probably turned down the heating again, she reflected as she headed for her office. All the tenants had been complaining about the rapid escalation not just in their rent but in their overheads as well. As she glanced down into the atrium itself she noticed that some of the plants looked over-green and slightly shiny, more as though they were artificial than real, she reflected with distaste, her attention caught by the sterile perfection of a white lily.

Such plants did not belong under London's sleet-laden grey skies, or imprisoned here, forced into life beneath their covering of glass and heat.

Claire, their receptionist, looked up with a relieved smile as Eleanor walked into the foyer.

She and Louise had chosen the décor for their offices with great care, calling on an interior designer friend of Eleanor's for confirmation of their choice, but what had seemed energetic and appropriate in the Eighties now looked brash and slightly harsh, as inappropriate for the grey skies of recession as the plants in the atrium were for the grey skies of London perhaps.

'Monsieur Colbert has arrived,' Claire told her. 'I offered him coffee but he refused.'

Thanking her, Eleanor went through into her own office, removing her coat and checking her appearance quickly before hurrying through into the room she and Louise used for negotiating with clients.

Pierre Colbert was French, with business connections which brought him regularly to London and which took him just as regularly to all the other major European cities. He acted as an agent for several large clothing designers and wholesalers, the type who were two steps down from the 'named' designers and two up from the general run of high street suppliers.

His business, if they could secure it, would prove an extremely valuable addition to their portfolio. Eleanor had heard via another client that he was unhappy with his existing translators, and she had made a tentative approach to him suggesting that it might be worthwhile their getting together.

She had been warned that as well as liking to get his pound of flesh he was also rather difficult to deal with, and, as she walked into the office and saw the impatience with which he was regarding her, her heart sank a little.

She didn't show her feelings, though, giving him a calm smile and extending her hand.

'I'm sorry I'm late,' she apologised. 'The traffic...'

'The English do not know how to drive,' he interrupted her brusquely. 'In Paris we have traffic; here in London you have chaos...'

'Perhaps you would like a cup of coffee,' Eleanor offered, side-stepping his aggression.

'Coffee?' He smiled sourly. 'I think not.'

Was he deliberately trying to goad her into a response, Eleanor wondered, or did he simply not realise how rude he was being? She had met other men like him, men who were plainly uncomfortable with and antagonistic towards women in business, and she had developed her own method of dealing with them.

Once, in the aftermath of a long, lazy afternoon of lovemaking, Marcus had told her with sleepy pleasure as he ran his hand lingeringly over her warm, relaxed flesh, pausing to cup her breast and slowly caress the still erect peak of her nipple, 'I love this peace you always carry with you, Nell. It's such a pleasure to be with a woman who is so calm and secure. It makes it so easy to love you.'

It had been shortly after that that he had proposed to her.

'No, we don't seem to have developed the skill of making really good coffee, do we?' she agreed with a smile. Another woman might have balked at using such placatory tactics, Eleanor admitted, but for her they were almost a way of life... peace and calm, good relationships, concord and harmony were important to her. Too important?

'Your coffee, like your bread, is uniquely irreplaceable,' she added, 'although I understand that Marks and Spencer are doing their best. Apparently they are actually importing the flour now from France for their croissants and French bread.'

'They are among your clients?' Pierre Colbert asked her with shrewd interest, dropping his earlier aggression.

Eleanor allowed herself a small surge of relief.

'Some of their suppliers are,' she told him, opening the file she had brought in with her. 'I see from your own client list that you have dealings with design houses in several major European cities, and that they in turn deal with manufacturers in the Far East. The clothes from the design houses you represent will sell best in our small exclusive country-town boutiques.'

'You have done your research well.'

Was that a hint of respect she could see overtaking his earlier churlishness? She hoped so!

Eleanor smiled gently at him, too wise in the ways of business to show her relief.

'I understand that at the moment you use translators domiciled in France, Germany, Italy and Spain. We, of course, could supply all your translation needs here under one roof.'

'As can the other companies I deal with,' he pointed out, watching her.

'True,' Eleanor agreed with another smile. It was going to be hard work persuading him to give them his business, she recognised as she quietly and calmly started to point out to him the advantages of using them.

'Additionally Louise, my partner, specialises in Middle Eastern languages. And Russian.'

'Ah, but remember,' he told her quickly, 'with the break-up of the Soviet Union into various independent states, each will want to revert to its own language.'

'A fact that we have taken into consideration,' Eleanor assured him.

It was true. She and Louise were actively recruiting on to their freelance books experienced translators who were able to work in these newly re-emerging languages.

Quite how she was going to continue to fit this additional commitment to interview and test their freelancers into her existing busy life, Eleanor wasn't sure, but somehow she would have to find a way.

She had tried to make a start on all the application forms this weekend, but it hadn't been easy. For one thing, the only place she had to work was the bedroom she shared with Marcus, and with Vanessa next door, her radio playing at full volume, it had been impossible for her to summon the necessary concentration, even knowing that it was vitally important to the continued success of the business that she and Louise secure an all-important head-start on their rivals in what promised to be the only genuinely expanding field open to them.

They *needed* that business if they were to continue to generate good profits, and yet with the ever-increasing demands on her time that marriage to Marcus had brought, never mind her own desire to have more time to spend personally with him, the actual hours she had left for expanding the company were alarmingly small.

She had already given up her two evening gym sessions and the once-a-month, long, leisurely Sunday lunch she used to share with her oldest woman friend, Jade Fensham; that had had to go because it conflicted with the weekend when Marcus had access to his daughter.

His daughter. She could understand why it was difficult for Vanessa to accept her, but surely it should not be so hard for her to accept Vanessa; she was after all a part of Marcus, and she loved him.

Jade told her she was too idealistic, and she had countered by telling Jade that she was too cynical.

Jade had shrugged those elegant shoulders and narrowed her long green cat's eyes.

'After two marriages and two divorces what do you expect? Take my advice: never, ever expect anything but trouble from a man's children, especially if they're teenage girls.'

The weekend before last, white-faced with a tension-induced migraine, she had asked herself what it was she was doing wrong and why it was that Vanessa was so antagonistic towards her. After all, it wasn't as though *she* was responsible for the break-up of her parents' marriage.

Perhaps Marcus was right. Perhaps she *ought* to try to arrange things so that Tom and Gavin stayed with their father when Vanessa came to stay. At least it would stop the interminable quarrels that seemed to break out when they were all together. Was she being unfair in suspecting that it was Vanessa who deliberately provoked them? It was true that Tom, over-sensitive and too vulnerable, tended to over-react—a legacy of her divorce from his father? But Gavin had a far calmer temperament; phlegmatic and easygoing, he had been a placid baby and was now a placid, sturdily resilient child.

Yes, it would make life easier if they kept them apart, but it wasn't what she had hoped for, what she had planned when she and Marcus had married. She had never assumed that merging their two families would be easy, but neither had she anticipated that her relationship with Vanessa would become so destructive. Her *relationship*? *What* relationship?

The last thing that Vanessa wanted was any kind of relationship with either Eleanor or her sons, but most especially with Eleanor. Sometimes she felt as though she and Vanessa were two rivals locked in a silent and deadly battle for Marcus. And yet the last thing she wanted was for Vanessa to feel that her marriage to Marcus in any way threatened his daughter's position in his life.

In fact *she* had been the one who had suggested to Marcus that he see more of his daughter. It had disturbed her a little, when she and Marcus had first become lovers, to discover how little he saw of his child.

'She's happy with her mother,' Marcus had told her.

'But she needs you in her life as well,' Eleanor had insisted gently.

'You have a husband and children,' she suddenly came out of her brief reverie to hear Pierre Colbert saying to her. 'Does this not affect your work?'

Eleanor refused to react, to allow him to provoke her into becoming defensive.

'I'm a woman, *monsieur*,' she told him quietly. 'And as such I am well used to balancing many demands upon my time.'

She saw from his expression that she had both surprised and amused him, and mentally congratulated herself for not falling into the trap of complaining that he would not have asked her such a question had she been a man. He was a Frenchman, undeniably chauvinistic and no doubt unashamedly proud to be. She would succeed far better with him by emphasising the virtues of her sex rather than by challenging him to accept her as the equal of any man.

She watched him thoughtfully as he smiled at her, and then said shrewdly, 'My partner and I like to think that we offer a very skilled and competitive service, and I believe that you must think so too, *monsieur*, otherwise you would not be here. You are not, I think, a man who need-lessly wastes his time.'

She watched the respect dawn in the clever brown eyes before he looked away from her.

'You are one of several agencies recommended to me,' he told her dismissively. 'It is always wise to consider several options, even though some of them must always be more favourable than others.'

He was standing up, terminating the meeting. Eleanor rose too, still outwardly calm and relaxed, although inwardly she was wryly aware that he would probably prefer not to give them the business. Had she been a man...or French...

As she escorted him to the door, she tried not to dwell on how much they needed the extra income his work would have given them. She had known when he first contacted them that it was extremely unlikely they would get the business. It made her feel a little bit better knowing that she had subtly challenged his initial attitude towards her, drawing respect from him in place of his original hostility.

After she had seen him off the premises, she went back to her office and picked up his file. She needed to put Louise in the picture *vis-à-vis* her meeting with him.

She got up and walked into the foyer. 'Is Louise in her office?' she asked Claire.

'Yes, she's just come in,' the receptionist told her.

Smiling her thanks at her, Eleanor walked across to her partner's office.

Claire watched her enviously. Eleanor was everything she herself longed to be. Attractive, successful, married to a man who exuded an almost magical charisma of sex and power; a man who, although he might be well into his forties, still had such an aura of compelling masculinity about him that he made *her* go weak at the knees. Not that he ever gave her so much as a second look. And even if he had...

Eleanor was so...so nice that she couldn't imagine anyone wanting to hurt her.

Yes, they were an ideal couple, with an ideal relationship; an ideal lifestyle.

Marriage, career, motherhood—Eleanor had them all.

Although she had knocked on Louise's door before going in, her partner obviously hadn't heard her, Eleanor realised as she saw Louise's dark head bent in absorbed concentration over some papers on her desk.

When Eleanor said her name she looked up, startled, quickly shuffling the papers out of sight, an embarrassed, almost furtive look crossing her face.

'Nell, I didn't hear you come in...'

'So I see.' Eleanor grinned at her. 'Planning your summer holidays?'

She had noticed, as Louise shuffled the papers out of sight, the photograph on one of them of a pretty and obviously French château-style farmhouse.

To her surprise a faintly haunted, almost guilty expression flickered through Louise's eyes before she turned her head and confirmed quickly, 'Yes...'

'I just wanted to bring you up to date on my interview with Pierre Colbert. Are you free for lunch?'

Once again Louise looked slightly uncomfortable.

'Er—no, I'm sorry, I'm not. I'm having lunch with Paul...'

Eleanor smiled at her. 'Lucky you,' she told her ruefully. 'I wish my husband could make time to have lunch with me. We're lucky if we manage to share a sandwich together these days.'

She broke off as she realised that Louise wasn't really listening to her.

'Louise, is something wrong?' she asked her quietly.

'No,' Louise assured her quickly.

Too quickly? Eleanor wondered, her intuition suddenly working overtime.

She knew that Louise and Paul had a very turbulent relationship, a relationship which had started while her then new business partner was still nursing wounds from her previous affair, and she was also uneasily aware of how much Paul tended to dominate her partner. He was that kind of man, needing to assert himself or perhaps to assure himself of the superiority of his masculinity by forcing the women in his life to assume an inferior position.

She had become increasingly aware of how often the words 'Paul says' or 'Paul thinks' had begun to preface Louise's comments since the two of them had married, but she had firmly dismissed her own dislike of the man by reminding herself that he was Louise's choice and not hers, and that it was after all just as well that different types of men appealed to different types of women. And besides, if she was honest with herself, didn't her dislike of Paul stem partly from the fact that his manner towards Louise was a little too reminiscent of her own first husband's domineering manner towards her?

Still, if there were problems with the relationship, she would hate to think that Louise did not feel she could confide in her.

She tried again. 'Louise——'

'Look, I must go. I promised to call and see a client before I meet Paul. I really must go, Nell.'

Louise was an adult woman and there was no way she could force her into giving her her confidence if she did not want to, Eleanor reminded herself wryly as she went back to her own office.

The trouble with her was that she had a strong maternal instinct, or so Jade said.

'What you need is to surround yourself with a large brood of children,' Jade had informed her once.

A large brood of children. To compensate for the loneliness of her own solitary childhood. She grimaced. Thirty-eight was no age to start suffering those sort of urges, she told herself.

There were women of course who did have babies at thirty-eight and older. Second families to go with their second husbands.

She and Marcus had discussed having children of their own. She had heard that a new baby was often a successful way of linking together all the tenuous branches of an extended family relationship.

But they had agreed that they did not need to cement their love in that way. It was out of the question in any case. The house wasn't big enough for them all as it was; and with the commitment she had made to the company, plus the extra demands made on her time as Marcus's wife... There were a surprisingly large number of events he was obliged to attend, and of course as his wife she wanted to go with him... to *be* with him.

The trouble was, their lives were so busy, so fast-paced, that despite the fact that they were married, sometimes they had less time to spend together now than they had done in the days when they had first met.

She was discovering within herself an increasing need for more time, more space; for a slower, less frenetic pace of life, one that gave her a chance to appreciate things more. There never seemed to be enough time to enjoy anything any more, to *savour* life's pleasures.

Even their lovemaking had increasingly become rushed and hurried; something they had to make a conscious effort to make time for.

Gone were the days when they could spend the whole afternoon, the whole evening, and even, luxuriously, the whole morning in bed, as they had done in the days before they had married. How much she had enjoyed them, those special intimate hours spent in the privacy of Marcus's house or her flat, hours when they had been completely and blissfully alone.

Now it seemed as though they were never alone.

Did Marcus feel as uncomfortable making love to her with her children under the same roof as she sometimes did with his, or was that something that only women suffered? Or perhaps only women with almost adult teenage stepdaughters.

She hoped that there was nothing wrong in Louise and Paul's relationship. She might not like him, but Louise loved him. He was a wonderful father, she had told Eleanor, almost doting on their two boys and fully involved in every aspect of their lives.

Yes, almost to the point where he was almost deliberately excluding Louise herself from the macho male world he was building around his sons, Eleanor reflected.

Marcus got on well enough with Tom and even better with Gavin, but he simply wasn't the kind of man who enjoyed exclusively male pursuits, and of course he was not after all their father. As Louise herself had rather unnecessarily remarked the other day when she had been contrasting Paul's almost excessive involvement in his sons' lives to Marcus's attitude towards Tom and Gavin.

Unnecessarily and tactlessly... Eleanor frowned, nibbling the nail of her index finger. As a child she had bitten her nails, and as a young adult... a young wife and mother. After her divorce she had told herself that she was going to stop biting her nails, and once she had done so she had told herself that if she could do that she could do anything; and yet here she was, happier and more fulfilled than she had ever been at any other time in her life, reverting to this destructive childhood habit.

What was the *matter* with her? In a month's time she and Marcus would have been married for exactly one year. On the day of their wedding she had been filled with such happiness, such optimism...such confidence.

But then she hadn't realised how difficult it was going to be to integrate their lives together fully, and not just their lives but those of their children as well.

Her phone rang and she reached out to pick up the receiver, her mouth curling into a delighted smile as she heard Marcus's voice on the other end of the line.

'Darling, what a lovely surprise.'

'Eleanor, can you come home? The school's been on the phone. Apparently Tom isn't very well. I'm going to collect him now, but I suspect that it's you he's going to want.'

'Tom? What's wrong with him? Did they say?'

'Don't panic. I doubt that it can be anything very serious, otherwise they'd have rung the hospital, not me. They did try to get in touch with you, apparently, but they were told you were in conference...'

In conference. They must have telephoned while she was with Pierre Colbert, Eleanor recognised. Guilt overwhelmed her. Was she imagining it or had that been irritation she had heard in Marcus's voice? She knew how much he hated being disturbed when he was working, and she was Tom's mother, after all.

She got up, grabbing her coat and bag and hurrying into the outer office. Claire wasn't there so she knocked briefly on Louise's door and walked in.

Louise was on the telephone.

'No, I haven't told her yet. I haven't——' When she looked up and saw her, Louise stared at her for a moment, her face flushing, and then she said quickly into the receiver, 'Look, I must go.'

'I'm sorry to disturb you,' Eleanor apologised. 'I've got to go home. Tom isn't well. He's been sent home from school. Luckily I don't have any appointments...'

Louise wasn't really listening to her, Eleanor realised. Her face was still flushed, and she seemed to be avoiding looking at her. She was uncomfortable with her, Eleanor recognised with a small stab of shock. At any other time she would have instantly queried that recognition, but her concern for Tom and her guilt over not being there, over perhaps even not having recognised earlier that he wasn't well, overrode everything else.

As she drove home, she cursed the traffic, heavy and congested even at this time of day, the smell of petrol and stale air rising chokingly inside her car. The tension which never seemed to totally leave her these days became an insistent demanding tattoo of impatience inside her head.

Although the house possessed a garage it was only large enough for Marcus's car, and irritatingly someone else was already parked outside their house, so that she had to drive halfway down the street before she could find anywhere to stop.

Her hand trembled as she unlocked the door. She hurried in, calling out to Marcus in a low voice.

'In here,' he told her, emerging from his study,

'Tom——?' she demanded quickly, glancing towards the stairs.

'He's in the kitchen,' Marcus told her.

'The kitchen!' Eleanor stared at him, tension and guilt exploding into a sudden surge of anger. Would he be taking this casual, laid-back attitude if it were his child who was sick?

Instantly she suppressed the thought, knowing it to be unfair and shaken that she could even have given birth to it.

Dropping her briefcase in the hall, she hurried into the kitchen. Tom was curled up in a chair in the living area, his attention focused on the flickering images on the television set.

'Tom?'

When he made no response, Eleanor called his name a little louder. Reluctantly he turned to look at her.

He did look pale, she acknowledged, her heart thumping sickeningly. *Why* hadn't she noticed that this morning? She *was* his mother, after all.

'How are you feeling, darling?' she asked him as she hurried over to him and placed her hand against his forehead. He didn't feel particularly hot.

'Sick. I feel sick,' he told her plaintively. 'I told you that this morning...'

Eleanor winced as she heard the accusation in his voice. He had said something about not wanting to go to school but she had put that down to the fact that it was Monday morning and that he was grumpy because he had overslept.

'I was sick after assembly,' he told her. 'In Mr Pringle's class.'

Her heart sank even further.

'I feel funny, Mum. My head hurts and my neck.'

Her stomach muscles tensed. The papers had recently been carrying details of several cases of meningitis.

'What about your eyes?' she asked him anxiously. 'Do they hurt?'

'Yes...a bit...'

Half an hour later, after she had got him into bed and telephoned the doctor, she asked Marcus anxiously, 'Do you think it *could* be meningitis?'

'I doubt it,' Marcus told her wryly. 'I suspect it's much more likely to be Mondayitis, plus the illicit carton of ice-cream he had for supper last night.'

Eleanor stared at him. 'What illicit carton of ice-cream?'

'The one I found this morning.'

Eleanor shook her head. 'I don't know. He says his eyes are hurting him.'

'He says, or you suggested?' Marcus asked her.

'I'm your wife, Marcus,' she snapped at him. 'Not an opposition witness.' She saw him frowning, but before she could apologise the doorbell rang.

'That will be the doctor. I'd better go and let her in.'

'There's no need to apologise,' the doctor soothed her fifteen minutes later. 'I'm a mother myself and I know what it's like. Besides, it's always better to be safe than sorry. Luckily this time it's nothing more serious than an upset tummy and a bit of attention-seeking.'

She smiled at Eleanor reassuringly.

So Marcus had been right, Eleanor reflected bleakly as she saw her to the door, and she had panicked unnecessarily. A panic increased by guilt because she had not been there...because Marcus had had to disrupt his working day to go and collect Tom, because *she* had been too busy this morning to notice that Tom was feeling off colour and because she had been too busy last night to notice that he had eaten the ice-cream.

What was happening to her? Where was the pleasure in a life that left her with so little time for her children, for her husband...for *herself*?

'You were right,' she told Marcus wryly later. 'It is just an upset tummy.' He looked up from his desk and smiled at her.

'I'm sorry I snapped at you earlier.'

'That's OK,' Marcus told her easily, adding, 'I should have remembered that mothers don't like having their judgement questioned.'

For some reason his comment jarred. What did he mean? Was he referring to mothers in general or one mother in particular, the mother of his own child, perhaps?

Eleanor had been pleased when Marcus had once commented on how different she was from his first wife; she didn't want to be a second Julia, a copy of another woman who had once been important in her husband's life. She had been fiercely glad that he loved her as an individual...as herself. Unlike Allan, who, after the initial enthusiasm of being married, had ceased to see her as a woman—a person—and had seen her only as a mother. Sexually he had found it hard to relate to her once she had had the children, and besides, he had accused her, they meant more to her than he did.

'By the way, the Lassiters want us there for eight. What time is the babysitter due?' Marcus asked her.

Eleanor froze.

The Lassiters' dinner party. She had forgotten all about it...forgotten to make any arrangements for someone to sit with the boys. How *could* she have forgotten? Harold Lassiter was the most senior barrister in Marcus's chambers. There was a strong rumour that he was about to be called to the bench as a senior judge.

Marcus might not have the sharklike instinct and drive, the personal and professional ambition that her first husband had possessed, but as a product of the British public school system, reinforced by the discipline of an army father, he was meticulous about observing a code of good manners which to many people was now hopelessly old-fashioned.

In fact, that had been one of the first things about him which had appealed to her.

Typically, Jade had laughed in disbelief when she had told her this, rolling her eyes and demanding, 'What? My God, trust you! You manage to find one of the most charismatic and sexy men I have ever set eyes on, and all *you* notice about him is that he held open the door for you. You realise that he probably only did that so that he could check out the view,' Jade had teased her, explaining when she had frowned, '*Your* rear view, idiot. Men like a nice, well-shaped female behind, didn't you know?'

Now, Eleanor's expression gave her away.

'You'd forgotten?' Marcus exclaimed sharply.

'Marcus, I'm *so* sorry. I meant to organise a babysitter last weekend and then Julia telephoned and asked if we could have Vanessa and somehow or other...'

'Damn!'

'I could ring Jade,' Eleanor suggested. 'She might be free.'

She had just picked up the receiver and started to dial Jade's number when she heard Tom calling, 'Mum...Mum...I don't feel well.'

Anxiously she replaced the receiver and hurried upstairs, just in time to hear him being violently sick.

It might only be ice-cream-induced and perhaps a fitting punishment for his greed, but there was no doubt that he was feeling extremely sorry for himself, Eleanor acknowledged as she tucked him back into bed.

At thirteen he was already beginning to consider himself too old and grown-up for maternal cuddles and fussing, but now he clung to her.

'Stay with me,' he begged her as she started to get up.

'I can't, darling. I've got to go and telephone Aunt Jade to ask her if she can come round to sit with you tonight.'

Immediately his face flushed and he sat bolt upright in bed, clinging fiercely to her.

'I don't want *her*. I want you,' he told her.

Dismayed, Eleanor put her arms round him. He normally never clung to her like this... perhaps the doctor had been wrong... perhaps he was more ill than any of them had recognised.

'Tom, darling, I have to go...'

'No, you don't,' he argued stubbornly. 'You don't want to be with us any more. You just want to be with *him*.'

Appalled, Eleanor hugged him tightly. 'Tom, that isn't true!'

There was no way she was going to be able to go to the Lassiters' dinner party, she recognised. Not with Tom so upset and unlike himself.

Marcus wouldn't be pleased. She could feel her heart growing heavy with despair mingled with anxiety and panic, a sense of somehow feeling as though her life was out of her own control...

What was happening to her? It shouldn't be like this... after all, she had everything a woman could possibly want. Yes, everything...

And some things that no sane woman would want. Like an accountant who was beginning to issue warnings about dropping profits and rising costs; a partner who had problems which seemed to be putting a strain on their business relationship. A stepdaughter who was growing increasingly hostile to her and who seemed to see her as some sort of rival for her father's affections; a son who had just destroyed her belief that she had finally slain her inner dragon of guilt about the effect her divorce from their father might have had on her children.

A house filled with antique furniture and carpets which might be the envy of her single friends, but which was no real home for two growing boys.

A growing feeling that there were too many things in her life over which she seemed not to have full control.

And a husband whom she loved and who loved her, and surely knowing that made up for everything else, didn't it? Didn't it?

CHAPTER TWO

TENSELY Fern checked her appearance in the bedroom mirror, already anticipating Nick's criticism. She smoothed the matt black fabric of her evening dress over her hips, anxiously aware of how much weight she had lost since she had last worn it for the round of Christmas parties.

Her mother's death had been partly responsible for that. It had been a strain taking care of her for those last weeks of her life, especially with Nick being so resentful of her absence.

She had tried to explain to him how she felt: that it was a mixture of love as well as duty and responsibility which made her feel that she had to be the one to nurse her mother; but Nick had demanded to know how he was supposed to manage in her absence. He had a business to run, he reminded her; she was his wife, and since she did not work, did not bring in any money herself, he felt he was not being unreasonable in expecting her to be there at home for him when he needed her.

She had tried to ignore the feelings of panic and misery his attitude caused her, smothering it beneath a thick blanket of anxious self-control, afraid of challenging him because she was afraid of where such a confrontation would lead.

With her mother so close to death, she had not been able to afford to provoke Nick because she had known she simply would not have either the physical or mental energy to cope with his reaction.

Her mother was dying and needed her, she had told Nick quietly.

'I need you too,' Nick had retaliated, and in the end she had compromised as best she could, spending the majority of her time with her mother, dashing home when she could, to ensure that Nick had clean shirts, a fridge and freezer full of food, and doing her best to placate him.

In the end her mother's death had come almost as a relief to her. She still felt guilty about that. About that and about so many other things as well, but most especially about...

She glanced back towards the mirror, grimacing as she studied her reflection. She looked far too tired and drained for a woman of only twenty-seven; the heavy, rippling mass of her hair, tawny brown with rich gold natural highlights in its thick waves, was almost too great a burden for the taut slenderness of her neck. In fact her hair with its rich tumbling mass of curls presented an almost grotesque contrast to her face and body, she acknowledged wearily. She really ought to have it cut short. She was too old now for its careless abundance, a legacy from a childhood governed by the views of much older parents, a mother who believed that all little girls should have long, neatly plaited hair.

She had toyed with the idea of having it cut years ago when she was at university. She remembered mentioning it to Adam.

'Don't,' he had told her in that strong but gently soft voice of his. And as he'd spoken, he had lifted his hand and slowly touched her, brushing the heaviness of her hair back from her face.

Trembling, she looked away from the mirror, her face flushing with guilty heat. What on earth was she doing? She had made a pact with herself years ago that she would never allow herself to give in to that kind of temptation. To do so was surely to break her marriage vows just as much as though she had . . .

The last thing she felt like doing tonight was going to a dinner party, especially this one.

For a start she barely knew Venice Dunstant. She was one of Nick's clients, the widow of an extremely wealthy local entrepreneur who had been much older than she was.

There had been a lot of gossip locally about her when she had originally married Bill.

Venice. Was that really her name, or had she simply appropriated it in the same way she had appropriated Bill Dunstant?

They had met on holiday. Bill, a widower of just over sixty, had gone away on his doctor's advice to recuperate after a heart attack. He had met Venice and married her within weeks of knowing her. They had been married just over two years when he had suffered his second and fatal heart attack, leaving Venice an extremely wealthy widow.

It had only been since his death that Nick had become involved with her. She had consulted him in his capacity as an insurance broker.

Prior to her husband's death, she had not been seen very much locally, apparently preferring to spend most of her time in London, but she was now becoming much more active in local affairs.

It had been she who had persuaded Nick to join the exclusive and very expensive new leisure complex which had recently opened.

'You ought to try exercising a bit more yourself,' he had commented critically to Fern only the other evening, eyeing her too slender body with obvious disapproval. 'Venice goes to classes almost every day, *and* she plays tennis as well.'

Fern had refrained from pointing out that, unlike Venice, she was not in a position to afford the kind of fees demanded by the leisure club, and that, even if she had been able to do so, her mother's illness and Nick's own insistence that in view of the fact that he supported her financially it was her duty to ensure that she put his wishes first meant that she wasn't free to enjoy the luxury of so many hours of personal freedom and self-indulgence.

Nick talked a lot about Venice. Too much? She frowned, her stomach muscles tensing. Was she guilty of being overly suspicious...too untrusting, imagining things which didn't exist...like another woman's scent on his skin?

Physically Nick was a very attractive man; a man, moreover, who knew how to make himself appealing to women, as she well knew.

The soft thickness of his blond hair, the boyish charm of his smile, the deep blue of his eyes, all added to his air of masculine appeal. Of just slightly above average height rather than tall, his body lean and slim, unlike Adam who was both tall and broad, and who looked what he was—a maturely male man—Nick looked slightly younger than his age. A fact of which he was secretly proud and tended to subtly emphasise.

Her husband could be described as a vain man, Fern acknowledged, who at thirty still cultivated the same aura of boyish appeal he had had when she first met him.

Nick could be very persuasive when he chose, as she well knew.

She had lost count of the number of times she had given way beneath the weight of his coaxing, dreading the sullen accusations which would follow if she did not.

When had she first realised that she didn't love him any longer; that she had in fact probably never really loved him, but had simply allowed him to persuade her that she did, flattered by his attention, aware of how anxious her parents were to see her happily and safely married, convinced by both Nick and them that marriage to him was the right thing for her?

She had genuinely believed she did love him then, she told herself miserably. Had genuinely believed that he needed and loved her. Why should she not have done? He had told her often enough how much he wanted her in his life...

And if, after their hurried courtship, she had bewilderedly discovered that his interpretation of loving and needing did not match hers, well, she had kept her thoughts to herself, reminding herself of the vows she had made, telling herself that she was expecting too much, hampered by the restrictions imposed on her by her upbringing from confiding in anyone else, much less seeking their help or advice.

The fact that she was not very sexually responsive to Nick she knew must be her fault, and she had struggled guiltily to overcome her lack of enthusiasm, miserably conscious of how much she must be disappointing Nick, of how he, as much as she, must dread the silent sexual intimacy they shared, which invariably resulted in her being left feeling tense and on edge, glad that it was over and yet guiltily unhappy at the same time as she lay there sleepless and dry-eyed, staring at the rejecting silence of Nick's back.

No wonder he turned away from her the moment it was over, no wonder he complained that she didn't know how to behave like a real woman.

No wonder that eighteen months into their marriage he had had an affair with someone else.

What *was* a wonder was that she had been so shocked, so disbelieving when she had first found out. Nick was her husband...they were married...had exchanged vows! Other people's marriages might involve a breaking of those vows, but not hers... And on top of her shock, underlining and heightening it, had been her awareness of how upset her parents would be if her marriage broke up...or how she had somehow let them down, broken faith with the standards they had set her.

It was over two years ago now and yet she could remember the events of that day as clearly as though it had only just happened. The arrival of the woman after Nick had gone to work, her own unsuspecting surprise at seeing her...the woman's tension slowly communicating itself to her as she refused the cup of coffee Fern had offered, wheeling round to confront her, nervously smoking the cigarette she had just lit.

Fern remembered how afterwards she had been surprised at Nick's choice, knowing how much he loathed people smoking—an odd, disconnected, sharply clear thought which had somehow lodged itself in her brain while other, far more important ones had been held tensely at bay.

She and Nick were lovers, the woman had told her, angrily claiming that she knew that Fern must be aware of the situation; that she, Fern, was deliberately holding on to Nick when she knew he no longer wanted her.

Shock and pride had prevented Fern from telling her the truth: that she had had no idea of what was going on.

Eventually the woman had left. Fern had watched her drive away, her body, her emotions, her mind almost completely numbed. She remembered walking upstairs and opening her wardrobe doors, removing a suitcase and starting to pack her things.

Then the phone had started to ring. She had gone downstairs intending to answer it, but instead she had walked right past it, through the back door which she had left unlocked and open, and out into the street.

She had no recollection of doing any of this...nor of how she had walked right into town...nor of what her purpose might have been in doing so.

It had been Adam who had found her, who had saved her from public humiliation, only to cause her to suffer later the most profound and intense personal humiliation—but that was something she could still not bear to think about, not now...not ever... He had taken her home—his home, not hers. She had started to cry, bewildered and shocked by the trauma which had overwhelmed her. She had started to tell him about Nick's affair...her shock...things she would never normally have dreamed of confiding to him.

Her days of confiding in Adam had ended with her marriage to his stepbrother, no matter that once it had been Adam who she had thought was her friend. Adam... Adam she had known first, not Nick.

But, as she had discovered when she met Nick, the Adam she had thought she knew must have been a figment of her own imagination.

'You didn't really think Adam was interested in you sexually, did you?' Nick had asked her incredulously. 'Oh, Fern.' He had laughed gently as he gave her a little shake. 'Did you really think...? Adam already has a girlfriend...or rather a woman friend. It's a very discreet relationship. Adam prefers it that way...it leaves his options open, if you know what I mean. I suppose I shouldn't criticise. After all, a man in his position, reasonably well off and with the kind of reputation Adam's built up for himself as a local do-gooder...he has to be seen to toe the moral line, even if what he does in private... He's something of a secret stud, my stepbrother. But you're quite safe from him, Fern. He likes his sexual partners to be women, not little girls... Little virgins...'

She could remember now how humiliated she had felt...how humiliated and self-conscious she had been from then on whenever she saw Adam. Had he actually discussed her with Nick...told Nick...? In fact, she had felt so uncomfortable, so betrayed almost, that she had deliberately started to avoid seeing him. And yet he had never given her any indication...done or said anything...

It had hurt her to know, though, as she now did know because of Nick's revelations, that Adam had probably been quite aware of the silly crush she had had on him. Aware of it and no doubt amused by it, discussing it probably with the unknown woman who shared his bed, the woman who Nick had implied was a world away from her own silly immaturity.

In the trauma of her shock, though, she had not had the strength to erect her normal defences against Adam. She had simply let him take her home with him, sit her down and gently coax from her what had happened.

She had started to cry, she remembered. And that was when it had happened...when she had broken faith with all that her parents had taught her to respect and revere, when she had done something that was far, far worse than Nick's merely sexual betrayal of her.

Even now she could not bear to think about it, pushing the memory fiercely out of sight, willing herself not to allow even a chink of light into that seething darkness of spirit and emotion into which she had locked the memories away.

She had known afterwards, of course, that there was no going back, that her marriage to Nick was over, but she hadn't said anything to Adam.

How could she, when she knew that he had simply acted out of pity, had just reacted as any man would have done to what she had said...what she had done?

She had insisted on returning home, even though Adam had tried to dissuade her. 'At least let me drive you,' he had said, but she had shaken her head, unable to bear to look at him, backing away from him in her panic in case he reached out and touched her, so shocked and ashamed by her own behaviour, her own wantonness, that all she had wanted to do was to escape from him and from it, taking advantage of the quirk of fate that decreed that his phone should start to ring just as he reached out towards her, distracting him long enough for her to turn and run.

He had come after her, calling out her name, but it was too late, she was already outside in the street, knowing that with others to see them, others who knew who both of them were and what their relationship to one another was, Adam could hardly run after her and force her physically back into the house.

And besides, why should he really want to? Despite the concern he seemed to feel for her, secretly he must surely have been only too relieved that she was leaving, saving him the necessity of pointing out to her that she had misunderstood . . . that he had never intended . . .

The phone had been ringing as she got home, but she had ignored it, knowing that it would be Adam. Instead she had gone straight upstairs to where her suitcase still lay open on the bed.

Methodically she had started to remove her clothes from the wardrobe and pack them into it, rehearsing what she was going to say to Nick, how she was going to tell him that she knew about his affair, knew he loved someone else; knew that their marriage had to end.

He had arrived home ten minutes later, returning much earlier than usual, and she had seen immediately from his expression that he knew his lover had been to see her.

She had opened her mouth to tell him that she was leaving but he'd forestalled her, bursting into an impassioned speech, reaching out to take hold of her, scarcely seeming to notice the way she tensed and flinched back from his touch.

'Fern . . . Fern . . . I'm so sorry. I never meant you to find out. She never meant anything to me, you must believe that,' he told her huskily.

He went on to beg her not to leave him, to tell her how much he still loved and needed her, to plead and cajole, making her head ache with the voluble force of his arguments and insistence.

'Think what this will do to your parents,' he said as he looked at her half-packed suitcase. 'You know how much it would hurt and upset them. Do you really want to do that to them, Fern, and all over a silly little fling that never meant anything important?

'You're so naïve . . . you see everything in black and white. How many marriages do you think would survive if every woman who learned that her husband had made a small mistake actually left him? I never intended it to happen, but, well, let's be honest—sexually . . .' He gave a small shrug. 'She made me feel wanted,' he told her, giving her his little-boy-lost smile. 'She made me feel that I was important to her. She wanted me, Fern. Oh, I know it isn't your fault that you aren't very responsive sexually, and believe me I do understand, but I am a man with all the normal male urges, and she...'

She felt sick then, sick and too filled with loathing and disgust to say anything, to do anything other than merely stand there and listen to him, knowing that he was right, knowing how upset her parents would be, how shocked, how devastated...how difficult they would find it to understand.

'I still need you,' Nick insisted. 'We can put things right...try again. Please, Fern. You must give me a second chance.'

In the end she gave in. What other option did she have? she asked herself bewilderedly. Nick loved her; he needed her; her parents would neither understand nor approve if she left him, and she herself was bitterly aware of her own guilt, her own betrayal of the vows she had made and had fully intended to keep.

Nick was right, she did owe it to him to give their marriage a second chance. But even as she was giving in, agreeing, aware of the huge weight of reasons why she ought to be pleased that he wanted to stay with her, she still felt an unfamiliar dangerous flare of panic and anger, a sense almost of being trapped and imprisoned.

She suppressed it, of course, quickly smothering it with the tight blanket of her parents' teachings and her own awareness of what she owed it to them and to Nick to do.

But that night in bed, after he had made love to her and she had lain dry-eyed and tense beside him, she knew she had to tell him about Adam.

The next morning she tried to do so.

'What do you mean, you can't stay with me?' he demanded angrily. 'Look, Fern, I've already told you, it...she meant nothing. It was just sex, that's all, just sex.'

'It isn't that,' she whispered miserably. 'It's me. I...'

Something in her expression must have given her away, because she heard him curse and then demand aggressively, 'It's Adam, isn't it? Well, if you think I'm going to let you leave me for him...'

'It isn't like that,' she protested, horrified by what he was saying. 'Adam isn't...doesn't...'

She wasn't able to continue, her voice breaking under the strain of what she was feeling, but Nick grabbed hold of her arm, insisting fiercely, 'Oh, no, you aren't stopping there. Adam isn't...doesn't *what*, Fern? Adam doesn't want to fuck you? Don't lie to me, Fern. I know how much he...'

He stopped then, releasing her so roughly that she half fell against the kitchen table.

'I'm not letting you go,' he repeated flatly. 'You've made a commitment to me, to our marriage, and if you think...'

He paused, watching her as she crouched against the table, her body shaking with shock and tension, tears slowly filling her eyes as her self-control started to splinter.

Suddenly his voice softened and became almost cajoling.

'Think, Fern. Think of how your parents would feel if we broke up...if I had to tell them that you've been unfaithful to me with Adam. How long have you been seeing him? How often?'

She stopped him immediately, the words falling over one another as she tried to explain what had happened, how upset she had been, how Adam had found her. How...

'You mean you did it just to pay me back...because of my affair,' Nick interrupted her before she could finish what she was saying. For some reason he had started to smile, his voice and body relaxing. 'Did you tell Adam that?' he asked her softly. 'Did he know you were coming back here to me?'

'I didn't tell him anything. Just that...just about her coming here...'

He was still smiling at her, almost crooning at her as he reached out to her, apparently unable to sense the tension and resistance in her body as he pulled her into his arms.

'Fern, Fern, don't you see? The only reason you went to Adam was because you wanted to get back at me. Of course I'm upset...jealous...hurt—what man wouldn't be? But I do understand. You love me...and because of that you wanted to hurt me...to pay me back for hurting you. But it's all over now and we're still together. And we're going to stay together. Let's both put the past behind us and make a fresh start...give our marriage a second chance. I want to. Don't you?'

What could she say? How could she refuse to accept the olive branch he was offering her? How many other husbands would be as generous...as forgiving? She owed it to him...to her parents...to the way they had brought her up and the standards they had inculcated in her, to do what he was suggesting.

'Yes,' she agreed listlessly. 'Yes, I do.' And yet somehow saying the words had hurt her throat, straining the muscles, making them ache with the same weary despair that had also invaded her body...

'Fern, what the hell are you doing? Aren't you ready yet?'

Guiltily Fern hurried towards the bedroom door, stepping back from it just in time as Nick thrust it open and walked in.

Formal clothes suited him, she acknowledged, as she studied the effect of his well-cut fair hair, and the healthy tan he had acquired since visiting the leisure centre, against the expensive fabric of his dinner suit and the crisp whiteness of his dress shirt.

Nick liked his dress shirts to be hand-laundered by her, and starched. It was a laborious job and one which she felt the local laundry could have performed far more efficiently, but she also knew that if she tried to point this out to Nick he would demand to know if she thought he was made of money, and what she did with her time. After all, she did not work.

Because Nick would not let her. Because every time she raised the subject of getting herself some sort of part-time paid work he told her furiously that he was not going to be humiliated in their local community by having his wife pretending that he kept her so short of money that she needed to earn the pathetically few pounds she would earn.

'And besides, what would you do?' he had taunted her. 'You've never held down a proper job.'

'I could train,' she had retorted. 'Some of the local shops...'

Nick had gone from contempt to fury, accusing her of deliberately trying to undermine him, his position.

Didn't she at least owe it to him to at least try to behave as a loyal wife? he had demanded bitterly.

A loyal wife... Her eyes bleak with despair, she turned to look at him, watching the irritation and contempt hardening his face as he studied her.

'Why the hell don't you find something decent to wear?' he demanded.

She could have retorted that she could not afford the luxury of anything other than the most basic of chain-store clothes, but to do so would reignite his grievance against her late parents, for using their modest wealth to purchase annuities which had died with them rather than investing their capital elsewhere so that it could have been passed on to her.

They must present a bizarre contrast, she admitted tiredly, Nick in his obviously expensive dinner suit, she in her shabby, well-worn, dull dress.

'My God, you love playing the martyr, don't you?' Nick accused her as he glared at her. 'Hurry up or we're going to be late. I don't know what the hell you're doing up here anyway.' He gave her another disparaging glance.

Comparing her with Venice, Fern wondered unhappily, or was she simply imagining things... looking for them, because...?

As she followed him downstairs, she wondered what Nick would say if she told him that she would rather stay at home.

Get even more angry with her than he already was, she imagined.

There had been a time when she had actually enjoyed going to dinner parties, had looked forward to the stimulation of conversation with other people, but that had been before Nick had pointed out to her on their way home one evening that she was boring people with her silly mundane conversation.

He had apologised to her later, but when she had refused to respond he had accused her of sulking and she had tried to tell him that she wasn't; that she just felt so weighed down by the burden of realising what people had privately been thinking of her that she simply couldn't raise the energy to respond to him.

'Don't lie to me, Fern,' he had told her bitterly. 'You're trying to punish me for telling you the truth. Just as you tried to punish me for having an affair by...'

She had run out of the room then, unable to bear to listen to him any more, knowing that she was behaving childishly and yet unable to trust herself to stay and hear him out.

It had been shortly after that that her father had died, and then her mother, who had suffered ill health for several years, had gradually started to grow worse, and she had had no energy left to do anything other than cope with her mother's decline.

'Fern, for heaven's sake come on,' Nick demanded irritably. Quietly she picked her bag up off the bed and walked towards the bedroom door.

Well, at least there was one thing she could be sure of about this evening's dinner party, Fern reflected, trying to resurrect her sense of humour, and that was that Venice would not be dressed in an out-of-date, dowdy black dress.

She was wrong, on one point at least. Venice *was* wearing black, but that was the only thing her own dress had in common with the outfit Venice had on, Fern remarked wryly as Venice opened her front door to them.

At closer to thirty-five than thirty Venice was older than Fern; older than Nick too, a tiny, vivacious, fragile-boned creature with a small oval face and enormous eyes. Where another woman might have self-consciously tried to conceal her lack of height, seeing it as a fault rather than an asset, Venice seemed to take pleasure in deliberately underlining the fact that she couldn't be much more than five feet tall, and Fern, who had in the past suffered several slighting comments from Nick about her own small frame and the fact that short women invariably lacked the elegant grace of their taller sisters, stifled a small pang of envy at Venice's abundant self-confidence.

The black dress she was wearing might almost have been painted on to her body. For someone so small-boned she had disconcertingly voluptuous breasts. Fern had overheard a couple of other women discussing Venice and her figure, one of them wondering out loud if her breasts might possibly owe more to man than nature.

Whatever the case, they were certainly catching Nick's eye, Fern recognised.

Had Venice deliberately chosen that trimming of black feathers for her dress, knowing that they not only provided an eye-catching contrast to her skin, but also that the sheen on the feathers reflected the pearly translucence of her bare skin?

The single pear-shaped diamond that nestled between her breasts was so large that it only just escaped being vulgar. When she moved, it blazed cold fire like the matching diamonds in her ears.

Tonight the almost white-blonde hair, which she normally wore in a perfectly shaped shoulder-length bob, was drawn up and back in a contemporary version of a Bardot-type beehive hairstyle, all careless, artful fronds of 'escaping' hair and tousled curls, half as though she had just come from her bed and the arms of her lover, piling her hair up carelessly on top of her head, more concerned with the pleasure of their love-making than her public appearance.

Only of course that particular type of artless sensuality could only be achieved with the aid of a very expensive hairdresser.

But even without the embellishments provided by her late husband's wealth Venice would have been a very beautiful woman, Fern admitted.

That she was also a very sensual and provocative one as well and that she enjoyed being so Fern also had little doubt.

Venice was obviously very much a man's woman and made no attempt to hide it, something that was reinforced by the cursory way she welcomed Fern, turning immediately and far more enthusiastically towards Nick, moving between Fern and her husband, her back almost but not quite turned towards Fern, almost deliberately excluding her from her welcome to Nick.

A welcome which was surely far more effusive than was warranted by the business relationship Nick claimed to have with her. Or was she being unfairly suspicious? Fern wondered, as she stood quietly to one side, politely waiting for Venice to finish her conversation with Nick.

'That's a beautiful diamond,' Fern heard Nick saying softly to her.

'Yes, isn't it?' Venice agreed.

As she smiled up at him, her index finger stroked over the hollow between her breasts just above where the diamond lay, almost deliberately drawing Nick's attention to her body.

Not that she needed to do so, Fern acknowledged. He had hardly taken his eyes off her since she opened the door to them.

The last time Nick had become involved with another woman, he had claimed that she, Fern, had driven him to it with her sexual coldness. If she, his wife, had been more responsive to him, if she had not forced him to find sexual solace in the arms of another woman, he would never have dreamed of being unfaithful to her.

It was her fault that he had had an affair.

And deep down inside herself Fern had believed him. After all, hadn't her parents brought her up to be aware that it was her female role in life to please and appease, to be gently and femininely aware of the needs of others, and to minister to them before her own?

She had married Nick without giving much thought to whether or not they might be sexually compatible, naïvely assuming that her inability to find much pleasure in their initial lovemaking had been because of her lack of experience.

And besides, she had not been marrying Nick for sex. She had been marrying him because he loved her... because he needed and wanted her.

It hadn't taken her very long to realise that the understanding with which Nick had appeared to treat her lack of sexuality before their marriage was an indulgence he might have been prepared to allow a fiancée but was most definitely not prepared to allow a wife.

She should never have stayed with him, she recognised now. Not once she realised she no longer loved him; but it had seemed more important then to put her parents' feelings before her own, and Nick had been so persuasive, so contrite, so sure that this time they would be able to make a go of it, that she simply hadn't had the heart to tell him that she no longer wanted to.

And then of course there had been the complication of Adam, and so she had given way.

Not just because she had wanted to protect her parents, not even because she was still torn between what she felt or rather did not feel for Nick, and what she firmly still believed—as she had been brought up to believe—that the sanctity of the state of marriage, of the commitment she had made, far, far outweighed the self-indulgence of giving way to her own feelings; but also, shamefully, she had given way because she could not face the thought of Adam knowing she had walked out on her marriage and suspecting why... feeling sorry for her that what had happened between them had in the end been at her instigation, and did not mean... *could* not mean that she could ever have any future with him...

No, she could not endure the humiliation of listening to Adam explaining in that careful, neutral voice of his that he did not really want her. As though she needed telling...

'Stay with me,' Nick had pleaded. 'We can make it work. I know we can...'

And she had allowed herself to believe him... because she had so desperately needed to believe him.

And now?

She could feel the panic starting to flood through her, the aching, cold, terrifying sensation of somehow having been asleep, only to wake up and find herself trapped in a world, a life that was totally alien to her.

She was still suffering from the effects of her parents' deaths, she told herself. That was why she was experiencing this sense of panic and loss... this sense of dislocation... of being not just a stranger to herself, but in some sense an outsider to her own life... someone who was dispossessed... alone... alien...

It was a relief when Venice finally turned to her, giving her a coolly appraising look as she commented with a feline smile, 'Fern... do come into the drawing-room. You look cold... and so thin.'

So plain, so dowdy, so patently undesirable, Fern added mentally to herself as Venice ushered them into the drawing-room, having handed their coats to the uniformed maid who had been standing silently just behind her.

Fern tried to think of anyone other than Venice who would give a small weekday dinner party for less than a dozen people and employ uniformed temporary staff.

Not even Lord Stanton up at the Hall did that. But then Lord Stanton probably couldn't afford to, and besides, he had the invaluable Phillips to take care of all his domestic arrangements. She had a feeling that Phillips would have been highly disdainful of Venice's maid, uniformed or not.

Venice's drawing-room, like the rest of Venice's house, had been decorated and furnished with one object in mind, and that was to provide the perfect backdrop for Venice herself.

If, in the recessionary environment-conscious Nineties some people might have balked at such an obvious display of wealth and consumerism, such an unabashed love of luxury, Venice was plainly made of sterner stuff.

The drawing-room had, Fern recognised, been redecorated since she had last seen it, and she blinked a little at the effect of so many subtly different shades of peach, layer upon layer of them, so that the room almost seemed to pulsate with the soft colour.

If chiffon curtains were not exactly what one might have expected to find in a drawing-room, they certainly created a very sensual effect, and it certainly took very little imagination to picture Venice lying naked on the thick fleecy peach-hued rug, smiling that slant-eyed provocative smile of hers at her lover.

And *her* husband? Fern wondered dully.

'I must show you my bathroom... It's wonderful,' she heard Venice saying. 'I've had a mural done of the Grand Canal with the bath framed so that it looks as though I'm looking out through one of the windows of one of those enormous old *palazzos*. So clever... and so naughty. Sometimes I almost feel as though the gondoliers are real and can actually see me.'

She laughed, batting her eyelashes at Nick, and ignoring her, Fern recognised.

Some of their fellow dinner guests had arrived ahead of them: the local doctor and his wife, both of whom Fern knew reasonably well. She had no really close friends in the town.

She had looked forward to making new friends when they had first moved into their house after their marriage, but Nick had proved to be unexpectedly jealous and possessive; so much so, in fact, that she had found it easier simply to give in to the emotional pressure he put on her rather than endure the unpleasant confrontations her attempts to establish an independent life for herself provoked.

Although she knew a lot of people, some through Nick's business and others through the work she did for a variety of local charities—Nick approved of this unpaid help she gave to others, not because it helped the charities she worked for, but because it increased his esteem within the area—she had no really close confidantes... no one to whom she could talk about the crisis she felt she was facing.

Was it her parents' deaths—a final severing of the physical links with her childhood—which had prompted this agonising and soul-searching, this belief that her life had become an empty wasteland with nothing to look forward to; these traumatic feelings of panic which threatened to engulf her whenever she was forced to confront the reality of her marriage? Or was it because she was afraid of facing up to that reality; afraid of stripping back the fiction and the deceit and seeing her marriage for what it really was? Afraid of admitting that she did not love her husband?

And if he was having an affair with Venice... She could feel her heart starting to beat faster, her throat starting to close up.

Don't think about it, she warned herself. Don't think about it.

Why not? Because she was terrified that, if she did, she would have to *do* something about it... that, without the necessity of protecting her parents to hide behind, she would be forced to confront the truth and ask herself, not just why, but also *how* she could bear to stay in a marriage that was so plainly a mockery of everything that such a commitment could be.

A commitment... That was the crux of all her agonising. When she'd married Nick she had made a commitment... a commitment she had truly believed to be given for life; she had made promises, vows, which were meant to last for life, not to be pushed to one side the moment things went wrong. And surely, just so long as Nick continued to claim that he needed and wanted her, she had no right to walk away from that commitment?

'Fern... how are you?'

Dizzily she broke free of her painful thoughts, smiling automatically, her tension tightening her face into an almost masklike rigidity as she turned towards the doctor's wife.

'I'm fine, Roberta... and you?'

'Relieved that the winter flu season is almost over,' Roberta Parkinson told her ruefully. 'It's been particularly bad this year, as well. John lost several of his older patients as an indirect result of it. Are you sure you're feeling all right?' she added with motherly concern. 'You're looking a bit pale.'

'It's just the heat in here,' Fern fibbed. In actual fact she was enjoying the warmth of the room. It was such a contrast to the cold chilliness of their own sitting-room at home.

Because he himself was often working in the evenings, Nick refused to allow her to have the central heating or the gas fires on, claiming that she was extravagantly wasteful with heat.

If it weren't for the Aga in the kitchen—not one of the brightly coloured modern ones, but the original old-fashioned dull cream type which had been in the house when they first moved in, and which Nick had claimed he was unable to afford to replace—Fern reflected that most evenings she would have been forced to go to bed at a ridiculously early hour just to keep warm.

Roberta excused herself, moving away to talk to the two other couples who had also arrived; Fern knew them both and smiled an acknowledgement of their greeting but remained where she was. One of the couples was a local entrepreneur and his wife, who had moved into the area in the last few years, and the other was their local MP and her husband.

Fern liked all four of them, but tonight she was feeling so on edge and tense that she wanted a few seconds to herself before going over to join them. Because she was afraid of what her expression might betray?

She could feel the panic welling up inside her again, and with it her increasing dread that she was losing all control, not just of her life, but of herself as well. Only yesterday, when Nick had ignored her request that they sit down and talk about their relationship, she had felt almost hysterically close to screaming her frustration out loud. Something... anything to make him listen to her instead of swamping her with his anger, his irritation, his indifference to what she was feeling.

'Only one more couple to arrive now,' she heard Venice saying from behind her. As she turned around, she noticed distantly that Nick was with her.

'Oh, Fern, you don't have a drink,' Venice commented, all mock hostessly concern.

'Fern's driving,' Nick announced before Fern herself could say anything. 'And besides, she has no head for alcohol.'

Fern was uncomfortably aware of the briefly appraising look Jennifer Bowers was giving them from the other side of the room; a look which said quite plainly what the MP thought of Nick's attitude towards her.

Hurt and humiliated, Fern could feel her colour rising as the anger and pain built up inside her, coupled with the knowledge that there was no way she could express what she was feeling; that even when they were back at home and on their own she would not be able to explain to Nick how his behaviour hurt her.

And that was surely her fault and not his, the result of her early upbringing and the loving but old-fashioned parents who had taught her with gentle insistence that little girls, especially nice, well-behaved little girls, did not behave aggressively, did not argue with others, did not express views which contradicted those of others, and always went out of their way to make life easier for others. Being polite and helpful, her parents had called it.

And since Nick insisted that he loved her, she must surely be the one at fault in feeling this frightening dislocation from life; this subversive awareness that she did not love him in return even though she knew she ought to.

In the distance she heard the doorbell ring, shifting her focus back from her introspective thoughts of the past and into the present.

'Ah, here are our final couple. They haven't been together for very long. I expect that's why they're late. They probably stopped on the way for...' Venice gave a small expressive shrug as she went to welcome them.

Fern turned away, smiling at Roberta as she came over to her and announced, 'I almost forgot...I wanted to have a word with you about the charity auction we're organising. You're still on to help sort out the jumble stuff, by the way?'

Fern was just about to answer when the drawing-room doors opened and Venice swept in, ushering the last arrivals inside.

Fern looked towards the doors automatically and then froze, paralysed with shock, her whole body going numb as she stared at the couple who had just walked in; or, rather, at the man who had just walked in.

Adam. She could feel the sound of his name pounding inside her skull, a silent, anguished protest of torment and pain that affected every single nerve-ending of her body; the sensation of her fear that it would be stronger than her self-control making her feel as physically sick as though she had actually let that silent private sound of torment become a physical nerve-jarring reality, revealing to everyone around her exactly what she was feeling...what she had been feeling for so long that suppressing those feelings had drained her energies to the point where there was simply nothing left over for anything else.

In those seconds of agonised confusion and fear it was as humiliating and terrifying as though she had been standing naked in front of them all...worse, in fact; but then she felt Nick's hand on the small of her back, heard the surprised chagrin and envy in his voice as he commented disbelievingly to her, 'Where the hell did Adam find *her*?'

And hard on the heels of the grateful realisation that somehow fate had been kind to her and that she had not betrayed her feelings came the sickening awareness, not just of the youth and prettiness of the girl who was with Adam, but also the way she stood uncertainly close to his side, and the way he moved closer, protectively towards her, smiling encouragingly down at her.

Fern could literally feel the knife-twist of jealousy and pain spearing inside her, the hot agony of longing and guilt that rose up so that she felt almost as though she was drowning in her own anguish.

'Fern...'

She heard Adam say her name...saw him coming towards her.

'Adam.'

Was that really her voice? It sounded so cool, so contained, so totally the opposite of all that she was feeling.

No one would ever guess, watching the wary way they greeted one another, that Adam was her brother-in-law, she recognised bleakly, or rather her stepbrother-in-law. There was after all no blood relationship between Nick and Adam; Nick's mother had married Adam's father when Nick had been in his early teens and Adam almost a young adult, and physically of course they could not have been more dissimilar.

Where Nick was all dapper blond elegance, Adam was...

She found she was having to swallow hard past the obstruction which had somehow lodged in her throat as her mind, her thoughts, her emotions, obviously resentful of the constrictions she had placed upon them, rebelled and relayed to her not the actual reality of Adam as he now stood before her, tall, distinguished in the formal evening clothes which subtly emphasised the essential maleness of him, his dark, normally slightly unruly thick hair firmly brushed—and newly cut—his eyes a calm, sober grey; but Adam as she had once seen him, his skin damp with sweat, tiny beads of it lodging in the hollow at the base of his throat, the scent of it, of *him*, filling her nostrils with a musky and body-trembling awareness of his masculinity, his eyes, so calm and steady now, burning with a molten silver heat, making her tremble, unleashing within her needs, desires, feelings she had never known she could possess.

For all his workouts at the gym, for all the obvious pride and self-satisfaction Nick took in his body and his sexuality, he had never, could never... She swallowed hard, forcing herself to ignore the taunting images filling her memory and to concentrate instead on the girl standing so shyly at Adam's side.

She couldn't have been a day over nineteen, Fern reflected, unable to stop herself from responding to the shy, hesitant smile she was giving her.

Enviably tall, with pretty dark hair, she had eyes which still held the doe-like innocence of extreme youth, her mouth its vulnerability and uncertainty.

The last time she had seen her, Fern remembered wryly, she had had a brace across those now perfect little white teeth and she had been wearing her school uniform.

'Fern, you remember Lily James, don't you?' Adam queried, gently bringing the younger girl forward.

'Yes...yes, of course I do. How are you, Lily? How are your parents?'

She sounded as though she was old enough to be Lily's grandmother, Fern recognised ruefully, but there was not even a decade between them.

It was totally contrary to Fern's own nature to be unkind to anyone, much less an obviously shy young girl like this, even if...when...

Even when what? Fern asked herself bitterly as she smiled warmly at the younger girl, gently trying to put her at her ease.

Even if Adam loved her...

Her heart seemed to jolt right up into her throat, its already nervous beating becoming a frantic distressed hammering.

The palms of her hands were damp with sweat, her nails curling painfully into their softness as she fought to suppress the cry of agony she could feel building in her throat.

What was wrong with her? She had always known that one day Adam would fall in love...that someone would eventually cause him to abandon the bachelor state which Nick had always claimed he would never voluntarily give up.

'If you really want my stepbrother,' he had told Fern once before they were married, 'then the only way you're likely to get him is by tricking him into getting you pregnant. Very keen on being seen to do the right thing, is our Adam. *Do* you want him, Fern?' he had added slyly.

'Adam is just a friend,' she had responded tautly. After all, no nice, decent girl ever admitted even to herself that she could possibly want a man who did not want her...or at least that was the message she had picked up from her mother's carefully protective teachings.

And she had believed it. And still believed it?

She could feel the pain stirring inside her again, tearing, wrenching, streaked with guilt and shame.

Adam was standing so close to her that she was actually conscious of the scent of him, not the faint cool hint of cologne he was wearing, but the basic personal male smell...

Despairingly she moved back from him, giving Lily a small apologetic smile as she started to excuse herself.

'Fern.'

She could hear the tension in Adam's voice and the anger, and her own stomach muscles clenched in response.

She couldn't look at him. She dared not...

'I think Venice wants us to go through into the dining-room,' she told him distantly as she turned away and looked for Nick.

The meal they were served was superbly presented, an exotic combination of all that was luxurious and first rate, which must have cost Venice as much as she probably spent on food in a year, Fern reflected tiredly, unable to face the richness of her food, nor the smell that rose up from her plate.

They had almost finished their pudding when without warning Venice turned to John Parkinson and asked, 'What do you think of this plan to bulldoze Broughton House and build shops and offices on the land?'

'What plan?' Roberta's husband asked with some concern.

'Oh, haven't you heard?' Venice queried. 'It's all over the town that someone local is planning to put in a bid for the place, ostensibly as a private home, but in reality because he...they have very different plans for it.

'Of course it would have to be someone with the right kind of local contacts and influence so that they could get planning permission pushed through, wouldn't you say so, Adam?'

Although she was smiling sweetly at Adam, no one could have been in any doubt that it was Adam to whom Venice was referring when she spoke of 'someone local' acquiring Broughton House. But surely Adam would never lend himself to that kind of scheme?

It was true that Adam, as an architect, was bound to be interested in anything which might lead to new commissions, and it was certainly no secret that he was part of a highly successful local conglomerate which had designed, built and now ran several small local shopping parades and housing schemes, but all of them had been completely above board and free from any taint of the kind of underhand usage of power and position which Venice was now none too subtly implying.

'Perhaps we ought to organise a committee to oppose it,' Venice continued without giving Adam any chance to reply. 'I have actually heard that what's being proposed isn't just a small parade of shops, but a huge hypermarket. Of course you have to admire whoever it is for his chutzpah. If he can pull it off, it will make him very, very wealthy, and I suppose to be fair there will be those who will say that the town does need that kind of facility. What do you think, Adam?'

'Broughton House is in an area of "outstanding natural beauty",' Adam told her quietly. 'I should imagine it would be impossible to get planning permission for that kind of venture.'

'Oh, but surely not if one had the right connections . . . knew whom to approach and how,' Venice persisted, smiling sweetly at him.

There was a small, uneasy silence which Nick broke by turning to Adam and saying silkily, 'You don't seem particularly surprised, Adam, but then perhaps you know more about what's going on than the rest of us. After all, as a member of the town council . . .'

'Like Venice, I have heard the rumours,' Adam countered, 'but that seems to be all they are . . . rumours.'

'But the house is up for sale and unliveable-in in its present state,' Venice persisted. 'And surely you, Adam, both as an architect and a councillor, must know something . . .'

'Mrs Broughton lived in it . . .'

Fern froze as she heard the unsteady huskiness in her own voice, her words cutting right across Venice's deliberate probing, deflecting attention away from Adam and towards herself, drawing not just an irritated little frown from Venice at her intervention, but an angry glare from Nick as well.

'Fern has always had a ridiculously sentimental attachment to the place,' Nick announced tersely, giving her a cold look.

'Well, I for one would be very surprised to hear that anyone would be foolish enough to imagine they could get planning permission for that kind of venture,' Jennifer Bowers announced briskly. 'And if anyone tried, I should certainly oppose it. After all, we haven't spent all these years protecting the character and history of the town only to go and have hypermarkets built on its unspoilt land.'

'Adam's the expert on the town's history and preservation,' Venice persisted. 'And I still have a sneaking suspicion that he knows more about what's going on than he wants to tell us.'

Because Adam himself was involved in some scheme or other to destroy the house? That was what Venice was implying, and Adam himself had done and said nothing that really contradicted her subtle accusations. Because he couldn't?

As she glanced round the table, Fern suspected that she wasn't the only one wishing that Adam would make a more definite and unequivocal rebuttal of Venice's hints.

'Have *you* heard anything about this supermarket business?' Roberta asked her later as they waited for Venice's maid to bring down their coats.

Fern shook her head.

Was what Venice had been suggesting true? *Was* Adam involved in some plan to secretly circumvent the planning controls operating locally? And what about Nick's earlier thoughts that Adam wanted the house to raise a family?

The maid came back downstairs, apparently unable to find Fern's jacket. Quietly she went upstairs to look for it herself.

The coats were all placed on a bed in one of the spare rooms. She had to move several before she could find her own thin jacket, and as she lifted one of them, a heavy, plain wool man's coat, she knew immediately that it was Adam's. Her fingers tightened into the fabric. She could feel the hot salt burn of the tears clogging her throat and for a moment the impulse, the need to bury her face in the soft black fabric and breathe in the scent of Adam from it was so strong that she had the coat halfway to her face, the fabric gripped tightly in her fingers, before she fully realised what she was doing.

Appalled, she dropped it, turning round quickly, her face flushed with guilt as she mechanically reached for her own jacket.

As she pulled it on, she realised that in dropping Adam's coat she had dislodged a heavy folded brochure from an inside pocket. She bent to pick it up and replace it and then stiffened as she realised what it was.

Through the tears which blurred her vision she could see the photograph of Broughton House on the front cover of the sale brochure.

She was twenty-seven years old, still a relatively young woman, but suddenly she wished with almost savage intensity that she were older, her life closer to its end, and with it the end of all the pain, the misery, the guilt which daily became an even greater burden to her.

She was Nick's wife, she reminded herself; she had no right to...

To what? To love another man?

'Stay with me, Fern,' Nick had begged her. And then later when she had told him about Adam he had said it again.

He must genuinely want and need her to overlook what she had done, mustn't he? And surely in view of that she owed it to him to stay.

And besides, what was the point in her leaving? she had recognised numbly. Where else was there for her to go—now that she had been all the way to hell and back again? And to heaven as well?

Shakily she turned away, almost running towards the door and down the stairs.

CHAPTER THREE

'MMM...nice,' Zoe murmured teasingly against Ben's mouth as she wrapped herself around him, curling her body into the sleepy morning warmth of his.

It hadn't been easy getting their precious time off to coincide; Monday was the one morning of the week when neither of them had to get up early for work, the restaurant where Ben was currently working closed on Mondays and Zoe having begged, cajoled and bribed the others at the London airport hotel where she was working so that she could have Mondays off as well.

She loved it when they were together like this, she thought drowsily as she snuggled deeper into Ben's naked warmth, rubbing her face against his skin and nuzzling him with lazy, appreciative sensuality.

Once, in their early days together, Ben had told her that she was just like a little cat with her soft fluid body and her habit of rubbing herself affectionately against him.

In truth there was something prettily feline about her small triangular face and the soft sinuous grace of her body.

But Zoe had an energy that had nothing catlike about it, an electric buzzing force that made her grey eyes sparkle with enthusiasm, and which seemed to crackle around her like a live force-field.

There was nothing kittenish about her either; she scorned such ploys and affectations. It was, Ben reflected wryly as he slid his fingers into the thick dark mass of curls haloing her face, only now, in these their most intimate moments, that her normal exuberance was calmed and tamed, to reveal her vulnerability and sensuality.

'Oh, no, you don't,' he told her as he felt her hand slide downwards over his body.

Zoe laughed, turning her face into the curve of his throat and kissing him lovingly.

She laughed again as she heard him groan and felt him turn his body in towards her, his actions running directly counter to his words.

It had always been like this between them right from the very start, Ben, cautious, concerned, wanting to hold back; take time and to be sure; she...

She made a voluptuous sound of appreciation against his skin as her fingers closed gently round him.

...She impatient, impulsive, knowing almost from the first moment they had met that she wanted him.

46

She felt him move against her, his body aroused, hard; she caressed him slowly, enjoying her own body's response to him, the taut, heavy feeling in her breasts; the sensitivity of her nipples especially when she rubbed herself rhythmically against his chest, the small betraying, knowing pulse that grew insistently urgent as she let herself absorb the hot silky texture of his skin, anticipating the pleasure that lay ahead, the pleasures they had already known.

Ben wrapped his arms around her, kissing the top of her head and then, when she lifted her face to look at him, her mouth.

His skin smelled of warmth and sleep and the faintly acrid scent of his sweat, and that special unmistakable scent that was his alone and which as always she found unbearably erotic. She wondered if her scent affected him in the same way. Ben didn't like talking about sex. In the northern city in which he had grown up, boys...men grew up with an attitude towards sex which was very different from the ones she had absorbed from her own middle-class parents.

And yet Ben was an unbelievably tender and caring lover, almost as though, if he was unable to talk to her about this most intimate side of their lives together, then at least he could make up for his inhibitions by *showing* her all he felt.

They knew each other well enough now, had been together long enough to recognise without words each other's signs of arousal, each other's sexual needs, and yet each time they made love it was different...special...familiar and yet still, for Zoe, achingly pleasurable.

Now, when Ben kissed her, he did so lingeringly, slowly, taking his time, as though the intimate caresses of their mouths were a total act of physical communication and satisfaction on their own, and not merely a preliminary act to his physical possession of her.

No, if anything *she* was the one who was the more impatient.

Not that there was any doubt that Ben wanted her, she acknowledged in satisfaction as she stroked her thumb along the underside of the rigid shaft of his penis and felt him shudder against her, his muscles tensing as his teeth tugged on her bottom lip.

She felt his hand touch her breast, cupping it, and she moved against him, enjoying the delicate friction of his palm against her nipple. Soon he would bend his head and kiss her throat, her shoulder and then her breast itself, taking his time, lingering over each caress, while she felt the urgent thud of his heartbeat against her body and savoured the delicious tension of her own growing need to feel his mouth against her nipple, tugging on the small hard peak of flesh.

Languorously she stroked her hands over his stomach and hips, sliding them down over his buttocks, caressing him lazily until she felt the sharp pins and needles of pleasure exploding inside her as his tongue rubbed over her nipple. Her fingers tightened on his skin, his mouth opened over her nipple. She shuddered in pleasure as the hot fierce surge of her own arousal overwhelmed her.

'Now, Ben,' she told him thickly. 'Now...now...now. I want you now...'

Half an hour later, when the sharp summons of the telephone broke into the luxurious pleasure of their shared post-coital relaxation, Zoe told Ben lazily, 'It's your turn.'

'Why on earth can't we get a telephone by the bed?' Ben grumbled as he pushed back the duvet and reached for and pulled on a clean pair of underpants.

'Because you said we couldn't afford one,' Zoe reminded him, watching him with unashamed pleasure.

He had a wonderful body, lean and powerfully male without being over-muscled. His arms and chest were taut with sinewy strength, his stomach flat and hard. She gave a small convulsive movement of sheer sensuality, remembering the sensation of the soft dark hair that grew on his body against her fingertips; fine and silky over his chest and stomach, it darkened and thickened into a heavier stomach-tensing line of more intense growth along the centre of his body, spreading wider and thicker above the base of his penis.

Idly she wondered if he derived as much pleasure in looking at her body, in thinking about it, in contrasting its femininity with his own masculinity, as she did his.

She was lucky in that, despite the exuberant thickness and wildness of the brunette curls that more than one envious friend had not been able to believe were actually natural and not the result of some expensive and enviable perm, the hair on her body was confined to a neatly demure triangle of soft hair that started just below the pretty mole where her body started to swell into sensual womanhood.

Thanks to her parents, she had no hang-ups about either her body or her sexuality. Unlike Ben.

She remembered how surprised she had been the first time they had made love and he had insisted on undressing in the dark, and even then on leaving on his underpants until they were actually in bed.

It had been many weeks before she had persuaded him to allow her to see him naked and in the daylight, and even more before she had ventured to tease him gently for his shyness.

What he had said in response to her then had for the first time in her life left her unable to make any verbal reply, unable to do anything other than smother back the anguish aching in her throat.

With five children, boys and girls, sharing one bedroom and two beds, such modesty was essential and necessary, especially when you were the eldest, especially when you were a particularly well developed teenage boy, especially when you had a gut-deep protective instinct towards your younger siblings which you had never been able to put into words but which led you to be fiercely protective, not so much of your own privacy, but of their innocence.

She had never teased him about his need for modesty again, just as she had never retaliated on those occasions when she'd grimaced in disgust over the tacky grubbiness of their rented flat with its damp patches on the walls, its bath which no matter how often she cleaned it never really seemed to her as though it was clean, and he turned on her and told her grimly that where he came from and to his family the privacy of the flat they shared would be considered a real luxury.

Most of the time, because there was just the two of them, because Ben had done his early training under one of the best chefs in the world and because that training had encompassed far, far more than the art of buying, preparing and serving good food, she was not conscious of any social differences between them and she was certainly not concerned about them. But Ben was.

She heard him pick up the receiver and say their number, and then, when he didn't call out to her, she snuggled back under the duvet.

They still had the whole day ahead of them and it would be fun to coax him into coming back to bed. She rolled over on to her stomach, smiling in reminiscent pleasure as she felt the soft pulsing echo of her orgasm.

It was five minutes before Ben came back. When he did and she saw his face, all thoughts of teasing him back into bed vanished. She sat up immediately, the duvet sliding unregarded off her body.

'What is it? What's wrong?'

'I don't know. That was Ma on the phone. She wants me to go up there.'

'To Manchester?'

'There's a train every hour.' He paused and looked at her. Immediately Zoe shook her head and told him quickly,

'No, it's all right. You go. I owe Mum and Dad a visit anyway.' She pulled a face. 'I haven't really seen them since Christmas... I haven't even told them our good news yet. I wonder when we're going to hear something definite about the hotel.

'Don't worry,' she told him softly, reaching out and taking hold of his hand. 'It can't be anything too catastrophic. Your mother would have told you over the phone if it had been.'

She didn't question his decision to go north. She knew him well enough by now to realise how seriously he took his role as the eldest in the family; substitute father-figure to his younger siblings in many ways since his parents' divorce. She had observed the way not just they but also his mother depended on him and, although her heart ached protectively for him when she saw how much he worried about them, she couldn't blame them for their dependence on him.

She had only met his family once. He hadn't really wanted her to...had argued angrily against her decision to accompany him on one of his visits home; but she had insisted, knowing intuitively that, if she gave in, his family and his openly ambivalent feelings towards them and the life he had left behind would act as a barrier between them.

He might have prepared her for their poverty, for the vast gulf that lay between him, with his energy for life, his ambition, his determination, his awareness and control over his life, and their poverty and apathy; but what he had not prepared her for, obviously because it had not occurred to him to do so, had been the shock of discovering that his mother could more easily have passed for his older sister.

He had been nearly twenty then and had looked older. His mother, who had given birth to him days after her sixteenth birthday, was still, amazingly after having five children, small and almost fragilely slender, her anxious eyes turning to her eldest son not just for his support, but for his approval as well, Zoe had recognised on a welling tide of her own emotion.

Ben had only told her the bare facts of his early upbringing, and then half reluctantly. His parents had divorced when he was in his early teens, his father disappearing, leaving the family completely without his emotional and financial support.

Reading between the lines, she had guessed that Ben had taken on to his own shoulders the role abandoned by his father, and *then*, without knowing her, she had resented Ben's mother on Ben's own behalf for her selfishness in allowing such a young child to take such an appalling burden.

Now that resentment had gone, but in its place had been born a determination never to treat Ben as his family did, using him as an emotional and financial support, *taking* from him instead of giving.

And with that in mind she smiled generously at him now and swallowed her own disappointment at the disruption of their precious shared time.

'You can have the bathroom first,' she told him. 'I'll go and make the coffee.'

On their days off breakfast together was normally a special leisurely ritual. She made the coffee while Ben went down to the small bakery a couple of streets away to buy fresh croissants still warm and buttery from the ovens.

Zoe acknowledged that she was lucky in never seeming to put on any extra weight no matter what she ate, but then her job was very physically demanding, with long hours and missed mealtimes.

She hadn't said anything at work yet about their plans. It had been hard enough getting her job as it was. Like everyone else, the large hotel chains were cutting back on expenses and staff. Only the fact that she had among the best exam results in her year had secured her a coveted job as a very junior trainee.

She had been with the company several years now, had completed their training scheme and had been lucky enough to be offered her present job as junior under-manager of their Heathrow hotel.

A plum job with a minute salary and the ferocious expense of travelling by car to work from the flat she and Ben shared. Silly perhaps, when she could have lived in or even at home with her parents, but it was worth all the hassle...all the time, all the travelling...all the hours she spent alone while Ben was still working...worth it for the precious wonderful time they did get to spend together.

Once Ben had gone, she rang her parents' number. Her mother answered the phone, pleasure quickening her voice when Zoe announced her plans.

'Darling, I'd love to see you. Will Ben be coming as well?'

'No. Not this time.'

'Oh, dear, what a shame. Never mind.'

Zoe grinned to herself as she heard the note of relief underlying her mother's pretended disappointment. As products of the Sixties, with all that the decade's culture had embraced, her parents had been determined to bring her up free of the shibboleths, the petty tyrannies and restrictions, the prejudices from whose shackles they and their whole generation had so enthusiastically and gloriously cut themselves free, and she knew how it both astonished and appalled them that they should have suffered such an extraordinary sea-change, such a reversion to the middle-class mores of their own parents, which they had assumed they had successfully thrown off where her own relationship with Ben was concerned.

Valiantly they battled to keep this horribly unegalitarian backsliding into middle-class morality hidden from their daughter, but Zoe was as much a product of *her* own decade as they were of theirs; she knew them too well, had lived with them too long, had grown to maturity alternately caught between amusement and disbelief at their naïveté and lack of awareness of what the real world, *her* world comprised to suffer any sense of ill-usage at their reaction to Ben.

As she had laughingly confided to one of her oldest friends, a girl like herself, born to the same kind of free-thinking, liberal if somewhat woolly-minded parents, 'I think the parents are more shocked at the way they're reacting to Ben than I am. Mummy said to me after the first time she'd met him, "Poor Ben... He's been so financially and socially disadvantaged." She can't even bring herself to say that he's working-class, poor darling. She still lives in a world where class differences aren't supposed to exist. I think she sees my relationship with Ben as some sort of physical desire for some rough manual worker type that will probably pass. She believes I'm oblivious to the class differences between us when of course I'm not. Neither of us is. Poor Mummy, she doesn't really understand that it's different now. Ben and I don't live in some dream-world where we think that love can conquer everything. We *know* it's going to be hard...that we're going to have to work at it. It's not like it was for our parents, going through life doped up to the eyeballs on pot and sex.'

'No,' Ann had agreed wryly. '*My* mother seems to think that because Matthew and I live together we spend our entire lives in bed having sex. She actually apologised for disturbing me the other day when she rang me up at eight in the evening. I nearly told her I'd only just come in from work; that I had a file of balance sheets I'd brought home with me to work on; that Matthew had gone to the supermarket to do the shopping and that we'd be lucky if either of us got to bed before midnight, and that once we did the last thing either of us would feel like doing would be making love. But you can't disillusion the poor darlings, can you?' Ann had added, wrinkling her nose.

Zoe's parents had a house in Hampstead, the fashionable part, bought just before the first of the big property booms with the help of a cash wedding present from both sets of parents who had been delighted and fervently relieved to discover that their offspring were finally legalising their union.

They had met at university; had taken the hippy trail to India together, returning with matching flowing locks and caftans. They had got married in them; scarlet ones. Zoe had seen the photographs, which were not among those now displayed in the plain tasteful heavy silver frames which decorated the pretty antique tables in her mother's sitting-room.

As an investment banker, her father had done well in the Seventies and Eighties. Zoe had gone to St Paul's, where she had worked hard enough to get a very satisfactory nine O levels. Her parents had confidently expected her to go on to university and had been shocked when she had told them what she wanted to do instead.

'Hotel management...but why, darling?' her mother had asked, obviously perplexed.

'Because I like looking after people,' Zoe had told her calmly. 'I enjoy organising them...being bossy and managing.' She had given them a wide laughing smile. 'Of course I won't always be working for someone else,' she had assured them. 'One day I shall have a hotel of my own. Perhaps somewhere abroad...Spain...Benidorm,' she added teasingly.

Of course they had been disappointed, but eventually they had given way, as she had known they would. They knew nothing of discipline or coercion and had no defences against her stubborn insistence that she knew what she wanted to do.

Against all the odds, Ben liked them, although he considered they were no match for her.

She knew that if she had wished it her father would gladly have financed her, giving her an allowance, buying her a better car than the ten-year-old Mini which took her to and from work...even paying the rent on a decent flat; but once she had made up her mind to move in with Ben she had decided that she would live on what she earned. Not that

Ben resented her parents' wealth. To do so, he had once told her, would harm him much more than it could harm them.

Her mother picked her up from the station. At forty-six she still showed traces of the pretty girl she had been, the prettiness now softened and transmuted into a polished elegance.

As she kissed her affectionately, Zoe said, 'You look good! I like the new hairstyle, it suits you.'

Heather Clinton smiled. 'I wore it like this in the Sixties, straight and bobbed.'

'Only then it was the same colour as mine,' Zoe teased. 'Not blonde.'

And then she had gone braless, and worn skimpy little shift dresses that showed more of her body than they concealed, and in those days her body had been worth showing, her skin glowing with health and youth, honey-tanned, sleek and firm.

Now, despite her aerobics classes, despite the expensive body preparation she used, she was beginning to be aware of the first beginnings of an unflattering loss of tone, an awareness that, no matter how hard she tried, it was impossible for her to recapture that golden, silky-skinned glow which David had loved so much.

Had he noticed its loss too? Did he, as she did herself, compare her to younger, fresher-skinned women and find her wanting?

She glanced at her daughter, half anxiously, half enviously. Zoe was all the things she had once been; so like her and yet so very different from her.

'Daddy's had to fly to Jersey,' she told Zoe. 'So I'm afraid it will just be the two of us.'

'Never mind,' Zoe told her. 'We'll be able to have a good gossip. How about having lunch somewhere together? That Italian place...I'm starving.'

She grinned to herself as she saw the uncertain sideways look her mother was giving her clothes: black leggings, black lace-up boots, a silk turtleneck sweater which she had swooped on with glee in a second-hand shop and, over the top of it, a thick bulky cotton-knit sweater which was really Ben's.

In contrast her mother was wearing a casual but very obviously expensive cream linen skirt and jacket, teamed with the plainest of plain ivory silk shirts, her nails elegantly buffed and free of polish, just as her hair was free of lacquer and her face of heavy clogging make-up. Her only jewellery was her wedding and engagement rings, and the pretty trio of gold Cartier bracelets Zoe's father had bought her for their twenty-fifth wedding anniversary.

Over lunch it was Zoe who skilfully controlled the conversation and who then, as a penance for not confiding in her mother about her own and Ben's hopes for the new restaurant-cum-hotel, allowed Heather to take her into her favourite dress shop and buy her a new outfit.

Her mother had pulled a slight face over her choice of brilliantly pat-terned Lycra cycling shorts and a top which she claimed clashed appall-ingly with it, but Zoe had smiled indulgently, refraining from pointing out that her generation had its own fashions and its own tastes and kissing her mother affectionately as they waited for her purchases to be wrapped up.

When her mother announced uncertainly that it was her evening for her bridge lesson, Zoe heroically concealed her amusement and gravely assured her that no, she did not mind at all.

'Ben will probably be home by the time I get back,' she assured her mother, hugging her warmly.

Only when she got back, Ben had not returned, and after the warmth of her parents' home, with its unpretentious and unfussy but oh, so dis-creetly expensive décor, the flat seemed even more unwelcoming than ever.

Here on the tatty basic furniture there were no carefully treasured silver-framed photographs, no pretty pieces of Chelseaware...no cleverly chosen *objets d'art*...no paintings. No, there were none of those things, but there *was* love, Zoe reminded herself, and then she stood still, frowning, the forefinger halting that she had been dragging lazily through the per-manent film of dust on the black ash table which Ben had assembled and which had joints which were nothing like true.

There was love in her parents' home as well, wasn't there? Of course there was, she reassured herself. All through her childhood and then her teenage years she had been aware of that love, and had taken it for granted. Too much for granted? After all, among their generation her parents were unusual in remaining together.

On her way up the stairs she had collected the post. Two bills, a bank statement and a thick white typed envelope which she was dying to open.

It was addressed to both of them, and she was nearly sure it was some-thing from their backer. What did it contain? News about the property he intended to purchase? She could feel the excitement starting to uncoil and fizz up inside her.

Hurry up, Ben, she pleaded silently. Hurry up. *She* could have opened the letter, of course, it was after all addressed to both of them, but like a little girl she wanted to share the surprise with him...to share the pleasure...or the disappointment.

It wasn't going to be a disappointment, she assured herself firmly. Ben was the one who was the pessimist, not she...

It was almost midnight before he came back, and she knew immedi-ately when she saw his face that whatever his mother had wanted to tell him could not have been good news.

'Ben!' she cried out in sympathetic alarm. 'What's wrong? Is someone ill? Is...?'

There were dark shadows under his eyes, and his skin looked drained and sallow, his blue eyes which could glow warmly with love and tenderness bleak and empty.

'What's wrong?' she asked him gently.

He sat down heavily on the old sofa they had inherited with the flat. Zoe's mother had wanted to have it re-covered for them, grimacing at the unknown identity of its many stains, but Zoe had firmly refused, flinging over it instead a richly patterned rug she had picked up from one of the street markets.

Now she sat down next to him, not touching him...waiting...

'It's Sharon,' he told her emptily. 'She's pregnant.' He turned his head and looked at her, but he wasn't seeing her, Zoe recognised, not really; his expression was too controlled, too hard and full of starkly bitter bleak despair.

Uncertainly Zoe waited, instinct telling her not to speak...not to touch...not to do anything; and then abruptly he seemed to focus properly on her, the blood surging into his face, burning it with a heat that left stains like bruises against his cheekbones.

'She's sixteen years old, for God's sake, and she's pregnant.

'Mum thought she was on the Pill, but apparently she forgot to take it and Sharon, of course, like the little fool that she is, didn't say a word to Mum about anything until she was just about bursting out of her school uniform.

'My God...hasn't she learned anything? Hasn't she *seen* from Mum? Doesn't she realise?'

Zoe swallowed painfully, knowing that his anguish was something private, something beyond the bonds that the two of them shared, caused by his knowledge and experience of a way of life that was totally alien to her.

Even so, she tried to reach out to him, asking hesitantly, 'And the father...the boy?'

'The *boy*...' The face he turned towards her was white now...not with exhaustion but with a bitter savage fury, the expression in his eyes one that made her shiver; one which she thought would always haunt her.

'The boys, not the boy,' he corrected her thickly. 'Sharon told me that she isn't sure just who is the father. And of course the stupid bitch has left it far, far too late to have an abortion. Mum can look after it, she told me. Either that or the council can rehouse her.'

Not knowing what to say, Zoe reached out and touched his arm gently.

'It might all work out for the best,' she began unsteadily, only to recoil in shock as Ben threw her hand off his arm so violently that she fell back against the settee. His eyes blazed fury and, even worse, contempt.

'What the hell do you know about it?' he demanded savagely. '*It might all work out for the best.*' She winced at the hatred in his voice as he mimicked her voice, her accent. 'How? Like it did for my mother, with three kids under five by the time she was twenty, an unfaithful husband...no income, no home, and no hope of ever doing anything but watching your life slide away from you, with no hope of ever getting out of the mess you're in; with no hope of *anything*, just the sickening reality of snotty-nosed kids dressed in other kids' cast-offs, and perhaps the odd few days of sex from some man you might happen to meet in the pub, who if you're lucky won't leave you with another unwanted and unsupported brat on your hands when he walks out on you. Is *that* what you call things working out for the best?'

'She...she could have the baby adopted,' Zoe suggested shakily, trying not to let him see how much his reaction had hurt her, how much it had excluded her...how much the starkness of the picture he had drawn for her contrasted with the home she had just left, the life and world her parents inhabited.

'She *could*, but she won't...girls like "our Sharon" don't. They haven't got that much sense...they love them, you see, the poor bitches, or at least they believe they do, and they can't even see that by loving them they're destroying them, submitting them to empty, wasted, dragged-out lifetimes of sterility and apathy. If they really loved them, they'd have them aborted.'

The ugliness of his comment took Zoe's breath away.

'And if they really loved themselves they wouldn't get pregnant in the first place. And who's to blame for that, do you think, Zoe...? The stupid little tarts for whom sex is about the only pleasure, the only excitement they'll ever have in their lives, if in fact it does give them any pleasure, or the middle-class liberals like your parents whose liberality took away the only things that used to protect them.

'Before your parents and their destruction of "the rules", girls like Sharon got married when they fell pregnant, or at least most of them did.'

'And was that any better for them?' Zoe asked him in a low voice. 'To be married at sixteen to someone they probably didn't love and to have to stay in that marriage for the rest of their lives? Were they really any happier?'

'Happier?' He looked at her in disgust. 'People like us, like me...like Sharon...like my mother...all my family...happiness doesn't come into our lives, Zoe. It isn't an option or a choice. No, Sharon might not have been "happier", but she'd have been a darn sight better off. She'd have a husband to support her, her child would have had a father...her *children* would *all* have had the same father. She wouldn't have been living alone in some grotty tower block isolated from her friends and family, driven to drink or depression, to drugs and sex...driven perhaps to abusing her children as much as she would be abusing herself.'

'It doesn't *have* to be like that,' Zoe cried out, horrified.

'No, it *doesn't* have to be,' Ben agreed. 'Maybe some fairy prince will ride up on a white charger and sweep her off to happy-ever-after land. Is that what you think?' he asked her in disgust.

There was nothing Zoe could say, no comfort she could offer.

'Do you know that when she was eleven Sharon was the top of her class...a clever girl, her teachers said, capable of going far, doing things; and then came puberty and suddenly Sharon wasn't clever any longer. Clever girls don't get pregnant and ruin their lives and the lives of everyone around them with unwanted babies. Only stupid, selfish girls do that.'

'And boys,' Zoe pointed out huskily to him without looking at him. 'It does take two, you know.'

He gave her a thin, bitter smile. 'She was supposed to be on the Pill, remember...' He got up abruptly, turning his back on her. 'I'm tired. I'm going to bed.'

As he walked into the bathroom, Zoe realised that she hadn't shown him the letter. She picked it up and stared at it and then slowly put it down again.

Perhaps tomorrow, when he felt a bit better. Tomorrow, when she had had time to forget how suddenly and frighteningly he had become a stranger to her, a stranger who it seemed almost hated and despised her.

But Ben didn't hate her and he didn't despise her. He loved her. She knew that.

Right now he was upset and shocked. She looked at the letter again and sighed quietly, blinking back the tears threatening to fill her eyes.

CHAPTER FOUR

ELEANOR frowned as she thought she heard a sound coming from the boys' room. She put down the text she had been studying and got out of bed, reaching for her robe. The Vivaldi tape she had been playing in the background as she worked was not on loud enough to have disturbed her sons, and, still concerned about Tom's bout of sickness, she hurried into their room.

Both of them were fast asleep and when she leaned over to place the back of her hand against Tom's forehead it felt reassuringly cool.

Straightening up, she watched them both for several seconds.

Both of them had been much wanted and dearly loved, by her at least. Allan, her first husband, had not really shared her joy in their conception, and had certainly never wanted her to have a second child. He had deeply resented their claims on her time and attention, half wanting to be mothered himself.

Things were very different now, and he was a far more responsible and participating father to his daughter with his second wife than he had ever been with his sons. But then, when they had married, he had been very young, and very ambitious, and with hindsight, and the calm detachment that came from recognising that both of them in their separate ways had been victims of their totally different perceptions of what marriage should be, she acknowledged that he had perhaps been justified in claiming that she had put the children before him, had loved them more intensely and more exclusively than she had him.

He still kept in touch with them, and she had been scrupulous about ensuring that they saw as much of him as was feasible. His new wife, Karen, was a maternal woman who made it clear she had enough love for everyone, and she and Eleanor got on very well, surprisingly. In fact, it had been Karen's idea that Tom and Gavin come to them during the day in the school holidays now that she was at home with her young baby, instead of rather impersonal childcare arrangements. Eleanor had even begun to pride herself a little on the way things had worked out, on the way *both* her sons had adapted so easily and contentedly to her marriage to Marcus.

But today, with his one brief sentence of accusation and unhappiness, Tom had totally destroyed that complacency.

'You don't want to be with us any more,' he had told her. 'You just want to be with *him*.'

And even allowing for a certain amount of childish exaggeration; even allowing for the fact that he had been feeling extremely sorry for himself,

58

and possibly subconsciously trying to offload his own share of responsibility for his sickness, there had still been enough real despair and fear in his voice to unleash the spectres of guilt and anxiety which were tormenting her now.

Marcus had been less than pleased when she had announced that she could not go to the Lassiters' with him, but he had accepted her decision without trying to pressure her into changing her mind.

That was one of the things about him which had first broken down her reserve, her doubts about the wisdom of embarking on a second attempt at marriage.

Allan had been inclined to behave petulantly and manipulatively when he couldn't get his own way, forcing her to make choices between him and their children, putting such an unbearable burden of pressure on her that in the end his announcement that there was someone else and that he wanted a divorce had come almost as a welcome relief.

Marcus wasn't like that, though. He respected her rights as an individual, even while he cherished her as a woman. In contrast to most other men, he seemed to know instinctively when she needed the reassurance of a certain amount of male possessiveness, a certain degree of proprietorial but wholly adult determination to have her undivided attention focused on their own very personal relationship, and when their relationship had to take a back seat to her maternal and professional duties.

Tonight, though, she had been aware that, beneath his outwardly relaxed calm acceptance of her decision to stay at home with Tom, inwardly he was irritated and annoyed.

'There is nothing really wrong with Tom,' he had pointed out coolly to her, and that, in giving in to his demands that she remain at home, she was potentially making a rod for her own back.

Logically he was quite right, Eleanor had admitted, but a small maggoty worm of resentment at his lack of understanding had made her wonder if he would have been quite so logical had it been his own child. Now, having satisfied herself that Tom was comfortably and healthily asleep, she acknowledged that at least part of her resentment had also been caused by her own totally illogical feelings of hurt because he had not recognised that it was more than Tom's sickness which had made her feel she must stay with her son.

Men were not like women, she reminded herself as she went back to their own bedroom and got back into bed. They did not possess a woman's understanding and intuition of emotions and needs that were not directly voiced.

Marcus was a pragmatist and it was surely unfair of her to expect him to read her mind, to know what she was thinking and feeling. After all, she had not known what was on Tom's mind, had she?

She frowned, pausing in the act of returning to her abandoned work. She found it easier to read like this, cocooned in the warm comfort of their bed.

Just as she liked feeling that she was cocooned in Marcus's love? But surely that kind of need belonged to someone lacking in maturity; someone who could not accept a genuinely equal partnership...someone who expected her partner to meet all her emotional needs?

Her frown deepened. She had been increasingly aware lately of a growing imbalance in the way she believed she ought to feel and react and the way she actually was doing. This unexpected chasm of self-doubt and insecurity which seemed to have opened up within her worried and confused her.

Of course there had been other times in her life when she had suffered from insecurity and lack of self-worth, but those times were behind her now. So why had Tom's unexpected accusation overset her so much? *Why* had it filled her with such panic and tension? *Why*, whenever she was confronted by Marcus's daughter's obvious aversion to her, did she feel she had to somehow conceal both the girl's behaviour and her own reaction to it from Marcus himself?

The Vivaldi tape had come to an end. She was not, she recognised, going to get any more work done now. She had too many other things on her mind.

After Marcus had gone out she tried to talk to Tom, to reassure him that he was wrong to believe that Marcus was any kind of threat to his relationship with her, but when she had gently tried to draw him out, to question him about why he should believe that she no longer loved him, he had clammed up on her, refusing to discuss the subject.

The antique grandfather clock in the hallway chimed midnight. Marcus should not be much longer, she comforted herself.

The clock reminded her of the one her grandparents had owned. They had lived in the country and every summer she had spent two weeks of her holidays with them, before flying out to join her parents in whichever part of the world her father happened to be stationed. As a career diplomat, he had been constantly on the move, and as their only child Eleanor had never felt particularly close to her parents. Her father's career had necessitated her spending most of her childhood at boarding-school, and, while she loved her parents and knew they loved her, they had never had the closeness she had promised herself she would share with her own children...a closeness she had genuinely believed they *did* have. Until this evening... How could they be close when she had not even known what Tom thought...when it had been Marcus who had correctly diagnosed the cause of his sickness and not her?

As a child she had looked forward all year to those holidays with her grandparents, to the unchanging security of their pretty house in its sleepy country setting.

Perhaps because of those childhood memories, she had been determined to maintain her own children's contact with Allan's parents. After all, they were their only set of grandparents; her own parents had died in an air crash before she and Allan married. But the last time they had visited, Tom had complained that things weren't the same.

She frowned now, remembering how upset he had been to discover that the room at his grandparents' which he had always thought of as his own was also the one Allan's new baby from his second marriage slept in when they were there.

At the time she had dismissed his complaint as mere childish possessiveness and jealousy, but now, aware of how disruptive she herself was finding it every time Marcus's daughter visited and she had to move her own sons out of their room, it suddenly struck her ominously that something more than mere childish resentment might have underlain Tom's complaint.

Children *needed* security...*needed* to feel that they had their own special and protected place in adults' lives, especially those children who had gone through the trauma of seeing their parents split up.

Now, when she thought seriously about it, she recognised that Tom had been increasingly truculent and withdrawn recently, especially when Vanessa visited, and it *was* unfair to expect him to give up his room to Vanessa... Just as it was unfair to expect Vanessa to be happy with the discovery that the room she had always thought of as her own was now someone else's.

The answer was of course to buy a larger house, but she and Marcus had already discussed this and agreed that it was financially impossible.

She glanced at her watch. Marcus should be home soon. Their large bed seemed empty without him. She smiled wryly to herself, acknowledging the direction her thoughts were taking.

When she and Allan had married she had been sexually naïve, and they had never really been sexually compatible. This had been another source of friction between them. Secretly she had always blamed herself for her inability to respond as fully and passionately to his lovemaking as Allan had wanted her to, and then, after the birth of the boys, he had become less and less interested in making love to her.

After their divorce she had been cautious about allowing herself to get involved with other men. Sex had been something she had pushed to the back of her mind and out of her life. She had the boys, and the excitement of a burgeoning career to keep her fulfilled and busy.

And then she had met Marcus. He had patiently encouraged her to put aside her wariness and caution and to learn to celebrate and enjoy her sexuality. He was a very sensual lover. And a very experienced one?

She frowned as she felt the tiny tremor of anxiety touch her spine. What was she worrying about now? Marcus had always been open and honest with her, making no secret of the fact that there had been other women in his life before they had met. He was not a promiscuous man but it would have been naïve of her to believe that he had lived a celibate life in the years between the break-up of his first marriage and their first meeting.

Her frown deepened as she remembered how, the last time she had visited them, Vanessa had asked her if she ever got jealous or worried that Marcus might leave her for someone younger.

'Most men Dad's age marry someone a lot younger,' Vanessa had commented. 'Women aren't attractive to men once they're middle-aged.'

'That's not true, Vanessa,' she had countered as firmly as she could, trying to dismiss her own personal feelings and to concentrate instead on her concern that already, while still only in her teens, Vanessa was being dragged into the female trap of perceiving her own sex as only being able to have a valid sense of self-worth when rated by their desirability to men; but Vanessa had shrugged her shoulders and walked away from her, telling her unkindly over her shoulder, 'You're only saying that because you're old.'

Old . . . at thirty-eight?

Marcus arrived home just after one. She had been asleep but she woke up when he walked into the bedroom, smiling sleepily at him as she asked, 'Did you have a good time?'

'Yes, but not as enjoyable as it would have been if you had been there,' he told her, coming over to the bed and bending his head to kiss her briefly.

'Did the Lassiters understand?'

'Yes. As luck would have it, they'd had an extra unexpected guest, a young American lawyer, who's over here on a year's sabbatical. She came with Paul Ferrar and his wife. Her parents are friends of theirs.'

'Pretty, was she?' Eleanor asked him, and then immediately wondered what on earth was wrong with her as she caught the acerbic, almost hostile note in her own voice.

No wonder Marcus was looking at her like that.

'Not exactly pretty,' he told her judiciously. 'She was very fresh and enthusiastic in the particularly American way. She seemed to find our legal system outdated and old-fashioned. When she returns home, she plans to specialise in international law.'

'Like you?'

Marcus gave her another thoughtful look. 'Yes,' he agreed. 'How's Tom?'

'He's fine,' Eleanor responded. Suddenly she wanted to talk to him about her concern for her son; about the doubts and guilt his accusation to her had aroused, but as she started to speak Marcus turned away from her. Her sons were not his problem, she reminded herself, and he had already hinted once today that he thought she was fussing too much; being over-protective.

'Hang on,' he told her. 'I'll just go and have a shower.'

She lay where she was for several seconds, and then, suddenly restless and wanting to be with him, she got up and followed him.

From the open bathroom door, she asked him, 'Marcus, this American girl. What was her name?'

'What?' He stepped out of the shower, shaking his head, smoothing his wet hair back from his face.

'The American girl—what was her name?'

He looked surprised. 'Oh, her...I...Sondra something. Cabot. Yes, that's it...Sondra Cabot.'

'Very WASP.'

His eyebrows rose slightly as he smiled at her. Silently Eleanor watched him, wondering if she would ever cease to be slightly astonished by the intensity of her own desire for him. When she and Allan had married, Allan's body had still had some of the thin gawkiness of youth, and in those days of course people had not been as aware of the importance of physical exercise...the fitness boom had not yet swept the country and she had assumed it was quite normal for a woman not to be particularly aroused by the sight of a man's naked body, that it was in fact necessary for the man to arouse the woman by touching her.

Of course she had learned long before she had met Marcus that this was not the case, but it was not until she *had* actually met him that she first experienced for herself her own arousal caused not by Marcus touching her, but simply by her own awareness of him and her desire for him.

They had been lovers for almost two months before he had told her how much it had turned him on to look at her and see in her eyes that she wanted him, and to know that she was doing her best to pretend that she didn't.

Marcus's body was nothing like Allan's. Once, when she had told him dreamily that for her, physically, he embodied all the sensuality and masculinity so admired by the ancient Greek sculptors, he had laughed gently at her, saying that no mere mortal man could hope to rival that sort of perfection, reminding her that he was forty-two years old.

Now he was forty-five and his body still had the power to make her hold her breath at the build-up of a slow, sweet tide of desire he caused to flow through her.

When he got into bed and turned to take her in his arms, she told herself that they could talk about Tom later.

'Mmm...' he told her softly as his hand cupped her breast and he started to feather small kisses along her throat. 'Have I told you lately how very sexy you are?'

Smiling, Eleanor moved closer to him.

'No,' she whispered back. 'But you can tell me now if you like.' She paused, her voice thickening a little as she added huskily, 'Tell me and show me...'

*　　*　　*

Eleanor bit off a sharp little sound of pleasure, voluptuously abandoning herself to the delightful sensations Marcus was giving her as his mouth slowly caressed her clitoris, his tongue stroking delicately over and over her receptive flesh in the way he knew she most liked. In another few seconds, her pleasure would become almost too intense for her to bear and then she would cry out to him that she wanted him; that she needed him; that she couldn't wait any longer to be a part of him.

She felt the orgasmic tension seize her and trembled deliciously.

'Marcus...'

She shuddered deeply and opened her eyes, and then froze as she saw their bedroom door opening, wrenching herself away from Marcus's embrace and pulling up the duvet in one quick automatic reflex action as Tom came into their room.

At her side, she heard Marcus groan. Her own body was reacting rebelliously and angrily to Tom's interruption, but emotionally she was already responding to Tom's entrance, pulling on her robe as she slid out of bed and hurried towards her son.

'What is it, Tom? Are you feeling sick again?' she asked him anxiously, guiding him back to his own room.

By the time she was able to leave Tom, Marcus had fallen asleep. He was lying on his side facing away from her side of the bed.

Quietly she slid in beside him and tiredly closed her own eyes.

'Nell, could you spare half an hour? There's something I need to discuss with you.'

'Louise—yes, of course.' Eleanor smiled warmly at her partner. 'If you want to ask me how I'm getting on with narrowing down the job application lists for the freelancers, I'm afraid I'm going to have to admit that I'm not making very much progress. What with Tom not being very well and one thing and another...'

'No...no, it isn't that,' Louise told her curtly. 'Well, that does sort of come into it, but...'

Eleanor could see how unhappy and ill-at-ease Louise looked as she sat down, and a feeling of disquiet began to ice up her own spine.

'Louise, what is it? What's wrong? Everything's all right at home, isn't it...with you and Paul...?'

'Yes, of course it is,' Louise told her almost snappily.

Her question had offended her partner, Eleanor recognised with concern as she saw the angry red flush staining Louise's skin.

She was on the point of apologising, but Louise didn't give her the chance.

'Why shouldn't everything be all right?' she demanded almost aggressively. 'Just because you've never liked Paul... Well, he's *my* husband, Eleanor, and I think he's right when he says that your antagonism towards him is bound to affect our business relationship. That's why I wanted to talk to you, as a matter of fact.'

Eleanor stared at her. It was true that she didn't particularly like Louise's husband, but she had certainly never said anything against him, not even when he had tried to interfere in the business.

'I'm sorry if you think that I'm antagonistic towards Paul,' she began quietly, 'and I guess that it's something we ought to have discussed before——'

'That's not what I want to talk about,' Louise interrupted her quickly. 'It's the business itself.'

A presentiment iced warningly down Eleanor's spine, her anxiety escalating as she waited for Louise to continue.

'Paul and I are moving to France.'

Louise couldn't quite meet her eyes, Eleanor noticed absently as her body absorbed the shock of what Louise was saying to her.

'It's something we've both wanted to do for a long time. Paul already has business connections there, several of our friends have moved there, and, as Paul says, with 1992 and the effects of the Common Market we owe it to ourselves and to the boys to do anything we can to make ourselves financially secure.

'I can work just as easily from France as I can from London—more easily really. We'll be so much more conveniently situated for Brussels, Paul says, than London. This whole country really will become a total backwater. And you've only got to think of our overheads here.' Louise was speaking much more quickly now as her words gathered momentum, her eyes sharp and defiant when she finally raised them to Eleanor's face.

So *this* was why Louise had been so on edge with her recently; so sensitive... Eleanor felt as though her brain had gone into slow motion as she tried to deal simultaneously with both the emotional shock and the practical aspects of the bombshell Louise had just dropped on her.

'But Louise, we're a partnership,' she protested quietly. 'We'd made plans... You never said anything...'

'We hadn't made up our minds then.' Louise flushed defensively. 'Besides, Paul feels that my Russian will have more commercial value than...after all, most European countries already speak English.'

Eleanor winced. What was Louise trying to say to her; that *her* language skills were of more value to the partnership than Eleanor's own?

She was tempted to point out what Pierre Colbert had said: that with the break-up of the Soviet Union no one as yet had any real idea of what language the re-emerging independent states would eventually choose to do business in, but what was the point in getting embroiled in a pointless battle of scoring off against one another?

If *only* she had recognised what was happening earlier; *before* Louise had made so many plans. If only Louise had had the consideration to tell her...give her some warning, she realised bleakly.

And she had thought they were such good friends...such good working partners. She had believed that they *trusted* one another...that she could rely on Louise to deal honestly with her.

'You do understand, don't you, Nell?'

Louise's voice had taken on a pleading note now, and Eleanor tensed, resenting her familiar use of her shortened name, the name by which those closest to her—her *friends*—knew her.

'It will be so much better for the children. London is no place for them to grow up. Paul and I have found the most marvellous château ... it's unbelievably cheap.' Louise was starting to gabble nervously now, Eleanor recognised numbly. No doubt with relief that she had discharged the task Paul had undoubtedly set her.

'You must all come out and see us once we're settled out there. I've enjoyed working with you, but you can, I'm sure, understand how it is ... and with our rent due to go up again ...' Louise gave a small shrug. 'As Paul says, we would be fools to pass up on this kind of opportunity.'

'Yes ... Well, I hope it all works out for you, Louise.'

Try as she might, Eleanor knew her voice lacked warmth and pleasure. Her face felt stiff and cold, her body wooden.

As Louise came towards her she found herself automatically stepping back from her, physically rejecting her, not wanting her anywhere near her.

It wasn't so much Louise's desire to end their partnership that was responsible for her feelings, Eleanor acknowledged, it was the feeling that Louise had been dishonest with her, that she had in fact betrayed her ... betrayed the relationship Eleanor had believed they shared.

She could remember so clearly now, when Louise and Paul had first married, Louise telling her vehemently, 'Of course our marriage won't make *any* difference to the business, Nell. Paul knows how important our partnership, our friendship is to me!'

Eleanor had sensed then that, whatever he might have said to Louise, Paul was the kind of man who liked to feel that *he* was in control of every aspect of his life and the people in it.

'You know, I'm surprised that you and Marcus haven't thought of moving to France,' Louise burbled on. 'The financial benefits alone are just too good to ignore and when I think of the freedom the boys will be able to have ... It isn't just that the French education system is far superior to ours ... The boys have been having extra French coaching and Paul has become amazingly fluent. We all speak French every evening during supper now and——'

'I'm sorry, Louise, but I have to go out,' Eleanor lied.

Her head was beginning to ache and her body still felt cold with shock. How *long* had Louise known that she was going to do this? Why couldn't she have said something earlier?

You know why, a small cynical inner voice told her. She ... Paul wanted to make sure, to secure their own future first.

A telephone call to their accountants later in the afternoon confirmed, as Eleanor had already suspected, that it was simply not financially viable for her to continue to work from their existing premises on her own, and that without a partner to share the load it was impossible for her to generate enough income on her own to service the costs involved.

Which meant... which meant what? she asked herself tiredly after she had replaced the receiver. She had a small amount of capital of her own, thriftily garnered over the years, a small bulwark to protect her and the boys, but nowhere near enough to cover all her existing expenses for any real length of time.

When she and Marcus had married she had been determinedly insistent that she wanted to be financially self-sufficient, at least as far as the boys were concerned. She knew from odd comments which Marcus had made that his first wife had been recklessly extravagant, using whatever income she earned as an actress for maintaining the kind of wardrobe and polished appearance she insisted was essential to her career.

And, while it was true that Marcus commanded high fees, he also had considerable expenses to meet. Vanessa attended an exclusive private school and Eleanor knew and applauded the fact that after the divorce he had assumed full financial responsibility for her.

Then there was also the Chelsea house which was expensive to run and maintain, and, while Eleanor knew that Marcus would willingly support both her and the boys, she did not want him to have to do so.

They had discussed her career before their marriage and she had told him that not only did she enjoy her work but she felt she needed the sense of self-worth and satisfaction she got from being financially self-sufficient; that she was proud of the fact that she was able to support both herself and her sons, that she did not *want* to go back to being financially dependent on someone else, no matter how generously that support might be given.

But how was she going to be able to maintain that financial independence now? As their accountant had pointed out, their expenses had risen uncomfortably high, and the number of commissions they were receiving was less than it had been; the recession meant that everyone was cutting back. Some of their smaller clients had even gone out of business altogether; everyone was having to fight hard just to survive.

The thought of working for someone else, even if she could have found a job, held no appeal for her; she was too used to being her own boss. And looking for another partner? The way the thought made her flinch was its own answer. Louise's defection was too new and raw for her to even think of risking entering another partnership. The reason she and Louise had worked so well together was because they operated in different but complementary fields. To find another partner like that would be time-consuming and probably impossible. No, she would be better off working alone.

Louise had disappeared after making her announcement. No doubt to inform Paul that she had broken the bad news, Eleanor reflected bitterly.

Why *hadn't* she realised what was happening...guessed what lay behind Louise's recent odd behaviour? It had never occurred to her that Louise might want to end their partnership. Nor had she realised that Louise felt resentful because she thought her languages were of more benefit, contributed more to the partnership than did Eleanor's own. Paul's handiwork, no doubt. But she couldn't put all the blame for Louise's perfidy on Paul's shoulders; Louise herself must bear some of the responsibility, and so perhaps must she.

She was uncomfortably aware of how blind she had been to what was happening. As blind as she had been to Tom's fear that somehow her relationship with Marcus threatened his place in her life; as blind as she had been to the fact that, with her marriage to Marcus, Vanessa would turn against her.

What was happening to her?

Had she been guilty of being over-confident of successfully handling all her diverse roles? Twice in the space of a few short days she had been forced to confront the knowledge that she had been completely unaware of what those whom she had thought of as being closest to her were really thinking.

Her heart thumped uncomfortably. She was beginning to feel as though she was losing control of her life and what was happening to it. The problem was that she had so little time and so many demands to meet.

How long was it, for instance, since she and Louise had shared an evening or even a lunchtime together, excitedly discussing their plans and their business? And yet once those occasions had been so much a part of the fabric of her life.

And how long had it been since she had been able to spend any real amount of time alone with her sons, concentrating on them exclusively?

These days her weekends seemed to flash past in a blur of frantic organisation for the following week, her conversations with her sons seemed to be limited to terse discussions about the need for football kits and enquiries about the whereabouts of the partners of the four or five odd socks disgorged from the washing-machine with monotonous regularity. And that was on a good week.

Take this evening, for instance... She would be working until six and then she would have to drive across the city to the boys' school to collect them and take them home for supper. She was lucky in that their school ran after-lessons sports and activities groups every evening, but it was not perhaps an ideal situation... Not like the one Louise had described so lyrically and which her children would enjoy.

Fresh air. The space to run free in proper open countryside, the security of a small close-knit community.

Only last week she had had to refuse Gavin's request that he be allowed to have some school friends over on Saturday because Marcus's daughter had been coming and there would have been nowhere for them all to play. Things were difficult enough with Vanessa as it was. Eleanor could imagine her reaction all too well had she arrived to find 'her' bedroom full of eleven-year-old boys.

Suddenly she ached almost physically for Marcus, and then guiltily she reminded herself that she had promised herself when they married that theirs would be an equal partnership and that she would never fall into the trap of using him as an emotional prop.

Tiredly she pushed her hair back off her face. Only another hour and she would have to leave to pick up the boys, and she still had this translation to finish.

'Marcus, what is it? What's wrong?'

Eleanor had just come downstairs from putting the boys to bed and had found Marcus standing in front of the window, staring into space.

He had been slightly withdrawn all evening, speaking curtly to Gavin when he and Tom had started arguing during supper.

'You aren't annoyed about last night, are you?'

'Last night?' He turned round to look at her, frowning.

'The dinner party, and then Tom.'

He shook his head.

'No, of course not. No... I had a phone call from Julia this afternoon. She's been offered a part in a film which necessitates her spending a month or so in Hollywood during the summer holidays. She wants me to have Vanessa.'

'Oh, no. How can we?' Eleanor protested. 'We haven't got the room, Marcus!'

'No, I know,' he agreed. He was frowning again, Eleanor noticed.

'Unfortunately, though, there isn't anywhere else for her to go. And after all, she is my child.'

Eleanor winced, sensitively aware of the slight edge of defensive irritation creeping into his voice. Was he privately thinking that had it not been for Tom and Gavin there would be room for Vanessa?

'Did you explain to Julia how difficult it would be for us to have her?'

'I tried,' he told her drily. 'But Julia has the gift of hearing only what she wants to hear. And it seems that she's already announced to Vanessa that she'll be coming here.'

Eleanor closed her eyes in helpless dismay. She felt no personal animosity towards Marcus's ex-wife, nor any deep jealousy of the relationship they had once shared—after all, she knew enough from what Marcus had told her about his first marriage to accept that he meant it when he said that the marriage had been a disaster from start to finish and that they had been so wildly incompatible that they should never have married in the first place. In a different moral climate they would probably have contented themselves with a brief affair, he had told Eleanor, but in those days such things were not as permissible or acceptable.

However, she was bitterly aware that when it suited her to do so Julia was inclined to feed Vanessa's suspicion and resentment by casting her in the traditional role of wicked stepmother, and if they refused to have Vanessa now, no doubt she would be blamed for that refusal.

'Oh, Marcus...' she protested helplessly, and then to her horror she did something she couldn't remember doing in years. She burst into tears.

'Hey, come on,' Marcus told her gently as he took her in his arms. 'Things aren't that bad...'

'No,' Eleanor contradicted him, as she looked up with a small sniff. 'They're worse than you think. Louise told me today that she wants to end our partnership. She and Paul are going to live in France. In a château...'

Half an hour later, having calmed down enough to have told Marcus the full story, she sipped the glass of wine he had poured her and asked him quietly, 'Marcus, what am I going to do? I *can't* afford to keep on the office and I can't work from here. There simply isn't room.'

'No,' he agreed. 'We don't really have much option, do we? We're going to have to find somewhere bigger, and soon. We'd better start making a trawl of the estate agents and arrange to have this place valued.'

'Oh, Marcus... I'm so sorry. I know how much you love this house.'

'Not as much as I love you,' he told her firmly, coming over to her and removing her wine glass from her hands as he took her in his arms.

'What do you think of our chances of remaining uninterrupted?' he murmured against her mouth as he kissed her. 'These days whenever we make love, I feel as though I'm holding my breath, wondering if we're going to make it. A race against the all too likely arrival of one or other of our offspring. When we do find a another house, I intend to ensure that our bedroom is fitted with an early warning system, and a lock.'

Later, lying in bed next to Marcus, Eleanor told him sadly, 'It isn't just the break-up of our partnership that bothers me. It's the fact that Louise so obviously didn't feel she could talk to me. The fact that she waited until virtually the very last minute to say anything to me. I feel such a fool for not realising... for not suspecting...'

'She deceived you,' Marcus told her quietly. 'And discovering any kind of deception on the part of someone we believe we know and trust is always hurtful. It hurts us where we're most vulnerable. In our emotions and in our pride...'

'Pride?' Eleanor questioned him, lifting her head to look at him.

'Mmm... Because it shows us that we've made an error of judgement... that our trust has been misplaced.'

'Yes,' Eleanor agreed, adding, 'At first I just wanted to blame Paul and then I realised that Louise must have wanted to end the partnership as well. If only she'd said something to me sooner...

'What's happening to me, Marcus? I feel as though my whole life is falling apart. First Tom and now this...'

'Tom?'

'I didn't even know he'd eaten the ice-cream,' she told him sadly. 'You knew, but I didn't. And I didn't...' She stopped abruptly, not wanting to burden Marcus with the rest of her problems. 'What kind of mother am I? What kind of wife when I can forget to organise a babysitter for a dinner party? What kind of partner when I don't know, can't see what's going on under my nose?'

'Hey, come on... You must accept that you can't take on the responsibility for everyone else around you. You're only human, Nell. Just like the rest of us... and, just like the rest of us, sometimes you get things wrong. You can't be perfect, you know. After all, perfection is often a very sterile and empty concept. It's our imperfections that make us human... loveable... and loving...'

He kissed her slowly and asked softly, 'Do you know how much I want to make love to you?'

'Again?' Eleanor asked him, smiling at him.

'Again,' he confirmed as he reached for her. 'Very, very definitely again.'

Three days later, when Eleanor was searching through her briefcase for something else and she inadvertently came across the advertisement she had torn from the magazine, it seemed almost like fate.

She told herself as she dialled the number of the estate agent that she was wasting her time, that the house was almost bound to have been sold.

When she discovered that the bids were still to come in, a feeling of unfamiliar and almost childlike excitement filled her.

She stared at the photograph again. It was the kind of house—the kind of *home* she had longed for so often as a child; solid, permanent, it offered the kind of security she had yearned for so desperately.

It would be a perfect home for them, close enough to London for Marcus to commute, rural enough to give Tom and Gavin the benefits of growing up in a country environment. More than enough room to accommodate them all comfortably, including Vanessa.

With a bit of careful planning there was no reason why she should not be able to work from there. Of course it would mean regular visits to London to collect and deliver translations, but the benefits of moving to the country far outweighed the disadvantages. She would have more time to spend with the children for one thing. More time to share with Marcus.

This would be a shared home, a new start for all of them, somewhere they could all have a stake in, feel a part of.

Vanessa would be able to choose her own room and its décor. Tom would feel secure in the knowledge that his room was solely his.

Surely with so much space at their disposal, with so much security, they would all be able to integrate far better. Life would be easier, free of the small but potentially very destructive tensions which now seemed to infuse it.

She couldn't wait to share her excitement with Marcus. It was the ideal solution to all their problems and she was surprised that she hadn't thought of it before.

She smiled to herself. Perhaps Louise had after all done her a favour in announcing that she intended to terminate their partnership.

She hummed happily under her breath, her face alight with happiness, and new purpose.

CHAPTER FIVE

'FERN?'

Anxiety prickled down Fern's spine as she heard Nick's voice. He walked into the kitchen, frowning when he saw that she was dressed for going out.

'Where are you going?' he demanded.

'I promised I'd help Roberta sort through the stuff she's collected for her jumble sale.'

'What time will you be back? I'm leaving for London this afternoon. You'll have to pack a case for me. I'll need my dinner suit. Did you remember to take it to the cleaners?'

'Yes,' she told him quietly. There had been lipstick on the collar of his dress shirt; bright scarlet lipstick, the colour Venice had been wearing the night of her dinner party.

People, even the most casual of acquaintances, did kiss these days, she reminded herself as she looked away from him.

Why didn't she just ask Nick if he was involved with Venice?

What was she so afraid of? Not the ending of their marriage, surely?

What was it, then? Having to confront the fact that all the effort she had put into holding their marriage together over these last two years had just been so much wasted time... Having to admit that she should never have married Nick in the first place... having to face up to the fact that her parents had not been omnipotent; that their way of living their lives was not necessarily right for her. Having to admit that she was married to a man who, despite the fact that he claimed to love and need her, increasingly behaved towards her in a way that suggested his feelings towards her held more contempt than love; that his need was more for a housekeeper than a wife.

Was it the realities of her marriage she was so afraid of confronting, or was it herself?

What was it she really wanted to do? Stay true to the way her parents had believed their daughter's life should be lived, or be true to herself, accepting herself with all her fallibilities; accepting that staying within her relationship with Nick as it was now was slowly destroying her, killing her self-respect, filling her with loathing for the woman she saw she had become.

'How long will you be away?' she asked Nick now before she opened the back door.

'I don't know!' His mouth tightened impatiently. 'Is my grey suit pressed? I'm taking a client out to lunch.'

73

'Venice?' Fern asked him.

She could see the angry colour seeping up under his skin.

'Yes, as a matter of fact it is.'

'You seem to be seeing rather a lot of her lately.'

'What the hell are you trying to say?' Nick exploded angrily. 'She's a *client*, that's all. A very rich client, I might add, and with business the way it is right now...

'My grey suit, Fern,' he added impatiently. 'Is it pressed?'

'Yes,' she told him.

They couldn't go on like this, she told herself as she left the house. They had to sit down and talk honestly with one another.

She smiled grimly to herself. Sit down and talk... The last time they had done that had been two years ago after she had found out about Nick's affair. She had thought then that he was being honest with her, had allowed him to convince her that their marriage could still work, and for a little while she had actually thought that it might; but then he had started to revert to his earlier behaviour, only this time it had been even worse, because this time, every time he was angry with her, he would taunt her with some viciously cruel remark about Adam.

Oh, afterwards he had always apologised, explained how difficult it was for a man... any man to come to terms with the fact that his wife had been unfaithful to him, told her how generous and heroic he was being in trying to forget what she had done... reminded her of how shocked and distressed her parents would be if they ever discovered the truth...pleaded with her to forgive him, promising that it wouldn't happen again; and because of the burden of her own guilt she had accepted what he had said, feeling in her heart that she deserved to suffer... to be punished for what she had done.

She was trembling so much she could scarcely see what she was doing, struggling with the latch on the front gate as she opened it.

One brief moment out of time, one careless action, one small error of judgement. Who would have thought that she... that Adam...?

Fiercely she blocked off the thought, denying it life. She must *not* think of that now. Not allow herself to remember...

That was, after all, part of her penance, part of the punishment she had inflicted on herself for what she had done.

The morning air was clear and sharp, the wind tempered by the promise of warmth in the spring sunshine.

The wind tugged at her hair, reminding her that she had intended to tie it back. Adam had liked her hair...he had once...

She stopped walking, her body freezing into immobility as she tried to reject her thoughts, pushing them fiercely to the back of her mind, trying not to acknowledge how afraid she was of their power.

It was quite a long walk into town, and she quickened her step a little. She had promised Roberta that she would meet her at the surgery at eleven.

The road where she and Nick lived was on the outskirts of the small market town, a pleasant cul-de-sac of Victorian villas built around the time the railway had first come to the area.

Theirs was one of a pair of good-sized semis which could have been turned into a very attractive and comfortable family home had Nick been willing to spend some money on it. It had the benefit of a large garden and an extra upper storey, and its previous owners had converted the small maze of kitchen, larder and scullery at the back of the property into a large kitchen.

Nick however had pointed out to her shortly after their marriage, when she had tentatively suggested that it might be nice to add a conservatory to the house, that since he was the only one of them working she must realise that he simply could not afford that sort of luxury.

She had done her best to update the décor, and had been quite proud of the dragged and stippled paint effects with which she had transformed the old-fashioned décor of the rooms, and of the curtains and loose covers she had painstakingly made from factory remnants of fabric bought as 'seconds', until Nick had commented to her how amateurish her skills were.

He had done it quite kindly and gently, but she could still remember how humiliated she had felt when, flushed with success and proud of what she had done, she had suggested they give a small dinner party to show off their home.

'Darling, it's impossible,' Nick had told her. 'Don't you see . . . anyone we invite could be a potential client? One look at what you've done to this place and they're going to wonder if my professional skills are as amateurish as your homemaking ones.'

His criticism, although perhaps justified, had taken from her all the pleasure and sense of achievement she had felt in what she had done, and when three weeks later Nick had suddenly announced that he had booked a firm of decorators to come and repaint the whole house she had quietly kept to herself her disappointment over the effect of the no doubt practical but very plain woodchip paper with which every internal wall had been covered.

It was obviously Nick's choice and no doubt he was right when he explained that it looked far better than what she had done.

After that it had never seemed to Fern that the house was really her home; only the kitchen was her domain, and she had tried to make it as cheerful and warm as she could, even though she could tell from Nick's face that he did not approve of the bowls of spring bulbs; the flowers from the garden, the soft yellow paint and the pretty curtains and chair covers she had made for the room.

From the outside the house looked neat and well cared for, just like all the others in the cul-de-sac, but inside it was empty and desolate of all that made a house a proper home, Fern reflected sadly as she turned into the road into town, her footsteps automatically slowing down slightly as she studied the view in front of her.

It didn't matter how many times she walked down here, or how familiar the view before her was; she always felt a fresh surge of pleasure at what she saw.

The town had originally been an important stopping-off point for stage-coaches and other carriage traffic, a vital link with the main arterial routes of the day, and although now modern roads and motorways had turned the town into a quiet backwater, bypassing it, the signs of its thriving, bustling past were clearly visible in its architecture.

One side of the town square was still dominated by the coaching inn which was said to date back to the fifteenth century, although its present exterior was that of a late Tudor building, herringbone-patterned brick insets between the beams replacing the original wattle and daub. Adjacent to it ran a line of similar buildings, once private homes, now mainly shops and offices. Next to them was the church crafted in local stone, its spire reaching up dizzyingly towards the sky.

There was a local legend that the original bells had been melted down at the time of the Civil War to make weapons and armour, but as far as Fern knew this had never actually been substantiated.

Like looking at the rings of a tree to discover its age, the various stages of the town's growth could be seen in the different styles of its architecture.

The third side of the square was lined with handsome Georgian town houses, originally the property of the wealthy tradesmen who had made their homes in the town, drawn there by the business generated from the coaching traffic.

Adam's office was in one of those buildings, beautifully renovated and lovingly restored to all its original elegance.

When it came to his work, no detail was too small to escape Adam's careful attention. Even the paint for the walls had had to be specially mixed to an old-fashioned recipe.

It had been Lord Stanton who had unearthed in his library an estimate and recipe for paint originally supplied for the new wing of the hall which had been built at the same time as the houses and by the same builder who had been responsible for the pretty Nash-type terrace of houses in Avondale.

As she crossed the square, heading for the church, and the surgery, Fern deliberately took the longer way round so that she wouldn't have to walk past Adam's office. The sun glinted on the leaded windows of the coaching inn, highlighting the uneven thickness of the old-fashioned glass, and picking out the detail on the pargeting decorating the upper storey of the building next to it.

In the centre of the square stood an open-arched two-storey stone building, a relic of the days when the town had marked one of the stopping-off places for drovers taking their flocks from one part of the country to another.

On a clear day from the top of the church tower it was possible to see out over the Bristol Channel to the west and to the spire of Salisbury cathedral to the south-east.

It had been Adam's gentle coercion of the local authorities, supported by Lord Stanton, that had been responsible for the removal of the square's tarmac road surface and the uncovering and restoration of the original cobbles which lay beneath it.

Adam's family had lived in the town since the late sixteenth century. Wheelwrights originally, they had prospered during the days of coach travel.

Fern had never met either Nick's mother or Adam's father, both of whom had been killed in a road accident a couple of years prior to her knowing the stepbrothers. However, while Adam had always spoken warmly of both Nick's mother as well as his own parents, Nick rarely mentioned his family at all.

Fern knew that Nick's father had deserted his wife and small son when Nick was barely three years old—Adam had told her that—but when she had once gently tried to sympathise with Nick over his father's defection he had rounded angrily on her.

Fern also knew from comments other people had made that Adam's father, like Adam himself, had been very highly thought of locally, and had been a very generous benefactor to local charities.

He had also been very good to Nick, treating him if anything more indulgently than he had his own son.

Fern remembered how surprised she had been when she first met Nick to discover that the expensive car he had been driving—far more expensive than the car Adam drove—had been a present to him from Adam's father.

The money Nick had used to set himself up in business had also come from Adam's father, via a legacy left to him in the older man's will, but despite this Nick seemed to begrudge the fact that Adam had inherited a far larger proportion of his father's wealth than Nick himself had done.

Fern remembered how shocked she had been the first time she had heard Nick voice this resentment, but then she had reminded herself that, bearing in mind the defection of his own father, it was perhaps understandable that Nick should react so badly, perhaps super-sensitively and totally erroneously seeing in Adam's father's willing of the larger part of his fortune to his natural son a rejection of Nick, his stepson.

And yet Fern had also heard Nick saying disarmingly how uncomfortable he had sometimes felt about the fact that Adam's father had seemed to relate far better to him than he had done to Adam himself.

'I think he felt more in tune with me than he did with Adam. Adam, worthy though he is, can be a bit lacking in humour at times.'

Fern had been surprised by this comment, since she had thought that Adam had an excellent sense of humour, rather dry and subtle perhaps, but he was an extremely perceptive and aware man, who made generous allowances for the vulnerability and frailties of others.

Was it perhaps because Nick had felt he was closer to Adam's father than Adam was himself that he had been so resentful of the fact that Adam had been left the larger portion of his wealth?

Nick had, after all, been the sole beneficiary of his mother's admittedly much more modest estate.

Fern carefully kept as much distance between herself and Adam's office as she could; was it really necessary for her heart to start thumping so furiously fast just at the mere thought that she might see him? Miserably she deliberately looked in the opposite direction, refusing to give in to the temptation to turn her head and see if that faint shadow she could see at one of the windows really was Adam.

Adam... She shivered convulsively, acknowledging how stupidly weak she was. Just mentally saying his name had such a powerful effect on her senses that she was half afraid she had said it out loud.

It was a relief to walk into the surgery and escape.

'Ah, good, there you are,' Roberta announced as she saw her. 'The stuff's already across at the church hall. I was just beginning to wonder if you weren't going to make it.'

'I left a little bit later than I planned,' Fern apologised as they crossed the narrow cobbled street separating the surgery from the church hall.

'Just look at all this stuff,' Roberta groaned after they had let themselves in and were standing surveying the bagged bundles heaped in the middle of the room. 'Heavens, these don't even look as though they've been worn,' she commented as she tackled the nearest of the bags, holding up a couple of dresses for Fern's inspection. 'These came from Amanda Bryant and they probably cost more than I spend on my wardrobe in a whole year...much more,' she added ruefully as Fern leaned forward to inspect the labels. 'I think I remember Amanda wearing this one for last year's vicarage garden party.'

'It is very striking,' Fern acknowledged.

Amanda Bryant and her husband Edward had been their fellow guests at Venice's dinner party, a very wealthy and flamboyant local couple who had made a good deal of money from a variety of shrewd investments. There were certain staid members of the local community who tended to disapprove of them, but Fern liked them both. Amanda made her laugh with her robust good-natured humour, and her very genuine and down-to-earth enjoyment of their new-found wealth. They were not in the least pretentious and their annual summer barbecue was one of the best attended and most popular local events, probably second only in popularity to Lord Stanton's New Year's Eve ball, ranking there with the river race which Adam organised each year to raise money for charity.

'Venice has given us masses of stuff as well. All of it designer-label by the looks of it and hardly worn. I only wish I were a smaller size,' Roberta added wistfully. 'There's a suit here that would fit you perfectly, Fern,' she added, eyeing her own plump figure with resignation. 'It's just your colouring.'

Fern could feel the tension crawling down her spine; revulsion at the thought of wearing something that Venice herself might have worn when she was with Nick... In her mind's eye, Fern could see Nick removing it from the other woman's body... touching her... caressing her...

She felt no sexual or emotional jealousy at the scene she had mentally conjured up, only a deadening sense of futility and despair.

Was it for this that she had spent the last two years of her life desperately trying to piece together her marriage... to convince herself that in staying in it she had made the right, the only decision... that ultimately what she was enduring would prove worthwhile once she and Nick were through the turbulence of these painful years; that ultimately the need he said he had for her would... *must* conjure up an answering spark within her, that would allow her to cease searching hopelessly for whatever it was that had drawn her to him in the first place and make her believe that she loved him?

Without turning round to see what Roberta was showing her, she said quietly, 'I'm afraid I'm not really the type for drop-dead glamour outfits. They're not really my style.'

As she watched her, Roberta repressed a small sigh. Fern might not have Venice's extrovert vibrant personality, but she had a marvellously slender and supple figure, a femininity which shone through the dullness of her clothes, a serenity and tranquillity which drew others to her in need of the gentle warmth of her personality.

She had a very pretty face as well, and as for her hair!

Roberta's own husband, a pragmatic and very down-to-earth Scot, had once confessed to Roberta that he was never able to look at Fern's hair without wondering if it felt as sensually warm and silkily luxurious to touch as it did to look at.

'It's the kind of hair that makes a man want to reach out and...'

He had stopped there looking slightly shame-faced and sheepish, while Roberta raised her eyebrows and commanded drily, 'Go on!'

He had not done so, of course; there had been no need, and neither had Roberta been annoyed or jealous. She knew him far too well, and Fern as well. Now, if it had been Venice they had been discussing... There was a woman who would enjoy nothing more than the challenge of taking another woman's man. Fern, on the other hand...

'There are one or two children's outfits here,' Fern commented, interrupting her train of thought.

'We'll keep them separate from the rest,' Roberta told her, 'although I don't think there will be very many. Most mothers these days seem to operate their own exchange system.'

'Well, it does make sense,' Fern pointed out. 'Children's things are very expensive and often they're not in them long enough to wear them out.'

'Mmm . . . it's all very different from when mine were young,' Roberta agreed. 'These days it's all designer trainers and the right kind of jeans virtually from the moment they can speak.'

Even with only a very short break for a sandwich and a cup of coffee, it took them until well into the afternoon to work their way through all the clothes which had been donated.

Fern's knees ached from the draught coming in under the church hall's ill-fitting doors when she eventually got to her feet. Outside the sun was still shining although it was chilly now inside the hall.

Nick had said that he wanted to leave at five, which meant that he would arrive at his London hotel in good time for dinner.

He hadn't told her where he would be staying, though. Fern frowned as she remembered how tense and on edge he had been earlier . . . how irritable with her.

After she had left Roberta and started to walk home, she wondered tiredly why it was that she and Nick just could not seem to grow closer to one another. It was after all what they both wanted.

Was it? a small bitter voice demanded. If it was, why was Nick paying so much attention to Venice?

She *was* one of his clients, Fern reminded herself firmly, and Nick was after all human and a man. It was only natural that he should be aware of Venice as a woman. What man would not be?

But Adam had not looked at Venice with the same barely concealed sexual interest that she had seen in Nick's eyes . . .

She tensed briefly, fighting off the wave of emotion she could feel threatening her.

As she had done on her arrival, she carefully skirted Adam's office, keeping her head averted as she hurried past it on the opposite side of the square, increasing her walking pace as she left the town behind her.

If she didn't linger too long, she just about had enough time to take in one of her favourite detours, to enjoy a special piece of self-indulgence. After all, if Nick was right, she wasn't going to be able to do so for much longer, she reflected.

Broughton House lay on the outskirts of the town, close enough to her own house for her to be able to turn off into the quiet lane which led to it.

The railway which had led to the erection of their own small cul-de-sac had also heralded the end of the town's busy prosperity, preserving it as it had been in the middle of the nineteenth century virtually so that it remained compact and neat, without the urban sprawl which had over-taken so many other towns.

Although it was less than a mile from the town, Broughton House was still surrounded by fields, with an outlook over open countryside, the builder having cleverly sited it so that the side overlooking the town had the least number of windows.

It had originally been built by a wealthy merchant, a 'nabob' returning from India, who, disdaining the existing properties, had commissioned himself a new one in the countryside surrounding the place which had been his original birthplace.

The grounds, which covered an area of almost four acres, had become overgrown during the last eighteen months or so of Mrs Broughton's life, but Fern liked the soft wildness of the over-long grass with its sprinkling of spring bulbs; the moss which coated the paths and the general air of what to others might be neglect but to her gave the place more a sense of somehow sleeping mysteriously, waiting for the magical touch of an owner who would love it to restore it to its original splendour, but these were thoughts she kept to herself, knowing how derisive Nick would be were she to voice them to him.

As she walked through the formal rose garden, bare now at this time of year, she paused to watch the young heron standing on the mossy edge of the round goldfish pond.

Somewhere within its depths lurked a dozen or more fat lazy goldfish, but Fern suspected they were far too wise and knowing to risk surfacing in such cool weather, and that the young marauder for all his bravura would have a disappointing wait for his dinner.

Through the rhododendron bushes now gone wild and desperately in need of some attention Fern could see the house itself, but today the house wasn't her destination.

Instead she turned away from it, finding her way through what had once been an attractively planted shrubbery.

Alongside the neglected path there flowered remnants of what must once have been a two- to three-foot-deep ribbon of spring bulbs naturalised in grass.

Today these survived only in broken patches and clumps.

It took Fern almost ten minutes to force her way through the tangled undergrowth obscuring the pathway to the small bowl-shaped enclosure at the centre of the shrubbery.

The stone seat set back from its rim was encrusted with lichen, the lion masks of the seat pedestals and arms badly weathered.

Today, at this time of the year, all that could be seen in the bowl were the emergent shoots of the lilies which when in flower filled the bowl with band after band of massed drifts of flowers in rings of colour from palest cream to deepest gold and from lightest blue to almost purple.

It was Mrs Broughton herself who had first brought her to this spot and told her its history, explaining to her how her husband's grandmother had had the bowl made and planted, having fallen in love with the same design but on a much grander scale on a visit to America.

The lilies had been in flower then and Fern remembered how the sight of them had made her catch her breath in wonder, tears stinging her eyes, her senses totally overwhelmed by their beauty.

If Nick was right and Adam was part of a consortium planning to buy the house and use the land, this would be the last year she would be able to witness the small miracle of the lilies blossoming.

As she sat down on the stone seat, tears blurred her eyes.

Tears for the destruction of this small oasis of beauty or tears for herself? she wondered cynically as she blinked them away.

'Fern!'

She tensed, automatically controlling and absorbing her shock, and, even more importantly, concealing it, knowing without having to turn her head to whom the quiet male voice belonged.

Why pretend to be shocked? an inner voice taunted her. You must have known that he might be here. That's really why you came, isn't it? Not to mourn the passing of the garden but because...

She got up quickly, her face tight with tension as she turned to face him.

'Adam!'

Her voice betrayed nothing of what she was feeling; of the unending destructive war within her that was so much a part of her life that the wounds it inflicted on her had long ago ceased consciously to hurt and were something she simply accepted as part of the price she had to pay for her own culpability.

Automatically she retreated into the shadows of the shrubbery, carefully distancing herself from him, protectively concealing her expression, her eyes from him just in case...

'So Venice was right,' she said lightly. 'You *are* planning to buy this place. What will you build here, Adam? Is it going to be a supermarket as she suggested?'

She could hear the brittle tension in her voice, feel the way her body was starting to tremble as she faced him across the distance which separated them.

It had been almost two years now and yet her senses, her emotions, her flesh could remember with devastating accuracy how it had felt to be held by him, to touch him, not with the knowingness which had come later and for which she must eternally pay the price of her own guilt and searing, suffocating loathing, but with the innocence of loving someone for that first precious and very special time; the wonder of experiencing that love, the joy, the tremulous seesawing between awed delight and disbelief.

He had been so tender with her, so caring...so protective...so careful not to hurry or rush her.

Had he really cared about her at all, or had she simply imagined that
he had, out of her own need? Was it merely pity which had motivated
him? Whatever he might have felt for her then in that moment of intimacy, she knew what he must feel for her now... how much he must
despise her. After all, what man could feel anything other than contempt
for a woman who...

Who what? Who went to him and begged him, pleaded with him to
make love to her, even after he had already tried to put her to one side,
to end what had accidentally and inadvertently begun. Only she hadn't
let him... She had...

She shuddered tensely, desperately trying to block off her self-
destructive thoughts, to channel the threatening power of what she was
feeling in less lethal directions, to remind herself that she was Nick's
wife.

And the only way she had of reinforcing the view the outside world
had to hold of her relationship with Adam, of reinforcing to Adam that
he need never *ever* fear that she would seek to humiliate herself in such
a way again, by repeating that idiotic, crazy behaviour of the past, was
to treat him with the coldness and distance behind which she had learned
to hide her true feelings.

Even when they did not have an audience. After all, it was even more
important that Adam did not guess the truth than it was that no one else
did.

What was left of her pride, a poor thin-skinned affair, she had somehow
managed to patch together, but it could never be wholly mended or
trusted, and would certainly never be strong enough to sustain any real
blows against it.

'Is that really what you think I would do, Fern?'

The harshness in his voice hurt her almost physically. She wanted to
flinch back from it, to cry out in protest, but stoically she refused to let
herself.

Physically Adam might not have that charmed, almost boyish look of
youth which made Nick so attractive, but there was something about him
in his maturity which appealed even more strongly to her feminine senses
now than it had done when they had been younger.

There was a sensuality, a sexuality about Adam which, although covert
and subtle rather than something which he himself was aware of and
deliberately flaunted, had an effect on her that made her so aware of
herself as a woman—aware of herself and aware of her need for him—
that just standing here, what should have been a perfectly ludicrously
safe distance away from him, was enough to raise the tiny hairs at the
nape of her neck and send a *frisson* of aching desire twisting painfully
through her body.

Adam had a masculinity, a maleness which no woman could possibly
ignore, she acknowledged tautly. Even now, with her brain and her body

screaming warnings of danger to her, she was intensely aware of it and of him.

Aware of it and achingly, desperately envious of the woman, the girl on whom it was bestowed.

Once she had thought she had been that girl, but Nick had questioned her, laughing at her as he asked her almost incredulously if she had really believed that Adam was attracted to her.

'Has he ever made love to you?' he had asked her, and she had shaken her head, wincing as Nick had shrugged and announced bluntly, 'Well, there you are, then. If he had wanted you...really wanted you, he would have done so. I want you, Fern,' he had added huskily. 'I want you very, very much.'

She shivered slightly, forcing herself back to the present and to Adam's question.

'You're a businessman,' she responded tiredly.

'I'm an architect,' he contradicted her flatly.

'But you *are* here,' Fern pointed out, flushing slightly as she heard the anger edging up under his voice. 'Something must have brought you.'

'*You're* here too,' Adam retaliated coolly. 'What brought *you*?'

Somehow Fern managed to swallow down the hard, hurting ball of tears which had locked in her throat. It was always like this when they met, their voices full of painful anger, her body stiff and tense with the effort of rejecting and controlling what she was really feeling, the indifference, the distance she forced herself to display taking so much out of her that she already knew that the moment he had gone she would be reduced to a trembling, shivering wreck, totally unable to do so much as put one foot properly in front of the other; that she would spend hours and not minutes trying to stop herself from reliving the past, from wishing...wanting...

'You're here,' he had said. Tension crawled along her spine and into her nerve-endings. Did he think she had known he would be here...that she had followed him here...that she might...?

'I wanted to see the garden, before you destroy it...'

Try as she might, she could not keep the pain out of her voice. She turned to face him, her chin tilting, the sunlight catching her hair so that for a moment she seemed so ethereally a part of her surroundings that Adam found himself holding his breath, afraid almost to breathe as he watched her, mentally reclothing her in soft greens and yellows, the colours, the fabrics flowing and harmonious, enhancing the feminine suppleness of her body, highlighting the almost fawnlike quality of her features, so delicate that they were cruelly swamped by the dullness of the clothes she was actually wearing. Only her hair... Her hair...

Abruptly he looked away from her. She was Nick's wife and she loved him, although how she...

As she watched him, Fern wondered what he would say if she told him that she had seen the brochure he had been carrying.

Pain flooded through her. It seemed unfairly cruel of fate that it should be Adam of all people who threatened the existence of somewhere that had come to mean so much to her...a solace...a refuge...a sanctuary...

From what? From life? From herself? From her marriage? Tiredly she knew that she wouldn't challenge him...just as she couldn't challenge Nick about Venice?

'I...I must go. Nick...Nick is...will be expecting me. He...he's leaving for London and...'

Without finishing her sentence she ducked her head to one side and hurriedly started to skirt a wide circle around him, heading back towards the path, sensing that he was watching her but knowing that she dared not look back at him.

Adam! She could feel the heavy, dreary feeling of despair starting to settle over her as she half ran and half stumbled back down the path. Her body was trembling and she felt icy cold even though at the same time her face felt as though it was burningly hot, and her heart was beating so fast that she was finding it difficult to breathe properly.

Too late now to wish she had gone straight home...to wish she had not given in to the temptation to go to Broughton House and in doing so inadvertently and so very, very dangerously and painfully she now risked opening the Pandora's box into which she had tried to lock away all her memories and thoughts of Adam.

CHAPTER SIX

ZOE woke up slowly and reluctantly, subconsciously aware of something unpleasant waiting for her, something she didn't really want to recognise. It hovered threateningly, oppressing her, making her want to resort to the childhood tactic of squeezing her eyes closed and refusing to acknowledge that she was actually awake.

She rolled over in the bed, instinctively seeking the empty space which had held Ben's body.

The bed felt cold and empty. It was gone ten o'clock. Ben would have been up at four to get to the markets early.

His original training had encompassed not only the preparation and cooking of food, but also the importance of its purchase; of knowing the difference between good fresh food and that which was sub-standard.

Her shift didn't start until two, and after their late night the previous evening she would have been grateful to Ben for not disturbing her had it not been for the row they had had last night.

Or, rather, the row she had tried to have.

She had known that he was still awake when she got into bed—his body had been too rigid, too tense for sleep—but he had kept his back to her, refusing to turn round, refusing even to acknowledge that she was justified in her anger against him.

It wasn't so much his attitude towards his sister's pregnancy, although that had shocked her. What had hurt her most of all had been his emotional rejection of *her*, his refusal to acknowledge that she might possibly be able to understand how he was feeling; his use against her of the barrier of 'class', which they had always promised one another they would never allow to come between them.

It had almost been as though he had wanted to reject her, to shock and even disgust her by what he was saying.

And yet at the same time she had been aware of his pain and despair; of his love for his family, and for his sister, even though he had tried desperately hard to conceal it.

But why should *she*, just because she was female, a woman, be the one to make allowances ... to understand ... to forgive?

Why should *he*, just because he was male, a man, be allowed to offload the pain of what he was experiencing on her by attacking her?

His sister's pregnancy and his reaction to it was something they should have been able to share, to talk about. Ben should have been able to accept that, even though she lacked his experience, his perception of what that pregnancy could mean, she was nevertheless capable of listening, comprehending . . . that she might even have a viable viewpoint to put, and one which, although different from his, was still worthy of being heard and discussed.

His final comment to her last night before he had flung away from her had been an acid, 'You don't really understand even now, do you? You just don't have a clue. Outwardly you're sympathetic, sorry; but inwardly you're recoiling from what I've just told you, just like a healthy man recoiling from a leper!

'Nothing's really changed in two thousand or more years of civilisation, has it, Zoe? You in your nice, clean, sanitised, privileged world— and it *is* a privileged world no matter how much you might want to deny it—you just don't have any conception of what life's really like for people like my sister.'

Hurt, and close to tears, she had tried to defend herself, and it was then that she had made her worst mistake of all.

'She could come here and stay with us,' she had suggested eagerly. 'I could find her a job. The hotel is always looking for——'

'Oh, for God's sake,' Ben had interrupted her in disgust. 'Have her here? She's damn near seven months pregnant, Zoe, and all she wants to do is sit watching television all day long. She doesn't *want* a job. She doesn't *want* anything other than this damned baby which she thinks is going to miraculously transform her life.

'And so it bloody well will, but not in the way she imagines, the little fool.

'Are all you women the same, so blindly prejudiced that you can't see what having a baby really means?'

She had tried hard to stand her ground, inviting him shakily, 'What *does* it mean, Ben? Tell me.'

He had given her a bitter, cynical look.

'It means an extra mouth to feed, and less money coming in; it means endless nights without any sleep, and the stink of sour milk and worse pervading everything. It means the total destruction of the relationship you thought you had with one another; that's if you're still together when the child arrives.

'It means . . . Oh, God, what the hell is the point in trying to explain to you, Zoe? Children, pregnancy . . . to you they mean giving birth in some fashionable private ward of a hospital and then going home with a clean cooing bundle wrapped in something expensive and impractical bought by Mummy. It means agonising endlessly over finding a nanny, and then agonising even more over finding the right school. You don't have any real idea.'

She had wanted to tell him that he was wrong, totally and utterly wrong, but instead she had asked him quietly, 'And what does parenthood, fatherhood mean to you, Ben?' But as she waited for his answer, she suspected she already knew.

Even so, his reply had shocked her.

'It doesn't mean anything,' he had told her harshly. 'Because I don't intend to *ever* be a father.'

And with that he had got into bed, put out the light and pointedly turned away from her.

Later, lying silently in bed beside him, she had waited for him to relent and turn to her; to take her in his arms and hold her.

Only he hadn't done, and now this morning she was alone in their flat with anger as well as misery, a cold, hard lump of indigestible solidity wedged firmly inside her.

She got out of bed reluctantly and headed for the bathroom.

She pushed open the door and then stopped, staring at the paper images pinned, taped to almost every surface.

Eyes widening, she went into the living-room. It was full of them as well, huge hearts cut from newspapers and magazines, with the words 'I love you' scrawled across them in red felt-tip pen, tiny smaller ones cut from silver kitchen foil and strung together like the tail of a kite, and hung from the doorframes so that they danced in the draught, big fat pigs with drawn-in tiny mean little eyes and droopy would-be-curly tails made from wrapping ribbons that made her laugh as the tears filled her eyes.

He must have spent hours doing this, hours when he should have been asleep. Hours when she *had* been asleep.

Across the largest pig of all, propped up against the kitchen taps, he had written the words, 'I'm sorry'.

Oh, Ben!

As she carefully collected every single heart, and every single pig, smoothing out the paper before gently folding it and then searching for a large envelope to put them in, she was still crying, her heart aching, not for herself but for him.

She knew how much his family meant to him, how fiercely protective of them he was. And she knew as well how much Sharon's pregnancy and all that it would mean to her life must hurt him. She had been a clever girl, he had told her, and in those words she had heard all his frustration and disappointment.

'It will be another mouth to feed,' he had told her and no doubt he had been thinking that he would be the one who would have to help to feed it.

Neither of them ever discussed the financial help he gave his mother. They didn't need to. Zoe felt no resentment of his loyalty towards his family.

'That's because you've never needed to worry about money,' he had told her cynically, and then she had smiled sunnily, refusing to allow him to aggravate her.

It wasn't until she had finished tidying away all the scraps of paper that she noticed the envelope on the table.

She had forgotten to mention it to Ben last night, and he obviously had not noticed it when he got up.

She picked it up, scanning it uncertainly. When she had seen it yesterday she had been so excited; now, like an opened forgotten bottle of champagne, her excitement had gone flat, superseded by other emotions.

For the first time she felt, if not resentment, then certainly a sudden awareness of irritation with Ben's family. She wriggled uncomfortably, frowning as she refocused on the envelope.

This was *their* future here in front of her. Hers and Ben's... The exciting, enticing, challenging future they had worked so hard together for. It belonged to *them*. They had worked for it...planned for it, and Ben...Ben deserved it; and yet now, because of his family, because of last night, somehow its promise was shadowed, her excitement doused, their right to share and anticipate the pleasure of taking their first major step into the future and success dulled by the sharp contrast between their future and that of Ben's sister and her child.

And if *she* was so aware of the discrepancies in those futures, then how much more so must Ben be?

She gave a small shiver of distress and guilt. Was she really so selfish, so shallow that she resented Sharon for inadvertently casting a shadow over their lives? By rights what she ought to be feeling was sympathy and concern, not wishing that Ben's sister had not spoiled this special moment in their lives by inflicting her problems on her brother.

She picked up the envelope and then put it down again.

She was not normally given to self-analysis or questioning her feelings— her life was too busy, her responses too immediate and instinctive. It was Ben who measured his reactions, who monitored everything he said and felt, measuring them against some personal and, to her, bewildering measuring stick of personal standards.

But now, forced to deal with her own shock at what she was feeling, she had to question whether Ben might be right when he accused her of not being able to really comprehend or understand, of not wanting to accept the reality of his family's lives.

How would she feel if she were in Sharon's shoes, for instance?

She gave a small cold shiver. It could never have happened to her, of course.

There *had* been girls at school who had disappeared for a brief period of time and who it was rumoured had been discreetly hustled off by their parents to some expensive private clinic to remove the evidence of their unplanned and unwanted conception long before their bodies showed any signs of it, and rumours were all there had been.

Parenthood out of wedlock and children born to middle-aged fathers with almost grown-up families and second wives, often as young as their own daughters, were a familiar pattern of life to her, of course, but her friends' unmarried parenthood was nothing like that so graphically described by Ben.

Her friends' babies were always 'desperately wanted' or 'an accident really, darling, but now both of us are thrilled and Mummy is simply over the moon', or the product of serious committed relationships between couples who shuddered in distaste at the thought of their commitment to one another needing anything so proletarian as a marriage ceremony to cement it.

No, there were no Sharons in her world, or, if there were, no one talked about them.

Ben was her friend and her lover; the differences in their upbringing gave her no qualms at all. She was proud of him, fiercely proud... of the person he was and the things he had achieved. She felt no sense of being his superior, nor of being his inferior; they were equals, true partners.

And normally she did not allow herself to brood on the fact that there was a part of Ben's life from which he seemed to want to exclude her.

Now she was angry with herself for the small-mindedness of her feelings, for her selfishness in her irritation at the way Sharon's problems had overshadowed their own happiness. And angry with Ben for letting them?

What would she have preferred him to do—come back from Manchester pretending that everything was all right, keep the truth from her so that it need not spoil her pleasure, shield her from his own pain?

No, of course not. She loved him. She *wanted* to share his pain as well as his pleasure; the bad things as well as the good.

Before she left for work, Zoe propped the letter up against the kettle and scrawled a note, which she put beside it, saying, 'I love you too,' and then drew a heart which she filled with tiny kisses.

Poor Sharon. Did she lie awake in bed at night with her hands on her swollen belly, dreaming of a man who would love her—and her baby? *She* was so lucky, Zoe admitted. If she were in Sharon's shoes...

Ben had made no secret of the fact that he felt that Sharon should have had her pregnancy terminated, and Zoe couldn't help agreeing with him. It would surely have been the best solution for everyone. But Sharon had not taken that option and now it was too late.

Another mouth to feed, Ben had said bitterly, and Zoe had sensed his anger, his frustration, his refusal to see the coming baby as anything other than an extra financial burden he did not want to have to shoulder.

'I don't want children,' he had told her, but then neither did she. Not at this stage in her life. Maybe later, much, much later, when she had done all the things she wanted to do.

Her shift started at two and finished officially at ten, but it was gone half-past eleven before she was finally able to leave the hotel and almost one before her battered but reliable Mini brought her back to the flat.

She had expected Ben to be in bed; after all, he had to be up at four. But as she searched for her key he surprised her by opening the door for her.

'Ben!' She smiled her happiness up at him.

'I'm sorry... About last night,' he told her gruffly as he opened his arms to her, kicking the door shut behind her.

'It doesn't matter,' she whispered back. 'You were upset. Did you see the letter?'

'What letter?' he murmured, lazily nuzzling the delicate vulnerable flesh just behind her ear, but his casual tone did not deceive Zoe. She knew him too well.

'You know which one,' she told him. 'Have you opened it?'

His tongue was slowly exploring the shape of her ear, sending small *frissons* of sensation racing down her spine, making her want to move her body against his, to stretch languorously and sensually against him like a cat being stroked.

'Of course I haven't.' Ben smiled at her as he released her. 'You didn't really think I'd open it without you, did you? Come on, let's open it now...'

'No,' Zoe told him, watching him frown. 'Let's open it in bed instead,' she suggested, her eyes narrowing with laughter and warmth as she added, 'Then we can really celebrate if it's good news.'

'And if it's not?' Ben cautioned.

She smiled lovingly at him.

'If it's not, then we'll be in the right place to commiserate with each other, won't we? But it *won't* be bad news,' she told him firmly.

She insisted that he should be the one to open it and then closed her eyes, urging him to hurry because she couldn't bear the suspense any longer, crossing her fingers behind her back as she listened to the sounds of him tearing open the envelope.

She could feel his tension and stillness as he read whatever was inside and then, unable to bear it any longer, she opened her eyes and begged.

'What does it say?'

Silently Ben handed her the contents of the envelope. She scanned the letter quickly before dropping it on to the bed to scrutinise the thick glossy brochure which it had been attached to.

'Oh, Ben! Look...it's perfect!'

'You haven't read it properly yet,' he derided her, but he was smiling and she could tell, although he was struggling hard to conceal it, that he was almost as excited as she was herself.

'Don't start getting your hopes too high,' Ben warned her later when the brochure had been read and re-read at least a dozen times. 'As Clive points out in his letter, there's a long way to go. We'll need planning permission to convert the stable block for one thing, and then...'

'But it's so perfect,' Zoe interrupted him excitedly. 'All that land...'

'Which will have to be maintained. Gardens are all very well, but they don't look after themselves, you know.'

'No. No, of course not, but that walled vegetable garden... You said yourself that with people becoming more aware of the importance of how their food is grown as well as prepared...' she began impatiently, but Ben shook his head.

'We're a long way from growing our own produce, Zoe. That's something that will be way, way ahead in the future.'

'But with a house like this at least we'll have the potential for that kind of future development, won't we?'

'We don't know that Clive will be able to buy the place yet,' Ben reminded her. 'He only says in his letter that the property is suitable and that, because of its situation, it won't be overpriced.'

'No, but he says that the surrounding area is reasonably prosperous, and that he believes that there will be a demand for a first-class restaurant, and then there'll be weddings and other functions. Oh, Ben...it's perfect. We'll be able to use the gardens for marquees, and it says here that there's a large pond...'

'Which we'll probably have to fill in, if we don't want to spend half our time fishing drunken wedding guests out of it,' Ben supplied drily.

Zoe made a small moue and flung her pillow at him.

'You don't fool me,' she told him. 'I *know* that you're just as excited about it all as I am. When shall we go and see it? Clive says he'll make arrangements for us to view it with him, if we can give him a date. Ben...Ben, what are you doing?' she protested as he took hold of her and started kissing her.

'Didn't you say something about us celebrating?' he asked her, his voice muffled as he kissed the soft curve of her breast.

'It's two o'clock in the morning and you've got to be up at four.'

'Who needs to wait until four?' he told her. 'I'm "up" right now; come and feel for yourself.'

Zoe laughed, enjoying his unusual mock-macho display. It wasn't like him to either talk or behave so playfully, and she felt her own spirits lift as she responded to his ebullience.

She repaid him for it later though, laughing as he protested at the delicate friction of her teeth against his skin.

'What are you doing?' he demanded as she released him, craning his head over his shoulder suspiciously as he saw her face.

'Nothing,' she fibbed innocently, her eyes full of laughter as she surveyed the results of her handiwork, the small neat heart-shaped outline of lovebites she had drawn quite deliberately across his buttocks.

'Will you be playing rugby on Sunday?' she asked him sleepily as she curled up next to him.

Whenever he could, he played in a small team made up in the main of fellow chefs, and when she could Zoe went along with him to cheer him on. This Sunday, though, she would be working. Which was probably just as well, she reflected, smiling to herself as she visualised the results of her ardent handiwork.

'Have you any days' holiday left?'

Sleepily Zoe opened her eyes, lifting her head off the pillow to stare through the darkness at Ben. She had thought he was already asleep.

'Yes, I think so. Why?'

'I was just thinking. When we go down to see the house, it might be a good idea to take a few days off, have a good look round and weigh up the competition.'

'A holiday?' Zoe was sitting bolt upright now, her eyes bright with enthusiasm. 'Oh, Ben, could we?'

She knew how careful he was with his budget. Careful but not mean— never that. She earned more than he did, and she also had her parents to turn to should she need to do so. Because of that she was careful not to offend his pride by offering to pay for too many extra 'treats'. She also knew how much he would be worrying about Sharon's coming baby— the extra mouth he would insist on helping to feed, no matter how much he might rail now against the child's conception.

'I don't see why not. We could always put it down to business expenses,' he added drily. 'Isn't that the way it's done? Mind you, why should *I* knock it? It will be all those executives with their hefty expense accounts that we'll need to attract if we're going to make this thing pay. Running a hotel isn't like running a restaurant.'

Zoe caught the underlying note of tension in his voice and frowned. She was fully awake now and so obviously was he.

This was something they had talked about when Clive had first offered to back them.

Ben had always wanted to open his own restaurant; he was after all virtually running the restaurant where he now worked, although Aldo, the Italian who owned it, would never have admitted it. He was a sour-tempered, mean-natured man, whose chefs didn't normally last very long, even though the restaurant itself was a popular one.

He was over fifty, married to an Englishwoman, and it was the marriage which was the root cause of his bad temper and general antagonism towards his employees, Ben believed.

He made no secret of the fact that had he not been stupid enough to believe himself in love with an English girl he would now be running the family's prestigious restaurants in Rome and not living here in London.

His parents had never approved of his marriage; elderly now, they were still alive, his mother very much the matriarch of the family. Aldo's half-British children were still treated with disdain and suspicion by Aldo's family.

Zoe felt sorry for the man's wife, but Ben was not as sympathetic.

'She could always leave him,' he had told her. 'In fact she should do, but she stays with him because she enjoys making him suffer...and he takes it out on us.'

'You could always change your job,' Zoe had suggested.

'It's not that easy at the moment,' Ben had told her. 'You might not have noticed it yet, not with the hotel being so close to the airport and still busy, but we have. We're not getting as many midweek bookings as we used to.'

She knew he was worrying about how the recession might affect their hotel—about his own ability to take on so much increased responsibility.

She had done her best to coax him out of it, reminding him that he was the only one who seemed to lack faith in himself and that he should perhaps follow the example of others like Clive and herself who felt very differently.

'I know you can do it,' she had assured him. 'And so does Clive.'

It had been Clive who had been convinced that they should look beyond the mere owning of their own restaurant to a small top-flight country hotel.

Initially Ben had been uncertain, unsure if they were ready for that kind of responsibility, and it had been Zoe who had convinced him, pointing out that the hotel gave them a chance to pool their abilities in a way that a restaurant would not.

With a restaurant there would be no real role for her, she had told him, other than that of part-time bookkeeper and accountant. She would still need to keep on her own job, otherwise she would lose the momentum of her own career, and if she did continue to work, given the shiftwork involved and the long hours, they would scarcely have any time together at all.

As she had known he would, Ben had soon seen the validity of her arguments, and now he was every bit as keen and excited about their future as she was herself, even if he did sometimes lapse into the cautious wariness which was so much a part of his personality.

Not that she would want him to be any other way, Zoe told herself sunnily now. She quite cheerfully admitted that she was sometimes inclined to be so over-optimistic, that she neglected to see genuine potential pitfalls.

She had no need to fear them, though, not with Ben standing patiently and protectively by, ready to keep her safe from them.

'I can't wait to see the house, can you?' she asked him eagerly. 'When can we go? When?'

'Don't get too excited,' Ben interrupted her warningly. 'There's a long way to go yet, Zoe.'

'Cautious, careful Ben... Always looking for problems,' she teased him light-heartedly.

'Well, one of us has to,' he pointed out. 'And since it certainly isn't going to be you...'

He paused and Zoe's smile changed to a small frown.

Did he *resent* the fact that he had to be cautious for both of them? Did he sometimes find her optimism a burden?

Did he sometimes find *her* a burden, a responsibility? Like his family.

Her frown deepened, her excitement evaporating.

'Ben...' she began uncertainly.

'Mmm...' he said sleepily. 'Leave it with me...I'll give Clive a ring and sort something out.'

He was already virtually asleep and it wouldn't be fair to wake him up just so that she could ask for his reassurance, Zoe admitted honestly, but it was a long, long time before she herself finally managed to fall asleep too.

CHAPTER SEVEN

'MARCUS, I think I might have found us a house.'

Eleanor had had the details of the Wiltshire property for three days now, but she had deliberately waited until she and Marcus were alone before broaching the subject with him, conscious of the fact not only that he was irritated by the disruption caused by Julia's announcement that he would have to provide a home for their daughter while she was in America, but also that the complexities of a new case he had recently taken on were demanding most of his time and attention.

She had known before she married him that he was the type of man to whom his work was not just a means of earning a living but something he genuinely enjoyed, and that once he became involved in a case it absorbed him to an extent which demanded a partner's patience and understanding.

It had been Julia's inability to accept that there were times when, on the surface at least, his work would appear to receive more of his time and attention than she did which had originally led to a rift developing between them. Marcus had made no secret of this aspect of his personality before their marriage and Eleanor had wisely forced herself to detach herself from the magnetic delirium caused by her enjoyment of the physical side of their relationship to ask herself if she could accept the importance of his work, and live with the consequences of it; not just immediately in the dizzying rose-coloured flush of so unexpectedly falling in love and being loved in return, but in the more mundane years ahead when that flush had retreated, leaving a world shaded in more prosaic colours.

She had decided that she could; after all, she was a woman in her thirties who had discovered for herself not just the importance of being financially independent, but also the thrill which came from self-achievement. Hadn't there, after all, especially in the initial days of establishing her own business, been times when she had worked long into the night, so totally absorbed by what she was doing that she forgot everything else?

In an ideal world it might be possible for a man and a woman to find a way of synchronising their affairs so that they could harmonise those periods when their need for one another totally eclipsed everything else, a world where with a look, a word, both were able to put aside all other matters and reach out to one another.

Unfortunately life just did not happen like that, Eleanor acknowledged wryly as she waited for Marcus to make some acknowledgement of her comment other than the brief automatic grunt she had already received.

96

'Marcus,' she repeated more insistently. 'Did you hear me? I said I think I've found us a house.'

'What? Oh, yes...sorry.' He smiled at her as he raised his head from his papers.

'I've made arrangements for us to view it this weekend.'

'*This* weekend?' He was frowning now as he looked at her.

'We've got Vanessa the weekend after,' Eleanor reminded him. 'And you did say you might have to go to The Hague.'

'The Hague... Oh, that's had to be postponed now. I need to clear up one or two things first. This Alexander case is proving a bit more complicated than we first thought. This view—what time...?'

'One-ish,' Eleanor told him. 'That will give us enough time to drive down there——'

'Drive down there? Drive down where?' Marcus questioned her.

'Wiltshire,' Eleanor told him.

'Wiltshire! I thought we were looking for something in London!'

Quickly Eleanor agreed. 'Yes, I know that's what we originally discussed, but I've been thinking it over, Marcus, and there are just so many advantages of moving out into the country that I'm surprised that we didn't think of it before.

'I'll be able to work from home for one thing, which means I'll be there full time for the children. The boys will be able to go to a local school...become part of a real community. No more ferrying them halfway across London.

'We'll be able to have all the space we need...not just for Vanessa but for friends as well, and Wiltshire isn't that far. The agents tell me there's an excellent train service into Waterloo from Salisbury, and best of all is the fact that we'll just get so much more for our money.

'I've got the details here...if you...'

'Eleanor, I...'

Marcus stopped speaking as the phone rang, getting up to answer it and then calling over to Eleanor, 'It's Jade for you. Look, I've got to go,' he added as he handed the receiver over to her. 'But...'

'Don't you dare say that Saturday is out,' Eleanor warned him as she kissed him. 'I'm so excited about this house, Marcus,' she added softly. 'I know it sounds silly, but the moment I saw the photograph, I was so drawn to it. It will be a real home for all of us...somewhere where we could be a real family,' she told him, leaning her hand on his shoulder.

Against her hand, she felt his muscles flex, and breathed in the sharp muted scent of his cologne. Beneath it she could also smell the warm, musky male scent that was purely his and her stomach muscles contracted slightly, her body signalling a subtle sensual response to her recognition of that scent.

A small smile of contentment curled her mouth. How many married women of her age could lay claim to that kind of sexual response to their husbands and at seven o'clock on a weekday morning?

Not that either of them could do anything about it, she acknowledged ruefully as she heard her son's footsteps clattering towards them and Marcus started to move away from her, saying briefly, 'Nell, I . . .'

'You have to go, I know,' she agreed, wryly adding mentally to herself, and I have to find out what Jade wants, take the boys to school . . . sort out with the accountant the best way to terminate our office lease, try to make these last few weeks with Louise as amicable as possible . . .

Marcus had gone before she was even halfway through her mental list.

She turned to the telephone and said warmly into the receiver, 'Jade, sorry about that . . . Marcus was just leaving.'

'Can you make lunch?' she heard her friend ask her. 'I'm off to New York at the end of the week and we haven't seen one another for ages.'

'Yes, I think so,' Eleanor confirmed, mentally reviewing her diary. 'What time and where?'

She smiled to herself as Jade predictably named an expensive and very high profile restaurant, agreeing to meet her friend there at one.

She took the house brochure to work with her, tucking it away inside her briefcase like a secret talisman, refusing to give in to the temptation to study its promised delights yet again.

She knew them off by heart by now anyway, from the allure of the dusty lofts above the garages, which in her mind's eye she had already turned into a spacious work area for herself plus a large study-cum-playroom for the boys, an ideal refuge for them on wet winter days, somewhere where they could study in peace—she smiled to herself again, mentally picturing their dark heads bent over their books, a cheerful fire crackling warmly in front of them, solid desks standing on a dark polished floor, dormer windows overlooking winter-furrowed fields—right through to the elegantly proportioned ground floor drawing-room where she and Marcus would entertain their friends.

The house had seven bedrooms, all of them large enough to allow for the addition of private bathrooms. A must both for guests and to keep the peace between the needs of a teenage girl and those of her stepbrothers.

Vanessa would choose her own décor, of course. As a teenager Eleanor herself had been an addict of historical novels and had dreamed secretly of a huge old-fashioned four-poster bed.

She had never had one, of course, and the kind of bed she had dreamed of was a world away from the over-fussy modern versions swathed, flounced, draped and beribboned in sugary sweet pastel fabrics.

Downstairs . . . A small, happy breath escaped her. Downstairs there would be the drawing-room, a sitting-room, a dining-room, a study for Marcus, and then there would be the kitchen. The kind of kitchen that was the whole heart of the family. It would be a large rectangular room with sensible solid wooden cupboards, and a large wooden table . . . the kind the children could sit round while she was cooking.

The sudden blaring sound of someone's car horn brought her sharply back to reality and the fact that the lights had changed.

There were few traffic lights in the country, she reminded herself as she ignored the other driver's impatience and set her car in motion.

As she parked her car and headed for the office, she was conscious of her walking pace slowing down. She paused, frowning slightly. Things had not been easy at work since Louise had made her announcement; the friendship and closeness they had once shared and which Eleanor had genuinely believed was something they would always share had gone and in its place was a sense of confusion and, if she was honest, a sense also of betrayal on her part; and Louise was increasingly belligerent.

Eleanor did not need the services of a psychologist to tell her that Louise's aggression was probably her way of dealing with the guilt she must surely be feeling at the way she had behaved. Eleanor could not imagine that anyone could act as Louise had done and not suffer at least some pangs of guilt, but Louise had moulded herself so much in Paul's image that Eleanor suspected she had, on the surface at least, ignored and denied any such feelings, channelling them instead into resentment and anger against Eleanor herself.

When she was not being smugly self-righteous about her desire to put the health and education of her children first by moving them to a better environment, Louise seemed to be continually making remarks designed to underline her belief that it was *her* linguistic skills which contributed the most to their business, *her* languages which were superior to Eleanor's; and now that her initial shock and distress had worn off Eleanor was finding she was increasingly having to grit her teeth and make a determined effort not to respond to Louise's petty-mindedness.

She tried to remind herself that this Louise was not the same Louise with whom she had originally set up in business, the same Louise with whom she had shared so many doubts and worries, so many hours of anxiety and heartache as they fought to establish themselves. And so much laughter as well, she admitted bleakly.

And it was losing that laughter that hurt, Eleanor acknowledged as she walked into her own office. There was something very special about the laughter, the feeling of fellowship, of closeness one shared with another woman that was uniquely special, something apart from one's relationship with a man no matter how good that relationship might be.

She and Marcus shared laughter as well, but it was a different kind of laughter.

Eleanor had always valued her women friends, and she had considered Louise to be among the closest of them. Not perhaps as close as Jade, but then she and Jade had known one another since their university days... had met in fact on the train carrying them both to their new lives as students.

Jade had not been Jade then but Janet Anne.

When Eleanor had bumped into her seat, jolted by the swaying movement of the carriage, Jade had been scowling over the huge capital letters in which she had written her name on the notebook on her lap.

Janet Anne Hewitt.

She had looked up at Eleanor, still scowling as Eleanor hastily apologised to her. Eleanor had spent her final holiday before going up to university with her grandparents and had been wearing the hand-knitted jade-green sweater her grandmother had presented her with.

'That's it,' Jade had announced, staring at her.

'Jade...Fensham. *That's* going to be my new name,' she had told Eleanor firmly. 'Jade Fensham. Oh, and by the way, that colour is disgusting on you. What on earth made you choose it?'

Eleanor smiled to herself as she recalled that first meeting.

It had been an unlikely friendship; they couldn't after all have been more different, but it was one which had endured, perhaps because of their differences.

Jade was now a fashion writer with one of the glossies, a bone-thin, elegant creature who despite all her efforts had never quite managed to tame the wild tangle of glossy black curls which Eleanor remembered so vividly from their first meeting.

Her olive skin-tone and thick black hair were the result of a secret liaison between her grandmother and a black American blues singer, Jade had once claimed. Whether or not it was true, Eleanor had no idea, but it was typical of Jade that she should lay claim to such a heritage.

Eleanor grinned now as she thought about her, the thought of seeing her momentarily lifting her spirits.

She and Louise were due to see their accountant at half-past ten to formalise the ending of their partnership and to sort out all the remaining financial details.

Their accountant was late, causing Louise to twitch irritably and remind Eleanor that Paul had suggested some time ago that they switch to *his* accountant, who in his view was far more efficient than their own.

'We've been with Charles ever since we started,' Eleanor pointed out equably.

'And of course he's a friend—of yours,' Louise told her shortly.

Grimly Eleanor refrained from pointing out that their decision to take him had been a joint one, and that it had been Charles who had negotiated the mortgage Paul and Louise had so desperately needed when they had bought their house—a mortgage which Paul's own accountant had seemed either unable or unwilling to find.

When Charles did arrive he immediately apologised, explaining that there had been a traffic accident which had delayed him.

The meeting proved to be every bit as unpleasant as Eleanor had dreaded. Despite the fact that she was the one who wanted to end the partnership, Louise seemed to take pleasure in being as obstructive and difficult as possible, arguing over every single point and making it plain that she felt their partnership had somehow been angled unfairly in Eleanor's direction and that she was determined in putting an end to it that this should be redressed.

Several times Eleanor had to bite her tongue and remind herself that it was *Paul* she was really listening to and not Louise, or at least not the Louise she knew or rather had thought she knew, but when Louise an-nounced that she ought to retain their partnership name for her sole use Eleanor finally rebelled. That name had been *her* invention, but when she firmly pointed this out Louise erupted into such a flood of invective and accusation that Eleanor was finally forced to acknowledge that she could not have really known her after all.

Half an hour later, sitting in her own office with Charles, she listened disbelievingly while he told her gently that Louise had always been jealous of her.

'No,' she denied vehemently. 'No. We were friends.'

'Well, yes, but *you* were always the leader, Eleanor, the innovator, while Louise was the follower. There's nothing wrong with that; the world, businesses need leaders and followers.

'Louise admired you and was quite happy to let you take the lead. The problems probably started when she met Paul. You see, he's a leader too, and I suspect he didn't like his follower, Louise, being your follower as well.'

'And because of that he's broken up our partnership... turned Louise against me? But that's ridiculous!'

'Is it?' Charles asked her mildly. 'You'd be surprised how often it happens. I suspect, though, that Louise is in for a rather unpleasant shock, and so too is Paul. He isn't the kind of man who takes advice easily. I've already tried to warn him that he's over-committing himself in taking on this château but... He has his own financial advisers and they, it seems, see things differently.

'How's Marcus, by the way?'

'Fine, but very busy.' Eleanor chewed on her bottom lip. 'Actually there's something else I need to discuss with you, Charles. Marcus and I are thinking of moving.'

'Are you?' He both sounded and looked surprised. 'The last time I saw Marcus, he was saying how ideal the house is.'

'Was,' Eleanor corrected him wryly. 'It just isn't large enough for all of us... and it's on the wrong side of London for the boys' schools. And now that I'm going to have to give up the lease on this place...' She gave a small shrug. 'We've both agreed that I simply can't generate the kind of income which would support London's rents, and there's nowhere for me to work at home so we have to find somewhere else.

'Actually I think we might already have done so,' she told him. 'Fingers crossed. We're going to see it this weekend.'

'Mmm... Which part of London is it?'

Eleanor shook her head.

'It's not in London, it's in Wiltshire—the Wiltshire-Dorset border to be exact, just outside Avondale.'

'Wiltshire?' Charles gave her a startled look. 'Won't that be a bit far out? For Marcus, I mean...'

Eleanor shook her head.

'No. There's an excellent commuter rail service. People do commute, you know, Charles,' she added teasingly as she saw his frown. 'And from further afield than Wiltshire.'

'Mmm... Look, I must go, and don't worry too much about Louise. If anything I think you've been over-generous, and as for the partnership name...'

'*Was* I wrong to insist on keeping it?' she asked him uncertainly.

'No,' he assured her. 'Louise can't have things all her own way. And nor can Paul.'

Predictably, Eleanor was the first to arrive at the restaurant Jade had nominated.

The head waiter gave her a bored, slightly irritated look until she mentioned Jade's name, the deference with which she was then treated causing her to smile slightly to herself.

Once seated, Eleanor studied the other diners, most of them women, all of them formidably fashionable and, to judge from the snatches of conversation she could hear going on around her, most of them connected in one way or another to the same world which Jade inhabited.

Jade arrived five minutes later, pausing briefly as though in acknowledgement of the sharp *frisson* her presence created among the onlookers.

At just under six feet, she would have drawn attention whatever milieu she inhabited, Eleanor acknowledged, but it was not just her height that drew this crowd's attention; it was Jade herself, the aura that not merely surrounded her but which she actively projected so that it cocooned her like a mini force-field.

She had always had it, right from the first moment Eleanor had known her, and, Eleanor suspected, even before that; initially perhaps as a means of defence, the tall, gawky girl whose height drew comment and sometimes derision from her peers, but who had learned to use her 'differentness', to turn it round and glory in it rather than retreating from it, ashamed and afraid of the way it set her apart.

Unlike many of the other women present in the restaurant, she was not wearing some outrageously fashionable and to Eleanor's eye physically uncomfortable, eye-catching outfit, but a simple pale creamy beige suit with a fluidly tailored skirt and an elegant unstructured jacket, the fabric so fluid and graceful that it seemed to hint with covert sensuality at the curves and hollows of her body rather than outline them with blatant sexuality.

Her hair, her trademark, was as always a wild unfettered tangle of thick curls, a deliberate aberration and deviation from the demands and restrictions of her chosen field, not, as many seemed to think, as an affectation but because, as Eleanor well knew, that hair had the texture and strength of unbreakable wire and could not be styled.

Eleanor watched her as she made her way between the tables, regally deigning to pause to acknowledge the odd favoured courtier.

'Nell,' she announced in her deep husky voice as she reached Eleanor. 'You're here.'

'You did say one,' Eleanor reminded her with a smile and then added, 'I love your suit.'

'Armani. I picked it up in Milan after his last show. I'm afraid I can't return the compliment,' she added drawlingly, standing back to study Eleanor. 'How on earth did you manage to find something so disgusting?'

She gave a theatrical shudder while Eleanor watched her wryly.

'This is a perfectly respectable outfit, Jade,' she told her firmly, glancing down at the pencil-slim skirt and toning blouse which looked attractive and were just what she needed for work. 'Not high fashion, perhaps...'

'Perhaps?' Jade rolled her eyes. 'My dear, there is no perhaps about it. Have you ordered yet?'

Eleanor raised her eyebrows. 'I didn't dare... I'd probably have chosen something completely un-"in".'

Jade ignored her small gibe and assured her blandly, 'Impossible. They don't serve anything like that here.'

And then she started to laugh and Eleanor joined in, catching her breath as Jade hugged her.

'Oh, God, Nell, I do miss you,' Jade told her fiercely. 'How are you? How's Marcus? And how are my godsons?'

'No, you tell me how *you* are first,' Eleanor demanded. 'I know you, J,' she added, using the college nickname. 'Something's bothering you.'

'Mmm... Clever, aren't we?' Jade pulled a face. 'You're right, of course. I've been offered a new job. Quite a prize plum, really. Editorship of American *Fashion*; a huge increase in salary; all the perks anyone could want, including the most fabulous Manhattan apartment you've ever seen in your life, plus a month's let on a duplex in Aspen for the winter, and a house on Fire Island for the summer.

'Career-wise, it's what I've always wanted. There's no denying that as jobs go this one is the top of the tree, and not just because of the financial advantages. American designers in particular pay far more attention to the kind of reviews a magazine like *Fashion* gives them than their European counterparts. They need it for their ready-to-wear collections, of course, and...' She gave a small shrug. 'All in all I'd be a fool not to snap their hand off.'

'So what's stopping you?' Eleanor asked her.

The arched eyebrows rose, the intelligent dark eyes wryly self-contemptuous. 'Need you ask?'

'A man?' Eleanor questioned her.

'*The* man,' Jade corrected her. 'And there happens to be a problem.'

'He's married,' Eleanor guessed.

Jade shook her head.

'Nope. That wouldn't be a problem. No, the problem is that he doesn't know that he's the man, and I'm not sure he will want to know it. And he's ten years younger than I am.'

Eleanor looked at her.

'So? You've dated younger men before.'

'Dated them, yes, but this one I want for keeps, Nell. And I'm not sure if that's what he wants. I've reached an age when my dignity has become very important to me. I could throw caution to the winds, tell him how I feel, ask him to go to New York with me. He's a photographer, a very talented one in fact and it certainly wouldn't do his career any harm to make that kind of move; far from it.' She made a small face. 'That's how we met, of course. Very predictable. Someone recommended him to me, so I took him on for a shoot, as a stand-in for someone else as a matter of fact. He's no fool. Up-and-coming photographers fight to the death for the kind of commissions I could put his way.

'I'm already getting as jealous as hell every time he does a modelling assignment, Nell. You know what I'm like...possessive as anything and paranoid with it. I'm not sure if I can take the kind of pressure I'll be putting myself under if I get any further involved with him. If I take on this job it's going to need all my time...all my attention...all my energy, and yet the thought of ending it, leaving him behind...'

Eleanor saw the sharp sparkle of tears in her eyes and reached out across the table to cover her hand with her own.

'Why don't you tell *him* all this and not me?' she suggested gently. 'Let him make up his own mind, Jade.'

'And if he rejects me?' Her mouth twisted. 'I don't think I can take that. Oh, God, Nell, *why* are we like this...screwing up our lives over men...sex...cursed by our own hormones almost from the first second of our birth? Do you know, I was reading this book the other day which claims that women are programmed for failure right from the moment of conception, that only those with an unusual amount of testosterone actually have what it takes to succeed.'

'Doesn't that depend on how you measure success?' Eleanor challenged her. 'If you measure it by men's standards, then yes, I suppose we are, but why should it be? Why don't *we* judge men by *our* standards instead?'

'Take control of the power? Mmm... Men don't like it, though, do they? Look what happened to Margaret Thatcher and Boadicea.'

'Boadicea...what?'

Eleanor broke off as their meal was served and before she could pick up the thread of their earlier conversation, Jade had changed the subject, reverting to the question she had asked her earlier.

'Everything's fine,' Eleanor assured her and then pulled a face. 'Well, sort of. Louise and I have come to the parting of the ways. She and Paul are moving to France and——'

'Are they? That's a bit unexpected, isn't it?'

'Paul's decision. He thinks it will be a better environment for the boys; that they'll be better integrated into the European Community and so on. He considers that Britain is destined to become an economic backwater. I must admit that it did come as a bit of a shock, though. However, I'm rather pleased in a way. It means that I'll have to work at home, so I'll be able to spend more time with my two. We'll have to move, of course. Not that I mind that. I've always wanted to live somewhere more rural.'

'Rural?' The dark eyebrows lifted again as Jade stared at her, her expression clearing as she exclaimed, 'Oh, you mean somewhere like Hampstead.'

Eleanor laughed. 'No. I mean the country, proper country, Jade. You know, as in green fields and——'

'Yes, I know,' Jade agreed, shuddering as she interrupted her. 'Rain, mud, boredom, more rain, more mud. I grew up there, I *know*. You can't be serious.'

'I am,' Eleanor assured her quietly. 'We need more space. We...*I* need to be able to breathe. The Chelsea house is beautiful, but there certainly isn't the space for me to work there; there isn't even really room for us all to *live* there. The boys and Marcus's daughter, especially Vanessa, just don't get on. In fact Vanessa...'

'Ah, Vanessa. Stepdaughters are hell, aren't they? Especially teenage stepdaughters. I know, I was one. I can understand your feeling you need more space, but moving to the country... Don't tell me you've fallen into this ridiculous "let's get back to nature" trap? Viewed through rose-tinted glasses from the safety of a city apartment, the country is fine, but *living* there... And what about Marcus? Somehow I just can't see him as the country type...or wearing green wellies.'

'You haven't seen the house,' Eleanor told her stubbornly. 'It's everything I've always wanted. Solid, permanent...a proper home, J...'

'A proper home for a proper family, presided over by a proper mother. Is that really what you want to be, Nell? Don't tell me you're falling for that media myth.'

'I feel I owe it to the boys. I don't want them to look back on their childhood with the same unhappiness I had in mine,' Eleanor told her defensively, ignoring her derisive comment.

'It's people, not places that make us happy, Nell,' Jade told her quietly.

'We've got to do *something*,' Eleanor told her unhappily. 'I haven't said anything to Marcus yet—he's so busy at the moment on this new case—but this constant moving in and out of his room to make way for Vanessa is upsetting Tom. Julia has announced that she'll be working in America throughout the summer and that we'll have to have Vanessa.

'It isn't easy just coping for a *weekend*, never mind the whole summer holidays. Vanessa is at a very difficult age.'

'So let Marcus deal with her. She's his daughter.'

'And *my* stepdaughter. I can't go running to Marcus every time there's a squabble and I can't refuse to have her. Marcus is her father.'

'You know your trouble, Nell—you try too hard. You're too accommodating... too willing to please others at your own expense. Let me give you a small warning. Don't. Especially not with Vanessa. It won't do you or her any good. She won't respect you for it. Once you let her think she's gained the upper hand, she'll use it on you.'

'She's at a vulnerable age. She needs to know that Marcus loves her... that there's a place for her with us.'

'She also needs to know that you're Marcus's wife,' Jade told her drily. 'Don't be too idealistic, Nell. It doesn't work. Let her know there's a place for her by all means, but make sure she knows what that place is, what its limitations are... and make sure that she doesn't make a take-over bid for *your* place.'

She saw Eleanor's face and raised her eyebrows.

'I'll bet you anything you like that Vanessa could have gone to America with her mother, if she'd wanted. Now ask yourself why she doesn't want to...'

'But she's never lived permanently with Marcus...not since the divorce. I haven't tried to come between her and her father at all.'

Jade shook her head pityingly. 'You don't know anything really, do you, you poor naïve thing? Vanessa means trouble, Nell.'

'But you've only met her a couple of times.'

'Yes, and recognised the type instantly. I should do. I was once a Vanessa myself. I almost drove my stepmother to the brink of a breakdown before she and my father divorced. It's a problem some teenage girls have. She'll grow out of it, but your marriage to Marcus might not,' Jade warned.

'Jade, you're wrong! Vanessa might not *like* me but she would never be deliberately vindictive.'

'No? Honestly, Nell, you...'

She stopped speaking abruptly, her body tensing, a barely discernible tinge of colour creeping up under her skin.

Fascinated, Eleanor followed the direction of her concentrated stare. A man had just entered the restaurant and was making his way towards their table. He was, Eleanor reflected in awe, possibly the most physically perfect male she had ever seen: closer to six feet six than six feet, he had the body to match his height, and yet for all its power he also had a physical grace reminiscent of that of a dancer.

Every woman in the place was watching him and no wonder, Eleanor acknowledged.

She had seen good-looking black men before, but never one like this. His features could have been sculpted, so perfect that you actually wanted to reach out and touch his skin just to see if it was real rather than hewn from polished marble.

Unlike most very tall and powerfully built men, he wore his clothes easily and comfortably, a softly structured suit that looked casually thrown on, but which Eleanor suspected was every bit as expensive as Jade's own.

He had reached them now and Jade was starting to introduce him.

No wonder she had said that this was *the* one, Eleanor reflected as she read the intelligence in his eyes. This was no fawning puppy; this was one full-grown, wholly adult male, and while it might be possible to guess from Jade's demeanour that they were lovers, there was nothing to be gauged from *his* manner as to what his feelings for her might be.

Whatever they were, Sam was a whole world away from Jade's previous lovers, Eleanor estimated as they all exchanged pleasantries and she thanked Jade for her lunch and prepared to take her leave.

'I'll ring you,' Jade promised as Eleanor got up.

They hugged one another briefly and then Eleanor turned to leave.

It was only when she was back in her office that Eleanor remembered that she hadn't shown Jade the details of the house.

Jade would surely have changed her mind had she seen them.

Almost like a child seeking comfort and reassurance in a favourite fairy-story, Eleanor reached into her briefcase, withdrew the brochure, and placed it on the desk in front of her.

CHAPTER EIGHT

'BUT where are we going?' Gavin persisted, leaning forward between the front seats of the Daimler.

'I've told you, it's a surprise,' Eleanor responded, adding firmly, 'Put your seatbelt back on, please, Gavin.'

'Yes, otherwise Marcus will have to go to prison,' Tom cut in with such a mixture of virtue and relish that Eleanor couldn't quite stop herself from laughing.

'Thanks very much,' Marcus murmured drily. 'I'm delighted to see that the prospect of my potential detention at Her Majesty's pleasure fills your offspring with so much despair.'

'Oh, it would never happen,' Eleanor assured him softly. 'You see, I know this wonderful Q.C.'

'Mmm... But can we afford him?'

Eleanor laughed, her fingertips resting briefly on his thigh as she whispered provocatively, 'Oh, I think I can come up with an appropriate way of rewarding him.'

It had been a long time since they had indulged in this kind of trivial, almost adolescent sexual banter, she recognised when Marcus made what was quite obviously an unnecessary change of gear, the muscles beneath her fingertips flexing slightly as he did so.

Last night they had made love with a passion and vigour which had been missing from their sex life for some months. She suspected that it was her excitement over the house which had helped to throw off the tension-induced restraint which had been inhibiting her lately.

Certainly Marcus had noticed the difference, murmuring appreciatively in her ear, 'Mmm... We really should do this more often, you know.'

It seemed he had meant it, too, because he had made love to her again this morning, not in the comfortable warmth of their bed, but in the shower, surprising her not just with the unexpectedness of his desire for her, but with its intensity as well.

How long was it since they had made love like that... quickly and impetuously, so eager and hungry for one another that she had been crying out to him to enter her almost within seconds of his touching her, and then still wanting him enough to go on to caress him slowly and deliberately into a second erection?

Not since the early days of their marriage. Not even last year, on holiday in Greece.

The villa they had hired had been beautifully situated, immaculately clean and more than large enough for all of them, but by some trick of Greek architecture it had also had an accoustic receptiveness more suited to an auditorium than a private home.

The holiday had been ruined for her on the second morning when over breakfast Vanessa had insisted on monotonously kicking her foot against the base of the table around which they were all seated eating their breakfast.

It had been Marcus who had suggested mildly that he would like her to stop, since the noise she was making was both intrusive and unnecessary, to which she had replied triumphantly, throwing a malicious look at Eleanor, 'Well, now *you* know what it was like for me last night listening to the two of you...'

Marcus's curt, 'Vanessa,' had stopped her before she could go any further, but her comment had ensured that the holiday was ruined for Eleanor, and if she was honest she would have to admit that ever since then, even if Vanessa was not in the house, she had felt slightly tense and on edge whenever they did make love.

But not last night and certainly not this morning, which was surely a good omen and proof that she was right to feel so confident and enthusiastic about the house. A small smile curled her mouth as she remembered the small betraying bruises she had found on her body this morning, the faint but very real and slightly provocative ache she could still feel within her body.

She remembered how with Allan she had always known when he had started a new affair because of the intensity with which he had made love to her. He had admitted to her after the divorce that it had been a volatile mixture of guilt and physical desire for his new lover which had been responsible for these bursts of passion.

Marcus, thank God, was not like Allan. He loved her. She and Allan had thought they were in love, but in reality they had married too quickly and too young, without really knowing enough about one another. She bore Allan no malice or resentment, and was just relieved that they had been able to develop an amicable enough post-divorce relationship to allow the boys to know that both of them loved them.

When the boys had first been born, Allan had been too immature to be a father, and she had transferred the love she had thought she felt for him to his sons. She had no personal regrets over the ending of their marriage. From a personal point of view at least she had felt guilty about depriving the boys of their father, even though they had been so young when they divorced that they had scarcely any memories of them actually living as a family.

Marcus was very good with them, and after an initial period of natural suspicion and resentment at his role in her life both of them were beginning to develop strong bonds with him, or so she had believed.

In the back of the Daimler the boys were squabbling amicably over which tape they wanted to listen to. The weather forecast had predicted rain, but nothing could obscure the glow of pleasure and elation which Eleanor could almost feel encapsulating her.

She turned her head and smiled at Marcus. 'I'm so excited,' she told him huskily.

'I know,' he agreed wryly. 'Eleanor, don't——'

'Mum, it's my turn to choose. Tom chose last time.'

'No, I didn't...you did.'

'Stop arguing, both of you,' Eleanor told them firmly. 'I'll choose.'

By the time she had sorted them out, it had started to rain quite heavily, and Marcus was frowning slightly as he concentrated on his driving.

The journey was taking them rather longer than the agent had indicated, Eleanor acknowledged as she glanced at the dashboard clock.

They had, the agents had told her, had several interested prospective purchasers who wanted to view Broughton House. It was after all very reasonably priced, and in a particularly attractive part of the country. Eleanor hoped that they were not going to be late for their appointment. She wanted to savour their tour of the house and its grounds and not have to rush it.

'We've got to be there for one,' she reminded Marcus as she tried to calculate how much further they had to travel.

'I'll do my best,' he told her, 'but it all depends on the traffic.'

'It won't take as long as this by train,' Eleanor assured him.

And of course Marcus wouldn't necessarily have to travel to London every day. Like her, he could work from the house as he already did sometimes from Chelsea. She closed her eyes, mentally picturing the future: a warm sunny afternoon, Marcus working in his study, its windows open to the garden while she took advantage of a break from her own work to join him. There was just time for the two of them to enjoy a short but leisurely stroll through the grounds before she set off to collect the boys from their local school, a duty she shared with a group of other mothers.

In the house, the downstairs rooms were filled with the scent of freshly cut garden roses and the lavender which was drying in bunches in the old-fashioned sunlit porch area at the rear.

In the kitchen you could still smell the cakes she had baked that morning and in the kitchen garden a long line of immaculate white washing flapped lazily in the soft breeze.

After supper she would iron it, breathing in its fresh, clean country smell, and then later, when it was on their bed, its scent would cling to Marcus's skin, mingling with his musky erotic maleness as they made love.

Reluctantly she opened her eyes, grimacing at the steady downpour soaking everywhere.

'How much further?' Tom demanded from the back seat.

'We'll be there soon now,' Eleanor promised him, her spirits lifting as she saw a signpost for Avondale.

She had read up on the town and was looking forward to exploring it. Enthusiastically she started to tell Marcus about its history.

'Mmm... Well, I doubt that we'll be seeing it today,' Marcus interrupted her. 'There's a diversion up ahead.'

It was just after a quarter past one when they finally turned into the drive of Broughton House.

The weed-infested gravel, the overgrown rhododendrons which had become too tall and leggy, and the heavy rain which was now falling, did not quite fit in with the picture she had drawn in her imagination, Eleanor admitted, and the house itself, without the sun on it, and perhaps viewed from a slightly different angle than that from which the photograph had been taken, was not quite as she had visualised it either.

As Marcus stopped the car, Tom stared out of his window and exclaimed in disgust, 'It's just a house.'

Another car was already parked in front of the house and as Eleanor chivvied her sons into their jackets and out of the car she glanced towards Marcus.

He was frowning slightly as he studied the building in front of him, but when he realised she was watching him he turned towards her, his face relaxing.

'How much land did you say it had?' he asked her as they got out of the car.

'Around four and a half acres,' Eleanor told him happily. 'There's a walled kitchen garden. We'll be able to grow our own vegetables; and then there's the formal gardens, plus a small copse...'

'Mmm...sounds expensive,' Marcus commented, adding wryly as they walked towards the house, 'Looks as if the last owner thought so as well, to judge from the way it's been neglected.'

'Mrs Broughton was very old, and the house has been empty for over six months,' Eleanor pointed out, adding eagerly, 'It will all look different in the summer. Gardens never look their best at this time of the year.'

'Hmm. I suspect that this one is going to need rather more than a change of season,' Marcus pointed out.

Eleanor frowned. Marcus was sounding rather tense and on edge, a note of terse irritation creeping into his voice, but then the drive down here hadn't been particularly pleasant, she reminded herself.

'It does all look a bit wild and forlorn,' she agreed, slipping her arm through his. 'And this rain doesn't help. I hope it stops long enough for us to have a good look round the grounds.'

'I doubt there'll be time for that,' Marcus told her as the front door of the house opened and the agent came towards them.

'I'm sorry we're late,' Eleanor apologised as he introduced himself.

'That's all right,' he assured them. 'My next viewing isn't until half-past two.'

'Oh, that doesn't leave us much time to look over the grounds,' Eleanor protested.

'Well, actually you can get a pretty good view of them from the attic windows,' he assured her.

As he held open the front door and stood back to allow them to walk inside, Eleanor caught her breath in pleasure.

The hall was large and rectangular with a polished wooden floor and a heavy carved wooden staircase with a galleried landing.

'It *is* magnificent, isn't it?' The agent smiled as Eleanor turned to express her admiration.

Marcus was also examining the staircase, but when he turned back to face her he was frowning rather than smiling.

'What's wrong?' Eleanor asked him.

'I may be wrong, but I think I can smell damp,' he told her quietly.

Damp! Eleanor stared at him, and the agent, who had obviously overheard him, stepped in quickly, saying lightly, 'Old houses often smell slightly of damp, especially when they have been empty for a while as this one has, but structurally the building is extremely sound. The Georgians knew how to build. There might be the odd patch of damp, but it's nothing serious.'

'Serious enough to cause the skirting to rot,' Marcus commented mildly, but he smiled at Eleanor when she looked across at him, and agreed with her when the agent opened the door into the sitting-room and she enthused on the amount of daylight that large windows to the front and side of the room allowed in.

'Oh, look, Marcus, it's still got all the original plasterwork on the ceiling, and the picture rails, and look how heavy these doors are. It will all need decorating, of course.'

In her mind's eye she could see it already. Excitedly she turned back to Marcus. 'It's perfect, isn't it?' she whispered to him.

'Mmm . . . We've only seen one room so far. How many bedrooms did you say it had?'

When Eleanor told him, he raised his eyebrows slightly.

'It's a very large house,' he pointed out to her.

'Yes, it's ideal, isn't it?' Eleanor enthused. She turned towards him, her face alight with excitement. 'It's just perfect for us, Marcus. Of course I know it will need a lot of work doing on it,' she added as they followed the agent into the large drawing-room, and from there into the dining-room, and then a further small sitting-room, which he told them had been Mrs Broughton's favourite room, because it overlooked the long borders which had been designed and planted by Gertrude Jekyll. 'But now that I'm not committed to going into the office every day, I'll have

enough free time on my hands to cope with that.' She paused as she saw
that Marcus was frowning again.

'What is it? What's wrong?' she asked him.

'I was just wondering if it was going to be as easy as you imagine to
oversee the kind of work that this place needs. You saw for yourself how
long it took us to drive down here today. If you were having to make
that kind of round trip several days a week... You said yourself that
one of the benefits of working from home would be that you would have
more time to spend with the boys, but with them at school...'

'Hopefully we could time things so that most of the work can be done
during the school holidays,' Eleanor told him cheerfully. 'That way they'll
be able to come with me.'

'Go where with you?' Gavin asked her.

'Come here,' Eleanor told him with a smile, touching the top of his
head with gentle fingers, mentally imagining the pleasure and the fun
they would have living somewhere like this...and not just them but
Vanessa as well.

'The kitchens, I'm afraid, are rather archaic,' the agent announced as
he led the way to the back of the house.

As he opened a door and they followed him inside, Eleanor realised
that her dream of a large family-sized kitchen had been exactly that.

The reality was a collection of small dark rooms obviously designed
in the days when only the servants inhabited such quarters.

'Potentially this area could be converted into an excellent kitchen-cum-
living area,' the agent told them.

'Potentially,' Marcus agreed, wandering over to one of the windows
and peering out.

'Is that the kitchen garden?' he asked.

Eleanor joined him at the window, staring excitedly through it to the
walled area beyond.

Vegetables gone wildly to seed showed here and there among the weeds,
and on the walls the once neatly espaliered fruit trees were beginning to
burst into new leaf.

'Until the last few months of her life, Mrs Broughton employed a full-
time gardener. He died six months before she did.'

As Eleanor strained eagerly to study the garden, she tried to imagine
how it must once have looked with rows of neatly cultivated vegetables,
all healthily free of chemicals, all deliciously organic and wholesomely
grown. She remembered her grandmother's store cupboard with its rows
of fruit-packed Kilner jars, the home-made soup she made in the winter.

Upstairs the bedrooms were well proportioned, although the bathrooms were in need of refitting, and the attics, although dusty and dirty,
did give the promised view of the grounds.

It was a pity they were shrouded in rain and looked so dismal that
even the boys seemed less than enthusiastic at the prospect of exploring

them, and since they still had the garage block to look over, a tour of the whole grounds would probably have to wait for another day, Eleanor acknowledged reluctantly as they all trooped back downstairs.

The garages had originally been stables, and comprised a long run of buildings, with an upper storey with steeply sloping eaves and small dormer windows.

'These would make offices for us,' Eleanor enthused as she watched Marcus having to bend to avoid bumping his head on one of the low door lintels.

'For *us*?'

'Mmm... You know, I've been thinking, Marcus... You know how you already do some work at home; well, if we bought this place, you could work from home two or three days a week. That would cut down the amount of time you would need to spend commuting; and you would have more time to spend at home with us.' She turned towards him, taking advantage of their privacy—the agent and the boys had gone back downstairs.

'Last night and this morning...' She leaned closer to him, resting her head briefly on his shoulder. 'I was thinking on the way here this morning... it's been so long since we had time to... to be together like this...to be able to concentrate exclusively on one another. Living here...I want us to be a real family, Marcus, close and supportive of one another. All of us,' she emphasised.

'And it isn't just the time, it's the privacy as well,' she added. 'There'll be enough space here for all of us. The children will get on so much better if they have their own rooms... their own space, I'm sure of it. I know how much Vanessa resents the fact that Tom and Gavin use her room, and it *is* very disruptive having to move them out every time she comes to stay. I thought we'd let Vanessa choose her own room. She's at that difficult, sensitive stage and...'

'Don't hope for too much where Vanessa's concerned,' Marcus warned her. 'You can't bribe her, Nell.'

'*Bribe* her?' Eleanor moved slightly away from him, looking indignantly at him, her face flushing slightly. 'Is that what you think I'm trying to do... bribe her? *I* just want to make her feel that she has a real place here with us. I know from my own experience how difficult things can be for a girl of that age. I *know* how unhappy and miserable it made me when I was growing up, not having a stable home, somewhere that was really mine. Every time I left school to join my parents, they were living somewhere else. I loathed it.'

'Vanessa *isn't* you, Nell,' Marcus told her. 'I know how disruptive she can be... but she is only a child, and sometimes I think that you——'

He broke off while Eleanor continued to frown at him.

'That I what? You can't stop there, Marcus,' she told him quietly, her euphoria suddenly vanishing, leaving in its place a sharp, chilly feeling.

She knew how much Marcus hated arguments and scenes, how much he disliked the quarrels and tension which seemed to erupt whenever all three of their children were together. He never interfered, nor favoured his own child above hers, but she was well aware that he was not the kind of man who enjoyed that kind of domestic disturbance.

That Vanessa knew it too and sometimes deliberately provoked her own sons into arguments and quarrels was a suspicion that Eleanor kept to herself.

She was not, she had already decided, going to be the kind of step-mother and second wife who was constantly finding fault with her step-daughter and constantly demanding the support of the girl's father against her.

Not that it was always easy; there were times, like last year in Greece, when Vanessa's attitude towards her had brought her perilously close to the edge of her self-control.

Who would have thought that a teenage girl had the power to make a grown woman feel so vulnerable about herself that she could actually bring her almost to the verge of tears? And yet last year that was exactly what Vanessa had done.

Before Eleanor could take the subject any further Gavin and Tom came rushing up the stairs, bursting into the room, Tom demanding excitedly, 'If we come to live here, can we have a puppy?'

She was so relieved to see their enthusiasm that Eleanor responded immediately without thinking, 'Yes, of course you can.'

As she turned around, she saw that Marcus was shaking his head.

'Vanessa is allergic to dogs,' he reminded her tersely.

Immediately Eleanor felt guilty. Of course she was. Why on earth hadn't *she* remembered that?

Quickly she corrected herself, explaining to Tom that it would be im-possible for them to have a dog inside the house because it would make Vanessa sick, but to her dismay, instead of accepting her explanation, Tom kicked moodily at the floor and demanded accusingly, 'Why is it that *she* can always have what she wants and we never can? She always gets what she wants,' he added sullenly. 'It's not fair.'

'Tom, that isn't true,' Eleanor protested.

'Yes, it is. Otherwise we wouldn't have to move out of our bedroom every time *she* comes to stay.'

'Tom, you *know* that that room was Vanessa's and you know why you have to sleep in the attic when she comes to stay. But it won't be for much longer. When we move here, you'll be able to have your own room.'

'I don't want my own room. I want a puppy.'

'Time we left, I think,' Eleanor said wryly to Marcus, but instead of returning her slight smile he had turned his head away and was looking through the window.

As he followed her towards the stairs, he stopped and Eleanor turned
back to look enquiringly at him as the boys went back downstairs.

'Do you think it's a good idea to tell them we're moving here at this
stage?' he asked her. 'I know how much you like the house, Nell, but
don't you feel that we could be taking on too much? You've seen for
yourself how much work needs doing, and personally I——'

'No...don't you see, that could be a plus point,' Eleanor interrupted
him eagerly. 'We'll be able to have the conversions designed specifically
to meet our own needs. It's offers by sealed bid, Marcus,' she added
anxiously. 'I'd like to get ours in just as soon as we can. I suppose we
ought to consult a valuer first.'

Marcus was frowning.

'We've only just seen the place, Nell. Surely you can see for yourself
that it will need a thorough structural survey, never mind a valuation. I
really think we should——'

'Marcus, it's wonderful, isn't it? I feel as though it's just been sitting
here waiting for us. I feel as though a huge weight's been lifted off my
shoulders. It's the answer to all our problems. You're very quiet...' She
smiled up at him. 'It's all the driving, I suppose, in the rain.' She made
a face. 'It's a pity we didn't get a better day to view it...'

Half an hour later, on the way home, his three passengers all asleep,
Marcus glanced into Eleanor's face and frowned to himself.

He had never seen her so excited about anything before—not even him?
It was so out of character for her; she was normally so calm and controlled. He could still remember the glow which had come to her eyes
when they had come across the pond in the ten minutes he had allowed
her to walk him round the grounds in the steady rain. This fantasy she
had about them all living in rural bliss, one big happy family—couldn't
she see how improbable it was...how impractical?

He knew she'd been under a lot of stress recently—hadn't they both?
But this need she seemed to have developed to become some kind of earth
mother, presiding over an impossibly perfect family... Did she really
believe that moving out to the country could actually achieve what anyone
in their senses could see was a totally unrealistic harmony?

He had thought that, like him, she enjoyed their London life; and it
disturbed him to discover that he knew her less well than he had thought.
What else was there about her that he did not know?

He could understand her concern for her sons. She was a good mother,
wise and fair as well as loving, and worked very hard to provide them
with a sense of security and the knowledge that they were loved.

Unlike Julia, who had always alternated wildly between ignoring
Vanessa almost totally when she had more important things to occupy
her time and attention, or spoiling her outrageously, showering her with
a, to him, nauseating false maternal affection, which was of course why
Vanessa...

He sighed under his breath. He loved his daughter, and was increasingly aware that her upbringing was having a detrimental effect on her personality. He acknowledged that it wasn't easy for Eleanor having to deal with her, but why couldn't Eleanor see that there was nothing she could do to alter Vanessa's attitude? Too old to have discipline imposed on her and too young as yet to understand the merits of self-discipline, Vanessa revelled in the power she had to hurt others, too immature to be able either to temper or balance her own feelings and needs against those of others.

How much of that was his fault? He had left his marriage to Julia, driven away from her by the constant seesawing of her moods, the debilitating arguments and theatrical and equally exhausting fits of remorse; the pressure of living life at such a constant high pitch of emotional intensity turned him off rather than on, his need to escape from his increasing loathing of Julia's moods and demands for attention overwhelming everything else.

He had not recognised then that her inability to control those moods might have as devastating an effect on his daughter as it had had on him. Had not realised, or had not wanted to realise?

Of course he was aware of Vanessa's hostility towards Eleanor and her sons, but this idealistic, sentimental belief Eleanor had developed that somehow by moving to Broughton House everything would miraculously change and that they would somehow be welded together as in some sickening sentimental pastiche of perfect family life...

Marcus was very wary of sentiment. His marriage to Julia had taught him to be. She had loved sentiment, had wallowed in it, manipulated it, projected and promoted it until she had grossly deformed and abused it, until he had felt as sickened by it as by a surfeit of sticky, cloying chocolate. Sentiment had no substance, no reality; it was simply a tool Julia had used to get her own way.

When he had first met Eleanor she had seemed like a breath of fresh clean air, bracing, invigorating in her honesty and naïveté, a woman who combined a very special kind of strength and self-worth with a disarming aura of femininity and sexuality.

He had known from the first moment they met that he wanted her, but he had also known that she was oblivious to that wanting, untouched by it, unaware of it in a way that Julia would never have been.

She had been recommended to him as an excellent language teacher, and he had approached her with a view to polishing up his schoolboy French and German, for the business law in which he specialised was increasingly taking him to the European courts, especially The Hague and Brussels, and he had decided that it would be no bad thing to become far more fluent in both languages.

He remembered the first time he had made love to her: she had been hesitant at first and slightly uncertain. He had soon discovered that it was a lack of self-confidence that inhibited her and not a lack of desire.

She had been divorced for five years and in that time had made love with only one other man, she had confessed, adding ruefully that the experience had not been a success.

'It was too soon after the divorce,' she had told him, 'and I was too anxious. I wanted to reassure myself that I was still desirable, I suppose, and so I made the classic mistake of going to bed with the first man who asked me.'

'And he was such an inadequate lover that you decided to be celibate?' he had suggested.

She had laughed then, that free, uninhibited laugh he loved so much.

'No,' she had admitted.

She had never made any conscious decision not to have sex. It was simply that the occasion and the desire had never arisen simultaneously.

'And now?' he had asked her, bending to caress her nipple with his mouth, amused to discover how quickly he wanted her again and filled with an unexpected tenderness at the way she trembled against him, her eyes closing, her teeth tugging on her bottom lip as she made no attempt to conceal from him what she was feeling. What she had given to him had been given totally freely and generously. And she had never made any attempt to use his feelings or her own to manipulate or coerce him. It was that honesty about her which had first made him love her; but marriage demanded more than love, more than desire. It demanded... What?

That he give up his comfortable London house to move out into the country?

He looked at Eleanor again.

There were a dozen or more reasons why this house was unsuitable, not least of them the fact that she was expecting it to perform impossible miracles. He did not particularly like the country and he certainly did not relish the travelling that would be involved in such a move, but as he looked at Eleanor's sleeping face he knew that he didn't want to be the one to have to disillusion her and point out the truth.

Even so, surely she must have sensed his lack of enthusiasm? She was normally an acutely sensitive person.

He frowned, irritated with himself for his attitude, for the awareness it gave him of a certain male streak of resentment and almost selfishness that she should not be aware of his feelings. And not just aware of them, but intent on putting them first?

His attitude was both illogical and unfair, he told himself.

Eleanor was so caught up in her own excitement about the house, it was only natural that she had missed spotting that his enthusiasm did not match her own. She was not, after all, a mind-reader, and could not be expected to know what he was feeling if he did not tell her. What did he want—for her to make it easy for him by recognising what he was feeling? And if she didn't he would have to tell her how he felt, he admitted.

She would be disappointed, but, being Eleanor, she would strive to understand. She would certainly not, as Julia would have done, attempt to force his hand with emotional blackmail, tears and scenes.

He could understand her desire to promote peace and harmony—after all, he shared it too—but this implausible idealistic idea she had that somehow... He shook his head. They would have to sit down and talk. He knew they needed to move; the Chelsea house *was* obviously too small for them, especially now that Eleanor was going to have to work from home.

Knowing they needed to talk was one thing, he admitted; finding the time to do so was another. His workload at the moment was such that finding time for anything else was virtually a luxury.

Take today; by rights he should have been working on the Alexander case. He had several cases coming to trial over the next few months, none of them simple and straightforward. International law never was, which was what had attracted him to it in the first place.

His frown deepened. From his point of view, all this upheaval with Eleanor's partnership and Julia's prolonged visit to America could not have come at a worse time.

He enjoyed his work, thrived on the challenges it gave him, and, if he was honest with himself, a part of him actively needed the tension-induced highs it gave him.

Sondra Cabot had said much the same thing when she had called round at his chambers yesterday to collect some papers.

He had seen the American girl on several occasions since his initial meeting with her at the Lassiters'.

In many ways she reminded him a little of Eleanor, or rather Eleanor as she had been when he first met her, a younger Eleanor, of course, and not quite as softly feminine as Eleanor; a little more forceful and spoiled. Used to having her own way, but not less attractive because of it. He smiled to himself.

She was quite obviously a young woman who was not only used to male admiration and appreciation, but who expected it as well.

She wore her sexuality with all the confidence of the very young, a bright, enticing banner that proclaimed her innocence of life rather than her experience of sex, even though she herself did not know it; there was an appeal about that kind of youthfulness, that kind of freshness, that kind of enthusiasm and optimism that was dangerously engaging.

She had lingered in his chambers for a while, hotly debating with him the contentious issue of 'date rape'. Her vehemence had amused him...and excited him?

His frown returned, deepening slightly as Eleanor stirred in her sleep and turned towards him.

CHAPTER NINE

'DID you manage to get the time off?' Zoe asked anxiously as Ben came in.

He nodded his head, grimacing a little as he did so.

'Aldo didn't like it, of course, but he owes me some time from last year, so...'

Zoe shook her head. 'He takes advantage of you, Ben. You *are* that restaurant—without you...'

'I'm the chef, that's all. Or at least, that's the way he sees it,' Ben reminded her. 'Chefs are ten a penny these days.'

'Not ones like you,' Zoe argued loyally. 'Do you think he's guessed that...?'

'No,' Ben told her. 'If he had, he'd have sacked me.'

He knew that he sounded curt and he could see some of the excitement and pleasure fading from Zoe's face as she listened to him. He knew that she thought he was being over-pessimistic in cautioning her to wait before getting too excited about the new restaurant.

In reality, he was just as keyed-up and excited about it as she was herself, probably more so; after all, this kind of opportunity had been his most secret and protected dream ever since that moment in that small back-street eating place in Manchester—to call it a restaurant would have been an insult to the name—when Henri Fontanel had walked into the dingy, ill-equipped kitchen and offered him an opportunity, opened for him a door into a world he had never dared dream he might enter.

The simple truth was that, unlike Zoe, he was not used to trusting fate, life... and yet in many ways both had been generous in their favours to him.

As a boy his main interest in food had been the feeling it gave him when it filled his stomach; eating had been a necessity rather than a pleasure. His mother was no cook and no nutritionist either. Fast foods and takeaways, biscuits and sweets, those had been all Ben had known of food until that fateful day he had walked home with David Bernstein.

Manchester had several large Jewish communities, but the area where Ben lived was not one of them.

David Bernstein was a thin, asthmatic boy who stuck out from the rest of the class like a sore thumb and was roughly tormented by the bullies among them because of it.

Ben neither liked nor disliked him, having more important things to worry about, like collecting the baby from the babyminder on his way home from school and making sure she didn't try to overcharge his mother, who seemed not to notice when the money she claimed was owed her amounted to more than the hours she actually minded the child. He had his other siblings to care for as well; the habit of taking charge, of being responsible had been instilled in him very early; it was an automatic habit, a reflex action, something which he neither directed nor controlled, but something which was so intrinsically a part of him that when he found David Bernstein sniffling outside the school gates, his clothes torn and blood staining the knees of his jeans—immaculately clean jeans, unlike those that most of the others wore—despite his irritation with the boy for allowing himself to be so tormented, Ben stopped beside him, chivvying him to his feet with the same brusque firmness he used towards his siblings, commanding him to 'stop skriking' and telling him that there was nothing really wrong.

David Bernstein seemed to think otherwise, though. He was afraid to walk home in case they attacked him again, he told Ben miserably, and, more out of irritation and impatience than anything else, and because it would not take him much out of his way, Ben announced that he would go with him.

David Bernstein lived not in the flats like Ben and most of the others, but in a small terraced house, in one of the few streets left undisturbed by the planners. His father worked in a delicatessen on the other side of the city and the house, Ben discovered later, had been left to his mother by a relative.

As he firmly marched David up to the front door, it never occurred to Ben that David's mother would interpret his actions as those of a rescuer and protector, a saviour who had been sent specifically to guard her precious son.

Ben was a solid, determined child, independent and stoical and reserved to the point that some adults found off-putting and unsettling.

Sarah Bernstein saw none of this. When she opened the door and saw her bedraggled, precious only son being firmly pushed in her direction by a pugnacious-jawed and very obviously non-Jewish boy, her first thought was that Ben was the one who was responsible for David's appearance; but David, who a little to Ben's surprise proved far more adept at dealing with his mother than he was with his peers, immediately corrected her, so that, instead of being castigated for his brutal attack on her defenceless child, Ben found to his horror that he was being swept up in a smothering embrace and hauled inside the house, despite all his protests and his attempts to regain his dignity and his male supremacy.

The first thing he noticed once Sarah Bernstein had released him was the smell coming from the kitchen. His nostrils twitched, his stomach rumbling so loudly that not only did he stare down at it, but Sarah Bernstein actually stopped talking.

From the moment of his birth, Sarah had been engaged in a losing battle between her desire to nourish her child and his stubborn refusal to do anything more than peck at the food she so lovingly prepared.

To Sarah, food was love. In giving food, she gave love; and when he rejected her food David rejected that love, but now here was a child...a goy child to be sure...but still a hungry boy-child, whose eyes glistened as he smelled her soup, whose stomach advertised his need.

Before he could even think of objecting, Ben was sitting in Sarah Bernstein's kitchen, drinking a bowl of her chicken soup, silenced not just by Sarah's ceaseless stream of instructions and questions to her son, but also by the discovery that what he had in front of him, what he could taste in his mouth, what was right now filling and warming his stomach, bore no resemblance whatsoever to anything he had previously eaten.

That discovery was the beginning of his interest in food, and his friendship with Sarah Bernstein, the knowledge and awareness she gave him, were what fuelled and fed it.

It was from Sarah that he learned that the raw ingredients he had seen in shops but which his mother always ignored in favour of ready-prepared foods could be transformed into meals, and it was also from her that he learned too the value and importance of freshly grown vegetables, of carefully chosen meats and fish.

Once he had also discovered the difference between the meals Sarah prepared and those his mother provided, as well as their nutritional benefits, there was no stopping him.

The first time he'd served his version of Sarah's chicken soup his mother had stared at him open-mouthed, and then she had laughed.

Ben had refused to be deterred and very soon he had taken over not just the preparation of their meals but the choosing and purchase of their ingredients as well.

With Sarah he visited the markets, learned to tell the difference between what was fresh and what was not.

There was no time when he made a conscious decision that food was to be his career; boys, young men like him did not look for careers, they simply found jobs—if they were lucky.

It was one of his teachers who suggested to him that by borrowing books from the library he could add to and extend what he had already learned from Sarah when she found him in the school yard one day, sternly berating his younger brother for selling off half of his home-made lunch to one of his friends.

Kevin was indignant and unrepentant. 'You don't understand. It's not fair,' he had accused his brother. 'I could have sold that for fifty pence. Everyone wants our Ben's dinners, miss,' he had added to the surprised teacher.

Long before he was sixteen, Ben was working weekends and after school to add to the family income, hard, often poorly paid jobs which Sarah found for him through her family connections, none of them paying much; but Ben was glad of what they did pay; work wasn't that easy to find.

And it was Sarah who, when he left school, managed to persuade one of her relatives to take him on in his restaurant.

The restaurant was more of a diner really, serving hot meals both to the people who worked in the nearby market and the drivers who brought in the fresh supplies of food.

The food was cheap and hot, and the diner was always busy. Ben was paid little more than a pittance but at least he was in work, and every now and again, when Solly's back was turned, he would alter the ingredients of whatever he was preparing, refining and experimenting.

He had become an avid reader of not just cookery books but magazine and newspaper articles as well, passionately interested in the way that food was changing, experimenting secretly whenever Solly wasn't around.

It was the long arm of coincidence and accident which brought Henri Fontanel into his life. The French restaurateur had been on his way to Scotland to hand-pick the first of the season's game when his hired car had broken down.

He had seen the diner from the opposite side of the road when he was telephoning for assistance and, rather than wait in the car, he had made his way to the restaurant, intending to do nothing more than order himself a cup of what he anticipated would be execrable coffee. But when he saw the meal the two men at an adjacent table were eating, his interest had been sufficiently aroused for him to order the same dish.

The sauce, although clumsy and unrefined, intrigued him; the vegetables were not the usual soggy overcooked English affair he had expected, but crisp and full of flavour, the meat, although far from an expensive cut, betraying an awareness of at least some knowledge of what was and was not good meat.

He was interested enough to ask if he could speak to the chef. Solly Bernstein was too astonished to stop him.

But when Ben discovered that Henri was actually offering him—*him!*— the chance to train in one of France's most famous restaurants, he thought at first that his brain was playing a cruel joke on him.

Once the euphoria had worn off, though, he knew that it would be impossible for him to accept. How would his family manage without him? The wages he earned would be no more than a pittance, Henri had told him that, but Ben knew that there were many hundreds who would gladly have paid for the chance to learn from such a master.

How could *he* live in Paris? He couldn't even speak French.

Surprisingly, it had been his mother who had changed his mind, who had insisted that this was his chance and that he must take it; who had reminded him that she *was* his mother and not his responsibility.

He had been full of doubts at first... not just about his family's ability to manage without him, but doubts that he could live up to the promise his mentor had claimed to see in him. What if Henri was wrong and he ended up being sent home in disgrace?

'Listen,' Sarah Bernstein told him when he confided his worries to her, 'what problems can this French cuisine give you? You learned how to make my chicken soup, didn't you?'

Ben smiled slightly, remembering that comment. Sarah lived in New York now. She had moved there after her husband died to live with David and his family. David was a doctor and Ben still kept in touch with the family.

Henri had sold the Paris restaurant after a spectacular—and very costly—quarrel with his cousin and partner Fabian, and had now opened a new restaurant in Provence. In the catering business, it was not the chefs who earned a good living but the restaurant owners. Ben had seen that when he'd worked in Paris and it was a fact which had been reinforced while he was working in London.

Owning his own restaurant had been his dream ever since he had left Paris, but, if he was honest, it was a dream he had never dared to envisage coming true, and now that it was on the point of doing so—more than doing so, in fact—his delight was tinged with apprehension and fear—a fear that sprang not from any lack of belief in his own talents, nor in Zoe's, but from a lack of trust in fate to be so beneficent to him; fear of allowing himself to believe that his dream was attainable only to have it snatched back from him at the last minute.

Zoe might tease him for his caution, but Zoe had never known what it was to be denied anything. He did not resent her for that. In fact it was the confidence, the sheer bubbling confidence in herself and in life which she possessed in such abundance that had drawn him to her in the first place. But he could not change the watchful caution of a lifetime's awareness of life's cruelty and unfairness no matter how much he wished he was able to do so.

'I've explained to Clive that we'd prefer to travel down there on our own so that we can spend a couple of days looking around and sussing out the competition. He was all for it. And I've booked us into a hotel.' Her nose wrinkled. 'It's closer to Salisbury than Bath and advertises itself as "An exclusive country house hotel designed to provide the discerning guest with every comfort and luxury." It's got its own indoor pool and gym and apparently a well-recommended restaurant.'

'It sounds gross,' Ben told her frankly. 'That official recommendation could be a problem, though.'

Zoe gave a small shrug. 'Well, hopefully it will be far enough away not to be any real competition, and if Clive gets the go-ahead to buy the extra land and build a golf course...'

'If...it's a big if, and anyway I'm not sure if it's a good idea to start expanding into that kind of market too soon. We don't want to overstretch ourselves. Let's get the restaurant established first.'

'And the hotel,' Zoe interrupted him.

'The house is too small to accommodate more than three or four couples at most as it stands at present, and even then it's going to need a lot of work on it. We shan't be able to call it a hotel until the extension has been built and we don't even know if we'll be able to get planning permission for that yet.'

'Clive has been in touch with a local architect and he hasn't said that we won't,' Zoe objected.

'No, but he hasn't said that we will either, has he? Don't get too excited yet, Zoe. We've still got a very long way to go.'

Zoe pulled a face at him.

'Why do you always have to be such a *pessimist*?'

'Because life's safer that way. Have you told your parents yet?'

Zoe shook her head. 'I was going to tell Ma when you were in Manchester, but by the time we'd had lunch and been shopping... She rang me this morning. She sounded a bit down; I...'

'She probably hasn't had her hair done this week,' Ben interrupted her.

Zoe glared at him. 'Ben, that isn't fair. I was going to suggest we drive out to see her. Dad's away on business again, but if you feel like that, I'll go on my own.'

A little to her surprise, Ben shook his head.

'No, I'll come with you—or would you prefer I didn't bother? After all, we don't want to embarrass Mummy with my uncivilised behaviour, do we?'

When he saw her face, he made a small grimace and apologised.

'OK, OK. I'm sorry but I can't help it. Your parents' life, their relationship, even that damned house—they're all so perfect, so—so politically correct. I sometimes wonder how they managed to produce you.'

'Oh, I think they did it just like everyone else; they did it with a good fuck,' Zoe told him, baring her teeth.

She knew he hated her saying anything like that, and while normally she was gently careful not to tread on the tenets of his upbringing which still subconsciously led him to think that 'nice girls' did not use that kind of language, his criticism of her parents had annoyed her so much that she wanted to hit back at him, and she saw from his face that she had done and that he was aware of what she was doing.

Her temper, quick to flare, was always equally quick to subside, remorse darkening her eyes as she hugged him and said ruefully, 'I'm sorry... I expect, or at least I hope, I was conceived with the same love and enjoyment that *we* share when we make love. Is that better?'

'Mmm... but somehow I can't see your mother... She always looks so perfect, so almost antiseptic that it's hard to imagine...' He shook his head. 'Come on, then, if we're going to Hampstead, we might as well start now before the rush-hour.'

*   *   *

'Just think...I can hardly believe it! In two days' time we'll be there, seeing it properly...'

'Where?' Ben teased her, pretending not to understand and then yelping in protest as she took her attention off the road to aim a playful fist at him and in doing so nearly hit a car emerging from a side-street.

'Idiot,' Zoe muttered under her breath, causing Ben to stare at her when he realised it was the innocent and affronted driver of the other car she was castigating and not herself.

If Zoe's mother was surprised to see both of them standing outside when she opened the front door, she did not show it.

'You didn't need to knock, darling,' she told Zoe gently as she kissed her. 'You've still got your key, haven't you?'

'Yes, but I don't like using it,' Zoe told her as she stepped past her into the house, adding with a grin, 'After all, for all I know you could be upstairs, enjoying a very private interlude with your lover!'

'Zoe!' her mother protested.

'All right, Ma,' Zoe laughed. 'We all know that you and Dad are boringly faithful to one another.'

Because he was still standing in front of her and because the light from the still open doorway was streaming fully into her face, it was Ben and not Zoe who saw the way her expression changed, shadowing so that for a handful of seconds she was suddenly stripped of the cool veneer which Ben always found so irritating, and for once he could see behind it to a woman who was suddenly far more like Zoe than he had realised.

Automatically he stepped forward, and then checked as her general veneer slid back into place. Silently he watched her retreat from him and turn towards Zoe.

'Ma, before we do anything else, Ben and I have something to tell you...'

Quickly and excitedly, before her mother could say a word, Zoe rattled on at high speed, delivering a complicated and muddled account of what was happening, leaving Ben to unravel the tangled threads of her conversation and to explain their plans.

When Heather interrupted quietly, 'Wiltshire?' it was Ben who picked up on the suppressed note of despair that contradicted the smile she was giving them, and cut through Zoe's excitement to say calmly,

'It sounds further than it is. Just a couple of hours' drive, really.'

He watched as the hazel eyes briefly met his, revealing conflicting emotions of pride and gratitude, and wondered why it was that he had felt impelled to reassure her.

He was not antagonistic towards Zoe's parents; at least, not as far as his relationship with Zoe went—there had never been any need. But if he was honest there was a small thread of atavistic, instinctive rejection of them within him that was more cultural than logical, something he normally tried to ignore but which surfaced occasionally, normally in the form of some acid comment about their cushioned, protected, cosseted lifestyle.

Zoe's mother in particular irritated and baffled him. She was so different from his own mother, different too from the women who came into the restaurant, career women in the main, efficiently businesslike and in control, without those odd flashes of vulnerability which Heather possessed and which disconcerted him so much, causing a shift in his perception of her, which made him feel unwantedly protective towards her, protective and irritated at the same time.

It was happening now, while Zoe chattered on excitedly about their plans and the future, apparently oblivious to the anxiety and panic her mother was suppressing. Those emotions were so clear to Ben that he felt angry with them both, Heather for imposing them on him and burdening him with them and Zoe for not recognising what her mother was feeling and thereby making *him* feel responsible for her emotions.

And yet as he looked away from her and glanced round the pristinely immaculate sitting-room with its fresh flowers and pastel colours, a prettiness and warmth which somehow only seemed to emphasise the loneliness of the small, slim, elegant woman who was its creator, he wondered as he had wondered so many times before how such a woman could ever have produced a child as vibrant and ebullient as Zoe, and, as he had been forced to do in the past, he had to admit that there must be something within Heather that he was missing, that he was simply not perceptive enough to see.

Now, as he saw the distress she quickly concealed from Zoe, he wondered if he was finally seeing it.

'Well, that's wonderful, darling,' he heard her saying warmly to Zoe. 'I only wish that Daddy were here to share your exciting news. Actually, though, I have something to tell you myself.'

Quickly Ben looked across at her, hearing the strain in her voice, but Zoe seemed oblivious to it.

'What is it, Ma?' Zoe teased. 'Are you planning to change your hairstyle?'

'I've been asked to consider working full-time for the housing charity. They're running a training programme and there's a place on it for me...' She paused uncertainly. 'I'm not sure what I should do. If I take the place and then it turns out that I'm not really suitable for the work, I'll have prevented someone else from training.'

'What does Dad think?' Zoe asked her.

There was a small pause and Ben watched as the small frown between Zoe's mother's neatly defined eyebrows increased. 'Well, I have discussed it with him, of course, but you know how busy he is. He's in Zurich at the moment—something to do with the IMF, some kind of conference.

'Of course, it is a big commitment to take on, but I will be doing something useful, something that's of benefit to others . . .'

'The Sixties teenager comes of age with a Nineties conscience,' Zoe teased, and Ben, who had been thinking much along the same lines, saw the brief flicker of pain in the older woman's eyes and said nothing.

Instead, as much to his own surprise as to hers, he went over to Heather and hugged her, telling her gruffly, 'You go for it, Heather. You've got one hell of a lot to offer.'

He saw the surprise in her eyes, the quick sheen of tears which she covered, the gratitude mingling with pain. He also felt the small slight tremble of her body; a totally non-personal reflex action of female to male which told him that her body was unfamiliar with that kind of spontaneous show of affection.

And yet Zoe had often commented how as a teenager she would regularly inadvertently interrupt her parents sharing a kiss, and that it was partially this awareness of their sexuality and their enjoyment of it which had given rise to her own belief that physical intimacy was a natural expression of emotion.

As Heather stepped back from him, Ben glanced across at Zoe. She seemed oblivious to her mother's tension, insisting instead on outlining to Heather all their plans for the future of the hotel.

'Well, I'm thrilled for both of you,' Heather announced when Zoe had finally run out of breath.

'It's all really thanks to you,' Ben told her quietly. 'After all, you were the one who recommended me to Clive Hargreaves in the first place, and if I hadn't been invited to cater for his daughter's wedding . . .'

'Clive is a businessman, not a philanthropist. If he didn't have faith in you, he would never have even contemplated backing you. So when are you going to see the house?' Heather asked them.

'This week,' Zoe told her excitedly. 'We're meeting Clive down there. Ben and I are having a couple of days off so that we can scout around and test out the competition.

'We're staying at this hotel near Salisbury. It seems to be the only close competition we're going to have, and of course the chef won't be anywhere as good as Ben.'

'Don't be too sure,' Ben advised her. 'The restaurant does have a good star rating, remember.'

'Oh, you. Why are you always such a pessimist?' Zoe objected, laughing at him.

It was gone midnight when they finally left. Heather had insisted on opening a bottle of champagne to toast their success. The phone had rung while they were drinking it and she had hurried to answer it, her face flushing with colour, the anticipation draining from her voice, leaving it flat and tired when she responded to the caller.

'I was hoping it might be your father,' she told Zoe as she replaced the receiver. 'He promised he'd try to call this evening, but obviously he's got tied up with something.'

Later on while they were driving home, Zoe commented happily to Ben, 'Ma seemed really pleased for us, didn't she? Not that I thought she wouldn't be. I was surprised about this extra work she's talking about taking on, though.'

'Perhaps she feels she needs something to fill her time with your father being away such a lot,' Ben responded cautiously.

Zoe seemed to have no perception of the undercurrents he had sensed in her parents' home, nor of the tension he had felt emanating from her mother, and he had no wish to distress her by outlining his own suspicions.

Was it because he didn't want to upset her, or was it because, selfishly, he didn't want her attention deflected from their own lives to her parents'?

What was the point in stirring up trouble? he asked himself, shifting a little uncomfortably in his seat as he suppressed the sharpness of his silent self-questioning.

After all he could be wrong. Heather Clinton could genuinely simply wish to find something to fill in her spare time. He could quite easily be wrong in suspecting that Zoe's parents' marriage was not after all as idyllically happy and secure as Zoe had always seemed to think.

Or was he just being over-cynical in suspecting that a husband who spent so much time away from home, plus a wife who was plainly unhappy and feeling rejected, was a recipe for marital problems?

And had it already gone further than merely being a slight problem; was Zoe's father...?

'Ben, come back,' Zoe called out, demanding his attention. 'You were miles away. Who were you thinking about? Sharon?'

'No,' he told her honestly as he smiled at her.

'Well, you were worrying about something...someone...' Zoe retorted.

Ben said nothing. Worrying? About her parents, her mother...? Why should he? He had problems enough worrying about his own family without taking on the additional burden of Zoe's parents as well.

And yet later, holding Zoe tight in the warm relaxation of post-coital intimacy, her head resting heavily on his arm, her body curled sensuously around his, her breathing slowing and evening out into sleep, he remembered how tense and oddly fragile Heather had felt when he hugged her; how struck he had been by his sharp awareness of her unhappiness and aloneness.

They were not his problem, he reminded himself as he closed his eyes. *She* was not his problem.

CHAPTER TEN

'WELL, what do you think?' Zoe demanded excitedly.

Clive had just driven off to go and see the architect and they were alone in Broughton House's grounds. From where they were standing it was possible to see the house through the tangled undergrowth that choked the small copse, and from this distance it looked solid and permanent, the signs of age and decay hidden.

'It's smaller than I'd imagined,' Ben commented, 'and one hell of a lot of work will have to be done before we can even think of using those kitchens.'

'Well, we knew that,' Zoe dismissed impatiently. 'And anyway, you've said all along that you'd prefer to have a say in the design of the kitchen.'

'Those don't just need redesigning,' Ben told her drily.

'But Ben, you've got to admit that it's got masses of potential. These grounds...the area... I hadn't realised the town was going to be so pretty. It will be a tremendous hit with American and Australian tourists.'

'American and Australian tourists? *What* American and Australian tourists? We don't get any any more!'

'We will,' Zoe told him firmly. 'You've got to admit that all this...' she waved an arm to embrace their surroundings '...is wonderful...'

'Is it?' Ben asked her wryly, but he was laughing, Zoe recognised, and behind his dour refusal to share her enthusiasm she could sense that secretly he was excited.

'I can see what Clive means about the stable block being extended to make perfect extra accommodation.'

'Yes, if we can get planning permission,' Ben reminded her.

Zoe refused to be deterred. She laughed, turning to him, flinging her arms round him and hugging him fiercely.

'Oh, Ben,' she teased him. 'How you do love to worry! Just look at all this.' She gestured to the grounds around them. 'And once people taste your food...'

'All right,' Ben admitted, hugging her back, his face breaking into a grin. 'All right... I love it. *Now* are you happy?'

'Yes, yes, yes!' Zoe laughed back.

'It's going to take a hell of a lot of time and money before we even get close to serving food, though, Zoe,' Ben warned her. 'And as to what it will cost to convert it to the type of place Clive has in mind...'

'Clive knows what he's doing. He's a millionaire,' Zoe interrupted him cheerfully. 'And,' she added with emphasis, 'he didn't get that way just by chance and with good luck.'

'Come on,' Ben urged her. 'I'm hungry...'

'Let's just have another look at the pool,' Zoe pleaded with him.

Ben shook his head, but he still followed her back down the path they had just taken, pausing with her as she stood entranced by the sight of a small kite's tail of ducklings following their mother across its placid surface.

'Oh, just look at them, aren't they gorgeous?'

'Gorgeous,' Ben echoed, keeping his face straight as he mused, 'Henri had a recipe for duckling. It——'

He yelped as Zoe aimed a small thump at his arm, and whispered teasingly in her ear, 'Ducklings... are you sure they're not really swans?'

Zoe made a face at him.

They talked the whole thing through excitedly as they drove away half an hour later. All right, so the house was badly affected by damp in places, and certainly, having looked at the rooms, she had been forced to agree with Ben's original comment that until they had planning permission for a conversion and extension of the stable block to provide more realistic accommodation, they could not hope to open the house as a hotel; but even Ben had had to agree that the place had potential.

Zoe sighed ecstatically.

She could see it all now: the house, carefully and sympathetically renovated, the new block perfectly in keeping with the original building, a large sunny conservatory added which could be used as an extra alfresco-type dining-room, the lawn perfectly manicured, sweeping down to the copse and its pretty hidden pool, the formal walkways and borders filled with the colour and scent of traditional summer flowers... What a setting it would make for summer weddings; the lawns were more than large enough for even the largest of marquees. Her imagination took fire; the weddings became charity balls, prestige events, the busy but very elegant reception area filled with eager visitors whom the smiling, very well-trained receptionist was having diplomatically to turn away. *Tatler* and *Harpers* mentioned them in their 'dining out' columns and they were inundated with floods of bookings...

Ben was in such popular demand that he was contemplating his own small cookery school in a new purpose-built block tucked away discreetly in the grounds...

She heaved a deep ecstatic sigh of pleasure and excitement.

She could see it all...everything they had ever talked about, dreamed about. Perhaps they might even expand, open a second restaurant... perhaps a château in France... But this place, their first hotel, would always remain special to them.

And one day, when they were old and about to retire, they would look back and she would remind Ben of how pessimistic he had been, of how needlessly he had agonised and worried.

'Mmm...' she heard Ben murmuring sexily in her ear. 'Bet I know what you're thinking about.'

She laughed as she shook her head, and told him with a grin, 'Bet you don't.'

'Is this it?'

Ben gave a small grimace as he stopped the car next to the hotel entrance.

To either side of the drive where once there must have been the kind of 'natural' rolling parkland beloved of Capability Brown there now stretched a golf course, all raw patches of earth and vistas which contained only unrealistically posed clumps of golfers instead of majestic stands of specimen trees.

'This course was probably designed in the days before they had to design them around existing landscape features,' Zoe pointed out.

'It does look pretty off-putting, though, doesn't it?' he said.

'Mmm... Unless of course you happen to be a golfer; but why on earth couldn't they put the course out of sight of the hotel's main entrance?'

'Are you sure this is the only place in the area that we're going to have to compete with?' he asked her thoughtfully.

'As far as I can tell.'

'Mind you, there's still that good food rating,' Ben pointed out as they parked the car in front of the hotel.

Inside, the reception area was cramped into what was obviously a sectioned-off portion of what had originally been a much larger room. The conversion had altered the room's proportions in a way that gave the reception area a boxed-in, unwelcoming feel to it, a mistake they were most definitely not going to make, Zoe assured herself as she contrasted its layout to the one she was mentally planning for Broughton House.

The reception desk was unattended, even though they could hear the sound of voices from the office area behind it—and so presumably could the people within it hear them.

In the end, Zoe had to ring the bell provided a couple of times, before a very young and rather flustered girl appeared.

She had to go through the registrations twice before she found their names, her manner changing slightly as she found them and commented with some surprise, 'Oh, you're booked into our special suite.'

'Are we?' Ben whispered to Zoe as she turned away from them.

'Clive's idea,' she whispered back. 'He said I was to book the most expensive suite they had so that we'd know exactly what we were competing with.'

'Well, I don't care how it advertises itself,' Ben told her. 'This place is no country retreat. It's more of a business complex-cum-conference centre.'

'It does have a large leisure complex attached to it,' Zoe pointed out fairly. 'Something we haven't even considered.'

'Nor do we intend to,' Ben countered firmly.

The girl behind the reception desk had found their key, but she seemed to be having trouble locating someone to take them and their luggage up to their rooms.

'I'm sorry,' she apologised, 'but we've got a conference on and we're rather short-staffed.'

'Permanently short-staffed would probably have been a better description,' Zoe murmured to Ben when she had eventually found someone to take them to their room.

It wasn't the girl's fault, she acknowledged; she was very young, probably only a part-timer. The hotel was several miles from the nearest village, and presumably had to bus its staff in and out.

The industry was notorious for paying low wages, and probably had a very high turnover of teenagers, who worked part-time for extra money while still at school. It was not part of one of the large chains and therefore probably did not have a thorough training scheme, none of which was very satisfactory from a potential guest's point of view, she decided as they eventually reached their suite, but very, very gratifying from their own.

Zoe smiled her thanks to the boy who had brought up their bags and waited until Ben had tipped him and he had left before delivering her professional opinion of his services.

'Mmm . . . very amateurish,' Ben agreed, asking her, 'And what is madam's opinion of her room?'

Zoe pulled a small face.

The sitting-room they were standing in was comfortably if somewhat unoriginally furnished with vast swaths of floral chintz, its décor an unenterprising mixture of pink and green.

'Pretty, but rather overdone.'

'Mmm...pretty sickly, I would have called it,' Ben corrected her. 'Let's go and have a look at the bedroom.'

The bedroom echoed the same colour scheme as the sitting-room, and they had, as Zoe pointed out fair-mindedly, been given a double bed as she had requested, and the view from their window, while it incorporated the golf course, did extend further afield to include some of the surrounding countryside.

'It's the bathroom I want to see, though,' she announced mysteriously, moving away from Ben to push open the *en-suite* bathroom door.

'Why?' Ben questioned her. 'What's so interesting about a bathroom? Ah...' He paused, standing behind her.

'It's a jacuzzi,' Zoe told him unnecessarily.

'So I can see,' he agreed drily. 'No wonder that girl on the reception desk gave us such a funny look. This suite is probably normally reserved by ageing businessmen accompanied by their secretaries.'

'Clive said we were to book their most expensive suite,' Zoe pointed out virtuously.

'Well, I hope you don't imagine that our hotel...'

'Aha! So it *is* going to be a hotel and not just a restaurant,' Zoe pounced.

'It could be, but it won't have bedrooms equipped with those things.'

'Not the bedrooms,' Zoe agreed.

Ben looked at her. 'What exactly does that mean?'

She turned towards him, and slowly started to unfasten the top buttons of his shirt.

'Well, you never know, do you?' she said slowly. 'We could always have one in our own private quarters.'

'Could we? What on earth for?' Ben asked her, but he was mumbling the words rather than saying them as Zoe wrapped her arms around him and started kissing him.

An hour later, when Ben was complaining that he was beginning to look and feel like a wrinkled prune, Zoe smiled lazily at him and said thoughtfully, 'Do you suppose it's true that these jets are strong enough to give...' She broke off, laughing, as Ben grabbed hold of her and hauled her to her feet, lifting her out of the water.

'Right now what I'm interested in is my dinner,' he told her firmly.

He paused as Zoe ran her fingernails against his skin and bent her head to playfully nibble his ear.

'Mmm... What time did you book dinner for?' he asked her indistinctly as his hand cupped her breast and the sensation of their damp bodies moving together caused Zoe to make a soft murmur of appreciation.

'Half-past eight,' she told him.

Making love with Zoe had right from the start always been something very special to him, Ben acknowledged later as her body relaxed into a luxuriously sensual appreciation of the orgasm she had just uninhibitedly enjoyed.

It had taken him a while though to get used to her open acceptance and appreciation of her sensuality, to her joyful enjoyment of it; to the way she felt no inhibitions, no reservations about showing him, sharing with him what she was feeling.

Zoe was not promiscuous, although at first he had wondered, even judged her openness as a sign that she might be; he had not realised then, in those early days, that the ease and delight with which she had instigated their lovemaking came not from a wealth of varied previous experience but from a much more simple and natural awareness of her own needs and desires.

In fact, he had discovered later that she had far less experience than he had imagined, much, much less than he had had himself, and that in wanting them to be lovers she was simply expressing physically her emotional reaction to him. Zoe had shown him an aspect to sex he had never previously known existed, a special shining beauty and purity in it, which others might think was at odds with her obvious enjoyment of the physical side of their relationship, but which he had come to recognise was a very rare form of honesty and trust.

Through her, he had gradually let go of his own inhibitions to discard the destructive sexual attitudes he had collected during his teens when girls who did 'it' were easy, and those who didn't too much hard work. Girls who did were for having fun with, those who didn't for marrying.

Zoe had taught him to see things from a very different perspective, to accept that a woman had a right to control her own sexuality and to feel free to enjoy it.

And Zoe did enjoy it. And through her enjoyment gave a very special and rare form of pleasure to him, he acknowledged as she kissed him sleepily and snuggled up to him.

'Oh, no, you don't,' he warned her, disengaging himself from her and giving her a small shake. 'We're not here to enjoy ourselves. It's eight o'clock and dinner's booked for half-past—remember?'

Zoe laughed and rolled on to her side, watching him. He had a wonderful body, she reflected as she studied him through half-closed eyes. His skin was firm and golden, warm both to look at and touch, his arms hard and well-muscled, and strong enough not just to hold her, but to pick her up as well. She smiled to herself at her own foolish femininity in finding that knowledge a small turn-on, but it *was* sexy knowing that the arms that held her were also strong enough to hold her safe.

Safe? From what? She laughed to herself as she sat up.

It had taken her a long time to coax Ben to be as relaxed and confident about this kind of shared intimacy as he was now. She could still remember a time when the moment they had finished making love he would reach for his clothes. Now...

She looked up at him as she ran a teasing fingertip along his thigh.

'Oh, no, you don't,' he checked her, covering her hand with his own and removing it as he reminded her mock sternly. 'Not this time. Dinner...'

Zoe pouted. 'How can you even think of food, when instead you could...?'

She paused deliberately, looking at him through her lashes, making Ben laugh even though he refused to give in to her teasing, getting off the bed, and collecting clean clothes as he headed for the bathroom.

'I'm a chef—that's how,' he told her. 'Oh, no,' he added as Zoe started to follow him. 'This time you can wait until I've finished. I'm not risking going in there with you. Not with that damned jacuzzi...'

'Coward,' Zoe called out after him mildly, as she stretched luxuriously on the bed.

Her body felt deliciously satisfied, sleek and relaxed, still warm from the intimacy of Ben's, still...

She touched her stomach lightly, smiling to herself, and then her smile widened into a blissful grin as she reflected on the sheer perfection of the day.

The house had been wonderful, everything she had imagined and more. Or at least it would be once it had been renovated, the kitchen redesigned, the new extension built.

She rolled over, breathing out a small ecstatic sigh of quiet happiness.

She was still lying there when Ben emerged from the bathroom, his hair damp, his skin glowing from the shower. It must be all that lifting and carrying of heavy sacks of food that had developed those powerful muscles that lay so tautly beneath the sleek healthiness of his skin, Zoe reflected appreciatively. She liked the way his body hair grew across his chest, and then arrowed narrowly downwards over his belly. Those Fifties women who had sighed over male film stars who had been instructed to shave off such evidence of their masculinity hadn't known what they were missing, she decided dreamily.

She loved the way the silky fineness of Ben's body hair felt against her fingertips and her breasts; sometimes, to tease him, she tugged tormentingly at it with her teeth, making him yelp in protest.

She smiled secretly to herself, remembering the occasion he had been tempted to retaliate, and what had followed; that had been in the early days of their relationship and she remembered how he had told her tautly afterwards how he had never known until then just what degree of intensity of sexual pleasure it was possible for him to experience in that kind of intimacy.

Now neither her body nor its responses held any secrets from him.

It didn't bother her that their sexual roles were reversed from what was generally and romantically considered the 'norm'; that she had originally been the one to initiate sex between them and that she had also been the one to draw him deeper into its shared intimacies; in fact she rather liked it, enjoying the sense of equality and rapport it gave her.

'You've got fifteen minutes,' Ben told her firmly.

Obligingly she got up, and headed for the bathroom; for all her teasing and playfulness, underneath she was just as conscious as he was of the real purpose of their stay here. What was even more important was that he knew she was aware of it as well. But of course, being Ben, he couldn't resist chivvying her, worrying around her like a sheepdog ever anxious about the potential silliness of its flock.

She liked that about him too, she admitted as she showered and then quickly dried herself. She had always prided herself on her independence, and fiercely rejected anyone, but especially any male, who attempted to control or curtail it, and yet there was something almost perversely reassuring, some deep-seated core of feminine instinct, not for her own preservation but for the preservation of the seeds of life she carried within her that made her feel reassured by Ben's conscientious worrying even while she teased him for it.

She paused in the act of drying her body to frown as she made a closer inspection of her own idle thoughts, but then, as she heard Ben calling out impatiently to her, she shrugged and dismissed them, hurrying into clean underclothes.

From a culinary point of view the meal was a disaster on a scale which could only be described as heroic. From the standpoint of a potential competitor it was a wonderful, mind-blowing, exhilarating confirmation of all that Zoe had been impressing upon Ben since Clive had first floated his offer to back them.

How could they be anything other than successful if this was their only competition? Zoe queried in exultation, watching Ben's expression as he tasted his soup.

They had had to wait until nine o'clock to be shown to their table by an obviously nervous waitress. The dining-room was half empty, the empty tables destroying any atmosphere the room might otherwise have had.

They were very busy with the people from the conference, the waitress told Zoe apologetically when she commented on the absence of other diners and the length of time they had had to wait for their meal.

The soup was described over-lavishly on the menu as 'A thick, home-made, nourishing soup of garden-grown vegetables, enhanced by the chef's special free-range chicken stock, and embellished with croutons from our own home-made bread'...

'The vegetables are canned and not fresh,' Ben exclaimed in disgust after just one spoonful, 'and as for the stock... Whatever it is, it isn't chicken, and I should know.'

'Sarah Bernstein, I know,' Zoe said, asking him cheerfully, 'Oh, Ben, is it really that bad?'

'Worse,' he assured her grimly.

Zoe had chosen the melon for her first course, not out of any preference but because, apart from a pâté which she didn't want, it was the only other thing on the menu, the other items no longer being available.

The melon was thinly sliced, and garnished with a sticky red sauce into which what looked like an uninspiring selection of small pieces of fruit had been thrown.

For her main course she had ordered *coquille St-Jacques*, much against Ben's recommendation.

'Have the duck,' he had suggested. 'You know you've got a sensitive stomach—look at that bout of sickness you had only a few weeks ago.'

Zoe had shaken her head and pulled a face. 'I couldn't... not after this afternoon...'

Ben had ordered the vegetarian dish for his main course, mainly to see what was being offered, and when their food finally arrived and he saw that he was being served with a very indifferent omelette Zoe could see the disgust curling his mouth.

So, it seemed, could the waitress because she flushed a little and apologised, explaining, 'It's because of the conference... We're very short-staffed.'

'I'm getting rather tired of hearing about this conference,' Ben commented when she had left them.

He reached over and picked up Zoe's plate, sniffing at it.

'Don't eat it,' he warned her. 'I think the fish is off.'

Zoe pulled a face at him, and laughed. 'Oh, come on,' she teased. 'That's taking rivalry a bit far.'

'Mmm... Well, I could be mistaken,' Ben admitted, 'but, if my soup was anything to go by, that fish has probably spent more time in the freezer than it ever did in the sea.'

Having discovered that his omelette had the texture of rubber and that the side-salad produced with it was boringly uninspirational, Ben was content to do nothing other than give a disbelieving shake of his head when they discovered that the sweet trolley contained nothing more than chocolate fudge cake and fresh fruit and ice-cream.

'I don't believe this,' he told Zoe in awe.

'Believe it,' she assured him. 'I've just seen the trolley.'

After they had finished their meal, Ben summoned the waitress and told her placidly that they had been rather disappointed in their meal.

'Your restaurant is advertised as recommended,' he pointed out gently.

The girl flushed and looked unhappily over her shoulder, but no one appeared to rescue her.

'Yes, but... Well, I'm afraid the chef left last week and as yet... Well, he hasn't been replaced, and then there's——'

'The conference... yes. You've already said,' Ben agreed.

But it was jubilation and not criticism that warmed his voice half an hour later when he and Zoe were sitting in the bar discussing their meal.

'They could always replace the chef with someone even better,' Zoe warned him, for once playing devil's advocate and taking on his role.

'They can, but something's got to be wrong for their chef to have left in the first place.'

'Mmm... Shall we see if we can find out what?' Zoe suggested, glancing over her shoulder towards the deserted bar and the teenager behind it.

It took her less than half an hour of skilful questioning to elicit the full story.

There had apparently been a clash of objectives between the chef and the hotel owner. The chef had been under the impression that he had full control in the kitchen, and this apparently included control of his own budget. The hotel owner had had other ideas, ideas which apparently consisted of budget-cutting to an extent which meant that the chef was having to make do with poor quality produce and was therefore unable to produce the kind of meals on which he had based his reputation. The kind of meal which had earned the restaurant its award, Ben commented wryly to Zoe.

The hotel owner had also apparently disapproved of the unusual sauces and flavourings the chef wanted to use, and had insisted on sticking with a *nouvelle cuisine*-type menu. 'Small portions, you see, and therefore cheaper to produce,' the boy told them.

'The chef, Armand, didn't want to do that, though. He said that *nouvelle cuisine* wasn't *nouvelle* any more and that it certainly wasn't *cuisine* either,' he told them with obvious relish at having remembered this part of the quarrel he had obviously overheard.

'He said that people, discerning people, were tired of *nouvelle* and wanted wholesome, nourishing food, food whose origins they could check, food that was wholesomely grown. He prided himself on his sauces being free from additives and fat. He said that if people wanted to clog up their arteries with cholesterol, they could do so over breakfast.'

The boy gave a small shrug. 'Mr Patrick, the owner, said afterwards that he had intended to sack him anyway, but he hasn't managed to replace him yet.

'The underchef is having to do the food for the conference and that means that there isn't anyone to run the kitchen properly. The food in the restaurant is just bought-in freezer stuff. In fact I think some of it was here when Mr Patrick took the place over... Ella, my girl-friend... she works in the kitchen, she said some of the stuff is so encrusted in ice that they're having to run the packets under the hot tap before they can find out what's in them.'

'I warned you not to have that *St-Jacques*,' Ben whispered to Zoe as she winced.

Four hours later, when she had got out of bed for the third time within an hour to be violently sick, he followed her into the bathroom, dealing as efficiently with her nausea and consequent weakness as she suspected he must once have done with his siblings' childhood illnesses, but at the same time he couldn't resist crowing triumphantly.

'I knew it... I knew that fish was off.'

'Thanks,' Zoe told him weakly, but she shook her head when he asked her if she would like him to ask the hotel to get hold of a doctor.

'It isn't that bad,' she told him.

'Bad? It's wonderful!' Ben corrected her with a grin. 'My God, I can hardly believe our luck. Food poisoning... Let's hope you aren't the only one to get it. They'll close this place down, and if it really is our closest competition...'

'It is,' Zoe assured him, adding triumphantly, 'See, I told you not to worry, didn't I? I told you everything was going to work out... that nothing...'

She gulped as another wave of nausea hit her, and as he waited for the spasm to leave her, Ben grinned down at her and told her, 'All right...so you were right. Nothing is going to go wrong. Nothing *can* go wrong. We're unstoppable...and we're going to succeed beyond our wildest dreams... *I believe you.* All right?'

'All right,' Zoe agreed weakly, wincing as she told Ben, 'Stop making me laugh. It hurts...'

Physically she might feel dreadful, she acknowledged, but mentally, emotionally, she was on the kind of high that made her feel giddy with excitement. She had never seen Ben in such a positive mood, so full of his own excitement, pushing all his doubts and caution aside, for once being the one to buoy her up instead of the other way around.

It was all working out perfectly, she acknowledged tiredly as Ben helped her back to bed.

Perfectly, perfectly, perfectly, and Ben was right. *She* was right. *Nothing* could stop them now. *Nothing!*

CHAPTER ELEVEN

'AH, FERN, my dear, do come in.' Lord Stanton beamed at Fern as Phillips, his butler, showed her into the library.

Lord Stanton and Phillips; impossible to imagine one of them without the other, Fern acknowledged. Phillips at seventy was Lord Stanton's junior in age, but in many other ways he was, if not his mentor, then certainly his guardian; not in any custodial sense of the word, for Phillips's guardianship of his employer had nothing of that about it; it was more that one could not see the two of them together without being aware of how seriously the butler took his responsibilities towards the older man. There was certainly more to their relationship than that of employer and employee, although Fern had neither seen nor heard either of them ever abandoning the correct and sometimes quaintly old-fashioned manner they had of addressing and communicating with one another, both of them always rigidly correct in their etiquette. Without Phillips to ensure that his household ran smoothly, Fern doubted that Lord Stanton could survive, and she also suspected that, without Lord Stanton to take care of, Phillips would lose the sense of purpose that motivated his own life.

'How delightful of you to call,' Lord Stanton added as he ushered her towards a chair.

The library was large and old-fashioned, essentially a man's room, with a huge pedestal desk, and two large fireside chairs complete with foot-stools, their covering of green velvet worn smooth on the arms, like the patches in the Turkish carpet which showed the familiar pathways of Lord Stanton's peregrinations from desk to window and back to the fireside again.

'You asked me to call so that we could update the list for the children's party,' Fern reminded him gently, shaking her head when he offered her a glass of sherry, knowing that despite the fact that she could see the decanter and glasses on the silver tray within arm's distance of her chair Lord Stanton would still ring for Phillips to come and perform the small task of pouring it for her, and that the butler would then be despatched to the kitchen to fetch a plate of the small sweet macaroon biscuits which had been Lady Stanton's favourite and without which Lord Stanton felt it was impossible for any woman to enjoy her sherry.

'Ah, yes, so I did. It's my age, I'm afraid, my dear,' Lord Stanton told her ruefully. 'One tends to find it far harder to recall the present than one does the past.

'Now, where did I put that list...?'

'I have a copy of it, Lord Stanton,' Fern told him diplomatically as he started to search through the mass of papers on his desk.

'Have you? My dear, you really are the most marvellous young woman—exemplary, in fact. Have we many more children to add this time?'

'Three,' Fern told him, 'but we're going to lose five; two who are moving away with their parents, and three who will be thirteen this year.'

'Thirteen. Oh, dear. Eugenie always used to say that we should extend the age to fifteen, but children of that age do so hate to be grouped with those younger than themselves. I had to remind her of how much she resented being grouped with the children when we were young.

'She was younger than me, you know, Fern. Ten years younger, and so full of life and laughter. I never thought...

'It's five years this week since she died, you know. Sometimes I still find it hard to remember that she's gone. We were married when she was seventeen. We didn't quite make it to our Golden Wedding...

'We were talking about it the night she died. She wanted to have a big party... to invite all those we'd invited to our wedding, or at least those of them who were still alive...'

Fern smiled understandingly. She knew how much he had loved his wife. Nick grew irritated when Lord Stanton talked about her, claiming that he was bored with hearing the same old stories over and over again. Fern had tried gently to point out to him that it was the older man's only way of dealing with his grief that he needed to talk about the woman who had after all shared virtually all of his life with him. They had been second cousins and had spent holidays together as children; she had always been there as part of his life and now he was finding it very difficult to cope without her.

'You must miss her,' Fern said softly now.

'Yes. Yes, I do...' He looked at her, emotion replaced by intelligent awareness as he studied her.

'You have a very gentle touch, Fern, very compassionate... very soothing on one's small sore places. You must be tired of hearing me talk so much about her.'

'No, I'm not,' Fern replied honestly. 'I know how close you both were.' Her own eyes shadowed slightly as she withdrew from making the uncomfortable comparison between the Stantons' marriage and her own.

'We had our difficult times as everyone does, but Eugenie wasn't just my wife, she was also my best friend, my closest confidante. Oh, not at first, perhaps, in the early years... but later, once we had both settled into our marriage.

'Friendship is a very under-estimated virtue in marriage,' he added quietly, shaking his head. 'These days so much attention seems to be focused on other aspects... but, as one gets older, one truly appreciates the importance of being good friends, and it is as my friend that I miss

Eugenie the most. As a woman...as my wife, she may not always have approved of what I did; but as my friend she accepted my frailties and fallibilities and made allowances for them.'

He raised his head and smiled at Fern, shaking his head a second time when he saw the tears in her eyes.

'There, now I have upset you,' he apologised patting her hand, 'and I certainly didn't mean to do so.'

'No, you haven't upset me,' Fern assured him, blowing her nose.

Her own parents had had a long and happy marriage, but they had been in their early forties when she was born, unexpected but very welcome. However, because of the age-gap between them, much as she had loved them and known that they loved her, she had never felt free to talk to them uninhibitedly, had always been conscious of a need not to disappoint them, not to slip from the high standards their own moral code set her. As a teenager and a young woman it had seemed to her that her parents inhabited a very different world from hers, and she had always been anxious not to disillusion them, not to bring the reality of her own life in to disturb the peaceful harmony of theirs.

Now she recognised that she had, perhaps naïvely, assumed that their lives had always been like that, not appreciating as she now did from listening to Lord Stanton that that harmony and peace could have been something which had grown with age and might not necessarily always have been there.

She had always found it difficult, impossible almost, to imagine her parents quarrelling or arguing, involved in the kind of turmoil, the kind of ugliness which sometimes seemed to pervade her own marriage, and certainly neither of them could ever have experienced the kind of guilt and shame which so tormented her.

But she was here to help Lord Stanton, not to brood on her own problems, she reminded herself sternly as she produced her own copy of the Christmas party list and started to go through it with him.

'Sally Broughton's presence will be sadly missed by the town this year,' he commented sadly when they had finished. 'Especially with the summer fête.'

'Yes,' Fern agreed, and was unable to stop herself from adding unhappily, 'I do hope that Broughton House isn't going to be demolished.'

'Demolished? Surely not,' Lord Stanton protested.

'Well, Nick seems to think it's a possibility, and Adam ...' She stopped and bit her lip.

'Adam what?' Lord Stanton pressed her.

'Well, I saw him in the grounds of Broughton House earlier and he...he had what looked like a set of plans with him. Nick says that Adam is part of some consortium that's hoping to buy the house and tear it down so that they can use the land for commercial purposes...a supermarket, shop units, that kind of thing.'

'Ridiculous,' Lord Stanton told her firmly. 'I know Nick is your husband, my dear, but I very much suspect that he is wrong. If Adam is involved in some way with the purchase of Broughton House, you may be sure that the last thing he will want is to lend his authority to any plan to demolish it. I'm rather surprised that you should have any doubts on the matter yourself. Adam is a man of great probity and sincerity. I can't think of anyone who is more committed to doing his best for the town and, in fact, for its residents. However, if you genuinely fear for the future of Broughton House, and if as you say Adam is in some way involved in that future, then I'm surprised that you haven't discussed it with Adam himself.'

Fern knew that she was flushing slightly. Instinctively she dipped her head, seeking behind the heavy fall of her hair protection for the embarrassment and guilt she feared was written in her eyes.

'Adam is very busy,' she murmured unsteadily. 'I... I... don't like to bother him, and besides... Well, I... if he is involved in some kind of speculative purchase, it's bound to be confidential, isn't it?'

'I'm sure you're wrong,' Lord Stanton replied. 'If he is... but I doubt very much that you need have any fears for the house's future if Adam is involved with it,' he assured her. 'I was pleased to hear, by the way, that he has been escorting that pretty young daughter of George James's around recently. It's high time he found himself a wife. I can't think why he hasn't done so before.'

'Yes, Lily is very attractive,' Fern agreed in a small, quiet voice.

'Are you all right, my dear?' Lord Stanton asked her with some concern. 'You look quite pale. Let me ring for Phillips and you can have that glass of sherry. It isn't very warm in here...'

In the end, it was over two hours before Fern actually left, having given way to Lord Stanton's insistence that she have a glass of sherry and having waited numbly while Phillips was summoned to pour it and to bring the essential sweet biscuits.

'You're a very kind young woman,' Lord Stanton told Fern when she finally stood up to go. 'And that husband of yours is a very lucky young man.'

Was he? Fern reflected as she walked home. She doubted that Nick himself thought so.

After all, if he had, would he need to lie to her, to deceive her, to tell her that he needed her as his wife with one breath, while with the next telling another woman that she was the one he wanted?

What hurt her the most, she wondered miserably: his infidelity or her own feeling that it was because of her, because of some failing, some lack of something within her?

Her heart started to beat faster with apprehension and misery, her unhappiness quickly wiping out the pleasantness of the time she had spent with Lord Stanton.

Was Nick being unfaithful to her with Venice, or was she simply imagining it? And if he was having another affair...

She tugged at her bottom lip, worrying at the soft inner flesh.

She had tried her best to make their marriage work, to put the past behind her, to forget... to love him.

She had loved her parents, too, and had wanted to please them out of that love... Had not wanted to disappoint their expectations of her.

And yet once she had come perilously close not just to doing that, but to breaking every moral law they had taught her.

A commitment made to another person was a commitment made for life, they had taught her. Marriage was the ultimate commitment, a vow made that should never be broken. And yet she had broken hers... And was still, within herself, breaking it?

Nick had once accused her of driving him into the arms of other women; of rejecting him not just with her physical inhibitions, her inability to arouse him as they could, but by not loving him.

And yet in almost the same breath he would then announce that she did love him, and that he loved her, that their marriage was important to him; that *she* was important to him.

How important? Certainly not important enough to stop him from having an affair with Venice.

If he was having an affair with her.

Fern shivered a little, knowing that she could not let the present situation persist for much longer without confronting him with her suspicions, and yet knowing that she was afraid to do so, afraid of the emotional trauma that would follow... afraid not just of his anger, but of her own guilt, the guilt she knew he would throw back at her.

Justifiably?

Tears stung her eyes and she half stumbled against an uneven piece of pavement.

There was no escape for her from the truth, certainly not within her own thoughts or conscience. She *had* been guilty of the ultimate marital sin. She had broken faith with him, with her marriage vows.

The evening was giving way to dusk. She paused to watch some housemartins sweeping up into the eaves of a house on the other side of the road—nest-building, no doubt.

A small, sharp pain caught at her heart, making her chest and throat feel tight with hurt. Quickly she turned away, bending her head so that she wasn't tempted to look back at them.

'Adam... My dear chap, what a pleasant surprise.'

Adam shook the hand the older man extended to him, noting as he did so the frailty of the bony wrist.

'I was just driving past and remembered that you thought you might have located the original bills submitted for the wheels made for the earlier Lord Stanton's curricle...'

'Ah, yes...now where did I put them?'

Adam waited patiently while the older man searched through the mound of papers on his desk.

It had been a comment he had overhead Fern make which had alerted him to the fact that Lord Stanton felt very much alone since his wife's death...not a comment to him, of course. He grimaced to himself. It was a rare occurrence indeed for Fern to make any kind of comment directly to him. What did she think he might do? Insult her...*assault* her? His mouth twisted again. No, he had overheard her saying something to Nick some months ago, and since then he had tried to make a point of calling round to see the older man when he could.

He was always careful to disguise his visits as being for his own benefit rather than his host's, and now, as he waited for Lord Stanton to unearth the bill, a record of a long-ago transaction between their mutual ancestors, he heard him saying conversationally, 'Fern was here earlier. You just missed her.'

'Yes, I know,' Adam agreed.

'Ah...you passed her on the lane, did you?'

'No, I...'

Automatically Adam checked, cursing himself under his breath. It was unlike him to forget, to let down his guard...to make that kind of mistake.

'I...remembered Nick saying she was coming to visit you,' he lied, wondering grimly what on earth the older man would have thought had he said that he had known Fern had been here because he could still smell her perfume in the air.

Not that Lord Stanton would have said anything. He was too much of the old school for that. But, even so, a seed would have been sown which could ultimately have resulted in someone leaping to the wrong conclusion...in Fern's being hurt... His mouth thinned, so that when Lord Stanton turned round and saw his expression he asked with some concern, 'My dear chap, is there something wrong?'

'Nothing,' Adam assured him.

'Actually it's a pity you didn't arrive while Fern was here. You could have put her mind at rest.' He paused and Adam forced his body into tense control, watching and waiting. If Nick had done something, anything to hurt or harm her...but, when Lord Stanton continued, Adam realised that it was not his stepbrother who had upset her but himself.

'She seemed to believe that Broughton House is to be destroyed, to make room for—a supermarket, I believe she said.'

Long, long ago Adam had thought he had taught himself to accept reality, to live with it and endure it, but now, listening to Lord Stanton, *knowing* that Fern had judged him guilty of what to her would be an aesthetic crime, and that she had done so without allowing him to defend or explain his actions, caused such a sharp flaring of pain and bitterness within him that he had to clench his teeth to stop himself from betraying what he was feeling.

'Needless to say, I assured her that she must be wrong.'

'I *am* working on a commission for a client,' Adam told him.

'You need say no more,' Lord Stanton assured him. 'Ah, here it is: "Four wheels for Lord Stanton's racing curricle, to be painted with yellow spokes and black rims." There is a family story that my ancestor, who was a notorious gamester, bet ten thousand guineas that he could beat an opponent in a London to Brighton race in the curricle carried by those wheels.'

'Did he win?' Adam asked him.

'Yes. Otherwise I doubt I would be living here today to tell this tale. It was on the strength of winning that bet that he was able to propose to the rich mill-owner's daughter whose fortune saved the estate. I often wonder what will happen to this place after I am gone. It's too small to be of any interest to the National Trust. I have no direct heir...

'In fact, I have been meaning to discuss it with you for some time, Adam. Beavers, my solicitor, seems to think something could be arranged whereby I could leave it in trust to the town. Eugenie would have liked that,' he added gruffly.

'That would be a very generous gesture, Lord Stanton,' Adam told him quietly.

'Nonsense. Know too well that the burden of all the damned paperwork and the like would fall on your shoulders. Told Beavers you'd already got enough on your plate, without taking on another responsibility. Wouldn't want to do it, though—unless you could be one of the trustees, Adam. Know I can rely on you to see that it is kept as Eugenie would have wanted. Loved this house, she did... right from being a small girl.

'Often used to say that it was the house she wanted to marry and not me...

'Still miss her dreadfully, you know, and won't be sorry when my time comes to "shuffle off this mortal coil". Have to keep going, though, for Phillips' sake.' He gave Adam a thoughtful look. 'Hear you've been seeing quite a lot of young Lily.'

'Her father and I are old friends,' Adam said firmly, adding pointedly, 'She's a nice child. Only just nineteen.'

'My Eugenie was only seventeen when we married.'

'Well, if Lily were my daughter I should be advising her to wait at least another ten years before she considered that kind of commitment,' Adam said easily.

Did Lord Stanton really think he could contemplate marriage to a girl... a *teenager* like Lily? He was thirty-four, almost thirty-five, and there had only ever been one woman whom he had wanted as his wife, whom he had loved enough to want to spend his whole life with.

Had loved?

Beneath the dry old smell of dust and leather books that filled the room, he could still smell quite distinctly the scent of Fern's perfume. *Her* perfume, he admitted tiredly, not the light, flowery scent which she always wore, although he could smell that too.

Fern... Even her name was evocative of fragility, vulnerability, of soft, hidden, secret places, of tenderness and delicacy, like the pale uncurling fronds of the plant after which she was named.

Over the years he had watched... had been *forced* to watch as his step-brother cruelly and he was sure deliberately bruised that delicacy with his abrasiveness, his public criticism of her, his unthinking and, to Adam, uncaring attitude towards her. But through it all Fern continued to love him, to see no fault in him, to give him all that she had so plainly never felt able to give Adam himself.

Apart from that one occasion, that one brief moment out of time when she had come to him, turned to him... needed him and appealed to him.

And had later withdrawn from him, rejecting him in horror and disgust, running from him, distraught, refusing to wait, to listen.

Sometimes, despite everything that it had meant to him, he wished it had never happened. It had changed their relationship irrevocably, denying him the friendship they might have shared, denying him the right even to take his place in her life as a member of her family; denying everything but her rejection and his own anguished pain.

Fern... As he took his leave of Lord Stanton and got into his car, he wondered bleakly how anyone could ever imagine that he could possibly find or even want to find happiness with a pretty child like Lily.

There had been women, attractive, intelligent, appealing women— available women—whom he had tried to love, but love was not something that could be forced. It either existed or it did not, and, perhaps because it had been so intense, his love for Fern had burned out of him any ability to feel that same emotion for anyone else.

But Fern loved Nick. Loved him and was married to him, and whenever she saw him, Adam, she treated him as though he were a leper. No...worse...Fern was not the type to turn away from a person who was afflicted in any kind of way. It was not in her nature.

Perhaps because of her upbringing, she had a compassion, a sense of awareness and responsibility towards others that some might see as old-fashioned and out of place, but which to Adam only emphasised all the qualities within her that he had originally fallen in love with.

No, Fern was not the sort to pass by someone in need. Unless that someone happened to be him.

He had a council meeting this evening and if he wasn't careful he was going to be late, he admitted as he drove back into town.

He lived in a small elegant town house off the main square of the town and in a quiet side-street. It had a long rear garden which stretched down to the river and it was an ideal base for him.

A base, but not a home... not like the home which Fern had made for Nick, even though his stepbrother seemed not to appreciate it, or spend much time in it with her. But if Fern loved him...

If! There was no 'if' about it, he reminded himself grimly as he drove homewards.

'So, Adam, what's all this about you being involved in some scheme to pull down Broughton House?'

'I'm sorry, Anthony, but my clients' affairs are not something I can discuss with you,' Adam told his fellow councillor evenly.

Anthony Quentin and he did not always see eye-to-eye on council matters and he suspected the other man's interest in Broughton House sprang more from the point of view of self-interest rather than out of genuine concern for the community, although he could always be wrong, Adam admitted fair-mindedly.

However, as the owner of the town's largest privately owned supermarket, Anthony was bound to have a vested interest in any information appertaining to a possible competitor.

The meeting was almost at an end and people were starting to drift away, but Adam stiffened suddenly as he heard Nick's name mentioned.

A quartet of people standing in front of him were discussing Venice, remarking on how determinedly she was insinuating herself into various aspects of local life.

'She's in London at the moment,' he heard one of them say, and Anthony Quentin, who was standing next to him still and who had also overheard their conversation, winked and dug Adam in the ribs, telling him,

'And she's not the only one either, is she? I saw Nick earlier. He said *he* was leaving for London... Quite a coincidence, eh?'

'Not really,' Adam contradicted him coldly. 'I should imagine that at any one time several inhabitants of the area could quite easily find themselves in London over a similar period.'

'Hey, come on... I'm not saying anything. I *like* Nick... always have done. Mind you, I wouldn't blame him if...'

'If what?' Adam asked him freezingly.

He stopped abruptly when he saw the look Adam was giving him and shrugged. 'Stuck-up bastard,' he muttered to himself five minutes later as he headed for his car. Of the two of them he always had preferred Nick. It had been good of him to tip him off about Adam's plans for Broughton House. He had seen what happened to local businesses when these large chains started operating huge hypermarkets on the outskirts of a town. Clever old Adam, to get himself involved. He wouldn't be surprised if Adam wasn't hoping to pick up an architectural contract as well as his share of the sale of the land, he reflected acidly to himself as he got into his car.

Just as well that Nick had warned him of what was in the wind and that had been a good idea of his to get up some sort of protest group. Adam Wheelwright wasn't the only one who had influence in this town, not by a long chalk he wasn't. Looking down his nose at him like that. Just as though half the damned town didn't know or guess what Nick was up to. Not that he blamed him. Fern was a nice enough woman . . . could have been quite pretty if she wore a bit more make-up, dressed herself up a bit . . . She was certainly a good wife, though . . . a bit like his own. Good, but dull. Not very exciting between the sheets; but then that wasn't always a bad thing in a wife. A nice, sensible, loyal wife who knew her place in life, leaving a man free to indulge himself— discreetly of course—with someone who could provide him with a little bit of excitement on the side. Yes, Nick was a man after his own heart, a lucky devil too if he was having it off with Venice. He wouldn't have minded taking an interest in that direction himself, although Venice was a bit too independent for his tastes, and a bit too fond of making her views and her presence known. That kind of woman couldn't always be relied on to know her place and to keep to it.

Shrewd, though. She must have been, to get old Dunstant to marry her in the first place, and to leave her all this money.

So Anthony Quentin thought that Nick was having an affair with Venice, Adam reflected bitterly.

Was he, or was the other man simply trying to stir up gossip? If so, it wouldn't be the first time that Nick had been unfaithful to Fern.

Did she know? If so, he was the last person she was likely to confide in. He could imagine how hurt she would be, though, and how fiercely determined not to allow anyone to see what she was suffering.

Dear God, *how* could Nick even think of wanting anyone else when . . . ?

But that had always been Nick's way. Adam could remember how, from being a boy, Nick would single-mindedly pursue something to the point of obsession, be it a new football or a new friend, only to lose interest in it virtually from the moment he possessed it.

They had never been close, had never really got on. Adam had been almost adult when their parents had married. He had liked and admired Nick's mother, who had been a friend of his father's for several years before they had actually decided to marry.

She had adored Nick, and for her sake and his father's he had made every attempt to get on with him, but he had realised almost from the start that Nick did not want to get on with him, and that in fact he took an almost perverse pleasure in thwarting his attempts to make friends with him.

In fact Adam had very quickly come to realise that Nick actually wanted to foster antagonism between them and he had discovered that Nick was very quick to run to their parents with exaggerated tales of imagined injustices and slights, which had always cast Adam in the role of aggressor.

The only way to deal with Nick's hostility was to ignore him, Adam had decided. For their parents' sake, he had striven to maintain a semblance of some kind of reasonable relationship between them, but he had very quickly learned not to put himself into a position where anything he said or did could be turned against him and used to hurt their parents.

It had taken a little longer for Adam to come to accept that Nick had a warped, defective personality which seemed to take delight in opposing and even actively hurting others.

So far as he could ascertain, there was no reason for this.

His mother adored him, and when he went out of his way to do so he could be so breathtakingly charming that Adam was not really surprised that no one else seemed to share his own view of him.

Neither had he been surprised when Fern had fallen victim to that charm.

He just hoped for her sake that the scales would never fall from her eyes and that she would never, ever see Nick as he saw him, because if she did, he knew it would break her heart and totally destroy her. And that was something he could not bear to contemplate.

He wished now that he had been less abrupt with Anthony Quentin. Who knew what gossip he might inadvertently start to spread? It would have been more tactful of him simply to have listened to what the man had to say and then found a way of defusing it rather than...

Venice... How could his stepbrother possibly want a woman like *that* when he was married to Fern?

CHAPTER TWELVE

NICK was in a good mood. Fern heard him humming under his breath as he came in. She went to the kitchen door and opened it, walking into the hall.

When he saw her, Nick stopped humming, and started to scowl instead.

Fern could feel her stomach muscles tightening. Ever since Laura Welch had commented innocently in the supermarket the previous day how much she envied Venice the ability to simply drop everything and take herself off to London for an impromptu shopping trip just whenever the mood struck her, Fern had known that Nick's interest in Venice and hers in him was not merely a fiction created by her own overworked and suspicious imagination, as Nick had implied.

The coincidence of both of them choosing to visit London at the same time; the fact that Nick had claimed that he was unable to tell her where or how she could get in touch with him; the hyped-up mood he had been in before he left...they were all signs that were familiar enough to her by now.

She didn't want to have to tackle him about it, she admitted cravenly as he glowered sullenly at her, but she couldn't just close her eyes and pretend it wasn't happening.

Listening to Lord Stanton talking about his wife, hearing the love, the loss, the respect in his voice had brought home to her how barren and sterile her own marriage was.

'She was my best friend,' Lord Stanton had said of his wife, and Fern had ached with a sense of loss and grief as she listened to him.

Friendship was something she and Nick had never shared, nor ever would share. She tried to imagine the kind of relationship they might have had if they had not married and acknowledged with a sickening sense of despair that friendship could never have existed between them. They had nothing really in common, no shared interests or hobbies, no past memories of shared happiness to treasure.

No matter how much he might claim that he needed her and refuse to discuss the state of their marriage, Nick surely could not be happy...could *not* love her.

She took a step towards him and then stopped as he pre-empted her and spoke first, his voice harsh and critical as he looked at her and demanded, 'For God's sake, Fern, can't you do something with yourself?' His mouth twisted contemptuously. 'You look closer to forty than thirty. Why don't you get your hair restyled...wear some make-up...?'

'Like Venice?' Fern suggested, her voice taut with humiliation, the words escaping from her before she could call them back, even though she knew from experience how much they would infuriate Nick.

'Like *Venice*! You couldn't look like her in a million years,' he told her scathingly.

'Good. I wouldn't want to,' Fern retorted. 'Did you see her while you were in London?' she asked him, attacking before she could lose her courage.

'See who?' Nick asked, turning away from her.

Fern gritted her teeth. He knew quite well who. 'Venice,' she told him, keeping her head up high as she added challengingly, 'Apparently she was in London these last few days as well.'

Nick turned round, his mouth cynical and hard, his eyes glittering slightly, but he was avoiding looking directly at her, Fern recognised as he turned to go upstairs.

'My dear Fern, it may have escaped your notice, but London is a *very* large place. No... I did not see Venice. Who told you she was in London, anyway? Adam?'

Fern could feel her skin starting to burn.

'No,' she told him woodenly. 'Laura Welch happened to mention it.'

'Interfering busybody. Still, a single woman of her age... I suppose she's so desperate for it that——'

Fern turned away, reopening the kitchen door. She loathed it when Nick behaved like this, reverting to the kind of crudity which made her cringe. In the early days of their marriage he had laughed at her for it, calling her a prude, telling her that it was simply the way that real men behaved, but that, since her experience of his sex was limited to her father and Adam, *she* was unlikely to be aware of it.

She had felt too humiliated then to counter that she did not believe a 'real' man as he termed it would ever find it necessary to reinforce his masculinity by the parading of that kind of verbal vulgarity and she still couldn't say so now, although her expression gave her away...

'What's wrong, Fern?' Nick called contemptuously after her. 'Don't you like hearing the truth?'

'I'm your wife, Nick,' she told him quietly. 'And after all it wouldn't be the first time you'd been unfaithful to me, would it?'

'And just who the hell is to blame for that?' Nick demanded aggressively, coming downstairs and following her into the kitchen. 'If you hadn't fucked my brother...'

Fern went white and then red, nausea erupting violently inside her stomach, her body tensing as Nick gripped hold of her arm and swung her back to face him.

'You're such a prissy little bitch, Fern. My God, you haven't a clue about what it means to be a real woman... and Adam wouldn't know what to do with one anyway.'

A real woman... They were back to where they had started, Fern recognised miserably. Back to Venice, who no doubt Nick considered to
be the epitome of what a 'real' woman should be.

'I'm not Venice, if that's what you mean,' she agreed dully, wishing
now that she had had the sense to keep silent and say nothing instead of
provoking all his aggression and malice... instead of reminding Nick of
her guilt, instead of giving him that guilt as a weapon to use against her.

'What *did* you do when you were with Adam, Fern?' Nick challenged
her thickly, ignoring her comment about Venice. His eyes were glittering
too sharply, like pieces of broken glass, a hectic dangerous flush surging
up under his skin. 'Were you as cold and boring in his bed as you've
always been in mine? Did you lie there unmoving and unexciting the way
you do with me, or did he make you scream with ecstasy when he touched
you? Did you beg him to lick you; to suck you; to fuck you... did you,
Fern... did you?'

She had gone so cold that her teeth were literally chattering, her body
gripped by such a storm of anguished pain that her throat muscles locked
against the protest, the denial she wanted to scream out loud...

How could Nick talk to her like that... accuse her... suggest...? But
it was her fault that he was doing so, she reminded herself as she shook
her head, fiercely trying to blink back the tears filling her eyes. *Her* fault
that he was drawing those ugly destructive images of her. *Her* fault that
he was deliberately defiling something which...

'Oh, for God's sake,' she heard him mutter as he released her and then
stormed out of the kitchen.

She heard him going upstairs and into their bedroom. She couldn't
move. She could only remain where she was, clinging to the back of the
chair she was holding on to for support.

Now she made no attempt to stem the weak tears of shock and shame
slowly running down her face.

Why on earth hadn't she simply kept quiet, said nothing, done nothing
to provoke him?

Perhaps after all she had been wrong... perhaps he hadn't been with
Venice.

From somewhere inside her a small, caustic, cynical presence she hadn't
known existed raised its voice and demanded tauntingly, 'That's it, give
in... take the easy way out. Of course he's been with her. He still smelled
of her perfume.'

She stayed in the kitchen until she heard Nick come downstairs and
go out again. She had known that this was what he would do. It was a
familiar pattern he followed every time they had a quarrel...

When he came back he would be contrite and apologetic. He would
remind her of how much she had hurt him... of how much she owed
him, of how difficult it was for him to live with the knowledge that she,

his wife, the woman he had married... revered... put up on a pedestal above other women, had betrayed him... and with his own stepbrother.

Was it any wonder, he would ask her, that he sometimes felt the need to prove his manhood, to lay claim to his own sense of masculinity and self-respect by occasionally flirting with a pretty woman? Flirting, that was all... She was his wife, wasn't she? He would never leave her, she knew that.

Oh, yes, she knew that, Fern acknowledged heavily.

Now, in the aftermath of her shock, she felt weak and shaky, oddly light-headed in a way that seemed to give her thoughts a relentless, unignorable clarity and intensity.

She should never have married Nick. She didn't love him and, for all his avowals to the contrary, she suspected that he did not love her. Their marriage was a sham, a deceit, a dishonesty that was slowly infecting not just their relationship with one another, but her whole attitude to life, Fern acknowledged.

She had been not just a fool, but a coward as well. During her parents' lifetime she had told herself that she could not upset and hurt them by revealing the truth about what she felt, but had she simply used them as an excuse because she had been too weak to tackle Nick and make him see that their marriage had to end?

Was the simplest, the easiest, the best thing to walk away from him?

She hugged her arms around her body, shivering still with shock and distress.

She had tried that once before and look what had happened. The discovery that their marriage was simply not working, the knowledge that Nick was involved with someone else—these had sent her running from him, a headlong, unplanned, unthinking flight with no direction to it, motivated solely by her need to escape a situation she could no longer contain or control.

If Adam had not seen her, stopped her, insisted on taking her home with him because he had seen how obviously upset she was...

He had thought it was the discovery of Nick's infidelity which was upsetting her; the shock of the visit from Nick's lover shaking her faith in her husband to the roots, never guessing that Fern had actually been on the verge of leaving Nick.

Afterwards she had known that she had to stay; that to leave then after what had happened would have been to make Adam feel responsible for her... to make him feel that he had to...

Men were not like women; men, even the nicest, the kindest, the most compassionate of them, took a very different view of sex from women.

It was not Adam's fault that he had succumbed to the physical desire she had obviously aroused in him. How could it be? Hadn't she after all been the one to instigate everything... to urge, encourage, incite and almost beg to complete what they had inadvertently started, when *he* would have stopped it?

She had been the one to push them both over the edge and into the abyss of guilt and shame from which she could never escape. No blame, no guilt, no responsibility could attach to Adam.

She could feel the slow, hot crawl of colour stinging her skin as she remembered the things she had said, the things she had done... things she had never, *could* never anticipate doing with Nick.

Nick was right to accuse her of that. She *had* been a cold, sexually unresponsive wife, unable to understand why Nick's caresses should leave her so unmoved, so inclined to tense her muscles and pray silently that it would soon be all over. She loved him, didn't she?

Some women were just not highly sexually motivated, she had comforted herself, and in some way she had felt that Nick was almost pleased by her lack of sexuality. She had tried to discuss it with him in the early days of their marriage, to apologise and ask him to help her understand why, when she knew from all he had told her that he was a very sexually experienced and gifted lover whose previous lovers had more than appreciated his prowess in bed, her body remained so cold and awkwardly unresponsive to his touch.

She had *wanted* to respond to him; had *wanted* to experience the pleasure, the knowledge she had heard other women talking about. She had even taken to furtively reading books, nervously purchased from a bookshop on a specially planned trip to London, hoping to discover within their covers something that would explain away the reasons for her lack of arousal.

All they had done had been to reinforce her sense of guilt and despair, even further diminishing her self-confidence and security.

Nick had turned away from her in bored irritation when she had talked to him about it. It was just his bad luck that he had married a woman who was frigid, he had told her. She had been grateful then when he had added that, despite her frigidity, he fully intended to stay married to her. Grateful because in overlooking her inadequacy he was saving her from having to face the humiliation and scorn of the outside world...in having to admit that her marriage was a failure and see the disappointment and pain reflected in her parents' eyes.

She hadn't noticed at first how Nick's tolerance was beginning to change to contempt and criticism... how the way he touched her in bed had started to change from a pattern of orchestrated and obviously knowledgeable caresses to an almost rough immediate penetration followed not only by his physical withdrawal from her and the sight of his hunched back and the back of his head as he turned away from her, but by his emotional and mental withdrawal from her as well.

She knew that it was her fault, of course, but she ached to be able to talk to Nick about what was happening to them, to ask him to be more patient with her... more... more tender, more loving... to give her time.

What was the point? he asked her brutally when she did. Nothing—no one could arouse her. Did she think he actually enjoyed it? he demanded cruelly. Because if so she was wrong. It was simply that as a man he had a need . . . and that she as his wife had an obligation to allow him to satisfy it.

She had cried herself to sleep the night he had told her that, and for several nights afterwards.

It had been less than a month later when she had begun to suspect that he was having an affair.

How much longer could she go on like this? Fern wondered wretchedly now. No matter how hard she tried to push it to the back of her mind with increasing intensity, the problems within her marriage would push past the mental barriers she had tried to erect against them, forcing themselves to the forefront of her mind, refusing to be ignored.

Nick might have needed her once, as he had claimed, but he didn't need her now. Living with him, knowing that their marriage was an empty sham, was eating away at her self-respect, adding self-dislike to her already heavy burden of guilt.

She had even begun to find she was avoiding looking at herself in the mirror, almost as though she could no longer face the accusation and misery in her own eyes.

The days were gone when a woman in her position had to remain locked into an unhappy marriage simply because she had no alternative. She was a healthy, intelligent woman of twenty-seven who was surely capable of living on her own and supporting herself financially.

All right, so maybe she had left it a little late to step into a high-powered career, but she could still earn her own living.

She had always disliked being financially dependent on Nick, she admitted when enough strength had returned to her body to enable her to complete the task she had been engaged in before Nick's return.

As she climbed back up the ladders and reapplied herself to cleaning the kitchen windows, she reflected on Nick's insistence right from the start of their marriage that he did not want her to work; that he wanted her at home.

Her parents had approved of this. Her mother had never worked and both she and Fern's father had seen in Nick's attitude confirmation of their old-fashioned belief in the traditional roles both sexes played within a marriage.

Faced with their united agreement with one another, it had seemed easier to simply accept what Nick had said.

'It isn't that I want to prevent you from having your own career,' Nick had told her winningly. 'It's just that my own job is so demanding and I have to work such odd hours that, selfishly, I don't want to come home and find you not there. Of course, if you're worried that I won't be able to support you properly, or if you think I'm going to turn into the kind of mean bastard who keeps his wife short of money and queries every penny she spends . . .'

Of course she didn't think that, Fern had quickly assured him.

He had kissed her then. In those days they had of course still been on kissing terms.

However, while Nick had never precisely kept her short of money, he had not exactly been generous with it either, neither in practicality nor, more importantly, in spirit.

How and when had it happened? Fern wondered, stopping work for a second to stare unseeingly out of the window, staring not out into the garden, but back into the past and the early days of their marriage. When had she started to feel apprehensive about spending Nick's money...about buying small luxuries? Not for herself...no, the kind of luxuries she meant were things like good quality food, fruit out of season, small delicacies and treats which, although he ate them with every appearance of relish, Nick always seemed to make small critical reference to, some small but sharp allusion to her inefficient financial housekeeping. It was never anything too abrasive, at least not in those early days...sometimes little more than a smiling, almost teasing reference to her love of luxuries, and the spoiling her parents had indulged in; but his words had hurt none the less.

As for her buying herself the sort of luxuries Venice enjoyed...the expensive clothes, the expertly painted nails, the make-up, the chic salon-styled hair, the real silk tights—or more probably stockings, Fern acknowledged—the exclusive health-club membership that provided her with a year-round tan and the slim, svelte shape to show off on the tennis courts, plus the opportunity to parade around in the most minute of bikinis...

It was laughable, a joke to imagine that *she* could ever indulge in those kind of self-centred enjoyments, even on the simplest of scales.

In the early days of their marriage, Nick had made a big virtue out of giving her her own allowance.

That allowance, so much discussed and paraded for the approval of her parents and their acquaintances, had barely covered the cost of her underwear and tights in the days when he had first allocated it to her, Fern acknowledged tiredly.

She had once tried to broach the subject of it with him, assuming that he was perhaps unaware of just how much things actually cost, but he had been so angry with her, accusing her of being spoilt and unrealistic; of expecting him to support her as generously as her parents had done, making her feel so greedy and thoughtless that she wished she had never raised the subject in the first place.

When all the legal formalities had been attended to, she would inherit a small sum from her mother's estate, but her parents had purchased an annuity with the bulk of their capital which had died with them.

But it wasn't any lack of money that was keeping her within the marriage, Fern knew. If necessary she was quite prepared to take on the most menial kind of work there was in order to support herself. After all, she had no children to worry about...no one dependent upon her.

Nor would she want to make any kind of financial claim on Nick. So why didn't she just go? Why *didn't* she simply go upstairs now, pack her things and leave before he came back?

Because she *couldn't*, she admitted...because she simply could not walk out on him without at least trying to understand why their marriage had gone wrong...without at least trying to explain to him how hurt and confused she was by his infidelity.

But you know what will happen, a small inner voice taunted her. Nick will simply say that it's your fault because of Adam.

But loving Adam had made no difference to her marriage...no difference to her determination to work as hard as she could to preserve it...

Loving Adam was an aberration, a mistake...a secret agony she could never, would never admit to anyone else. It was her private torment and punishment, the burden she must carry in silence and alone.

Just thinking about him caused the familiar pain to start unravelling slowly inside her.

Adam... Why had she not known...realised...recognised...but, even if she had done all of those things, what good would it have done her? Adam did not love her, had never loved her.

Oh, he had been kind to her, concerned for her, anxious to help her— but then, that was Adam. Kind, compassionate, caring for everyone. Look at the work he did for local charities, and not just officially... All over the town there were people who could attest to his small acts of personal kindness and generosity.

It had been Adam she had met first, known him in fact before she had known Nick. Actually, had it not been for her friendship with Adam, she would never have met Nick at all.

She gave a small shudder. She didn't want to think back, to remember the innocence of those early days.

It had been a chance remark of a fellow student on the same university course about the town of Avondale which had brought her here in the first place. History had always fascinated her; her father was a keen amateur archaeologist and as a child she had spent many contented and happy hours exploring a variety of historical sites.

The town, with its examples of so many different types of urban architecture, gathered together within such a small area and so fortuitously unaltered from their original state, had naturally interested her. It was near enough to Bristol for her to visit, driving herself there in the small car her parents had bought her as an eighteenth birthday present.

She had fallen in love with the town almost at first sight.

And with Adam?

If so, she herself had certainly not recognised it. She remembered how she had been slightly in awe of him the first time they met, and how embarrassed she had been.

She had been standing in the town square, studying the church. She had stepped back without turning round and had walked right into Adam, whom she had not seen crossing the square.

Crimson-faced, she had apologised, awkwardly aware of the contrast between them. She had been wearing her students' garb of black woolly tights, an equally dark-hued skirt and an old baggy sweater she had bought in a second-hand shop.

Secretly she still felt slightly uncomfortable in these clothes, so very different from the ones she had worn while still living at home, and yet without them, in the university environment that was now her home, she had stuck out like a sore thumb, the neatly pressed pleated skirts, the crisp blouses, the good quality woollens that followed the example set by her mother marking her out as a curiosity, an object of amusement and friendly derision.

She had learned to find anonymity and safety in the uniform of dark-coloured baggy clothes so beloved of her peers.

Today, though, she was not with any of her fellow students, she was on her own, and Adam was wearing an immaculate dark wool suit, the jacket unfastened to reveal a crisply laundered white shirt on which she could almost smell the clean scent of starch, and an equally formal striped tie.

Looking at him, she had assumed automatically that he was some kind of successful businessman, although when he had put his hand out to steady her she had been subconsciously aware of a certain powerful muscularity about his body that belied the image cast by the formality of his clothes.

His hair too had confused her, sending out a different signal from that given by his clothes. Thick, with a natural inclination to curl slightly, it had had something endearingly untidy and informal about it, a tousled, windblown unkemptness which had matched the lean ruggedness of his face, and the fan of small lines that rayed out from his grey eyes.

His face and hair were those of a man used to spending a good deal of his time out of doors, she had recognised, but his clothes . . . that suit . . . they belonged to a man who spent his days sitting at some impressive boardroom desk, sternly overseeing the lives of other less powerful mortals. Initially it had been the effect of that suit which she had reacted to, mumbling her apology, turning to hurry away from him, feeling both awkward and uncomfortable as she stared down at the floor and saw the small dusty imprint her shoe had left on the shiny glossiness of his.

However, instead of chastising her for her clumsiness as she had anticipated, he had asked her totally unexpectedly instead, 'Are you interested in the church?'

The warmth in his voice had caused her to look up at him, and when she saw the way he was smiling at her, the genuine friendliness of his demeanour, her self-consciousness had miraculously vanished.

After she had explained her interest in the town's architectural history, he had introduced himself to her and had offered to act as her guide to its buildings.

Shyly she had accepted, sensing with an instinct she hadn't known she possessed that she would be safe with him.

In the event he had proved so informative, and so interesting, that she had soon forgotten her initial embarrassment and had found herself talking with him as easily as though she had known him for years.

When the afternoon had ended and it was time for her to return to Bristol, she had felt oddly bereft, although it hadn't occurred to her to connect this feeling with the same emotions she had heard other girls describing in connection with their sexual and emotional feelings for the men in their lives.

It had come as quite a shock ten days later to receive a telephone call from Adam saying that he had some business in Bristol later in the week and asking if she would like to have lunch with him.

She had agreed to meet him—a shock perhaps, but not an unpleasant one. There was nothing to fear in having lunch with him, none of the anxiety and uncertainty that so frequently made her refuse the invitations of her male peers in case, in accepting them, she inadvertently found herself the recipient of sexual advances she did not want.

Fern knew that she was regarded, if not as something of a prude, then certainly as slightly sexually out of step with everyone else; but her gentleness and kindness made her popular not only with the male students but the female ones as well, who good-naturedly accepted her shyness and good-heartedly did their best to protect her from the sexual machinations of the more sexually aggressive male undergraduates.

Only the previous weekend she had gone with a group of friends to the Union Bar, where she had been left scarlet-faced with embarrassment by one man coming up to her and announcing with a leer, 'The campus virgin. I like virgins... I eat them up... I love the way they taste. Would you like me to eat you up, little virgin?'

The other males with him had laughed and cheered and despite her embarrassment Fern had managed to stand her ground and ignore the comments he was making to her. She knew there was no real malice in them and that he was more playing to the crowd than trying to intimidate her, but nevertheless she had been left feeling vulnerable and slightly bruised, aware of the gulf that lay between the world her parents had brought her up to inhabit and the one which actually existed.

Her school days attending a small village school and then an equally small and protective all-girls' private school had not really equipped her for the sexually energetic lifestyle of her fellow students, but underneath her shyness Fern had a strong enough personality to allow her to take things at her own pace.

The male students she responded best to and felt most at ease with were the ones who treated her more as a sister than a potential bed partner, the ones who brought her not only their dirty washing, but their problems as well, and she would quite happily spend an evening listening to them complaining about the unfairness of a particular tutor or the cruelty of another girl while she ironed and cooked for them. Knowing that they wanted . . . that they needed her to perform these tasks for them soothed and comforted her, confirming the role her parents had brought her up to play, even if this was a subconscious and hidden awareness rather than a conscious one.

Adam took her to an Italian restaurant for lunch. She had mentioned to him the previous week how much she loved Italian food.

The family atmosphere of the place, the joviality and warmth of the waiters made her feel instantly relaxed and at home.

Adam was good company, quickly putting her at her ease and banishing her initial uncertainty that she had done the right thing, so that very quickly she felt so comfortable with him that she found herself answering his questions, telling him things about herself with an openness and ease that was completely contrary to her normal reticence.

Long before the lunch was over, Adam knew about her family background, as well as her interests and her hobbies.

She had not decided exactly what she wanted to do once she had her degree, she told him.

His quiet, 'Perhaps some kind of counselling work, something where you would be able to help others,' surprised her with its astuteness, and she flushed slightly as he smiled at her and told her that he suspected she would be particularly well suited to that kind of work.

At no time during their lunch had Adam said or done anything to suggest that he had any kind of personal or sexual interest in her, and *then* she had been relieved that this should be the case.

Then?

When was it that she had started, instead of being grateful and relieved that Adam did not show any sexual interest in her, feeling hurt, slighted...humiliated almost by this lack of awareness of her as a woman?

After she had met Nick?

Because of the contrast with Nick's attitude towards her, flirting with her, complimenting her, standing unfamiliarly and unnervingly close to her in a way which Adam never did, his whole demeanour somehow underlining not only his sexual interest in her, but Adam's slight withdrawal from her.

That had hurt and confused her, making her draw back instinctively from her relationship with Adam, too immature to question his behaviour or to ask for an explanation, taking comfort instead in the contrasting warmth of Nick's attention and interest in her.

She could remember how surprised she had been when Adam first introduced Nick to her as his brother.

Adam had told her that he had business in Bristol which brought him to the city fairly regularly. He had telephoned and arranged to meet Fern earlier in the week, but for the first time since she had met him he had been late.

It was his fault, Nick had apologised winsomely after Adam had introduced them. He had friends in the city and had decided to take advantage of Adam's journey there to visit them, his own car being out of action. 'Adam's done the brotherly thing by helping me out today although I can't say it's easy being dependent on someone else's set of wheels.'

He had made an expressive gesture with his hands and out of the corner of her eye Fern had noticed the way Adam was frowning.

Immediately she had felt that she must have done something wrong, a feeling which was reinforced later when they were alone and Adam seemed withdrawn and quieter than usual.

Was he perhaps growing bored with her, regretting arranging to see her?

Nervously she had tried to fill the silences between them, asking him about Nick, not because she was curious about his brother, but because she could think of nothing else to say.

He had responded to her questions with unfamiliar terseness.

Nick was his stepbrother, he had told her.

For the rest of the afternoon he had seemed preoccupied and distant. Fern had been stupidly close to tears when he left.

She remembered looking up at him, vulnerably aware of her own emotions and his apparent lack of them. She remembered the way she had accidentally looked at his mouth, looked at it and suddenly, startlingly, shockingly ached to press herself up against him and feel it moving against her own.

She could remember too the hot, scarlet waves of guilt which had swept up over her whole body.

Adam had frowned, stepping towards her. Immediately she had stepped backwards, appalled by what she was thinking, turning and almost running away from him, barely managing to stammer a goodbye.

After that things had changed between them. Adam had grown increasingly remote.

On one visit he had had a message for her from Nick.

Fern hadn't been able to make much sense of it. It seemed to refer to a date she had had with Nick which had not in fact existed, but insecurity, shyness and hesitancy had stopped her from saying anything.

And one of her worst memories of all was being told by Nick, with what she now suspected had been a spurious and totally false concern, that, while Adam might not be sexually interested in her, he was both aware of and very sexually interested in other women.

She remembered even now the cold, jarring shock of the moment Nick had told her that Adam had a girlfriend...a woman friend, with whom he had sex...made love...

She could remember quite distinctly how angry she had felt...how hurt...how betrayed almost, and yet Adam had given her no reason to feel any of those things. At no time had he indicated that he felt anything for her other than friendship. Yes, he had always been kind to her, always made her feel special, protected, wanted when she was with him, but he had made no physical overtures to her, other than to occasionally brush her hair out of her eyes, or to touch her arm lightly...things that any man might have done.

'I hope you aren't falling in love with him,' Nick had said lightly. 'Because if you are, I ought to warn you that you'd be wasting your time.'

Wasting her time...

Just as she had wasted her life...in marrying Nick. Had wasted his as well.

She gave a deep, wrenching shudder. Why on earth hadn't she had the courage to face up to the truth then, to recognise her real feelings for what they were, to recognise that she was falling in love with Adam, instead of denying those feelings, burying them deep inside her and clinging stubbornly instead to the belief that because Nick said he needed and wanted her she must somehow automatically be able to return his feelings, to respond to them...to reward him by loving him?

'I want you, Fern,' he had told her. 'I want you to love me. You *are* going to love me. Do you understand...?' he had told her fiercely and she had nodded, solemnly accepting what he was saying, *believing* what he was saying, just as she had believed the lies she had told herself when she had denied that she loved Adam.

It was all *her* fault, she told herself. *She* was the one who was to blame...the one who carried the guilt.

Perhaps Nick was right when he said that she had driven him to being unfaithful to her, although in those early days of their marriage she had still been clinging with desperate sincerity to the belief that she loved him.

CHAPTER THIRTEEN

'BUT why have we got to sleep in the attic? I hate sleeping up there. It's too hot and Gavin keeps waking me up.'

Guiltily Eleanor stifled the small urge of irritation caused by the half-whining tone of Tom's voice. He had started doing that lately. Was it a mannerism he had unwittingly picked up from someone else at school, like the term when all the children in his class had started to subconsciously copy the child who lisped slightly, or, more dangerously, was it perhaps a warning of some deeper dissatisfaction and unhappiness?

'Tom, *please* don't be difficult. You know why. Vanessa is coming this weekend.'

Tom wasn't looking at her, his face averted as he scuffed the toe of his trainer along the floor. She had an appointment with the agent from whom they had rented the offices in half an hour; she had had to ask her if she could come round to the house and had sensed from the cool disdain in the other woman's voice as she'd explained that she had her sons at home for a 'Founder's Day' holiday that the agent was not herself a mother.

'Get yourself an au pair or a nanny,' Jade had suggested when Eleanor had mentioned to her how increasingly difficult she was finding it to juggle her home life and her work. She couldn't always rely on Karen's kindness in taking her two sons in. 'Or are you worried that she might discover it's more rewarding looking after Marcus than looking after the kids?' Jade had teased her.

'No, of course I'm not,' Eleanor had denied. 'It's just that we don't have room for someone to live in.'

It would all be different once they had moved to the new house, Eleanor promised herself. Then she wouldn't feel so irritated, so pressured and overwhelmed somehow by all the things she had to do.

It wasn't, after all, Tom's fault that she had forgotten about Founder's Day, and really Louise was the one who ought to have been seeing the agent, but Louise was in France, having left Eleanor a hastily typed note in the office announcing that she would be gone for two weeks and conveniently forgetting to leave any number or address where Eleanor could get in touch with her.

'Tell the agent that you can't see her until Louise gets back,' Marcus had suggested mildly, when Eleanor had expressed to him her anger at being left to cope with the winding up of the partnership on her own. 'Louise is, after all, jointly responsible for the business,' he had added.

'But the agents are pressing us to finalise everything now and then the accountant wants to go through the final partnership figures, and I've got to arrange to have the office emptied and the services...'

Marcus had not been as sympathetic towards her as she had expected. In fact he had been almost dismissive of the burdens she was having to carry... impatient and irritated by them... and by her?

It was all very well for Marcus to say leave it until Louise gets back and thus oblige her to share the responsibility for winding up the partnership; *he* wasn't the one being subjected to the subtle and not so subtle pressures that were being put on her. Like Louise, she too wanted to get on with her new life, but, unlike Louise, she was not selfish enough to simply walk off and leave someone else to sort out the loose ends of the old one for her.

And she had hoped to have time to talk to the surveyor this morning. He had promised her that he would give priority to inspecting Broughton House, although he had warned her that it could be several days before he could get a written report to her.

She also needed to discuss financing the purchase with Marcus, but he had been so tied up with his work recently that she had not really been able to talk to him very much about the house, and was therefore having to do most of the organisational work herself.

Not that she would have minded that, if only she had had a little more time.

It was her frustration in not being able to be free to get on with their plans for the future that was making her so irritable and tense, she admitted.

To the point where her own sons were an intrusion? Guiltily she looked down at Tom.

'I know how difficult it is for you when Vanessa comes to stay,' she sympathised. 'But it won't be for much longer, Tom. We'll soon be moving to the new house.'

'I don't want a new house,' Tom told her angrily. 'I just want it to be like it was before, when it was just us!'

'Oh, Tom...' Eleanor dropped to her feet and put her arms round him, giving him a hug and ruffling his hair. 'I thought you liked Marcus...'

'He's OK, but I don't like *her*. I hate her and she hates us. She hates everyone. Why does she have to come?'

How was it that children seemed to know by instinct how to pick the very worst possible time to demand one's attention? Eleanor wondered despairingly, mentally pushing to one side her own problems and abandoning the small luxury she had promised herself of fifteen minutes before the agent arrived to 'do' her face and hair and get changed into something a little bit more businesslike than the jeans and sweatshirt she had put on to move the boys' things up into the attic.

Gently she again went through the reasons why he and Gavin had to move into the attic when Marcus's daughter came to stay with Tom, sensing that, while he already knew them, it might help to reassure him to hear them again and to understand that being moved into the attic was in no way a reflection of any lack of love for them, or in any sense a matter of putting Vanessa first and them second.

'Vanessa is a girl,' she told him quietly. 'And because of that she needs a room to herself.'

'So why can't *she* sleep in the attic and leave me and Gavin in our own room?'

'Tom, you know why. *Your* room was Vanessa's room. She's always slept there when she comes to stay with her father...'

'We always used to sleep in our room when we went to Dad's, but now it's Hannah's room and Gavin and I have to sleep on bunk beds.'

Eleanor checked, frowning slightly. This wasn't the first time that Tom had mentioned the change in sleeping arrangements at his father's house, but it was the first time she had been so clearly aware of the resentment and anger she could now see and hear.

'Daddy got those bunk beds especially for you,' she reminded him. 'You went with him to choose them yourselves.'

'He doesn't want us any more, not now that he's got her. He loves her more than he does us. Just like you and Marcus love Vanessa more. Nobody cares about us any more. Not even Nanna and Grandad. All they ever talk about is babies...'

Eleanor stared at him. When had the idea that he was not loved begun to take root in his mind... and how long might it be before he started to convince himself, and perhaps Gavin along with him, that girls were the preferred sex; that parents loved their daughters more than they did their sons? How long before the anger and resentment he was expressing now became suppressed and hidden, distorting his personality and, with it, potentially his life? A cold chill of shock and panic ran through her.

In the hall, the clock chimed the quarter-hour and her stomach muscles automatically tensed.

It was too late now to ring the agent and put her off. She would be here in fifteen minutes, but what Tom had just revealed about what he was thinking and feeling needed dealing with now and could not be pushed to one side.

'Of course I don't love Vanessa more than I do you,' she told him fiercely, adding huskily, 'Oh, Tom, how could you think that?' her words almost more for herself than for him as she added emotionally, 'You and Gavin are my children... my sons. No one, least of all Vanessa, could ever change the way I feel about you... or alter how much I love you.'

'Not even if you had a baby?' Tom questioned her.

A baby? Where on earth had he got that idea from? She and Marcus had discussed the question of whether or not to have a child of their own and both of them had agreed that neither of them felt any need to bind their relationship in that way; that their love for one another was more than strong enough just as it was.

'I know families where the birth of a baby has helped to bring all the stepchildren together,' Eleanor had commented.

'Mmm...and I know just as many where it has caused problems. I love *you*, Eleanor—I'm not a paternal man. I married you because I love you and because I want to spend my life with you, not because I want to start a second family. I've got enough problems with Vanessa as it is.'

And she had fully agreed with all that he had said. It wasn't that she wasn't aware of the allure of having his child—she was; what woman could not be?—but she refused to allow herself to be seduced by the mirage of perfect glowing motherhood, or adoring stepchildren clustering round the cradle, and most especially of subconsciously using that child as a means of adding cohesion to all their relationships and perhaps unwittingly making it responsible for being the family's peace-keeper.

'A baby?' She focused abruptly on her son. 'Marcus and I aren't planning to have a baby, Tom. What made you think we might be?'

For a few seconds he said nothing, and then, when she had thought he wasn't going to answer her, he turned towards her and burst out, 'Vanessa said you would. She said that you wouldn't want us any more; that we'd have to go and live in a place where they send children who nobody wants. She said that we'd have to do what we were told by the other children there, otherwise they'd beat us up, and that we wouldn't get anything to eat.'

Eleanor could feel herself going cold with shock and anger. How dared Vanessa do this to her children? She must have known what she was doing. She was an intelligent girl, aware beyond her years, sometimes to the extent that the calculating, knowing look in her eyes often made Eleanor herself feel slightly unnerved; and fuelling her anger, heating and swelling it, was also her own guilt, her own awareness that somehow in refusing to confront Vanessa earlier, in taking the softer option, the easier line, in trying to placate her, in allowing her in fact to subtly gain ascendancy over her, she herself was indirectly responsible for what she was doing to her sons.

'Vanessa is talking nonsense,' she told Tom robustly, but she could hear the tremor of anger underlying her words, and knew that, had Vanessa been there, she would have been hard put to it not to confront the girl and demand an explanation for her behaviour.

Vanessa might not be her child and as such it was not perhaps permissible for her to criticise or correct her—the role of a step-parent was always complex and difficult, fraught with potential hazard and danger—but when it came to Vanessa deliberately trying to hurt and upset her own children... And it was not as though Vanessa had not *known* what she was doing...

As she felt the anger twist and coil inside her, demanding release, surprising her both with its force and its intensity, Eleanor heard the doorbell ring.

'I've got a business meeting now, Tom,' she told her son as she got up. 'But you mustn't worry about anything Vanessa says to you. The next time Vanessa tells you something, just ignore her... and don't worry about your room. It won't be long before both you and Gavin will be able to have your own rooms, and I promise you that no one will share them; they will be *your* rooms.'

As he smiled at her, she found herself silently cursing Louise for the second time that morning. If she had taken a more responsible attitude towards the ending of their partnership she would have been able to spend more time with her sons, instead of rushing around trying to fit far too many things into far too few hours. *Why* had she not noticed before what was happening between Vanessa and her sons? She had known that they did not get on, but, as Marcus had pointed out, it would have been odd if they had; at fourteen she had virtually nothing in common with two boys of Tom's and Gavin's age. Given the fact that Vanessa was very much her daughter, Julia had told Eleanor once, 'It's a pity she's got Marcus's nose, though. A strong nose looks good on a man, but not on a woman. I've told her not to worry too much about it. I know this marvellous plastic surgeon...'

Eleanor had been so taken aback by what she was saying that she had made no response, but afterwards she had wondered if some of the disruptive behaviour Vanessa exhibited might not be caused by her mother's unthinking personal criticism of her; but she had warned herself that it would be wrong of her to criticise Vanessa's mother, and that it was not up to her to interfere. She only had to think of how she would feel if Julia started trying to tell her how to bring up her sons.

The interview with the agent took longer than Eleanor had expected, and it was the middle of the afternoon before Eleanor was able to ring the surveyor to ask for his views on the house.

'I would describe it more as an expensive luxury than a good buy,' he told her. 'It's a lovely house, in an idyllic setting, but it needs a lot of money spending on it and then there's the upkeep...'

'What do you think we should offer for it?' Eleanor asked him quickly, not wanting to listen to the doubt he was raising.

He named a figure that was rather more than she had expected and then pointed out that, while at the moment there was no question of any of the land being used for building purposes, no one could guarantee what might happen in the next decade, and that the possibility that the land could be developed was bound to send the price up.

'And what in your view is the essential work that needs to be carried out?' Eleanor asked.

'Well, the dry rot has to be tackled, the whole place has to be re-wired... If you can get it, I would recommend you have gas piped to the house, and then of course you'll need bathrooms; extensive altera-tions to provide a decent kitchen...

'Still, with a bit of luck, you could be talking about moving in this time next year. The building trade is quite slack at the moment so you won't have to wait as long as normal to get a good builder...'

'Next year!' Eleanor was aghast, her rosy mental images of long, sunny summer days spent enjoying the miraculously immaculate gardens swiftly disappearing, to be replaced by the unwanted and far more prosaic picture of builders' skips and detritus, of mud and dirt and endless pleading discussions for the work to be finished quickly.

Disheartened, she thanked him and replaced the receiver.

Ten minutes later when the phone rang and the estate agents were on the end of the line asking her if they were still interested in the property since they had several other very keen enquiries, Eleanor suppressed the pessimistic views the surveyor had expressed and confirmed that they were. The sealed bids were not due in immediately, but the agents, never one to miss an opportunity of putting on the pressure, said that they couldn't afford to delay too long.

It would be madness to submit a bid without knowing how much they could expect to receive for this house; how much the essential building work was going to cost, and how much loan-finance they could raise to pay for it.

By the time Marcus returned home halfway through the evening she was in a fever of anxiety to discuss the house with him, rushing into quick speech as soon as he walked into the kitchen.

'Within a few months?' he interrupted her when she had quickly re-lated her conversation with the estate agent to him. 'For a moment I thought you were going to tell me the deadline was midnight tonight.'

Eleanor stared at him, wondering if she had imagined the sarcasm in his voice, but one look at his face assured her that she had not.

Surprise and confusion were quickly followed by hurt and then re-sentment. It was not, after all, her fault that Marcus seemed to have less and less time to talk with her these days. She was doing all she could to spare him hassle. She was the one who had sorted out the surveyor... she was the one who was dealing with the agents; and no doubt she would be the one who would have to find builders and other tradesmen'... the one who would have to worry about organising the financing, while Marcus claimed immunity from such mundane traumas through the im-portance of his work.

What about *her* work? She had a career too, and she had the additional responsibility of looking after the children full-time.

When she and Marcus had married, they had both agreed that they wanted their relationship to be as equal a partnership as they could make it; that they would make sure they did not fall into the trap of subconsciously entrenching themselves and each other into stereotyped and outdated roles.

Later Eleanor tried to put aside her own resentments, but Marcus was so brusque and withdrawn that she found herself retreating into a resentful silence and only just managed to bite back an accusatory reminder of the promises they had made one another on their marriage.

What kind of equal partnership was this, when she was left to deal single-handedly with all the problems? What kind of mutual awareness of one another's rights as individuals?

At bedtime she discovered she was deliberately delaying going upstairs, almost deliberately holding on to her anger and irritation, and when Marcus announced that he was going to bed she told him coolly that she still had some work to do.

As he showered and cleaned his teeth, Marcus wondered tiredly if Eleanor had any idea of the pressure he was under. She was so preoccupied with that damned house that she seemed completely oblivious to everything else, especially him.

He checked, staring at his reflection in the bathroom mirror.

Of course she was preoccupied. She had one hell of a lot on her mind, what with the break-up of the partnership and Louise swanning off to France and leaving her to sort everything out.

He knew that Vanessa had been particularly difficult to deal with recently.

And he knew how much this house meant to her... how many hopes she had pinned on it.

Too many? He was still not convinced that it was the right move, but every time he tried to point this out to her Eleanor swamped him with her enthusiastic plans.

Marcus had grown up in a household where his mother and maternal grandmother, who had lived with them, had totally dominated his quiet father, between them overruling every decision that he tried to make. The garden shed had been his father's retreat, a place he vanished to whenever the criticism and carping of his wife and mother-in-law grew too much for him.

Marcus had learned early in his life that the best way to make an easy life for himself was simply not to argue with his mother and grandmother, but to let their forceful opinions wash over him in silence and then to make up his own mind what he wished to do.

The day he realised that in her way his first wife bore many similar characteristics to his mother, he questioned whether he really had any intelligence at all, and one of the first things that had drawn him to Eleanor—apart from the sharp keenness of his sexual desire for her—had been the gentle calmness of her nature; the way she always seemed prepared to listen and accept that he might have views which differed from her own. But suddenly she didn't seem to be listening to him any more.

She *was* under a lot of pressure, he reminded himself.

But so was he. As he had explained to Sondra Cabot when she called into his office to collect some papers this afternoon, the case he was presently involved with was proving a good deal more complex than he had initially anticipated; and he was due over in The Hague at the end of the month on a long-running case that was being heard by the European court.

He smiled to himself, remembering Sondra's enthusiasm as she had asked him about it. The complexity of both British and European law fascinated her, she had told him, and Marcus had seen from the small half-smile she had given him that he was also becoming a part of that fascination.

It had happened before and no doubt would happen again, but this was the first time since he had met Eleanor that he had felt any tug of answering attraction.

She was far too young for him, of course, and not really what he wanted. He knew he loved Eleanor. But he seemed to be losing her, or rather he seemed to be losing the Eleanor he had married to an Eleanor who seemed to have more time and emotion for a house than she did for him.

Just listening to her talking about it this evening, he had seen her face start to glow, and her eyes start to shine. The way they had once done for him. He could hear her coming upstairs.

Quickly he finished cleaning his teeth, not questioning why he wanted to be out of the bathroom before she could join him.

When Eleanor walked into the bedroom and saw the humped still shape of Marcus's body beneath the duvet she felt a mixture of resentment and relief.

What had happened to them? she wondered uneasily as she prepared for bed. Tonight she had actually felt as though she could no longer talk to Marcus . . . could no longer share things with him.

She thought back to when they had first met and admitted their mutual attraction for one another, how eagerly she had looked forward to her dates with him; the way she had saved up all the interesting and funny happenings of her day to relate to him; the way no day seemed fully complete without his goodnight phone call . . . Phone calls which had often extended well into the early hours, especially when either of them was working away.

There had been more real contact between them then than there was now that they were married and living together.

How had that happened? *When* had it happened? she wondered unhappily.

Take this evening, for instance...the way Marcus had made her feel so irritable and on edge that she had felt unable to discuss Vanessa with him, afraid of being unfairly critical of the girl, because of the lack of harmony between herself and Marcus.

The last thing she wanted to do was to try to alienate him from his daughter. She knew how much Vanessa needed her father and, even if Marcus himself did not realise it, he needed her too. Fatherhood did not come easily to him, Eleanor recognised, and he had confided to her once that he suspected himself of lacking the necessary gene to be a good parent.

Eleanor suspected that what he had lacked was more likely to be an example of good parenting set by his own parents.

Both of them in their different ways had suffered from that, and she appreciated that Marcus very genuinely did his best for both sets of children.

As she got into bed beside him, Eleanor hesitated, wanting to reach out and touch him, to reassure herself that, despite the brusqueness he had exhibited this evening, Marcus still loved and wanted her; but then she remembered the self-destructiveness of that kind of conciliatory behaviour and the way it had ultimately led to the break-up of her first marriage, and reminding herself instead of how difficult *her* day had been, and how Marcus did not like her to have to combine the pressures of career, family and running a home. All she had wanted was for him to listen while she confided her anxieties to him and yet instead he had cut her off with irritation and impatience, plainly not wanting to listen to what she had to say.

As she turned her back on him, her mind was ignoring the small forlorn voice that questioned whether standing on her principles was really worth the loss of the warmth of his arms, and the pleasure of snuggling up next to him; the sensation of the soft furriness of his body hair against her skin; the delicious friction it caused when he breathed; the smell and warmth of him; the lovely male solidness of his body...the giveaway instinctive male possessiveness with which he would in his sleep sometimes throw one leg across her body, holding her against him as though he wanted to keep her securely there next to him even while he slept.

When she felt tears unexpectedly prickling the backs of her eyes, she blinked them away irritably. She was a woman, not a child; a woman moreover who was surely old enough to accept that even within the best of marriages and relationships there were bound to be points of conflict. Perhaps she had been a bit thoughtless in rushing straight into a list of problems and complaints almost before Marcus had walked through the door, but she was not about to turn into the kind of woman who felt she had to pander to a man's need to have his ego soothed and cosseted, and Marcus was too mature and intelligent to want her to do so.

She would ring the surveyor in the morning and get him to supply her with a list of all the essential work the house needed, and then she would ask him to recommend some suitable builders, she comforted herself.

And perhaps she had been a little bit over-sensitive to be so hurt when Marcus had demanded accusingly earlier, 'For God's sake, Nell, can't we discuss... can't you think about anything bar that damned house?'

Just before she fell asleep, she reminded herself that she would have to ask Mrs Garvey if she could give them a couple of extra hours tomorrow. Because of all the problems and delays she had had today, she had not had time to move the boys' things up into the attic, and Vanessa was due to arrive after school for the weekend.

Eleanor was halfway through the delicate negotiation required to persuade Mrs Garvey to work the additional two hours when the telephone rang.

She answered it, expecting her caller to be the surveyor who had promised to ring her, but instead it was Marcus.

'Nell, can you do me a favour? I'm going to be tied up in a meeting on a case all afternoon. Could you pick Vanessa up from the station for me?'

She had already promised to take Tom and Gavin to McDonald's after school, but when she explained this to Marcus she could hear the impatience and lack of understanding colouring his voice as he demanded, 'Well, can't you take all three of them after you've picked up Van?'

How could she explain to him, especially with Mrs Garvey within earshot, that the visit to McDonald's had been both a conscience-soother and a small unadmitted bribe to her own sons to make up for the upheaval the arrival of his daughter would inevitably cause them?

Even if Mrs Garvey had not been there, could she have explained? Would Marcus have understood?

It was obvious that in Marcus's eyes her children's visit to McDonald's rated far far lower in his list of priorities than his meeting.

Curtly agreeing to his request, she replaced the receiver and reflected half an hour later that, in view of the way her life was going at the moment, it was perhaps not surprising that Mrs Garvey had announced that it was impossible for her to work over.

Which meant that *she* would have to clear out the boys' room, Eleanor acknowledged.

Why was it that all members of the male sex seemed to share the same habit of misplacing one of a pair of socks? And why, additionally, was it that half a dozen pairs of grey socks all bought at the same time and all washed in the same way should ultimately end up in so many varying shades, so that each sock could only be matched to its own specific partner? Irritably she surveyed the three very definitely off-grey socks she had found beneath Tom's bed.

Of the two of them, Gavin was definitely the neater; his possessions, unlike Tom's, were not strewn haphazardly all over the room but stacked neatly in his 'half'.

Children, like adults, could be very territorial animals. All the more so when they felt that the security of tenure of that territory was threatened? Gavin was a much more independent and self-reliant child than Tom, far less sensitive and imaginative, a sturdy sports enthusiast, who took most things easily in his stride.

She had spent all morning trying to convince herself that the surveyor was being unduly pessimistic in quoting a period of almost a year before the house was fit to move into. A year... She tried to calculate how many weekends, how many holidays, how many nerve-shredding hours of animosity and tension that would comprise. Too many. That would be Marcus's opinion... The whole idea of moving was to find as immediate a solution as they presently could to their present lack of space.

Working here at home was proving even more impossible than she had imagined. Like her sons, she resented the fact that she had no private, personal space of her own. The kitchen table was not an adequate substitute for her own office and, while Marcus had said she could use his study, she felt reluctant to do so.

Marcus's method of working was neat and methodical, everything in its place and a place for everything; she on the other hand liked to strew things haphazardly all over the place, something it was impossible to do in a work space that was not really one's own.

As she surveyed the possessions Tom had strewn all over the bedroom, she recognised wryly that she knew full well to whom he owed that particular trait.

The visit to McDonald's was not a success. Tom sulked and picked at his food, refusing to look at her, kicking Gavin under the table. Gavin retaliated in kind, and as for Vanessa...

Watching her stepdaughter's disdainful, contemptuous expression as she complained in a voice loud enough for those sitting near enough to them to hear about both the health value of the menu and the intelligence of those choosing to eat there, Eleanor gritted her teeth and tried to hold on to both her temper and her sense of humour.

When she and Marcus had first married on her visits to them, the only things Vanessa would eat had been burgers and fries. From Marcus, Eleanor had learned that Julia was not the kind of mother to be interested in the nutritional value of her children's diet.

Vanessa's conception had apparently been 'an accident' and it seemed to Eleanor that Marcus had never enjoyed that closeness with his daughter which she shared with her own sons.

It had, oddly enough, been Jade who had been responsible for the change in Vanessa's eating habits, shrugging impatiently when Eleanor had begged her not to say anything that might hurt or antagonise Vanessa.

'She's got you just where she wants you, Nell,' Jade had told her forthrightly. 'You'd never let Tom or Gavin get away with the things she does and she knows it. She also knows that you love them,' she had added tellingly, but, despite what she had said, Eleanor had still not felt able to comment adversely on Vanessa's behaviour.

'Haven't you finished yet?' Vanessa demanded now, glowering at Tom, adding under her breath, 'God, this place is so juvenile. Why didn't Dad pick me up?' she demanded curtly, turning to Eleanor.

'He had a meeting,' Eleanor told her quietly.

Vanessa smirked, giving her a knowing look. 'I suppose that means he's got a mistress. Men always tell their wives they're in meetings when they're having affairs.'

Eleanor stared at her. Did Vanessa have any idea of what she was saying, or was she simply reacting too naïvely to comments she had heard other girls make, assuming a sophistication she did not yet possess? Taking a deep breath, Eleanor looked at her and said calmly, 'I doubt that that's true, Vanessa. If it was, the country would quite simply grind to a halt and, since it hasn't, we must assume that there are men who, when they say they have business meetings, are actually telling the truth. Your father is one of those men.'

Vanessa said nothing, but she was still smirking. Irritated, Eleanor turned back to the table and snapped unfairly at Gavin, who was still stoically munching his way through his burger.

'For goodness' sake hurry up and finish, will you, Gavin?'

When they got back to the house, Vanessa went straight to her room, firmly closing the door behind her. Gavin was watching television and Tom was doing his homework on the kitchen table. There was a small desk upstairs in the attic bedroom, but Tom complained that there wasn't enough room for him to work on it.

They had been back about half an hour when Gavin suddenly looked up from his work and announced that he had football practice in the morning and that he had left his football kit at school.

Subduing her exasperation, Eleanor told him that he would just have to make do with his spare kit.

'But the shirt is too tight,' he complained.

'It wouldn't be if you had remembered to bring your kit home with you. I've told you before, Gavin, you've got a calendar in your room. You know that you're supposed to write down on it all your school "extras".'

'I did,' he told her indignantly.

Eleanor sighed. The hypermarket would still be open. She could buy him a new shirt; it might not be strictly school regulation but at least it would fit him. He would probably need boots as well. If she remembered correctly, his old pair had been getting too small for him...

She tensed as she suddenly heard the noise from upstairs; Tom's out-raged shriek of, 'Give it to me, it's mine,' and Vanessa's answering,

'Well, what is it doing in *my* room, then?'

Quickly she hurried upstairs to find Tom standing on the landing, his face scarlet with temper, while Vanessa stood in the doorway of the bedroom, holding aloft a poster.

'Stop it, both of you,' Eleanor commanded. 'Tom, stop making that noise. Vanessa, please give Tom his poster.'

'Is *that* what it is?' Vanessa smiled at her and then, so deliberately that Eleanor could scarcely believe she was doing it, she ripped the poster into four and dropped the pieces on to the floor, apologising with in-solent insincerity, 'Oh, sorry, Tom. I've torn it.'

Before Eleanor could say a word, she was turning her back on them and closing the bedroom door.

'I hate you,' she heard Tom crying shrilly. 'And when we move house and I have my own room I'm never, ever going to let you in it...'

'Move house?' Vanessa shot out of the bedroom, slamming the door back against the wall, and stared at Eleanor, her expression so bitterly hostile that for a moment Eleanor was too shocked to speak.

'Who's moving house?'

'We are,' Eleanor told her as calmly as she could, inwardly helplessly aware that this was neither the time nor the place to explain to Vanessa what they were planning.

She knew immediately that she was right. The look of fury and fear on Vanessa's face made her wince and, at the same time, it also made her ache for the vulnerability she had witnessed in her eyes, but before she could say a word Vanessa had disappeared back into the bedroom, returning with the rest of Tom's prized football posters which were always removed from the wall for her visit and stored in the wardrobe.

'Here,' she told Tom savagely, handing him the rolled-up posters. 'Seeing as you're going to have your own room, you won't need to con-taminate mine any more with this junk, will you?'

But as Tom reached out to take them from her, instead of relinquishing them, she held on to them, deliberately twisting and screwing them up, a smile of such unkind, almost malevolent satisfaction in her eyes as she heard Tom's anguished protest that for the first time in her life Eleanor experienced a direct and very urgent desire to retaliate in kind and to subject her to the same kind of cruel demonstration of superior power the girl was showing to her son.

Anger swept through her, fiercely protective maternal anger, and a more subtle but just as overwhelming female recognition of the challenge Vanessa was throwing out, not at Tom, but at her.

Her patience already strained long past breaking point, Eleanor reacted instinctively to it, reaching out to grab hold of Vanessa by her wrist, her own shock at what she was doing mingling with Vanessa's as her stepdaughter froze, surprise, confusion and then bitter resentment blazing in her eyes as she pulled back against Eleanor's hold.

'What do you think you're doing? Give Tom his posters at once.'

Eleanor could hear the fury trembling in her voice; it made her whole body shake.

'*You* can't make me,' Vanessa defied her. '*You* can't tell me what to do. This isn't even your house. It's Dad's...'

The shock of hearing the venom in her voice instantly sprang Eleanor from the trap of her own anger. Shakily she released Vanessa, stepping slowly back from her, watching as Vanessa rubbed her wrist.

'I hate you,' Vanessa hurled at her. 'I hate all of you and I wish Dad had never married you.'

Ignoring the pain her words were causing her, Eleanor gritted her teeth and said quietly, 'Please give Tom his posters back, Vanessa.'

She watched as the girl turned away from her and towards Tom.

'You want them...you really want them?' she taunted him. 'Well, here you are—you can have them.'

With a savage motion she ripped the posters in half, laughing as Tom howled in outraged anguish, throwing the ruined things at Tom's feet before turning back to Eleanor and demanding insolently, 'Happy now? That *was* what you wanted, wasn't it?'

She couldn't let her get away with it, Eleanor recognised. If she did...if she did, she would have even more of a problem with her than she already had.

Taking a deep breath, she took a step towards her. Behind her, Tom was crying noisily, protesting about what Vanessa had done. There was a sound in the hallway, but Eleanor ignored it, concentrating instead on what she was going to say to Vanessa.

As she moved towards her, Vanessa's expression suddenly changed, the gloating, triumphant look obliterated by the shrinking, almost cowering look of fear which took its place.

'No! No, don't. I didn't mean to do it... Please don't hit me.'

Hit her? Eleanor stopped, her body suddenly ice-cold. Surely Vanessa hadn't really thought...

'Eleanor, for God's sake, what the hell's going on? You can hear the noise in the street.'

Marcus... Thankfully Eleanor turned to greet her husband, but Vanessa beat her to it, darting past Eleanor to fling herself into her father's arms, sobbing half hysterically, 'Daddy, Daddy...don't let her hit me.'

Vanessa had obviously inherited her mother's love of acting, Eleanor reflected tiredly as she met the look Marcus was giving her.

Later she would explain the whole situation to him; later when they were alone, not here, allowing herself to be manipulated by Vanessa into defending herself.

Vanessa was a child, that was all, she tried to remind herself. A child...

Numbly she realised that Tom was still complaining loudly about his posters and that Marcus, who had disentangled himself from Vanessa's tearful embrace, was giving her an irritated, impatient, frowning look.

'It's not fair,' Tom wailed. 'She can do just what she likes... I wish I didn't have to live here with you. You always take her side in everything...'

As she saw the tears standing out in his eyes, saw the accusation in his face, heard the dented male pride in his voice, Eleanor looked helplessly from his flushed, angry face to Vanessa's smooth, triumphant one.

A child? No. Vanessa's actions had not been those of a child motivated by a misunderstood reactionary impulse; it had been deliberate and spiteful; its result carefully planned and understood.

A sick sensation of despair overwhelmed her as she stood there, knowing that there was no reasonable explanation she could give her son to help him to understand why it seemed that Vanessa received more favourable treatment and was therefore more 'loved' any more than she could explain to Marcus just why his teenage daughter made her feel so vulnerable and so on edge; so wary of saying or doing the wrong things in case it prejudiced her own relationship with him.

Her body tensed. Where had that thought come from? Surely she didn't really think that Vanessa had that kind of influence over Marcus? To do so was an insult both to him and to their relationship, and yet the thought... the fear must have come from somewhere...

A relic from the days of always coming second best... of always feeling that she was not important enough in her own right to be unconditionally loved... of feeling that she must always work hard to deserve love.

Surely she had thrown off those old shackles years ago?

If so, what were those old doubts and fears doing resurfacing now?

She looked at Marcus, searching his face for some sign that he understood what she was going through, that he could see past the mayhem Vanessa had caused to her own pain and confusion, but the only thing she could see in his eyes was her own reflection, its defensive, drooping posture and his irritation with the scene around him—and her!

CHAPTER FOURTEEN

FERN heard the post dropping through the letterbox on her way downstairs. She picked up the letters and took them with her into the kitchen. Most of them were for Nick and, of the three addressed to her, two were from charities asking for money.

The third one, though, was a fat, bulky envelope, and the sight of her oldest friend's handwriting made her mouth curl into an anticipatory smile as she methodically placed Nick's post on one side, quickly making herself a cup of coffee before sitting down to open and read Cressy's letter.

She and Cressy had met while they were still at school and their friendship had survived not only their very different temperaments and upbringings, but also their university days and the widely diverging lives they had had since.

Admittedly, since she had married Nick, their friendship had been conducted more through letters and telephone calls than in person.

Cressy, a committed environmentalist, had opted for a career which involved her in projects which took her to some of the most remote parts of the world. This letter, though, was postmarked Lincolnshire. Normally, when she was in England, Cressy stayed in Cambridge, where she had done her post-degree studies and where she had several friends among the university fraternity.

Nick had never really taken to Cressy, considering her to be too outspoken and objective for a woman; too inclined to challenge him on issues on which he considered that he as a man held a much more valid and well balanced view than any woman.

Fern had tried to protest that he was being unfair to her friend, who was not only highly qualified and knowledgeable in her field, but who was also genuinely concerned about the effect the modern industrialised nations were having on the earth's environment, but Nick had turned on her, claiming that she didn't know what she was talking about; he had, she remembered, even tried to suggest that Cressy's affection for her had some kind of lesbian undertones to it.

It had been one of the few times when Fern had actually been angry enough to want to argue with him. She suspected that, had she known Cressy less well, his insinuations would have undermined their friendship completely. As it was, Fern, who had grown up alongside Cressy, knew quite well that his innuendoes were unfounded: Cressy, although not promiscuous, was enthusiastically heterosexual.

The letter was so typical of Cressy's breezy, no-nonsense manner that, as she read the opening line, Fern felt almost as though she was there in the room with her.

Guess what! I'm getting married! Graham and I met last year when we were both with a team working in Russia studying the effects that Chernobyl has had on the environment. He's a Scot—Presbyterian ancestry and hugely conventional and moral—and he's said that it's to be marriage or nothing. Since the nothing was impossible to live with, I've given in, less than gracefully, I must tell you. However, *having* given in, we've bought a rectory here in the Fens, with enough land for us to try some experimental crops. The wedding isn't until October— I did say he was conventional, didn't I?—and since Graham is away at the moment with a team studying the effects of sea pollution on plankton I was wondering if you could spare the time to come and spend a few days with me here.

It's been too long since we last had any time together, and it would give us an opportunity to catch up on one another's news. I'm sorry I missed your mother's funeral, by the way.

I know how devoted to one another your parents were, but I know it still must have been a shock to lose her so soon after your father's death.

Thoughtfully Fern put the letter down. What Cressy was suggesting was impossible, of course. Nick would never agree.

She remembered how difficult he had been in the weeks before her mother's death, when the pneumonia which had finally killed her had meant that she was confined to bed and Fern had had to go and stay with her to take care of her.

She sighed, closing her eyes. Cressy's letter had brought back all the pain and unhappiness she had felt when her mother died.

She had badly needed Nick's support then, his support and under-standing... his mature acceptance of the fact that her mother needed her. Instead he had behaved like a spoiled, possessive child.

Adam would never...

Abruptly she got up and walked over to the window, staring blindly out of it.

She had worked hard in the long, narrow garden, transforming it into a series of separate, almost secret gardens. A betrayal of her own need sometimes to seek sanctuary... to conceal herself not just from Nick but from her own fears and doubts?

'I'm sorry if you think I'm being over-possessive,' Nick had told her bitterly after her mother's death. 'But whose fault is that, Fern?'

No, he would never agree to her going to visit Cressy.

She glanced at the top of the letter. There was a telephone number there as well as the address.

She walked over to the phone, carefully pressing the numbers. She would have to lie, of course, to tell Cressy that unfortunately she just couldn't spare the time to visit her.

She could feel her stomach muscles tensing at the thought, as she heard the phone ring, her tension increasing slightly as she heard the receiver being picked up at the other end and then her friend's voice.

'Cressy, it's me ... Fern.'

'Fern! Wonderful ... When can you come? You *are* coming, aren't you?' Fern heard her pleading when she made no response.

Cressy had always had a distinctively husky, almost vibrant voice and now, listening to it, it was almost as though she were in the kitchen with her, her intelligent eyes brimming with the enthusiasm for life which made her so compellingly attractive.

Cressy was one of those people whom others instinctively warmed to, a vibrant, decisive personality that could be sharp and impatient at times and yet which was so essentially and obviously compassionate that she drew others to her.

'I ... I don't think I can make it, Cressy,' Fern apologised. 'You see——'

'No, dammit, Fern, I don't. I *need* you. I've never been married before, remember ... I'm feeling a bit jittery and ... oh, all right, if you want the truth, I'm downright terrified and I desperately need someone to come and hold my hand. There's no one better than you at doing that, Fern. Please ... please come!' she coaxed ... and, as she listened to her, Fern could almost see her smiling that wide-mouthed smile of hers, her lips curling back from her teeth, her hand lifting to rake impatiently through her hair.

Fern laughed in spite of herself. If ever there was anyone who needed her hand holding less than Cressy, she had yet to meet her, but then, as though she had read her mind, Cressy's tone suddenly became serious and she said quietly, 'I *do* need you, Fern. You're my oldest friend. You know me better than anyone else. I can be honest with you in a way that I can't with others. I love Graham more than I ever imagined I could love anyone and yet I'm terrified at the thought of committing myself to marriage. Crazy, isn't it?'

Not when you knew Cressy's family history, it wasn't, Fern reflected inwardly.

Her mother had left Cressy's father when Cressy was eight years old, and precociously intelligent enough to understand the shocked gossip that spread through the village.

Cressy's mother had aristocratic connections; very distant connections as it happened, but none the less the gossips had remembered this fact and embroidered on it, remembering also that Cressy's mother had a very, very distant and long-dead family relative who had been notorious for her affairs and for the very mixed percentage of the large brood of children she produced, while her husband turned a blind eye to what she was doing.

There had been much talk of 'blood coming out' and Fern could vividly remember Cressy solemnly announcing that she would never marry in case she turned out like her mother.

That had been when Cressy was eight, but childhood traumas could cast long shadows even over the lives of mature and intelligent adults.

'I'd love to come, Cressy,' she said regretfully, 'but I can't. Nick has only just returned from a business trip to London and things are rather hectic...'

'You mean he wouldn't approve of you coming to stay with me,' Cressy contradicted her, the flat, crisp tone of her voice making Fern wince slightly. 'Oh, it's all right, Fern. I know that Nick doesn't approve of me. I suppose he's afraid that my bad influence on you might encourage you to break out of that prison he keeps you in. I only wish it could.'

'Cressy...' Fern objected uncomfortably.

'Oh, all right. I'm sorry, Fern, but...' She broke off and then said quietly, 'Please try to come. I meant what I said about being terrified. I do need you.'

'I'll try,' Fern agreed, but as she replaced the receiver she suspected that Cressy knew as well as she did herself that she would not be going.

Half an hour later, she was just about to start the ironing when someone rang the doorbell.

When she went to open the door, the sight of Venice standing there took her completely by surprise.

It was a pleasantly warm day, warm enough for Fern to feel slightly uncomfortable in the jumper and skirt she was wearing.

Venice, in contrast, was wearing a tight-fitting scoop-necked short-sleeved cerise top, patterned with bright yellow coin-sized spots, with matching equally clinging leggings, and, seeing her standing there, her hair and make-up immaculate as always, her skin prettily tanned, her hands and nails looking as though any form of domestic activity was completely unknown to them, Fern felt a momentary and totally alien thrill of envy and resentment.

It didn't need the amused contempt which narrowed Venice's cat-shaped eyes nor the pleased smile that curled her mouth to highlight the contrast in their appearances to make Fern suddenly feel not merely dowdy, but somehow old and tired as well.

As she stepped back to allow Venice to walk into the hall, she pushed her hand into her hair, a defensive reflex action which betrayed her feelings.

'Oh, dear, have I called at a bad time?' Venice cooed, flashing Fern an openly insincere smile. 'Goodness, how wonderfully clean everywhere looks. Almost antiseptic. You must give me the name of your cleaner.

My woman is good enough in her way, but...' She wrinkled her nose, her sharp glance everywhere, assessing, judging...analysing...

'I don't have a cleaner,' Fern told her flatly. She could feel her colour rising as Venice looked at her. She was pretty sure that the older woman knew that quite well, and she had not missed the acid abrasiveness of the word 'antiseptic'.

'I shan't stay. I only called to bring this back,' Venice told her, opening the shoulder-bag she was carrying and handing Fern a carelessly folded and very creased tie. 'Nick left it at my place the other day. He came round to discuss my investments. My central heating has been causing problems recently and the house was so hot he asked if I wouldn't mind if he took off his tie. My woman found it this morning, and as I was driving past I thought I ought to return it...'

Fern said nothing. Bleakly she wondered if Venice thought she was actually deceiving her. How much pleasure had the other woman derived from making up that outrageous tissue of lies?

Fern knew quite well that the tie Venice had just handed her was one of the ones Nick had taken to London with him. She knew it, because it was a new one. Pure silk; it had cost more than her 'monthly allowance'.

There was only one possible explanation as to how it had come into Venice's possession and it certainly wasn't the one Venice had given her.

After Venice had gone, Fern stood in the kitchen, her hands icy cold whilst her face burned with humiliation and anguish.

There was no doubt whatsoever in her mind now. Nick was having an affair with Venice.

As she reached for the telephone, Fern realised that she was physically shaking. Not with pain but with anger; anger because Nick had so obviously and so callously deceived her, lied to her when he had told her that he valued their marriage and that he valued her.

And somewhere, as she punched in the numbers and waited to hear the phone ring, not quite smothered beneath her anger was a small still pool of coldness, of inevitability, as though she had always known that this would and must happen.

No matter how much he might protest otherwise, Nick did not want her. How could he? And, unlike her, Venice would not passively allow him to control their relationship. As she had shown today.

Venice was no fool—she had known what she was doing when she returned that tie.

At the other end of the line someone picked up the receiver and it was only when she heard her friend's voice announcing the number that Fern realised with a small start of shock that instead of dialling Nick's number as she had intended she had in fact dialled Cressy's.

A deliberate subconscious error on her part, or a random act of fate? Whichever way one chose to look at it, there was a definite message somewhere in what had happened.

Fern took a deep breath.

'Cressy, I've changed my mind,' she announced shakily. 'When do you want me to come?'

'As soon as possible,' Cressy responded.

It didn't take her long to pack; there wasn't after all much for her to take, and the unwanted visual memory of Venice standing in the sunlight in her pretty, casual clothes sharpened the revulsion she felt for her own shabby, old-fashioned things.

She left Nick a note explaining where she had gone and after signing her name to it added a footnote to the effect that Venice had returned his tie.

Let him make of that what he wanted, she decided grimly. It hadn't escaped her notice that the writing in the footnote was slightly bolder and larger than her normal neat, controlled script.

Would Nick notice? She smiled mirthlessly.

She wasn't running away, she told herself as she packed her small case into her car. She was simply giving herself space to come to terms with things and to decide upon her future.

A future which would no longer include Nick?

She took a deep shaky breath as she started her car and released the handbrake.

She stopped for lunch in a small country town. It was market day, the streets busy with people. As she walked back outside Fern noticed a young mother walking past with her baby. She was about Fern's own age, but, unlike her, she was dressed in a brightly coloured Lycra-based outfit in a similar style to, although nothing like as expensive as, the top and leggings Venice had been wearing earlier.

They were totally unsuitable for her, of course. Nick would have a fit if... She stopped abruptly, and then, without allowing herself to analyse what she was doing, she turned round and made her way back along the busy street to the branch of an inexpensive nationwide fashion chain she had passed a few minutes earlier.

Fifteen minutes later, when she emerged from its open doorway, her face flushed and her hands trembling slightly, she was no longer wearing the dowdy skirt and sweater.

Instead she had on a pair of pretty multi-coloured leggings and a matching 'body', as the girl had called the all-in-one she had recommended.

She had even been able to buy a matching pair of casual canvas shoes to go with them.

And she had paid for them out of her month's housekeeping money which Nick had only handed over to her the previous day.

Hardly the act of a supposedly responsible and mature woman, and one moreover who was actively considering leaving her husband and who morally therefore had no right to be spending his money, especially on something so frivolous...especially when she knew how much he would disapprove of her purchases.

They were comfortable, too, though. It was remarkable how different they made her feel...how light and unfettered. How free...She paused, entranced by the unexpected sight of her reflection in a shop window, blinked a little as she studied herself surreptitiously.

The salesgirl had commented enviously on the slimness of her figure, saying that she would need their smallest size, adding ruefully that she was lucky because their Lycra range tended to reveal every unwanted bulge.

It was only when she glanced at herself again that Fern realised she was grinning almost idiotically. No wonder that man had paused to stare at her. Quickly she hurried back to her parked car, part of her still shocked by her wasteful extravagance.

She was nearly there now, the flat Fenlands stretching out apparently endlessly in front of her.

Unlike others, Fern did not find this monotony boring; instead, the very regularity and predictability of the landscape seemed to offer a calming, soothing panacea to both her senses and her emotions.

What must they once have been like, these Fenlands, before they were drained? In her mind's eye she could see them, a land of mystery and secrecy, cloaked in protective mists, whose safe paths were only known to those who lived there and within whose quiet, silent half-land, half-marshland lurked danger and death for those unwise enough to treat it without caution and respect.

Cressy had told her during their earlier conversation that, in addition to the old rectory and the farmland they had bought with it, the Institute for whom they both worked was in the process of buying a small acreage of one of the few remaining remote Fens with a view to Cressy and Graham taking charge of the protection and development of this land in its natural state.

'When you see the house, you'll wonder what on earth possessed us to buy it,' Cressy had laughed. 'It's a huge old barn of a place, built early on in the nineteenth century and owned by the church ever since, although no one has actually lived in it for several years. It's far too big for us, but it's ideally situated for our work, and, as Graham says, once we've got the project properly under way at least it means we'll be able to house any students wanting to do fieldwork. It will be a wonderful opportunity to recreate a very special natural habitat, and one that was in danger of becoming completely lost to us.

'Of course, Graham keeps on joking that we could always fill the empty rooms with our children, but I've told him he can forget that. One, or possibly two, is my limit.'

As Fern drove through the final small village on her route, she glanced at her watch. Nick would be arriving home about now and reading her note. It was too late for her to change her mind and go back, and as she turned on to the long, straight road that disappeared in the misty distance of the low horizon she acknowledged that a part of her was actually glad, almost savouring the strange sensation which against all logic was lifting her spirits.

It took her several seconds to work out what it was and, once she had, she said the word aloud, experimentally.

'Freedom . . .'

Ahead of her she could see the house, a gaunt, almost gothically structured building, thrown up incongruously against the flat pale skyline, a building which was almost ugly in many ways and yet, because of its obvious strength, its tenacity in clinging to existence here in this fey, half-solid, half-watery environment, it only appeared as an object of admiration rather than contempt.

As she drove in through the open gateway, Fern recognised the almost typical rectory-style garden, with its balding lawns and neglected tennis courts. It was a far cry indeed from Broughton House and its environment.

And yet, for all its almost theatrical air of brooding heaviness, the startling contrast between its heavy stone bulk and the almost ethereal, misty weightlessness of a landscape which seemed more sky and water than land, the house possessed an unexpected and endearing aura of warmth and welcome.

Fern was halfway towards it when the front door was suddenly flung open and Cressy appeared, running down the steps, whooping triumphantly as she did so and then hugging Fern fiercely before exclaiming, 'You're here! I was half expecting that you might get cold feet and change your mind. Wow!' she added, releasing her and standing back from her a little bit, openly studying her appearance. 'Things *have* changed. I'll bet Nick didn't sanction that outfit,' she added wryly.

Fern could feel herself flushing defensively.

'It's too young for me, isn't it? I shouldn't have——'

'Too young for you? Don't be such an idiot,' Cressy interrupted her. 'It looks great on you. Much better than that dowdy middle-aged stuff you usually wear. Sorry,' she added. 'But you know me, Fern. I always speak my mind. I know your mother brought you up to believe that "nice girls" wear tweed skirts, twinsets and pearls, but you're a woman now and it's good to see you taking charge of your own life and dressing like one . . .' She grinned as she saw Fern's expression.

'OK, OK, I know what you're thinking. I'm a fine one to talk . . .' She glanced wryly at her dungarees and bush shirt and then said gently, 'But these are *my* choice, Fern, and no one else's, and if Graham, much as I love him, started to dictate to me what he thought I should wear . . .'

She shook her head. '*Listen* to me! You've only just arrived and I'm lecturing you already. Come on inside...'

Cressy hadn't changed, Fern reflected as she followed her into the lofty stone-flagged hallway, dim and cool after the translucent clarity of the light outside. Beams of sunlight picked out the dust spinning lazily in the air; a couple of brilliantly coloured woven rugs had been thrown casually over the battered leather chesterfield in front of the huge stone fireplace. Above it, on the wall, the mounted heads of what looked like a small herd of deer gazed glassy-eyed and moulting into space.

'Gruesome, aren't they?' Cressy commented, following her gaze. 'Not my choice, needless to say. They came with the house. Graham said they reminded him of a particularly awful holiday he once spent in the Scottish Highlands with his grandparents. We're going to take the poor things down and give them a decent burial.

'It's hard, isn't it, imagining the kind of society where that kind of wanton killing was not just sanctioned but actively praised? Look at them: a tribute to man's dexterity with a gun; and an indictment against his heart and soul.'

No, she hadn't changed, Fern reflected, listening to the passion in her old friend's voice. The wild mane of strawberry-blonde hair, the high-cheekboned face with its tanned skin, the intelligent hazel eyes, the lean, athletic body and the sharp, trained mind—they were all the same.

And so was the warmth, the humanity, the generosity of spirit and the affection, she recognised as Cressy looked at her and said vehemently, 'Fern, I'm so glad you're here. I still can't believe I'm actually doing it... actually getting married. You know how I've always felt about that kind of commitment... how afraid I've always been of repeating my mother's pattern of broken promises and broken marriages.'

'But you do love Graham...'

'Oh, yes.'

She said it so quietly, so simply, but with such a look of such softness and warmth on her face, that Fern felt her own heart move achingly inside her.

It wasn't that she envied her friend her happiness... nor even her capacity to recognise it and to cherish it; it was just that looking at Cressy, listening to her, brought so sharply into focus the emptiness of her own life.

The delicate protective tissue of self-deceit and self-denial with which she had cloaked the paucity of her marriage could not withstand the force of Cressy's almost brutal honesty.

What was Nick doing now? she wondered later as Cressy gave her a brief tour of the house coupled with an excited and enthusiastic description of the plans she and Graham had for its and their own future.

Was he pacing the house, raging against her defection, her deceit, her cowardice, or was he taking advantage of her absence to be with Venice?

She hadn't realised how closely Cressy was watching her until she heard her friend asking quietly, 'Fern, what is it? What's wrong?'

'It's...it's nothing. I was just thinking about Nick.'

'But not very happily, if your expression is anything to go by,' Cressy commented gently. 'Do you want to talk about it?'

Fern shook her head. She was here to listen to Cressy, to support her, not the other way round; but to her dismay she could feel her eyes beginning to fill with tears and she knew that Cressy had seen them as well.

'Come on,' Cressy insisted. 'I want to know what's going on.'

Unresistingly Fern let her take hold of her arm and guide her back to the spacious kitchen, a large, cluttered but very comfortable room on which Cressy had already managed to stamp her indefinable mark.

It was a room Nick would have hated, Fern acknowledged as Cressy unceremoniously swept a large pile of books off the kitchen table and pulled out one of the chairs, firmly but very kindly pushing Fern into it.

'Now,' she insisted, pulling out another chair for herself, 'I want to hear all about it.'

'There isn't anything to tell...' Fern began, and then, to her own shock, because it was the last thing she had intended to do, she heard herself adding quietly, 'Nick's having an affair.'

There was a small silence, and when she looked uncertainly at her friend Fern realised that her announcement had not come as any surprise to her.

'I know what you're thinking,' she said despairingly. 'It probably isn't that important. These things do happen...men *do* have affairs... It probably doesn't mean anything, and if I keep quiet it will probably all blow over... It's probably all my fault anyway. I——'

'*Your* fault!' Cressy exploded, standing up and looking at her. '*Your* fault? For God's sake, Fern, what the hell have you let him do to you? I always knew that he was a manipulative bastard, but if he's having an affair there's only one person responsible for him making the decision and it certainly isn't *you*. I don't think I've ever met *anyone* who takes her marriage more seriously than you do, or who puts more into it...'

Fern winced, but Cressy obviously didn't notice; she was pacing the kitchen now, her eyes stormily angry as she turned round and announced grimly, 'I know I shouldn't say it, and I've always promised myself that I wouldn't, but that husband of yours is one of, if not *the* most selfish and manipulative people I have *ever* met. Right from the moment the two of you met, he's blinded you to reality, Fern; he's used you and manipulated you, playing on your vulnerabilities...hurting you. Oh, yes, he *has* hurt you, Fern. I watched the way he deliberately took over your life, took over you, and I wanted to tell you then...to warn you...but you were so blindly in love with him...'

Fern made a small choking sound of distress and guilt.

'Do you *still* love him?' Cressy asked her fiercely.

Fern shook her head, unable even now to vocally admit the truth, the teachings of her parents and her own guilt still holding her too tightly to allow her to do so.

'Well, thank God for that.'

As she watched, Cressy marched over to the fridge and opened it, removing a bottle of wine, which she uncorked and poured into two large glasses.

'It may not be champagne, but...' As she raised her own glass, she paused and stated rather than asked, 'You *are* going to leave him, I hope.'

Leave him! Fern stared at her.

'We're *married*, Cressy. I made *vows*...gave a commitment. I...'

Cressy put down her glass. 'Fern, for God's sake, how much more of yourself do you have to give him? What the *hell* has *he* ever given *you*? You say he's having an affair; well, I'll bet it isn't his first. He's the kind of man who needs the constant ego-boost of entrapping another victim... Not for the sex. No, definitely not for that. You know, when you first knew him, I used to look at him and wonder exactly what it was you saw in him. He always struck me as being so sexually and emotionally cold... Although I must admit you had to admire the way he pushed Adam out of your life. Whatever *did* you see in him, Fern? And when you had Adam, who was so plainly the complete opposite, so very much everything that Nick wasn't... I have to confess there were moments, more of them than I wanted to admit, when I actually found myself fantasising about what it would be like to go to bed with your Adam.'

'He was never "my" Adam,' Fern protested, 'and you're wrong about Nick's pushing him out of my life. Adam was never anything more than a friend.'

'A *friend*? I saw the way he used to look at you. Adam wanted you, Fern. Make no mistake about that.'

'You're wrong,' Fern insisted. 'He already had a girlfriend... Someone much older and far more experienced than me. Nick——'

'Nick wanted you the way he's wanted everything else in his life,' Cressy interrupted her ruthlessly, refilling their glasses, but Fern knew it wasn't just the wine that was making her so loquacious, so almost brutally honest. She sensed as she listened to her friend that Cressy was giving voice to things she had suppressed for a very long time, and she sensed as well that her motivation was purely that of friendship and concern for her.

'He wanted you because he wanted to take you away from Adam.'

Fern felt her fingers curling protestingly round the stem of her wine glass. She could feel the blood draining out of her face, and the dizzying, disorientating shock of disbelief that filled the chasm which had opened up within her.

'That's not true. He wanted me...needed *me*...'

But even as she said it she knew that Cressy was right. In a sickening jolt of perception, the barriers of delusion she had used to protect both herself and her marriage suddenly came down and for the first time she saw her relationship with Nick for what it really was.

'I'm sorry, Fern...I'm so sorry,' she heard Cressy saying roughly. 'I didn't mean...I thought you must know...that you must have seen how bitterly jealous and resentful of Adam Nick has always been.'

Nick, jealous of Adam? The room, which had briefly slipped out of focus, spun round her dizzily. She blinked and forced herself to concentrate on the dresser against the wall, fixing her gaze on the primitive design of the unglazed jug in the middle of one of the shelves. Were the tribesmen on it hunters; were...those raised spears raised to kill their prey; were...?

She shivered tensely and turned her face towards Cressy.

'All these years and I never knew...never realised. I thought Nick wanted me...needed me...but all the time he was just using me because he thought Adam wanted me. Is that really what you're trying to say?' she asked Cressy in revulsion.

'Basically, yes,' Cressy admitted huskily. 'But there's more to it than that. People like Nick are like...like plants such as ivy; like bindweed. They need a host plant to cling to, to draw their life-force from, to use and draw the strength from while they slowly smother and destroy it. And the stronger the host plant is, the greater the appeal.'

'But I'm not strong,' Fern protested.

Cressy came over to her, kneeling beside her chair and wrapping her arms tightly round her.

'Fern, you're so wrong. You are one of the strongest, most courageous, most moral people I've ever known. Why do you think it's you I want here with me now, if not because I need your strength?'

'You need *my* strength!'

Fern could feel her body starting to shake with the onset of semi-hysterical laughter. 'But I'm nothing. I've done nothing with my life...seen nothing...been nowhere.'

'You have compassion, love and understanding; people turn to you instinctively for help. You don't know yourself, Fern. You don't know your own value. Do you think anyone who was genuinely weak, who genuinely lacked the virtues I've just described, would ever have stuck by someone like Nick, never mind been attracted to him in the first place? I'll bet you anything you like, despite this affair, he still won't want to let you go. Oh, he'll make you suffer...make you think it's your fault...claim some lack in you is responsible for his infidelity, some need you haven't fulfilled. Oh, yes, he'll use it to manipulate and control you, but he won't let you go. He can't afford to let you go, Fern. He needs you too much to support his ego.'

'But he's the one...' Fern started to protest and then fell silent as her brain observed the truth of what Cressy was saying to her.

'Do you still love him?' Cressy repeated.

Fern shook her head, unable to deny the truth any longer. 'No.'

'Thank God for that,' Cressy said again, adding emphatically, 'Leave him, Fern. You owe it to yourself.'

Leave him! How could she? And yet if Cressy was right how could she not? And Cressy was right, she knew that instinctively, and knew also that she had deliberately blinded herself to the truth.

Why? Out of fear? Out of guilt? Out of loyalty to her parents and the beliefs they had instilled in her?

They talked until the early hours of the morning, eating the chilli Cressy had made earlier, finishing the bottle of wine she had opened and then another.

Oddly Fern did not feel drunk, just more clear-headed and aware than she could remember ever feeling at any other time in her life.

As well as her marriage, they discussed Cressy's relationship with Graham and with her parents; her wariness of the kind of commitment marriage would bring; her fear of not being able to live up to Graham's expectations of her.

'I can't live without him,' she confessed to Fern, 'and yet I'm terrified that once we're married I shan't be able to live with him.'

'You will,' Fern assured her, and, oddly, as she said it, not only did she herself know that it was true, but she could see as well that Cressy believed her.

'Do you see much of Adam?' Cressy asked her idly as they finished their last glass of wine.

Fern tensed automatically, her whole body stiff and wary until she remembered that this was Cressy she was talking to and not Nick, and that with Cressy there was no reason for her to feel afraid of what her face might reveal.

'Not really. He and Nick have never been close and now with this business of Broughton House...'

'What business with Broughton House?' Cressy asked her. Briefly Fern explained.

'But surely Adam would never do anything like that? He's always been such a keen conservationist.'

'Yes, I know, but he is involved in several similar projects and I suppose as a businessman...an architect...well, no one is finding it easy these days, are they? Adam has his staff to think of as well as himself.'

'Even so... Have you discussed it with him, Fern?'

Now Fern did dip her head, avoiding looking directly at Cressy. There were still some things she had not told her, confidences she had not given, could not give anyone, not even the oldest and closest of her friends.

'No. No, I haven't. Tell me some more about how you met Graham,' she encouraged, changing the subject. 'I know you said you were both working on the same project...'

'Yes. Well, we were...'

Thankfully Fern listened as Cressy proceeded to describe her first meeting with her husband-to-be, congratulating herself on successfully deflecting her attention.

Out on the dykes, where water met sky, dawn was just beginning to pearl the horizon when they finally went to bed, leaving the detritus of the evening meal, the empty bottles of wine and even the cocoa mugs, so reminiscent of their earlier days together that Fern smiled ruefully over them as Cressy refused to allow her to clean up, announcing that they would have plenty of time for that when they got up.

'I suppose once I'm actually a wife I'll start getting like you and feel totally unable to go to bed unless the kitchen's spotless,' Cressy told her drily. 'But I'm not a wife yet, and Graham, thank God, is not one of these men who puts a premium on housewifely efficiency.'

'Really?' Fern teased her rounding her eyes in mock naïveté. 'You do surprise me.'

Laughing, they went upstairs together.

But half an hour later, as she slipped between the cold linen sheets of her bed, Fern wasn't laughing any longer.

'Leave Nick,' Cressy had advised her again later in the evening. 'Otherwise, he will destroy you completely, Fern.'

Leave Nick. As she closed her eyes, Fern could feel the unfamiliarly frantic panicky beating sensation deep within her chest. Not fear, she recognised, but the desire, the need, the overwhelmingly urgent and compelling ache to be free.

Why had she never recognised it before...never realised...never seen...? *Why* had it taken someone else to show her Nick as he really was; to set her free from the intolerable burden of her own sense of failure and despair?

And her guilt?

She opened her eyes abruptly. No, Cressy had not done that. How could she? She did not, after all, know the whole truth. Did not know that Nick had not been the only one to break their marriage vows.

But, even despite that, she could not stay with him now, she recognised.

Their marriage was over. But would she have the strength to tell Nick that?

CHAPTER FIFTEEN

'WHAT'S wrong with you? You've been pushing that pasta round your plate without touching it for ages. I thought you loved Italian food.'

Zoe smiled wanly at the mock accusatory tone of her friend's voice.

'I do—normally,' she agreed. 'It's just that I've been feeling so off colour lately.' She pulled a wry face. 'Virtually everything I eat seems to make me feel and be sick, and sometimes...'

'Oh, I see,' Ann interrupted with a grin. 'You're not trying to tell me that you're pregnant, are you?'

Pregnant! Zoe stared at her. 'No...no, of course I'm not. It's just the after-effects of this bout of food poisoning I had the other week.'

She broke off, irritated by the wryly arch expression on her friend's face.

'Look, just because you couldn't wait to produce,' she began, and then stopped as she saw Ann's archness give way to genuine concern.

'Sorry,' she apologised gruffly. 'It's just that feeling so rotten is beginning to get me down. What with that and Ben's boss being so demanding and picky... I've hardly seen Ben for the last couple of weeks, he's been working so hard.'

'That's the trouble with the restaurant trade,' Ann sympathised. 'What you could do with is setting up in business on your own.'

Zoe said nothing. Normally that kind of comment from one of her oldest and closest friends would have immediately led to her aching to confide their plans, almost bursting with the effort of controlling her excitement and elation, but since their return from their foray into Wiltshire she had felt so sick and tired that she had not been able to raise any enthusiasm for anything. Not even for sex, as Ben had remarked only last night when she had withdrawn from his arms, irritably claiming that she was too tired and then immediately feeling so tearful and emotional that she had longed for him to take hold of her again; to wrap his arms round her and keep her safe.

Safe from what? From the sudden unpredictability of her unfamiliar moods and emotions?

Pregnant! She grimaced to herself as she left the restaurant and headed back to the flat.

Ann was an old and close friend, but she had tended to become rather baby-orientated since the arrival of her first child six months previously.

Normally Zoe, who was godmother to little William, enjoyed hearing about his exploits, even if when she was alone she sometimes secretly marvelled at the change in her old friend from madcap girl-about-town to environmentally aware and concerned mother, and felt relieved that she was not in her friend's shoes, but today for some reason Ann's conversation had jarred uncomfortably on her.

It must be because of her anxiety about the house, and the fact that they could not go ahead and make any real firm plans until they had confirmation that planning permission would be granted, that she was feeling so on edge and out of sorts, Zoe reflected tiredly. She had always been inclined to be impatient of delays.

Pregnant... That was a joke, and impossible, thank goodness. She never missed taking her Pill, wanting the responsibility of an unplanned pregnancy as little as Ben did. That was something they both shared: their awareness of how impossible it would be for them to have a child at this stage in their lives.

Ben had made it more than clear that he never wanted children, and if she had ever doubted that he meant it she only had to think of his reaction to the news of his sister Sharon's pregnancy.

Her head was beginning to ache muzzily, the nausea she had experienced over lunch returning in a suddenly sharply urgent queasy wave. Oh, God, she wasn't going to pass out here in the street, was she?

She stopped walking, clutching dizzily at a nearby lamp-post, irritably aware of the curious looks passers-by were giving her, the careful way they were skirting round her, their expressions sharply in focus one minute and distantly blurred the next, strangers' faces, some expressing disdain, some apprehension, others curiosity or uninterest.

'Are you all right, dear?'

Shakily Zoe focused on the old woman who was addressing her, rejecting her initial impression that the woman was one of the city's growing army of bag ladies as her brain slowly registered the shopping in the tired-looking plastic bag and the fact that the woman's clothes, although shabby, were scrupulously clean.

'I'm fine,' Zoe lied. 'I just felt a bit sick...'

The old woman nodded sympathetically. 'I was like that with my first. Sick as a dog, I was, morning, noon and night. Course, it was different in them days...'

Nauseously Zoe let her conversation wash over her, too busy fighting off the invasive clammy feeling of fear which was now beginning to permeate her nausea.

Pregnant. She couldn't be. Must not be!

She was still thinking the same thing two hours later as she stood in the bathroom shivering with shock and disbelief as she stared at the incontrovertible evidence of the home pregnancy test she had just done.

Behind her on the floor lay the test she had done earlier. Like its fellow, it had shown the tell-tale evidence of what she had truly believed was impossible.

Sickly she kneeled down to pick up the small piece of plastic. Such an innocuous, almost innocent thing and yet it had changed her whole life. Destroyed her whole life.

Perhaps it was wrong, perhaps she had done the test incorrectly.

Feverishly she hurried towards the door. She had to go out and buy another test, try again. She must have done something wrong . . . yes, that was definitely it. She was letting Ann with all her silly talk of pregnancy get to her . . . that was all it was.

She was halfway across the room when she heard Ben's key in the lock.

Immediately panic hit her, and she rushed back into the bathroom frantically gathering up the box and the betraying test wands, wrapping them in a towel she grabbed off the rail, her stomach muscles clenching anxiously as she heard Ben calling her name.

As she opened the bathroom door she knew that the moment he looked at her he would be able to tell something was wrong; a brief glimpse of her own reflection in the bathroom mirror had betrayed her over-bright eyes and flushed face, and with it the tension and the fear she could feel churning sickly through her. What was she panicking for? What was she trying to hide? She had done nothing wrong—it was not her fault. If she was pregnant then it was a joint problem, something they would share as they had shared everything else—thank God Ben was here. As she ran towards him, she recognised with a small shock of surprise how vulnerable she felt, how uncharacteristically in need of his support, his strength; how dependent and afraid . . . how desperately in need of his love and comfort.

As she ran towards him she was conscious of a sudden lightening of the pressure and tension tightening her body, a sudden lifting of the burden which had descended so heavily and unexpectedly on to her shoulders.

'Ben . . .'

'I've got to go to Manchester, Zoe.'

He barely seemed even to look at her as he hurried past her and into the bedroom.

'I had a phone call at work from Ma. Apparently Sharon's been rushed into the hospital. Some complications with the baby . . .'

'But Ben, I need . . .'

She stopped as he emerged from the bedroom and she realised that he hadn't heard her, wasn't even listening to her, seemed in fact virtually oblivious to her presence, other than as a sounding-board to bounce off his own irritation and ire.

'This is all I need,' she heard him muttering angrily. 'I've already got Aldo on my back about the time I've had off and now he's started complaining that customers are getting bored with the menus. Whose fault is that? Not mine,' Ben told her forcefully. 'I've been pressing him for months now to let me change things, but would he? Not a chance in hell, but now suddenly, when things go wrong, it's all my fault.

'Any news from Clive?' he asked her, focusing on her.

Zoe held her breath. He must see now surely how upset she was; must realise that something was seriously wrong... Must know how desperately she needed him to reach out and help her to rescue her from the panic and fear which engulfed her.

His gaze was sharpening now, a small frown appearing between his eyebrows as his eyes narrowed on her. She held her breath, her heart beating as relief poured through her. He must see now how upset she was.

'*Clive*, Zoe,' he repeated snappily, oblivious to her need. Zoe could hear the irritation in his voice quite plainly, but it was several seconds before first her body and then her emotions reacted to it, her muscles tensing, her throat clogging with unfamiliar and wholly unexpected tears.

'Zoe, for God's sake,' Ben demanded exasperatedly. 'What's got into you? What's wrong?'

'Nothing,' she told him, turning away from him. It was too late for him to ask her that question now. He should have asked it before...should have seen...should have recognised...

'Look, I've got to go,' she heard him saying. 'I'll give you a ring as soon as I know what's happening... I might have to stay up there for a couple of days.

'God, of all the times for this to happen...' The irritation was back in his voice, but Zoe had distanced herself from it now.

What was wrong with her, anyway? she asked herself numbly as she watched him flinging a change of clothes into an overnight bag, her emotions still deadened by the shock of his inability to recognise her need.

She was always the one who had been the strong one, the one who had directed their relationship, who had supported him. And yet now, the first time she required help, what happened? He couldn't even recognise her need, never mind respond to it... He didn't even know, never mind care... All *he* was concerned about was whether or not they had heard from Clive.

Didn't he realise what was happening? She was pregnant! Pregnant with their child, the child that could ruin all their plans...all their hopes. The child who should never have been conceived. She needed him to share her fear with. She was so afraid, so filled with panic and shock, so in need of his support, of him; of being able to share her disbelief and fear with him, but he didn't want to know...couldn't see... Didn't *want* to see.

He was coming towards her, carrying his bag in one hand, his jacket in the other, his forehead still creased in that harsh rejecting frown.

As he stopped beside her and bent his head, she turned her own face away so that his mouth touched her cheek and not her lips. She could feel the pain and fear burning through her body, tight with the tension of not vocally giving way to what she was feeling.

'This is all we want right now, isn't it?' he muttered grimly as he straightened up. 'Sharon and her damned baby...'

As she heard the bitterness in his voice Zoe's body trembled, her heartbeat a fierce kick of sensation slamming sickly against her ribs.

A sensation of icy cold shock poured over her, thrilling her with the fearful realisation of the truth.

Ben had not realised or recognised her need because subconsciously he did not want to recognise it. Just as he would not want to recognise her pregnancy, her child—her child—her problem, not theirs?

For a long time after Ben had gone she stood in the middle of the small living-room simply staring emptily into space, and then, with a small shudder, she focused abruptly on the open door to the bedroom.

What was the matter with her? She had always known that Ben did not want children and neither did she. They had both agreed on what they wanted from their lives, had both shared the same heady thrill of excitement in planning their immediate future.

Zoe remembered how sorry she had felt for Ann when the latter had first told her she was pregnant, and how strongly supportive she herself had always been of a woman's right to choose whether or not she decided to go ahead with a pregnancy accidentally started.

There had never been the slightest shadow of doubt in her mind that, should she ever find herself in such a situation, she would be strong enough to make the only logical and appropriate decision.

What need was there after all to discuss anything with Ben? She already knew what his views would be, already knew what action he would want her to take.

She had always prided herself on her strength of mind, on her ability to make her own decisions and to stand by them. She was a modern, independent woman who did not need to cling helplessly and smotheringly to the man in her life.

In fact, of the two of them, she had always thought of Ben as being the less self-assured and confident, the more 'needy' one in their relationship, and yet now... She shivered slightly, suddenly aware of feeling very cold and tired—and very alone.

So that was it, then. Her own diagnosis had been confirmed. She was most definitely pregnant.

They had asked her at the clinic if she would like to talk with one of their counsellors, but she had shaken her head. After all, she knew exactly what course of action must be taken, didn't she?

Her earlier panic and fear had subsided now. She had had time to think logically and to plan, firmly pushing to the back of her mind the emotional reaction she now saw as a form of self-betrayal.

What, after all, could Ben do for her that she couldn't do for herself? She already knew what his reaction would be; why burden him with the responsibility of making the decision which she knew must be made?

It had been silly of her to expect him to somehow know intuitively what had happened. He had enough problems of his own to contend with without her adding to them.

She reminded herself of how she had always been the one to take the lead in their relationship, to direct and even in some way to control it. *She* had been the one to suggest they live together; she had been the one to urge him to give serious consideration to Clive's offer, and she had also been the one to tell herself privately that she would never treat him as his mother and family did; that she would never place on his shoulders the burden of responsibility for her emotional or physical happiness.

Just as, as a new lover, she had not expected him to know automatically how to arouse and satisfy her sexually, so she had prided herself on not expecting him to 'know' her emotional or mental requirements either.

Now, calmly, she sat down to analyse her situation. Not that it needed a great deal of analysis. The facts were simple enough. She was pregnant with a child which was neither planned nor wanted—by either Ben or herself.

She was not maternally inclined and never had been. The sight of babies in prams, no matter how adorable, did not move her to do anything other than smile with relief that they were not her responsibility.

It was just as well that Ben had been too preoccupied to guess that anything was wrong, she told herself firmly. Thank goodness she had come to her senses in time to stop herself from acting like some wimpy idiot.

And what good would crying all over Ben have done, anyway? What could he do for her that she could not do for herself?

It was her decision, her body... Her child?

She got up, wrapping her arms tightly around herself, fiercely pushing away such a dangerously emotive thought. No. Her course of action was simple and clear, and the sooner she got the whole business over and done with, the better.

She squared her shoulders, her chin tilting determinedly. She did not need to drag Ben into this. She was perfectly capable of dealing with it on her own. He already had enough to worry about. Remorsefully she remembered how tired and anxious he had looked as he left, how baffled by her behaviour. How irritated and angered by his mother's plea for help.

Guiltily Zoe wondered what was wrong with Sharon. She had been rushed into hospital, Ben had said tersely. Because her health was in danger, or because the baby...?

With a start Zoe looked down at her own body, and the left hand was pressed hard against her still flat stomach, the fingers splayed protectively over the space her child would ultimately inhabit.

Only there was not going to be a child.

The phone rang, bringing a welcome interruption to her thoughts. She picked up the receiver, her spirits lifting when she heard Ben's voice.

'How's Sharon?' she asked him quickly, determined to make up for her earlier moodiness. To assure him that she was not like his sister, clinging, dependent, draining him and forcing him to accept responsibility for her. To assure him... or to assure herself?

'She's stable, at the moment. They're keeping her in for observation.' He sounded tired and tense. 'Ma's in a bit of a state. Apparently she and Sharon had had a row and she feels responsible for what's happened, although the doctor said that it was a physical problem and nothing at all to do with their quarrel. I'm going to have to stay up here tonight, Zoe. Could you ring the restaurant for me?'

'Of course I will,' she assured him. 'There hasn't been any news from Clive yet, but I'm sure we'll hear something soon.'

'I hope so.' She caught the sound of tiredness and pessimism in his voice. 'If it falls through it looks as if I'm going to be out of work. I think Aldo suspects that something's going on...'

'It won't come to that,' Zoe comforted him. 'And even if he did fire you, we can live off what I earn for a few weeks...'

She heard the small explosive sound Ben made and gripped the receiver tightly. Some views became so entrenched in the human psyche that nothing would remove them, and she already knew how Ben felt about any suggestion that she should support him financially.

Ten minutes later, after she had replaced the receiver, a wave of nausea struck her.

When she emerged from the bathroom, her stomach empty and her head dizzy and light, she leaned against the wall, closing her eyes.

Of course she was doing the right thing. Of course there was no real choice... even less now than before, if Ben actually was made redundant and they had to live on her salary.

Of course there was no question of her getting all sentimental and silly about a baby she had never planned or wanted to conceive in the first place, but that did not stop the hot salt trickle of tears piercing the barrier of her tightly locked eyelids, nor the dull ache of loneliness and sorrow welling up past all the positive and determined thoughts she was trying to focus her mind on.

She wouldn't be feeling like this if Ben were here with her because she wouldn't be able to wallow in self-pity and self-indulgence, or dwell on things. She would have been far too busy worrying about Ben and making sure *he* didn't guess what had happened.

But Ben wasn't here. Ben was in Manchester. Ben was with his pregnant, dependent sister.

What she needed right now was some company, she told herself firmly. First thing in the morning she would ring the clinic and make the necessary appointment and arrangements, but now... She would drive over and see her mother, she decided. That would take her mind off things.

She was not a child, she did not need Ben with her to hold her hand and give her reassurance and comfort. She knew, after all, what had to be done. There was no choice to be made, only a simply logical sequence of events to be followed.

No choice... She shivered as she let herself out of the flat. Was *that* what was disturbing her so much, making her feel so uncharacteristically full of nebulous, difficult-to-understand emotions and needs? The fact that she had no choice?

The sight of her father's car parked in the drive of her parents' house lifted her spirits and, on impulse, instead of knocking on the door as she normally did, she decided to do as her mother was always urging her to do and use her key, give them both a surprise.

As she unlocked the door she was smiling, for the first time since she had realised she was pregnant, but then her smile disappeared, to be replaced by a cold chill of shock as she walked into the hall, her arrival masked by the sound of her parents' angry raised voices.

They were quarrelling! But her parents never quarrelled. Never!

Through the half-open kitchen door she heard her mother saying bitterly, 'Don't you understand... I *want* to work, to do something with my life other than sit around here waiting for you to come home? After all, it isn't something you do very often these days, is it?'

Zoe heard the sound of a chair scraping back over the tiled kitchen floor and then her father's voice, unfamiliarly sharp and edged.

'You, *work*? Don't make me laugh. What would you do? You don't have any qualifications...'

'And whose fault is that? Who was the one who always insisted that you needed and wanted me here? You complain now that I'm too dependent on you, that you don't have time to run the business and to entertain me, but *you* were the one who always insisted that you wanted me here at home. At home...' Zoe heard her mother laugh acidly. 'This place isn't a home any more. It hasn't been since Zoe left and we both know it. She's the only thing that really held us together. Oh, I've gone along with the pretence, made sure the rest of the world believed we were happy...'

'We *were* happy, dammit. We are...'

'You may be, but *I'm* not. I need something much more in my life than a husband who complains he's too tired and too busy to spend any time with me. Who says he's too tired to make love to me, who lies about where he is and with whom...'

As Zoe stiffened in disbelief she heard her father slam his hand down on the table and protest, 'Look, I've already told you that was a mistake. I was there, the receptionist had changed shifts and...'

'It's always the idiotic wife who's the last to know about these things, isn't it? The classic situation ... The affair ...'

'I am *not* having an affair.'

'Whether you are or not doesn't make any difference. Not to my plans. I still intend to go ahead with this training programme. I need to do it; I need to feel that I'm of value to someone. Even if I'm no longer of any value to you.'

Quietly Zoe turned round and slowly reopened the front door, letting herself out, her movements jerky and filled with tension as she hurried back to her car.

Her parents, *quarrelling. Her* parents betraying a side to their relationship, their marriage she had never ever dreamed existed; she had laughed at them so many times for their devotion to one another, never guessing ... never dreaming ... She was shivering as she started her car and reversed out into the road.

As she drove back to the flat, the tight knot of tension in the middle of her chest seemed to expand and ache, a hard, threatening ball of fear and confusion that was slowly turning to fierce anger and resentment.

Her parents ... Ben ... She was always there when *they* wanted or needed her, but when she was the one who was wanting, who was in need, where were they? When she needed someone to turn to, to lean on ...

To lean on? But she never needed to lean on anyone. She was the strong one.

What was *wrong* with her? Why was she so afraid, so angry; why was she torn between the calm and logical awareness that there was no reason for her to need to share her knowledge with anyone, that it would after all be much simpler and easier if she just went ahead with what had to be done and then got on with her life, and this terrifyingly and illogical sense of injustice and anger that the people who were supposed to be closest to her should be so oblivious to what was happening to her?

Did she really expect Ben, her parents to somehow possess the ability to see into her mind, to sense intuitively what had happened?

No, of course not. How could they? *She* had always been the one who had insisted to Ben that they could not be expected to know what one another felt, who had laughed at the idea of even the closest of lovers being able to read one another's thoughts. And yet here she was, beneath the smothering blanket of control she had thrown over the panic and fear she had felt earlier, still fighting to suppress an anger whose intensity totally bewildered her.

But what was she angry about? The fact that her parents were quarrelling ... the fact that Ben had gone rushing off to Manchester to be with his mother and sister, when she needed him here with her?

But he did not know she needed him, did he? And why did she need him? It wasn't as though she was facing anything particularly traumatic, after all. All she was doing was simply correcting a mistake; putting right something which should not have gone wrong in the first place. It wasn't as though the pregnancy had any real significance for her...

And yet here she was...

Here she was what? Full of anger and self-pity because no one but she would ever know of the sacrifice she was making... The life she was destroying... For Ben's sake... for the sake of their plans...

She was making? No, she wasn't the one making that sacrifice. It was her child who...

No... As she thumped the side of the steering-wheel with her hand she didn't even feel the pain of the impact, only the shock caused by the direction of her thoughts.

This was stupid. More than stupid, it was dangerous and self-destructive.

What was the matter with her, anyway?

Nothing. There was nothing at all wrong with her. Tomorrow she would ring the clinic, make the necessary appointment and with luck by the time Ben returned it would all be over and everything would be back to normal. The whole thing over and done with and safely out of the way, so that she could concentrate on their new venture, their new life.

It would be up to her to provide the optimism and the strength to support Ben through his doubts and pessimism, she had always known that—had in a way almost been pleased by his dependence on her. She could not give Ben and the business the time and attention they needed and have a child as well.

It was all so unfair—she did not *want* the complications this pregnancy were causing her, she told herself angrily later as she let herself into the flat.

Why was life doing this to her... testing her like this? Why her?

CHAPTER SIXTEEN

'I'M OFF now, Nell...'

Eleanor paused on the stairs, tensing as she watched Marcus disappearing through the front door. Couldn't he have waited until she got downstairs and said goodbye properly to her?

Angrily she walked into the kitchen and started clearing up the breakfast things. There had been tension between them ever since the traumatic events of the previous weekend. The reverberations from the scene Marcus had walked into still echoed uncomfortably in her head.

'Of course *you* want to move,' Vanessa had accused her bitterly. 'This isn't your home. It never has been...'

It wasn't true, of course. Or was it? *Had* a part of her always perhaps secretly felt insecure of her tenure here somehow—her right to Marcus's love?

She frowned, disliking the thought and the doubts, the emotions they aroused.

Why was it that Vanessa possessed this skilful ability to enmesh her in the trap of her own insecurities and fears...insecurities and fears she did not always even know she possessed until Vanessa underlined them for her?

Sometimes it seemed as though Vanessa was actually trying to undermine her relationship with Marcus...their marriage. And yet why should she? Her parents' marriage had been over and their divorce complete long before Eleanor had ever met Marcus, and initially Vanessa had seemed to accept her readily enough.

Vanessa was a teenager, she reminded herself, and, like all teenagers, she was subject to unpredictable moods and emotions.

And besides, it was not her relationship with Vanessa she ought to be focusing on but her relationship with Marcus.

This week they had been treating one another with the kind of careful, almost hostile neutrality which would have seemed laughable at one time.

Was it really only a month or so ago that she had been congratulating herself on the success of their marriage, fully believing that there was nothing, no one that could come between them? Laughing about the doubts which had initially held her back from committing herself to Marcus.

It was not the quarrel between their children that was the cause of the resentment she could sense between them now. Not on her part, anyway. What *she* resented was not Marcus's irritability with their inability to get on with one another, but the fact that he seemed to assume that she was somehow, if not directly to blame for this state of affairs, then at least remiss in not somehow being able to remedy it. Why, after all, should she be the one to take on the responsibility for solving the problem? Couldn't he see that his very attitude towards it, towards her was making the whole situation worse? And it wasn't even as though she was not trying to do something. It was not her fault that Vanessa had taken such a violent dislike to the idea of their moving to Broughton House—a dislike which Eleanor suspected sprang partly from the fact that Tom had announced the news to her so unexpectedly, and partly because she herself had been the one to propose it.

'I did warn you,' Marcus had told her almost curtly when she had complained to him that Vanessa seemed to be deliberately trying to poison Tom and Gavin's minds against the move.

'But they're the ones we're doing this for,' Eleanor had protested. 'It's for their benefit as well as ours. Vanessa complains violently about the boys having to use her room. At Broughton House she'll be able to have her own privacy——'

'I can't make her like the idea, any more than you can,' Marcus had interrupted her flatly, his voice impatient and irritated.

Why was it that suddenly they seemed to be pulling in opposite directions instead of pulling together? It couldn't just be because of Vanessa, surely?

In the past, whatever differences they had had they had managed to compromise on quickly and tolerantly, but somehow now...

Was it because secretly she resented the way that, instead of helping her with the problem of their children's mutual antagonism, he seemed to be cutting himself off from it and leaving her to deal with it alone...was that why she was almost deliberately allowing the distance between them to harden and grow?

All he had said to her when she had confided to him her concern about Tom's fears was a brief injunction to contact both her ex-in-laws and Allan and Karen to discuss her concern with them.

'It's no good blaming Vanessa for the fact that Tom feels insecure,' he had pointed out logically.

Logic was one thing, but where was the compassion, the concern, the love which should have softened his judgement?

Listening to him, she had suddenly felt as though not just her sons but perhaps she as well had become a nuisance to him, a problem, interfering with the smooth flowing of his life. She had felt, for the first time since their relationship had begun, the cold, destructive sensation of wondering if he did really love her.

This quarrel between their children had done more than provoke them both into taking a defensive stance to protect their own offspring; it had opened up areas of vulnerability within their relationship she had never ever suspected could exist.

The phone rang just as she was finishing loading the dishwasher. She picked up the receiver, surprised to hear the sound of her ex-mother-in-law's voice.

Despite the problems of her first marriage and its eventual break-up, she had always remained on good terms with her ex-in-laws.

'It's the boys,' Mary told her now. 'You haven't been in touch to confirm that they'll be coming to us as usual for half-term, so I thought I'd better give you a ring. Actually, I wanted to have a chat with you anyway... I don't want you to think I'm fussing, but the last time they were here Tom was very quiet and withdrawn. Not a bit like his normal self...'

'Ring Mary and Jim and talk to them about Tom's feelings,' Marcus had told her, and because she had been annoyed with him, and hurt, because she had somehow, almost childishly, felt that he was supporting Vanessa over her, sweeping Tom's feelings to one side as unimportant, she had ignored his advice.

Quickly now and half guiltily she explained what had happened and how Tom felt that because of the new baby he and Gavin were no longer important to their grandparents.

'Oh, no... poor little Tom. We thought he and Gavin would enjoy having a larger room. I should have realised how he might feel, though. I feel so cross with myself for being so insensitive. Thank goodness you discovered how he felt... perhaps if Jim and I drove up to London to collect them this time instead of you bringing them down it might re-assure him a bit...'

After they had finished making all the necessary arrangements for Mary and Jim to collect the boys for their week's holiday with them, Eleanor rang Karen, her ex-husband's wife.

Since they had never been rivals there was no animosity between them. From what the boys said to her and from what she herself had seen until Karen's daughter had been born, she had established a very good and caring relationship with her stepsons.

Bearing this in mind, and heartened by what Mary had told her, Eleanor explained to Karen why she was ringing.

'I thought Tom was a bit quiet the last time he was here,' Karen confirmed. 'I did wonder if it was the baby. I've got a younger stepbrother myself, so I *do* know what it's like, but he's so loving with her that I thought I must be wrong...'

'It isn't the baby he resents,' Eleanor told her. 'It's more that he's frightened that he isn't going to be loved any more. I've tried to explain to him that when a new baby arrives in a family, for a while all the attention and excitement is focused on it. I think part of the problem is that he feels there isn't anywhere he can really call his own. His bedroom here is really Vanessa's...'

'And we've put the baby in the room here that used to be his. Oh, dear... I am glad you've told me about this Eleanor. The last thing I want is to alienate the boys from their father. I know myself how devastating that can be for a child.'

What was wrong with her? Eleanor wondered sadly once she had replaced the receiver. She had thought of herself as a mature, responsible, aware woman and yet here she had been, deliberately refusing to accept the validity of what Marcus was suggesting, almost as though she were a sulky child trying to punish an adult for some imagined crime.

All right, so she *was* under a lot of pressure, what with the business and the house and Vanessa, and a part of her *did* feel resentful that Marcus seemed to be leaving everything to her and abdicating his responsibilities as a partner in their shared lives; but to adopt such a childish and pointless attitude, like a child seeking attention... wanting to be coaxed and cajoled...

She prowled irritably round the kitchen, trying to come to terms with the discovery she had just made about herself, irritated by her reactions—and afraid of them.

'Nell? What are you doing up here?'

Eleanor tensed as Marcus walked into their bedroom.

'You said you had some work you wanted to do,' she reminded him. '*And* that you'd appreciate being allowed to get on with it in peace and quiet.'

She was sitting on the bed, brushing her hair, but now she stopped, watching him. Couldn't he see her anger and tension?

She saw from his face that he could.

'All I wanted was for the boys to turn the television down a bit—you've got to admit they do tend to have the volume turned up too loud...'

'Well, at least you can talk above it, which is more than can be said for Vanessa's radio,' she retaliated acidly. She saw the irritation tensing Marcus's body.

'Look, Nell, I know it isn't easy for you having Vanessa here, but what am I supposed to do? She's going through a bad patch at the moment.'

'And because of that the rest of us have to suffer? Don't *our* feelings and needs matter at all, Marcus... Mine and the boys'? I've tried my best to be patient and understanding with her. Do you think I'd ever stand by and let Tom or Gavin speak to you the way she did to me the other day?' she demanded bitterly, switching tack. 'Do you think I'd let *them* manipulate you... us... our relationship... or try to come between us?'

'Don't you, though?' Marcus challenged her quietly. 'Look at the way you're behaving now just because I asked them to keep the noise down. I told you before we married that I'm not the paternal type, Nell.'

'So what am I supposed to do, turn my back on my sons, abandon them? You can see the effect Vanessa is already having on Tom.'

'Is it Vanessa, or is it you?'

Eleanor stared at him. 'What do you mean...?'

'Think, Nell. Tom is a very sensitive child, too sensitive perhaps. Don't you think he's picked up on your ambivalent feelings towards Vanessa? Add to that the fact that he sees me as a rival for his mother's time and affection, and he's bound to feel resentful and confused.'

'Tom is *not* resentful,' Eleanor denied. 'Both he and Gavin were very happy when I told them we were getting married.'

'When you told them we were *getting* married perhaps. Look, I'm not saying they don't like me personally, but obviously they're bound to feel some resentment and apprehension—any child would. You do tend to look at relationships through rose-coloured glasses sometimes, Nell. I think I understand why, but there's nothing wrong with accepting that all of us at times have negative feelings about situations and people. In attempting to deny that, in not allowing Tom and Gavin the chance to admit and accept that there are times when they resent me and want to go back to having you exclusively for themselves, you're teaching them to suppress feelings it would be far healthier to acknowledge.'

'Like the way Vanessa acknowledges her dislike and resentment of me, do you mean?' Eleanor asked him bitterly. 'Is that what *you* think *I* should do, Marcus? Encourage my children to behave like your daughter?'

She was so angry that she was shaking, Eleanor recognised as the pressure of the last few days built up inside her, exploding into a fury she could scarcely control. 'And what makes you such an expert on childcare all of a sudden?'

She stood up, brushing vigorously at her hair and then wincing as it got tangled up in her brush, tears of anger and pain blurring her eyes.

'Vanessa's right, this place isn't my home. It's yours! Is it any wonder that the boys play up? They can probably sense that you don't want them here...'

'That's not true.'

Eleanor tensed as Marcus caught hold of her. 'Look, Nell, I know how difficult things are for you at the moment, but can't you understand, I'm under a lot of pressure as well. The last thing I need right now is...'

'The last thing *you* need?' Eleanor interrupted him. 'What about what I need...what about what Tom and Gavin need? They're unhappy, Marcus. They think we don't love them...that *I* don't love them.'

She pulled herself out of his arms, the frustration of what she was feeling welling up inside her as she flung her brush on to the bed and cried out fiercely, 'I can't live like this, Marcus. I——'

She tensed as he took hold of her again, turning her round to face him. Her heart was beating twice as fast as normal and she could feel the adrenalin-boosted surge of emotional reaction racing through her veins. Her senses suddenly seemed so much sharper, her awareness. She could smell the male heat of Marcus's anger, see the small beads of perspiration dotting the flesh in the open V of his shirt. It pleased her somehow that she had made him as angry as she was herself; that she had jolted him out of his normal calm control.

'Let go of me,' she told him furiously, pulling sharply back from him, but then, as he did so, her mood changed, startling her with its abrupt switch from hot, almost violent anger to equally uncharacteristic and uncontrollable tears.

'Nell.' She heard the echo of her own shock in Marcus's voice as he took hold of her.

'Nell. What is it...what's wrong?'

He was brushing the tears off her face, kissing her gently. Too gently.

She reached up, wrapping her arms around him, opening her mouth beneath his with a fierce urgency which took them both off guard.

His body responded immediately, challenging and exciting her.

Somewhere at the back of her mind lay the knowledge that their arousal, and its intensity, for the first time in their relationship had its roots in anger; but the need within her to release what she was feeling wouldn't let her listen to any warning voices.

When she touched Marcus, when she kissed him, when she pressed her body demandingly into his, it wasn't just with the knowledge of what she knew would arouse him but with an unfamiliar, satisfying selfish urgency.

Clothes were shed, quickly, almost roughly, her teeth impatiently savaging his bottom lip as she tugged at the barrier of his shirt, spreading her hands against his chest.

His skin felt hot and damp, the rapid hammer-beat of his heart echoing her own urgency.

He kissed the side of her neck, her breasts, not with his normal slow tenderness but with an intensity, a savagery almost that fell just short of pain.

In the morning she would be bruised; bruised and just a little shocked by the way they had both behaved. But right now...right now all she wanted was the compelling, urgent thrust of him deep within her body; now...now...not after he had tenderly and carefully aroused her with his loving gentle foreplay, but now!

Neither of them spoke, both of them caught up in the same explosive physical expression of their mutual anger.

They fell across the bed, Marcus rolling her beneath him. Eleanor could taste blood in her mouth. Hers? Marcus's? From when she had bitten his lip?

As he moved against her, she opened her legs, wrapping them demandingly around him, shivering in her fierce spasm of physical pleasure as he entered her.

Her nails raked his back, urging him deeper, deeper, her abandonment to her own need and to the release of the furies inside her so total that nothing else mattered.

Was it nature, some primeval illogical instinct, that caused this fierce need to feel him so deeply inside her, to experience a penetration so intense that when he came it would be virtually right into her womb? Nature's way of balancing fate in favour of conception rather than against it?

It was alien to her to want such a deeply physical form of love-making—her normal route to orgasm was a much gentler and slower affair; and yet now, fuelled by her anger and by Marcus's, her body was convulsing in fierce contracting waves so intense that they were almost as much a pain as a pleasure.

She could feel Marcus still shuddering as he held her in his arms, their sweat-slick bodies rapidly cooling. Just like their physical passion, and yet, as explosive as the physical desire between them had been, it had not really resolved anything.

The cold, unwanted thought crept into her brain that in encouraging, wanting him to make love to her like that, to overwhelm him so that he in turn would overwhelm her, she had perhaps been trying to prove to herself that she was more important to him than anything or anyone else... Anyone else... or Vanessa?

Cold now, she shivered.

'What is it... what's wrong?' Marcus asked her tersely.

She turned to look at him, wanting to explain how she felt and yet at the same time a part of her still feeling angry and resentful that she should need to... that she should feel that she had to somehow justify herself and her feelings, her actions to him.

'Look, forget about our mutual offspring for a few minutes...'

Irrationally, now that he had recognised what she was thinking, Eleanor felt even more irritated.

'Forget about them? It isn't that easy, Marcus. Vanessa is doing her level best to come between us, to——'

'Vanessa—why?'

'Vanessa is *your* child,' Eleanor pressed on fiercely, 'Not mine. I can't...'

'My child, my creation, my blame, is that what you're trying to say?' he asked her quietly. 'Vanessa, like every child ever created, is an individual, Nell. Yes, in some part her personality, her faults if you like, are genetic, inherited... a gift or a curse depending upon how you look at it. But she is a human being... not a piece of machinery I can programme and control. I don't like what's happening any more than you do but we can't force her compliance. The best we can hope for is that tolerance and awareness will develop with maturity. In the meantime... In the meantime,' he sighed wearily, 'it might help if she were offered a little less provocation. Couldn't you have seen to it that Tom's posters were removed before she arrived?'

'Yes. Perhaps I could,' Eleanor agreed irritably, swamped by her own anger and sense of ill-usage. 'If you had stuck to our original arrangement and picked Vanessa up, then I might have had time to get the bedrooms properly organised. I *might* have had time to spend with the agent as well... and time to finish the translation I've been working on all week...'

The dark mobile eyebrows lifted slightly, the cool grey eyes suddenly cold and hard. 'All that in less than an hour. What a marvel you are, Nell. You must teach me how you do it.'

They made it up later, of course... on the surface at least; but underneath... Eleanor sighed under her breath. What was the matter with her? She was behaving almost as much like a teenager at times as Vanessa.

Tonight when Marcus came home she would talk to him, try to explain. Perhaps if she could persuade the boys to have supper early and watch television in their own room she and Marcus could eat alone... She could make his favourite pasta dish, open a bottle of wine... wash her hair and put on something special... that red jersey dress he had bought her from Jean Muir, the one he had once whispered that he preferred her to wear without undies.

Suddenly feeling a lot more cheerful, she started humming. If she was going to cook she'd better check the fridge... a little bribery for the boys might not be a bad idea either. After all, burgers once in a while weren't going to mean the end of the world.

'What's that?' Tom demanded suspiciously, pulling a face over the sauce on the hob.

'It's not for you,' Eleanor assured him. 'By the way,' she added, 'Nanna rang this morning. She and Grandad are going to come and pick you up on Saturday morning for half-term, so anything you want to take with you... It will just be the two of you, by the way. Daddy will probably call round to see you, but Karen and the baby...'

She broke off as she saw the look they were exchanging, her heart sinking a little.

'What is it? What's wrong?' she asked them.

'Nothing,' Tom told her.

'No... we don't mind about the baby any more,' Gavin piped up. 'Not now that Marcus has explained to us that Dad wouldn't stop loving us just because we weren't there all the time and she was, and that people always made a big fuss about babies but that it didn't mean they loved them more.'

Eleanor put down the spoon she had been using to stir the sauce.

'When did Marcus tell you that, Gavin?' she asked him quietly. Marcus had said nothing to *her* about speaking to the children. In fact, when she had lost her temper with him and accused him of leaving dealing with the problems they were having to her she had gained the impression that he felt she was making a fuss about nothing and that her concern was simply exacerbating the situation.

'On Sunday. After he had explained to us about Vanessa being angry with you and tearing up Tom's poster. He said he knew it was difficult for us when Vanessa came to stay. When he was a little boy he didn't have any brothers or sisters and his mother would never let him have his friends round to play in case they made a mess. He said that that made him so cross that one day he deliberately broke one of his grandmother's ornaments.

'He spoke to you as well, didn't he, Tom?'

Eleanor turned towards her elder son, who nodded. 'And to Vanessa,' he told her. 'And then he spoke to all of us together. He said that we were a family now and that in families people were allowed not to like one another sometimes and to get angry and that it didn't mean that we would always be angry and not like each other... I don't think I'm ever going to like Vanessa, though——'

'Yes,' Gavin interrupted excitedly. 'And then Tom said that he would hate Vanessa forever for what she did to his posters, and Marcus said that that was OK but that he would have to be careful because hating people got to be a habit and before he knew it he could end up hating everyone—even himself.

'Marcus said that hating people was like carrying a heavy parcel, and that the longer you had to carry it, the heavier it got until it got so heavy that you couldn't do anything any more.'

'Vanessa said she was sick of people always telling her what to do, and that she was sick of us as well,' Tom said.

'Yes, and then she burst into tears,' Gavin added. 'And she said that she knew that none of us wanted her here and that was all right because she didn't want to be here. She said she wished she'd never been born and then she ran upstairs and shut herself in her bedroom and wouldn't come out.

'Marcus said girls did things like that sometimes...'

Why had Marcus said nothing to her about any of this...why had he let her think that he was indifferent to what was going on...irritated and impatient with it?

Perhaps because she had not given him the opportunity to say anything to the contrary?

Marcus was not the kind of man who relished arguments or emotional scenes.

He had never really discussed his family background with her early on in their relationship, and it was only after they had been lovers for some time that he had finally and almost reluctantly told her about his childhood and the confusion... the tug of loyalties he had felt, witnessing the relationship which existed between his parents and the way his mother and grandmother appeared constantly to demean and criticise his father.

'I used to wonder why he allowed them to do it. It was only as I grew older myself that I realised it was probably because he had discovered, as I was doing, that there was nothing my grandmother in particular loved more than to provoke an argument...that she actually seemed to derive some sort of perverse enjoyment from the verbal battle.

'Had her arguments been logical I could have understood it, but they never were and she always had to win, no matter what kind of underhand or destructive emotional cruelty she had to use to do so. It was no wonder my father simply gave up and opted for peace and quiet.'

'It must have been very upsetting for you,' Eleanor had said gently, sensing that too much sympathy would be construed as pity and knowing that his pride would flinch away from that kind of emotion.

'It was certainly very educational. It taught me a good deal about human psychology. Men as much as women are equally capable of that kind of emotional and verbal bullying. One thing it did give me, though, and that was a lasting dislike of emotional scenes and outbursts.'

Eleanor bit her lip fretfully now. She could understand Marcus's dislike of scenes, given his childhood, but surely he could understand how upset she had been...? Vanessa was not her child. She could not discipline her in the same way she could the boys.

But she could perhaps have stayed a little calmer. If she had not been so on edge about the business and the house...

The house. She closed her eyes and took a deep breath. Nothing in her life seemed straightforward at the moment.

But it would all be different, better once they had moved house, she promised herself as she tried to quell her feelings of guilt.

Tonight over dinner she would talk to Marcus, ask him why he had not told her he had spoken with the boys and Vanessa. Explain how vulnerable and overstretched she was feeling. She frowned... Would she? One of the things Marcus had always said he admired about her was her calmness, her ability to cope and run her life smoothly. Marcus liked efficiency, calmness and order.

How would he feel if she tried to explain to him that panic she some-times felt these days...the feeling that her life was running out of control, that she was being swamped by a slow, stultifying tide of calls upon her time, of things she never seemed to have time to do properly? She felt sometimes as though that tide was so oppressive that it was actually squeezing the breath out of her lungs, the life out of her body. She felt cramped, constricted...imprisoned by it to an extent that her need for the space, the peace, the harmony that Broughton House would bring had become as necessary mentally as it was physically.

By eight o'clock the boys had had their supper and were upstairs watching television. The dining-room table was laid with silver and crystal. She had done her face and hair, and when she walked to the wardrobe to get the Jean Muir she caught the tantalising fragrance of the layers of bath oil, body cream and perfume that clung to her skin.

Was it really only such a short time ago that she had taken this much care every evening ... that she had spent almost as long getting ready for, anticipating her dates with Marcus as she actually had with him?

That had been in the early days of their relationship, of course. A time of greatly heightened excitement and intensity, which now somehow seemed slightly unreal. She smiled a little wryly to herself, remembering that other Eleanor and Marcus.

At half-past eight, when Marcus had still not come home, she dialled the number of his chambers.

The telephone rang for a long time before he answered it, his voice crisp and slightly impatient. Was it thinking about the past and when she had first known him that caused her heart to lurch with that half-forgotten sensation of pleasure and panic? Eleanor wondered.

'You're late,' she told him. 'I thought you'd be home by now.'

There was a small, almost sharp pause, alerting her senses, chilling the warm, sensuous anticipation.

'We're having a meeting here in chambers,' Marcus told her tersely. 'I did tell you, Nell. I shan't be back until late. We've got one or two important things to discuss...'

Eleanor could sense his impatience and irritation. He had said something about a meeting, she remembered guiltily, but she had obviously not registered it properly. She had also, she suspected, interrupted him at a bad moment, to judge from the tone of his voice. She was about to apologise when he continued grimly, 'Perhaps if you weren't so wrapped up in other things you might have remembered...'

And then, before she could say a word, he had replaced the receiver.

Slowly Eleanor replaced hers. She was *not* going to cry, she told herself fiercely. It was a misunderstanding, that was all. They were both adults. They both loved one another. They were both mature and understood that sometimes things were said ... things were done ... No, she was not going to cry, she repeated tiredly to herself as she lifted her hand to wipe the dampness from her face.

CHAPTER SEVENTEEN

'ELEANOR, is that you?'

Eleanor tensed as she heard the pretty, girlish tones of Marcus's ex-wife's voice.

'I've been trying to get hold of Marcus for ages but they keep on telling me he isn't there. Something about him being in conference with a client. You'd think his own daughter would be more important to him than someone he doesn't even really know...' Peevishness was spoiling the girlishness now.

'Logic is a concept Julia simply doesn't accept,' Marcus had once told her, and, listening to her now, Eleanor could understand what he meant.

'Is something wrong with Vanessa?' she asked. 'Is she ill?'

'Not ill, no. It's just that I'm going to have to fly out to LA earlier than expected—this weekend in fact, which means that Vanessa will have to come to you and I wanted to tell Marcus that he'd have to pick her up on Friday evening because my flight is early on Saturday morning. I can't bring her down. She can't come down on the train. If she's going to be with you for several months she'll need...'

'Several *months*?' Eleanor could hear the sharpness of her own voice.

'Well, Marcus had already agreed to have her for the summer, and now that I'm leaving a few weeks early...'

'But what about her schooling?' Eleanor protested.

'Oh, I've explained everything to her headmistress and she's arranging for her teachers to provide her with some coursework she can do at home. She'll only be missing a few weeks, after all...what with half-term and then the time she'd have off while they're preparing the upper classes for their exams. Oh, and by the way, she'll be bringing a friend with her...just for the week of half-term. Look, I must go, Eleanor, I've got a thousand and one things to do before I leave. You won't forget to tell Marcus about picking Vanessa up, will you?'

'She can't do this to us. You can't let her,' Eleanor protested bitterly to Marcus later. 'I *know* you agreed we would have her for the summer, but this...'

'Well, at least the boys won't be here.'

'No, but can't you see how this is going to look to them? They'll think that they're being pushed out of the way to make room for Vanessa and her friend. It's too much, Marcus. I'm way behind with my work and then there's the house...I've had to go down there twice this week already. The architect's worried that there might be problems with the kitchen conversion...something about the danger of removing too many internal walls, and he thinks the septic tank might be leaking as well. Spring's now become early summer and we don't seem to be much further on.'

Tiredly she pushed her hand into her hair, her face tense. 'I was looking forward to us having this week on our own.'

'Were you?' His voice sounded dry. 'It doesn't sound as though there would have been much time. Have you heard anything from Louise recently about the winding up of the business?'

'Only an acknowledgement of my letter setting out the details of my meeting with the agent. I need Louise's signature on some cheques. At least she's now given me an address and phone number for the times when she's away setting things up in France. I'll have to try and ring her...' She chewed anxiously on her bottom lip.

'I've got a better idea. Why don't you get the agent and everyone else to get in touch with Louise direct, instead of shouldering her responsibilities for her? You can't do everything, Nell, you're not omnipotent,' Marcus told her tersely. 'That way perhaps you and I can have a bit more time for other things.'

Other things? Like looking after his daughter? 'No,' she agreed lightly, suppressing her thoughts. 'If I were omnipotent, the boys wouldn't end up with so many pairs of odd socks.'

Why was it she felt that his comment was more a criticism than an expression of concern?

'That's something else I've got to do...pack their stuff for half-term. It's going to be chaos here on Friday night with four of them.'

'If you didn't want Vanessa here you should have told Julia so,' Marcus interrupted her, coldly.

Eleanor stared at him. 'Marcus! How could I...?'

'Quite easily. All you had to do was to tell Julia that it wasn't possible for us to have Vanessa and that she would have to delay her departure until it was. As it is, you've agreed now and it's too late.'

'There wasn't anything else I *could* do,' Eleanor protested, adding sharply, 'Perhaps if she'd been able to speak to you...' She stopped abruptly.

What were they *doing*? What was happening to them lately? There seemed to be so much tension in their relationship, so much irritation. And it wasn't just caused by Vanessa's unexpected and unwanted visit.

There had been a growing distance between them recently, a growing feeling on her part of having to cope with things on her own, of Marcus somehow detaching himself from the myriad irritating problems that continued to spring up over their house move, so that she felt increasingly isolated from him and increasingly resentful about his lack of awareness of the pressure she was under.

She had been looking forward to a few days on their own; looking forward to having time to discuss their plans for the house, to even perhaps persuading him to take some time off and go down there with her.

It irked her that Marcus seemed to think that she was at fault for agreeing to have Vanessa. What else could she have done, faced with the relentless pressure from Julia?

In the end she had to ring her ex-in-laws and ask if it was possible for them to pick up the boys on Friday. Luckily it was. She then had to work until gone midnight on Thursday evening—the only evening of the week when Marcus managed to get home early—in order to finish a translation she had promised a client for Friday, so that on Friday she could spend the day getting the boys' things ready, and then preparing their room for Vanessa and her friend.

When the architect rang halfway through Friday afternoon to announce that he needed to meet her at the house the following week to discuss several things with her she did some mental calculations with her schedule, acknowledging to herself that the only way she could do so would be if she were to take Vanessa and her friend with her.

Which might not be a bad idea, she told herself when she replaced the receiver. It would give Vanessa a chance to see the house for herself and Eleanor was convinced that once she had seen it she would stop being so difficult about the move.

Vanessa, the boys, and even it sometimes seemed Marcus himself to some extent... why *couldn't* they see and appreciate what she was trying to do?

That evening, as she waved the boys off, she told herself that it was ridiculous to feel hurt by the excited eagerness with which they had greeted their grandparents.

She had told them about Vanessa's visit but Tom had simply shrugged and said that he didn't care.

'Grandad is going to build a new garden shed and we're going to help him,' he had added excitedly. 'He wrote to me and told me.'

It was later than she had expected when Marcus returned with the two girls, and as the three of them walked into the hall and Eleanor saw Vanessa's friend her heart sank.

The other girl looked at least two years older than Vanessa and far more sophisticated, her face covered in thick pale make-up, her eyes outlined in dark kohl and her lips a vivid pouting scarlet. The eyes between the thickly mascaraed lashes were surely far too knowing and cynical for a girl of her age, and the short skirt and tight-fitting skimpy top, like the body they barely covered, so blatantly sexual that Eleanor felt not so much shocked by them as somehow slightly intimidated and embarrassed.

And the girl seemed to know it too. The look she gave Eleanor was both challenging and hostile, causing Eleanor's heart to sink even further. Did Julia honestly believe that this girl was a suitable friend for someone as impressionable as Vanessa?

Marcus, who had walked into the hall behind the girls, looked irritable and tense. As he put down their cases Vanessa's friend turned and sidled up to him, smiling archly at him as she thanked him.

'Come on, Sasha. My room's this way,' Vanessa announced, totally ignoring Eleanor as she headed for the stairs. After another lingeringly sexual look at Marcus the other girl followed.

'Don't say a word,' Marcus warned her as the bedroom door closed behind them. 'Just remember this was your idea, not mine.'

She was too tired to argue with him and point out to him that all she had done was take his ex-wife's phone call. Eleanor still felt both angry and hurt.

The weekend was a nightmare, culminating in Vanessa's locking herself in her bedroom, playing music so loudly that Eleanor felt as though the whole fabric of the house was shaking with it, when she was forbidden to accompany her friend to a nightclub the other girl apparently knew.

In the end Sasha announced that since Vanessa had to stay in she might as well stay with her. She seemed more condescendingly amused by them than anything else, Eleanor recognised. From odd comments she made it became clear that she had only recently moved to Vanessa's school and that she was living in a foster home.

'It was Mum's new fella. She didn't like the fact that he fancied me so she got the council to take me. Said I was getting out of control.' She had shrugged, apparently unconcerned, leaving Eleanor to question just how much Julia knew about her daughter's new friend.

By Monday morning, Eleanor didn't know how on earth she was going to get through the week.

The combination of Vanessa's sullen defiance and Sasha's aggressive sexuality were beginning to wear her nerves as raw as sandpaper on fine skin.

On Monday, when Eleanor announced that she had to meet the architect at the house and that she intended taking them with her, Vanessa immediately objected.

'We're not children, you know,' she told Eleanor bitterly. 'We don't need *you* standing over us all day long like a guard dog.'

Sasha leaned across the table and made some whispered comment to Vanessa that made her both flush and laugh. Eleanor could feel her own skin start to burn. Marcus had left early before the girls had come down.

'You're not my mother,' Vanessa added challengingly. 'I don't have to do what *you* say.' For a moment Eleanor was tempted to retaliate by pointing out that neither was she obliged to put up with her rudeness...or even her presence, but somehow she managed to stop herself.

Instead Eleanor forced herself to ignore Vanessa's unpleasantness and aggressiveness and say calmly instead, 'I'd really like you to come with me, Vanessa. I thought you'd like to see the house and we could stop somewhere nice for lunch if you like.'

'I don't know. What do you think, Sasha?'

Eleanor tried not to let her real feelings show as the other girl shifted her chewing gum from one side of her mouth to the other and then shrugged.

'Might as well, I suppose. Where is it, then, this house?'

'It's in Wiltshire,' Eleanor told her as pleasantly as she could. 'Just outside a very pretty country town.'

'Country...' The thin shoulders moved again. 'You wouldn't catch me moving from a place like this to the country. Wicked, this is,' she added admiringly, 'right in the middle of London. The country's gross.'

'Oh, is this it?'

Eleanor could hear the contempt in Vanessa's voice as she stared round the town square.

'This is Avondale, yes,' Eleanor responded as evenly as she could. 'I thought we'd have lunch in the pub here. It dates back to the fifteenth century and——'

'Just like the people who live here,' Sasha interrupted before she could finish, sniggering as she pointed out a couple of young girls standing on the opposite side of the square to Vanessa.

'Are they gross, or what?' she demanded. 'Just look at their clothes.'

'But why can't we eat in the bar?' Vanessa protested as Eleanor ushered them towards the dining-room. 'It's so stuffy in here.'

The bar had been crowded with several groups of men and youths, but even if it hadn't been *she* would not have chosen to eat there, Eleanor admitted as she compared the noise and discomfort of the busy bar area to the comfort and peace of the dining-room.

She had eaten at the pub before on a previous visit. The waiter remembered her and smiled shyly at her. He was only young and obviously a little nervous, but he was pleasant despite that. Pleasant and well-mannered.

Unlike Vanessa and Sasha, who were having a whispered conversation punctuated with giggles.

She suspected that the boy knew as well as she did that he was the subject of their amusement.

If Vanessa had been her own daughter there was no way she would have tolerated such rude behaviour, but then, if Vanessa had been her daughter, she would not have felt so hampered by her need to constantly remind herself that good and wise stepmothers did not attempt to take over the real mother's role.

Throughout the meal Vanessa and Sasha continued to giggle and whisper to each other. Something in the main bar seemed to be amusing them but since Eleanor had her back to the open doorway she could not see who or what it was.

It was a relief to Eleanor when the meal was finally over. While the girls went to the cloakroom, Eleanor stayed behind to pay the bill.

Because of some confusion over exactly what they had ordered—hardly surprising really in view of the number of times the girls had changed their minds—it was a good fifteen minutes before the bill was actually settled. More than time enough, surely, for the girls to have rejoined her?

Frowning, Eleanor left the dining-room and headed for the cloakroom, stopping abruptly when she saw Vanessa standing with her back to her, apparently deep in conversation with a leather-clad boy. Sasha was standing next to her talking with two others.

Suppressing her real feelings, Eleanor made her way towards them, forcing herself to smile as she firmly stepped between Vanessa and the boy and, facing Vanessa, said calmly, 'Ready? It's time we were going otherwise we'll be late for the architect.'

She hadn't missed the glass in Vanessa's hand but since she didn't want to provoke an argument she didn't ask her what had been in it. Vanessa was under age and so too, for all her aggressive sophistication, was Sasha.

When both girls followed her without comment she was so relieved that she decided to say nothing about their behaviour, although she suspected that Marcus would not have been so reticent.

As she drove towards the house she tried to quieten the conscience that told her that for Vanessa's own sake she ought to say something to her about the dangers of being picked up by unknown men, to warn her of the risks she could be taking in engaging in what on the surface might appear to be a harmless flirtation.

At fourteen Vanessa was still too young for any kind of emotional or sexual relationship and experimentation. But not too young to be very sexually aware and curious. Vanessa and Sasha probably considered her to be old-fashioned and out of touch, but Eleanor could remember from her own school days the handful of girls who had been sexually active at well below the legally permitted age.

The architect's car was already parked outside the house when they got there and he was waiting for them.

Within minutes of them going inside, Eleanor recognised that, far from being impressed and excited about the house, Vanessa was doing her best to be as destructive as possible.

'Do we have to stay in here with you? Can't we go outside?' she complained.

Exasperated and embarrassed and sensing the architect's impatience, Eleanor nodded her head.

When they had gone Eleanor listened to the architect, her heart sinking. It was obvious from what he was saying that he had serious doubts about the viability of the alterations they needed to carry out.

'Are you saying that we can't convert this area into one large living kitchen?' she asked him.

'I'm afraid not. Too many of the existing walls are load-bearing supports. I know how keen you are on the house,' he added quietly. 'And it *is* a lovely setting, but quite honestly...' He paused and looked thoughtfully at her. 'I don't want to seem a pessimist, but in your shoes I'd seriously consider looking for somewhere else.'

Tiredly Eleanor thanked him and walked with him to his car. Her dreams of buying the house and living within its walls, her dreams of what family life and togetherness should really be, were becoming so tarnished and bruised that she couldn't even close her eyes any more and visualise the transformations she had originally been so happily confident could be made.

As she walked back to the house and locked it with the set of keys the agent had lent her, she glanced at her watch and frowned.

Where *were* the girls? She had warned them not to be gone more than half an hour.

She turned round, scanning what she could see of the grounds.

They couldn't have gone very far, surely? Like her, neither of them were dressed for wandering through the garden's wildly overgrown undergrowth.

She called their names, her frown deepening when there was no response. In view of the contempt both of them had expressed for the countryside she was surprised that they were so keen to explore it rather than look round the house.

She had brought Vanessa with her in the hope that once she saw the house she would become more proprietorial about it, feel more involved in their plans.

She had envisaged discussing with her which room she would like, what kind of bathroom, what kind of décor and colour schemes, hoping by discussing these aspects of the move with her to win her interest and enthusiasm, but she had quickly recognised that as long as Sasha was with her this was impossible.

She called their names again and when there was no response she sighed under her breath. Where on earth were they?

Grimly she set off down the path which led to the boundary wall of the property and circled round inside it, linking the small iris-filled dell and the pool with small copses of trees and cleverly planned vistas.

Eleanor had explored this path on a previous visit, marvelling at the patience and care which had gone into its planning; even now, when so much was overgrown and out of control, it was still possible to see how it must have once been; flowers carpeting the ground beneath the trees, carefully planned seats and even a small, almost secret arbour all designed to encourage the walker to pause to admire the way the garden had been planned to almost reluctantly and shyly reveal its pleasures and secrets. But on that occasion she had been dressed for that kind of exploration.

Today she wasn't. Today, because she had had to spend so much time chivvying the girls to get ready, she hadn't even remembered to put a pair of low-heeled shoes in the boot of the car. Instead she was having to negotiate the path wearing an almost brand new pair of matt black Charles Jourdan court shoes with thin, delicate heels. Her equally fragile and expensive tights didn't last beyond the first few yards of the overgrown path; the bramble which ripped them lacerated her leg as well, leaving a long, ugly scratch from which blood was already starting to ooze.

As she stood up from stooping to check and examine it, a whippy branch of elder stung against her cheek and left a dark mark on the sleeve of her cream silk shirt. It was a new one, a Donna Karan Jade had persuaded her to buy in Harvey Nichols' sale.

She had worn it this morning on impulse, because Marcus had liked the way the soft fabric hung, telling her that it was not just the silk itself that was so subtly provocative, but that the way it outlined her breasts had an immediate eye and touch appeal that he found difficult to resist.

And so this morning, when her fingers had brushed against it in the wardrobe, her eyes had softened with the memories it evoked and she had impulsively put it on.

To give her confidence ... to remind her of Marcus's desire for her?

She tensed briefly. Why should she need to do either? To impress Vanessa and her friend, then? Her mouth curled ruefully into the smile that Marcus had first fallen in love with, the smile that said she was a woman who was tender with other people's vanities and vulnerabilities and aware of her own.

This resurgence of her sense of humour, though, was only brief—all it took to banish it once again was the sound of the girls' voices, and not just theirs, but male voices as well.

She saw them before they saw her, and it only added to her anger that it was the pretty dell which had so appealed to her that they had chosen for their rendezvous; and an arranged rendezvous it must have been, because there was no way these leather-clad youths with their pallid skin and loose-muscled bodies could ever have simply happened to be walking past.

As they turned to watch her, Vanessa's expression hostile and aggressive, Sasha's openly contemptuous and amused, the boys' wary, uncertain, the silence seemed to press down on her.

She could feel her heart beating and her body tensing, her clothes clinging stickily to her body. She felt slightly sick, anger and relief warring inside her.

Vanessa was Marcus's daughter, but *her* responsibility, and as she looked into her stepdaughter's hostile, tense face she could feel the bitter taste of failure and guilt rising up in her throat.

'Vanessa ...' She could hear the harshness in her voice, feel it tearing at her throat. 'Didn't you hear me calling you? What's going on?'

She could see Sasha smirking at her and cursed herself for the banality, the predictability of her reactions, but how could she explain to Vanessa how afraid she was, how shocked not just by her behaviour but by her own inability to predict it, to protect her from the consequences of it? What if she had not found them...what if those boys...?

She shuddered, visualising herself going back to tell Marcus that Vanessa had disappeared...

Out of the corner of her eye she saw the smoke curling up from the cigarette Vanessa was still holding awkwardly in her hand as though unfamiliar with the act of smoking it, unlike Sasha, who took a deliberate lungful of smoke and exhaled it with casual expertise, challenging her...daring her to say or do anything.

The boys, less aggressive and dangerous than she had first feared, were already melting away. As she saw the vulnerable, almost panicky look Vanessa gave their disappearing backs, Eleanor felt her own heart soften in quick sympathy, but when Vanessa turned back to look at her the resentment and loathing in her eyes quickly reminded Eleanor of reality.

'Vanessa——' she repeated quietly, but she wasn't allowed to continue.

'*You* can't tell me what to do,' Vanessa interrupted her hotly. 'I wasn't doing anything wrong, anyway.'

Nothing wrong. Eleanor looked pointedly at the cigarette Vanessa was still holding.

'I don't think your father would agree with that defence, do you, Vanessa?'

'Oh, trust you to bring Dad into it. I'll bet you just can't wait to tell him, can you? I hate you and I wish he'd never married you, but you can't stop me doing what I want. Tell Dad if you like, I don't care. It was you who made us come here. Boring, dull place.'

Her face was flushed with anger and defiance now, the hot colour overlying the greenish hue it had had earlier.

How long had she been smoking? Only recently, Eleanor suspected. Surely she knew the dangers of what she was doing? She couldn't not, she was an intelligent girl—and as for the other danger...

Eleanor looked round the small, enclosed place trying not to ignore the images her imagination was creating. Two girls on their own, vulnerable and provocative...those boys...her skin felt clammy and cold.

'Have you any idea of what could have happened?' she demanded, unable to hold back her feelings any longer. 'Those boys...'

'We were *talking*, that's all,' Vanessa told her.

'You had no right to arrange to meet them without asking me,' Eleanor countered. 'I may not be your mother,' she added, anticipating Vanessa's familiar protest, 'but while you're with me you *are* my responsibility. Have you any idea how I would feel if I had to go back and tell your father...?'

'Oh, yes...that's all you care about, isn't it? What *Dad* thinks. You don't care about me at all, really. Go on, admit it—secretly you'd love it if I just disappeared...if someone did murder me. Well...'

'Vanessa, that's *not* true!'

'Liar,' Vanessa taunted her softly, throwing down her cigarette and adding angrily, 'Well, go ahead. Tell Dad what you like...*I* don't care.'

Eleanor closed her eyes, warning herself that there was no point in provoking Vanessa into a full-scale row, especially not in front of Sasha.

Was it that, she asked herself tiredly, or was it more that she simply felt too overwhelmed to tackle all the issues Vanessa's behaviour had raised...?

What would she have done, *said* had Vanessa been her own daughter? Or did she secretly believe that her own child would never have behaved in such a way?

As she turned back down the path, shepherding them in front of her, Eleanor wondered what was worse: their deliberate deceit or the fact that, despite her intelligence, Vanessa was apparently either unaware or un-caring of the damage smoking would do to her health? And added to that was the spine-chilling cold shock of very real fear Eleanor had ex-perienced when she had first seen them.

No doubt the boys were harmless enough, for all their unappealing physical appearance. They had certainly, unlike Sasha, showed no incli-nation to force any kind of confrontation when they saw her; but what if things had been different...what if they had been more worldly...more aggressive? Was she being hyper-cynical in feeling that it hadn't just been for a cigarette and a chat that they had followed up on the invitation which either Sasha or Vanessa or both had issued to them?

She did not for a moment believe that Vanessa had had anything sexual in mind, but that was the whole point. From the look on her face after she had thrown her cigarette away, the greenish pallor of her skin, Eleanor suspected that the smoking had been more out of bravado and peer pressure than anything else.

Just supposing another kind of peer pressure had been put on her— or, even worse, actual physical force?

Her stomach churning with anxiety and with guilt as well, Eleanor didn't notice the tangle of roots until she tripped over them.

As she put out her hand to steady herself she saw Sasha and Vanessa turn round to watch her, and heard Sasha sniggering at her as a rough tear was added to the existing damage to her clothes.

The drive back to London was completed in a silence that was only broken when Vanessa demanded challengingly, 'I suppose you're going to go running to Dad now. Well, we weren't doing anything wrong. Just talking... It must be true that middle-aged women get all hysterical about things,' she added insultingly.

'Look, Vanessa,' Eleanor began impatiently, and then stopped. On another occasion she might have just laughed; as it was she felt too drained, too shaken by her own fears about what might have happened, her own guilt for not being more aware, for being so gullible and foolish, to do anything other than to remain silent.

She would *have* to tell Marcus, of course. Not to punish Vanessa but for her own protection. There was obviously no point in her trying to explain to the girl the very real danger she could have been inviting, never mind discuss with her how she really felt about the deceit involved in setting up the meeting in the first place.

Teenage girls liked and even needed secrets they could share with one another, giggles, whispered conversations, long, deep talks about boys and 'things'. Letting them have secrets, respecting their privacy and acknowledging their transition from the protected dependency of childhood to the independence of adulthood were one thing; tolerating and accepting outright deceit, coupled with the teenagers' awareness that they were being deceitful and why, was another.

Eleanor tensed as she picked up the post which had been delivered while they were out. Almost immediately on their return to the house the two girls had gone upstairs to Vanessa's room and the loudness of the music now coming from it was beginning to make Eleanor's teeth ache as well as her head.

As she looked through the mail she wondered how long it would be before the neighbours started to complain about the noise.

Perhaps *that* was something she ought to have pointed out to Vanessa, she decided ruefully—the advantages of living in isolation with no one to complain about any noisy teenage predilection for over-loud music!

She frowned, pausing to study a typed envelope addressed to her in French bearing a French stamp.

Assuming it was from Louise and would contain the signed papers she needed to complete the final winding up of the partnership, Eleanor put the rest of the post down and opened it.

It wasn't from Louise. Much to her astonishment it was from Pierre Colbert, a totally unexpected follow-up to their meeting, explaining that since he had been unable to get a response from her partner to his request for her private fax or telephone number he was having to write to her.

What he wanted to know was whether she would still be interested in taking on some of his translation work. He had contacted her partner—who had written to him informing him of the dissolution of their partnership in the first instance—hoping to discover whether he could get in touch with Eleanor, since he had been unable to get any reply from her office telephone. Eleanor's frown intensified as she read this, since one of the few duties Louise had taken on after they had agreed to end the partnership had been that she would make arrangements for their telephone and fax calls to be diverted to Eleanor's home number. Now it seemed that, instead, not just her own calls but Eleanor's as well were being diverted, but to Louise's number.

Now, though, there was some urgency in the matter, as he was due to begin a business trip to the Far East at the end of the month and had really wished to have a meeting with her before this in order that they could talk. If Eleanor was interested in his translation work, he went on to say, he had hoped that she would be able to travel to Provence where he had his headquarters, at his expense of course, so that they could discuss everything. If she *was* interested and felt able to take the work on he asked that she telephone him, adding that, unfortunately, the only time he would be able to see her now would be during the following ten days.

Shakily Eleanor put down the letter. She had had to accept the rift which had developed between herself and Louise and the loss of someone whom she hadn't seen just as a business partner but as a friend as well, but this new evidence of Louise's underhandedness still had the power to hurt her.

Louise was not proficient in modern European languages and could surely never have hoped to get Pierre Colbert to give her the contract, which meant that her only purpose in neglecting to organise the passing on of her own telephone number to him had been mean-spiritedness and nastiness. She had obviously felt obliged to give him her home address, but Louise must have hoped the news of the work would come too late— if at all.

What hurt even more was that Louise knew how concerned she had been about losing work through the break-up of their partnership; she had even admitted then that she was especially anxious to do as much as she could to maintain the level of her income because of the expense of moving house.

Yes, Louise knew how much this contract would have meant to her, and if she had been able to be in contact with Pierre Colbert in time she could perhaps have arranged to see him earlier. As it was . . . She sighed as she studied the date of the letter. As it was, there was no way she could go to France while she had Vanessa and Sasha here, and since Pierre Colbert specified that he wanted to have something sorted out before he left for the Far East that must surely mean that he already had someone else in mind should she not be able to take on the contract.

Later in the evening, when she was discussing the letter with Marcus, she told him tiredly, 'It's impossible for me to go, of course. I shall have to ring Monsieur Colbert and tell him.'

Marcus frowned as he listened to her. What had happened to the Eleanor he had fallen in love with and married; the Eleanor who had charmed and delighted him with her laughter and her happy, confident, positive attitude towards life? *That* Eleanor had always had time to listen to his problems, to be interested and involved in his life. *That* Eleanor had made him feel that he featured prominently in her life. This Eleanor seemed to be more interested in a house than she was in him. A house and their children. Even when they were in bed together at night she talked about it, about them, worried about it.

What was wrong with him? he asked himself irritably. He was a man, not a boy, who ought to know himself well enough to understand that the irritation, the resentment, the jealousy almost he was feeling now came not from Eleanor's preoccupation with Broughton House, but with the spill-over from his own childhood feeling that his mother did not love him; that the mere fact that he belonged to the same sex as his poor despised father made it impossible for her to love him.

His grandmother's attitude towards him had reinforced this feeling, and so had his first marriage to Julia.

It had taken him a long time to accept that a part of him must have deliberately chosen as his first wife a woman who he should have known instinctively would cause him to repeat within his relationship with her the same needy rejected role he had experienced with his mother and grandmother.

With Eleanor it had been different; right from the start he had not merely been attracted to her physically, but had also been aware of how very different she was from the other women who had taken prominent roles in his life. Eleanor had a vulnerability, a gentleness, a warmth and genuine compassion for others that he now recognised they had lacked.

In the initial stages of their relationship, her sexual hesitancy and insecurity had helped to bond them together, his awareness of her insecurity making it easier for him to acknowledge, even if it was only privately to himself, his own emotional need. Her relationship with her sons, her love and care of them had never made him feel threatened or jealous. Her agreement that their relationship, their love for one another was strong enough not to need any additional cementing with the conception of a child of their own had strengthened not just his love for her, but his feeling of security as well.

And yet now, he recognised, he not only felt angry and resentful, he also felt threatened somehow too.

Because of a house? Because of the way Vanessa spoke to her? Why were they important enough to her to dominate their relationship? Wasn't what they shared enough? Did she, despite all she had said to him, perhaps not love him as totally as he had thought? Was this obsession she had over the house just a way of trying to conceal from herself, from them both her awareness that their relationship, their love was not enough for her? Marcus's legal training had taught him to be analytical and logical, just as his early upbringing had taught him to conceal his emotions and to deny the pain they caused him.

Now, as he listened to Eleanor listing all the things she had to do, all the small problems which were beginning to dominate her life, he tried to confront the tidal swell of resentment and fear sweeping through him with calm logic, to tell himself that it was ridiculous to feel such resentment. But *was* he being ridiculous? Look at the way she was now denying herself the opportunity of taking on this new contract, and all because she had to be here for the house...

He took a deep, supposedly calming breath and then to his own shock heard himself exclaiming harshly, 'For God's sake, Nell, forget the house! The whole purpose of buying the damn thing in the first place was to ease our problems, not cause us more.'

He winced as he heard the tension in his own voice and saw the way Eleanor reacted to him, almost physically flinching back from him, shock and hurt registering in her eyes as she glanced at him and then looked quickly away again... almost as though she couldn't bear to look at him.

'Go away...just go away... I can't even bring myself to look at you.' That was what his mother had said to him, on more than one occasion when he had done something wrong: broken one of the many rules which had governed his childhood.

His mother? He was a man now... approaching middle age. What the hell was the matter with him? It must be the pressure he was under at work. He had taken on a very heavy workload recently, anticipating the increased expenses they would have if they moved. He had worked hard before, he reminded himself harshly, and it had never had this kind of effect on him.

He looked at Eleanor. Her face was set and pale. She was angry with him... and no wonder. He *had* over-reacted. What was it they had promised each other when they'd married... that they would also find the time to talk... to explain... to listen? Well, Eleanor seemed to have precious little time to do any of those things for him these days, he thought, guilt smothered by an atavistic male reluctance to admit to being at fault.

'Forget the house,' he repeated curtly. 'And as for Vanessa, the girls...I *am* capable of looking after them... her. She is, after all, as you never seem to tire of pointing out to me, Nell, my daughter.'

The antagonism in his voice was like a blow against her heart, making her wince with the anguish it caused her before she felt the reviving tide of responsive anger surging through her.

'What are you trying to tell me, Marcus? That you would prefer me not to be here?'

'For God's sake, Nell, what's got into you? You complained that you couldn't go to Provence because of Vanessa; I'm simply trying——'

'I suppose you think I'm taking the cowardly way out...that I'm running away. Well, I'm not. I *need* the money this commission will bring in, Marcus. *We* need it. I'm not having Vanessa or anyone else accusing me and my sons of being financially dependent on you as well as——'

'Stop it, Nell. When have I ever suggested anything like that? My understanding was that you would keep on the business because you enjoyed it, because you wanted, not *financial* independence, but some degree of *personal* independence, and not just from me but from the boys as well. I respected and admired you for that...I never thought you'd try to use it against me to make me feel guilty.'

'I'm *not* trying to make you feel guilty. You're the one doing that.'

'*Me?*'

'Yes,' Eleanor told him fiercely. 'It's easy enough for you to criticise me...to blame me for not being able to deal with Vanessa, but what am I supposed to do? She doesn't want me here, Marcus. Everything I try to do to bring us all together she deliberately undermines, and you let her. It's your fault she resents me, that she feels that I threaten her position in her life, that she feels so insecure.'

'Mine?'

'Yes,' Eleanor said sadly, 'she loves you so much, Marcus, and she's afraid of losing you. She's so insecure.'

'She's almost an adult,' Marcus protested curtly. 'You're letting your imagination run away with you, Nell. Children might cling to their parents, but teenagers...adults—they don't.'

'Not if they're secure enough, perhaps,' Eleanor agreed. 'But Vanessa isn't secure...she——'

'Leave it, Nell. Stop looking for someone else to blame because the pair of you don't get on. Perhaps you're trying too hard. You can't force these things. They take time and even then it's all a matter of luck. You have to accept that. You can't force Vanessa to accept or want your rosy view of the future or Broughton House, the way you can't...'

He stopped abruptly. Eleanor stared at him, the anger and pain she felt bringing sharp tears to her eyes. She blinked them away, demanding hoarsely, 'Go on...'

Marcus shook his head.

'No. It doesn't matter.' He rubbed his forehead tiredly. 'This isn't getting us anywhere, Nell. Perhaps a few days apart will do us all good. Give us both time to...'

'So you think I'm to blame,' Eleanor challenged him shakily.

'Nell, for God's sake. I don't have *time* to think about anything other than my work. I'm up to my eyes in it. This case...' He made a small explosive sound of impatience. 'I don't think I can take much more of this. What's happening to us...? What's happening to you?'

'To me?' Why did he make her feel as though everything was her fault, her responsibility?

What had happened to the harmony, the closeness they had once shared and which she had so smugly taken for granted? Where had it gone? How had they lost it?

An anguished sadness overwhelmed her anger. She gave a small forlorn shiver. She felt vulnerable and afraid, and, although she tried to hide from it, at the back of her mind lay the knowledge that somehow their quarrel had spoiled and soured their relationship and that she was angrily resentful of Marcus for allowing it to do so.

Was he equally disenchanted with her; did seeing her vulnerable and hurt diminish her in his eyes?

He had always praised her calmness and self-control. Where had they gone now?

It was a new experience for her, this anger and intensity, something she had never experienced with Allan; their relationship, their marriage had simply faded, died. There had not been any violent quarrels, any emotion of any kind as they had slowly drifted apart.

It hurt her more than she wanted to admit that Marcus had not denied immediately that he wanted her to go to Provence.

What had she really wanted? For him to beg her to stay, to tell her that she was indispensable?

Those were the thoughts, the vulnerabilities of a woman low in self-esteem and self-worth. She was not that kind of woman, was she?

'Look,' Marcus told her wearily, 'all I'm trying to do is help to make things easier for you. You want to go to Provence but you say you can't because of Vanessa, but then, when I say that I'll look after her, you accuse me of wanting to get rid of you.'

Eleanor looked away from him. How would she tell him how afraid she felt, that she didn't want to go and leave him alone with Vanessa in case... In case what? In case Vanessa turned him completely against her? Wasn't she doing a good enough job on her own? And besides, *why* should she feel suddenly that his love was less strong than her own, his need of her less than hers of him?

'I don't understand, Nell. I'm doing my best.' She took a deep breath, closing her eyes, willing back the sharp tears burning behind her closed eyelids.

'I'm sorry, Marcus. It's just...' She shook her head. 'You're right. It probably will be better for Vanessa if she has you to herself for a few days.

'For God's sake, Nell. It's not *Vanessa* I'm doing this for, it's you...'

She smiled crookedly at him, wondering why she felt as though the assurance had somehow come too late; as though it had no power to smooth the pain away from the raw, hurting place inside her.

'Why do these things always have to come at the wrong time? I need the business so badly, Marcus, but I need to be here as well—the house...'

She caught herself up as she heard his smothered exclamation of impatience.

She felt achingly empty and sore inside and wondered if he was concealing the same suppressed feelings of resentment and pain from her as she was from him...

They made love that night—if you could call it that—perfunctorily and silently, and afterwards, when she was sure Marcus was asleep, Eleanor lay on her back, letting the tears trickle silently on to her pillow, contrasting the silent distancing act with the ecstatic intimacy they had once shared.

The first time they had made love she had been so nervous...and uncertain—not of loving and wanting Marcus, but of not disappointing him or herself.

Life as a successful single woman might have taught her that it was not her or any other woman's duty to do anything, material, emotional or sexual, to please a man, and that she had as much right to expect to receive as she had to give, but her early conditioning, the feeling of constantly having to work for her parents' love and approval, a burden which she had carried with her into her marriage and which she knew had contributed greatly to its failure, was still there, lurking ogre-like in the deep subterranean caves of her psyche. She never felt it more forcefully than at that point in their relationship, when she knew she was going to have to strip herself, not merely physically of her clothes, but mentally as well of the protection of her success, her calm control, her so hard-won self-confidence, and to reveal herself to another human being as she really was.

It was this fear which had held her back from committing herself to the possibility of several earlier relationships with men whom she had liked but for whom she had never allowed herself to feel strongly enough to put aside her self-made protection.

Liking was not what she felt for Marcus, though. She had surprised herself with the intensity of her physical and emotional need for him.

But she was not an accomplished lover, not skilled or experienced in the way that she felt a woman of her age ought to be.

The act of coition was after all a very simple and basic one, but all the nuances of desire and arousal that went with it—they represented a vast and, to her, unfamiliar territory, which she wasn't sure she had the skills or instincts to traverse successfully.

It was only since the break-up of their marriage that, paradoxically, she had been able to talk with her ex-husband freely about the causes of their problems, both of them now free to admit that they had mistaken other emotions for the kind of love needed to bond two people together and be strong enough to endure the pressures of staying together. Allan had told her that part of the reason he had wanted to marry her was because she had seemed so suitable as a wife.

'I knew that my parents approved of you, that you were a "nice" girl. The problem was that every time we made love I still thought of you as a "nice" girl and to initiate between us the kind of sexual intensity I wanted seemed to be a violation of that niceness...'

Marcus knew, of course, the history of her life, her marriage and the years since then, just as he had told her, briefly, about his own childhood and marriage. About his relationships since his marriage ended he had said very little, but she had learned from friends that there could have been far, far more of them than there had been; that he had the reputation of being not just a sexually skilled lover, but a truly loving and appreciative one as well.

Marcus had been open with her about his desire for her, but he had not rushed or pressured her.

It was after one evening out that he had driven her home, and told her, after slowly releasing her from the passionate kiss they had been sharing, 'You know I'm not going to be able to stand much more of this, don't you?' and she had known that she must make up her mind one way or another, although it hadn't been until she had found herself in her doctor's surgery discussing various methods of birth control that she realised she actually had.

She had vaguely imagined that their first time together would be one evening after they had been out together, here at Marcus's house, a slow, skilled seduction to which she had no doubt at all that she would respond as helplessly and overwhelmingly as she did when he kissed her; but how would she fare when it was her turn to repay his skilled pleasuring of her? However, in the end it was nothing like that, nothing at all...

She turned her head in the darkness, her body chilled by the knowledge of how insecure and frightened she must feel to need to relive those memories... to cling to them. To remember and cherish them was one thing; to need to relive them because they now seemed to be all she had was another.

But it had been so good... so natural and easy. She had been in the kitchen at home, cleaning out some cupboards; the boys were spending the weekend with their father and Marcus was away in The Hague.

It was a hot, sticky day, she had had her hair tied back in a ponytail and she had been wearing an old T-shirt she kept for household chores. *Just* the T-shirt... nothing else apart from her briefs.

She had gone to answer the doorbell in some irritation at being interrupted, padding to the door, too stunned to see Marcus standing outside to do anything other than stare at him.

When she did find her voice, all she could manage was an inane, 'You're supposed to be in The Hague...'

'I know.' He had smiled at her but her heart had suddenly given a little unsteady beat; part of her subconsciously aware of the silent messages his body was giving off, the tension behind his smile, the way he had looked at her as she opened the door.

Self-consciously she stepped back so that he could come in, her hand going to her hair, her face flushing as she started to apologise for her appearance, explaining what she was doing.

In the kitchen the tap was running. As she went to turn it off Marcus followed her, standing behind her.

She could feel herself starting to tremble, her body caught up in the sexual surge of shock and excitement.

She heard him say her name, felt his arms come round her as he bent to kiss the side of her neck.

Instinctively she leaned back against him, sharply conscious of the feel of his suit-clad body, the fabric of his suit dark and slightly rough against her thin T-shirt, her bare skin, conscious too of a certain unexpected *frisson* of arousal at the contrast between the fabric of their clothes, the way they were dressed. There was something unfamiliarly erotic to her about their fulfilment of the rules of sexual stereotyping: Marcus, so powerfully male, in his formal business clothes; she, so vulnerably female, in her half-undressed state.

Silently she acknowledged to herself that there *was* something—some unexpected part of *her* that actually responded to that awareness, that the contrast between them was heightening her arousal; and that her apparent vulnerability was exciting to her.

And to him?

As she moved against him she could feel the hardness of his body and its tension.

'Mmm...you feel good—very good,' he added as he slid his hands up over her breasts. Her nipples, already hard and erect, responded to his touch, her breath locking in her lungs as he turned her round to face him and started to kiss her with real urgency.

Later she felt it must have been something about that naked, uncontrived, uncontrolled urgency which had broken down the barriers of self-consciousness. His touch...his words, but most of all his clearly demonstrated desire, made her feel that she could perhaps after all be not only a 'nice' girl, but a woman as well...and a woman who could wantonly take her lover's hand and urge him to touch her naked skin, to discover for himself how responsibly aware and aroused she felt.

They didn't make love right there and then in the kitchen, too impatient to remove all their clothes, too hungrily eager for one another to care, but that was only because Marcus's awareness of how close to her orgasm the hot suckling of his mouth against her breast and the eager, urgent stroke of his fingers against her flesh had brought her.

'Not here,' he had told her thickly when she had clung to him, reaching down to hold his hand against her body, arching herself into it, trembling with a mixture of arousal, need and fear of deprivation.

Yes—here, now. Now...she had wanted to protest as her body screamed its need for him, but old habits, old ingrained inhibitions held the words back, old ingrained beliefs that it was men who experienced uncontrollable desire while women...*nice* girls...controlled and ignored what they felt.

She had expected Marcus to release her, to let her lead him into the bedroom where they would both undress and then decorously make love, like adults, not like two crazy out-of-control teenagers, desperate to touch each other and be touched, as they had done in the kitchen.

With this in mind she started to turn away from him, but he stopped her, pulling her against him, picking her up, kissing her mouth as he pushed open the door, pausing just past it to run his free hand up over her body, his kiss deepening, hardening as he reached her breast.

Her body quickened, tensed, trembled, taut with urgency. The flat wasn't large, the bedroom door open, the room itself quite small, but it seemed a lifetime to Eleanor before they reached it, Marcus's mouth, Marcus's body, Marcus's hand as it travelled over her, stroking and touching her, absorbing her to the exclusion of everything else.

Later she hadn't been able to piece together just how he had managed to go on touching and kissing her while undressing, but somehow he had; somehow he had undressed her as well without ever losing contact with her, so that by the time they were lying naked together on the bed she was so aroused that every touch, every sensation was acutely heightened, every smallest breath she took seeming to cause the tiny quivers of sensation rippling through her to increase. Just the touch of Marcus's hands as he slid them into her hair, holding her head as he bent to kiss her, just the tiny abrasive movement of his body against hers, the thick, silky stroke of his body hair against her nipples, the slightly rough rasp of his jaw against her breast, the difference between the softness of her inner thigh and the abrasion of his fingertips, were all explosively sexually stimulating to her in her heightened state of arousal. In the end, just the feeling of the warmth of his breath against her body as he slowly stroked open the swollen outer lips of her sex, lingeringly caressing her flesh as though he not only derived pleasure from her ecstatic delight and arousal but as though the physical contact with her, the act of touching her was as intensely emotionally and sexually necessary for him as it was for her, was enough to bring her body to orgasm in a series of intensely powerful, visible physical contractions that left her shuddering helplessly, tears stinging her eyes, her throat raw, torn between elation over what she had experienced and guilt because she had enjoyed her own pleasure so selfishly and hedonistically, while Marcus...

'You don't know how much I've wanted to see you like this,' she heard him telling her thickly as he held her. 'How much I've wanted to know your body's responsiveness to me...its arousal and desire.' He bent his head and kissed her slowly, and then kissed her again.

Unexpectedly she felt her senses, her body quicken. She opened her eyes and stared at him, too startled to conceal what she was thinking and feeling, flushing a little when he looked back at her and she read in his eyes his recognition of her thoughts...her need...

Yes, it had all been very different then. Silently Eleanor closed her eyes, willing herself to try and sleep.

CHAPTER EIGHTEEN

FERN woke up abruptly, momentarily disorientated by the unfamiliarity of her surroundings and the intensity of the dream she had just been having.

It had been a long time since she had even thought about her wedding, never mind dreamed about it, but tonight... She shivered, sitting up in the high old-fashioned bed and pulling the bedclothes securely around her body.

Now that she was properly awake she could detect the cold, sharp, slightly damp smell of the house's age. Oddly, it wasn't unpleasant, unlike her dream.

Hugging her arms around her knees, she stared towards the uncurtained window. Cressy had explained that as yet she had not had time to do anything other than make the most basic attempts to furnish and clothe the place.

'Let's face it,' she had told Fern with a grin, 'neither Graham nor I are the frilly, flowery furnishings type...'

'No,' Fern agreed. 'What you need for here is masses and masses of old brocades; embroidered hangings, that kind of thing.' Her artistic senses were already busy clothing the empty rooms.

Outside the window the landscape was still cloaked in darkness like the church in her dream, the figures around her vague and shadowy, all apart from the one she had cried out to in anguish as she heard the vicar pronouncing the word which had made her and Nick husband and wife.

Adam! She could still taste his name on her lips, feel the icy cold shock of her own despair and panic.

Adam... Adam... She had cried out in fear as she turned towards him. Towards him and away from Nick, the man to whom she had just made the most binding and compelling of life's emotional vows.

She had married Nick knowing that she loved Adam.

She could feel the slow, hot crawl of the tears that burned her skin, the ache of knowledge and sadness that filled her body.

It had taken Cressy to make her unwittingly confront the reality which she had so determinedly buried beneath layers of duty and responsibility. And fear? Perhaps most of all fear. Not of acknowledging her love for Adam, but of where that admission would lead her.

Cressy had made her see tonight that she could no longer stay married to Nick.

Strange how it had taken someone else to show her what Nick really was; how he had manipulated and controlled her... used her.

'But why?' she had asked Cressy helplessly as she listened to her.

'Why? Because that's the kind of person he is,' Cressy told her flatly. 'There is no logical reason, Fern. I've stood by and watched over the years as Nick has loaded you down with guilt and fear, forcing you to carry burdens you had no need to bear, simply for the pleasure of making you do so. For some reason you've managed to convince yourself that you owe him that kind of sacrifice, of self-immolation almost, but you don't. *He's* the one who should feel guilty, not you. What the hell have *you* got to feel guilty about?'

Fern leaned her head on her knees, closing her eyes briefly. Cressy didn't know the full story.

She didn't know how she, Fern, had broken her marriage vows, betrayed her marriage and herself, forcing Adam, out of pity and compassion and automatic male reaction, to...

Abruptly she opened her eyes, her body tensing as though she could physically prevent her thoughts from forming; as though by the fierce compression of her body she could deny her memories.

But did she really want to? Didn't some treacherous, aching part of her want to hold on to them, to keep and savour them, carefully and jealously guarding them, protecting them from Nick's malice and from her own guilt?

Didn't some dangerously self-deluded part of her remember, not the way she had wept and begged Adam to hold her, to touch her and finally and, most shamefully of all, to make love to her, but instead the gentleness of his touch, the joy and pleasure he had given her, the tenderness he had shown her; and then, finally, ultimately, the passion? Just as though his desire for her, his need for her had been so intense that he hadn't been able to hold back, to control himself any longer? Just as though he loved her.

And even then she had tried to deny what she really felt; had tried to convince herself that she could somehow impose her will on her body and compel it, force it to respond to Nick's touch the way it had done to Adam's. But of course it never had. Nor ever would.

She had never dreamed until that day that her body was capable of that kind of physical intensity, never imagined that she could feel such desire, such need, never mind actually reach out past the barriers her upbringing had built up to separate her from her sexuality and be the one to initiate...to want...to beg.

She made a small, angry sound of protest deep in her throat, but it was too late, the memories were too strong for her; she was being dragged relentlessly back to the past, to Adam's comfortably furnished, welcoming sitting-room, once again experiencing the sense of relief, of safety she had always felt in Adam's presence.

Initially she had been too distraught to protest or object when he had taken hold of her arm in the street, but as he gently guided her into the soft comfort of the deeply upholstered sofa, quietly insisting that she tell him what was wrong, she had suddenly come to her senses, struggling against the firm pressure of the hands which had so carefully brought her to this sanctuary.

How *could* she tell Adam what was wrong; how *could* she admit to him that she had failed as a wife, as a woman...that Nick, her husband, was having an affair with someone else?

Before their marriage Nick had once told her cruelly that Adam would be pleased to hear that they were getting engaged.

'It seems he's been a bit concerned that you might be getting too...fond of him...that you might have misinterpreted things...imagined that...taken him more seriously than he intended.'

How she had writhed in embarrassment and mortification then as she listened to Nick, her face, her whole body consumed with the heat of the blush that burned through her as she pictured Adam confiding his concern to his stepbrother.

After that she had gone out of her way to make sure that Adam knew that he had been wrong, that she had *never* been foolish enough to believe that he had been interested in her in any emotional or sexual way, determinedly playing up to Nick's proprietorial manner towards her, grateful to him for saving her from the embarrassment she would have faced if he had not warned her.

'I must go,' she had told Adam shakily, but he had shaken his head, refusing to move, blocking her exit with the male bulk of his body as he said quietly,

'Not until you tell me what's wrong. I mean it, Fern,' he had added gently.

'It's nothing...nothing,' she had told him, but his mouth had tightened, the bone-structure sharply revealed against his skin as he leaned forward and gently touched his fingertips to her damp face.

'Nothing?' he queried, watching her. 'Then why have you been crying?'

It was then that she should have pulled herself together, reminded herself of exactly what his relationship with her was: of what his relationship with *Nick* was, and got up and walked out; but instead, as though his words, his touch had somehow turned the key and unlocked the floodgates behind which she had suppressed everything that she had been feeling, she had burst into tears, crying so hard that her body had physically shaken with the force of her pent-up emotions.

It had been impossible for her to speak, impossible for her to explain or to protest when Adam had suddenly cursed roughly beneath his breath and then gathered her up into his arms, pressing her face into the curve of his shoulder, his hand sliding into the thick mass of her hair, his arms wrapping round her, holding her tightly and safely against him.

It had been like coming home, finding a safe harbour, being given sanctuary...being let back into her own special Eden, and as she breathed in the familiar male scent of him, felt the warmth of his body against her own, felt the tension ease from her flesh as it recognised the feel of his, she had quite simply given in.

She had told him everything. How Nick had lied to her, deceived her; how he had betrayed her with someone else... She had even told him how much of a failure she was as a wife... a woman, the words choked out between her tears as she purged herself of her pain and fear, the self-consciousness and guilt she had become accustomed to feeling in Adam's presence gone and in its place an overwhelming sense of peace and security.

'It's all my fault,' she told him helplessly, lifting her head from his shoulder and looking up at him.

'No. That's not true...'

The harshness in his voice silenced her, her body stilling as she looked into his eyes and saw herself reflected there: saw the intimacy of their embrace, felt the sudden shift in her own emotional balance, the thrill of electric sensation that ran through her as she recognised what she was experiencing.

Helplessly her gaze slid from his eyes to his mouth and lingered there, her need, her hunger so overwhelming that it totally obliterated everything else.

She heard him saying her name, his voice unsteady, urgent with a warning she deliberately chose to ignore.

In the past when they had kissed it had been with the chasteness of friendship and she had not known how to communicate to him her desire.

But she was a woman now, not a girl, and she ached so sharply and intensely inside to know the touch of his mouth on hers as a lover, to experience the taste and texture of his passion, that she was already leaning towards him, her breath constricting in her throat as she whispered his name and placed her mouth against his.

He was not to blame for what had followed. He was after all human, and a man—very much a man, as she discovered when she moved her mouth delicately over his, her body trembling as she gave in to her need to explore the texture of his lips, the response of her senses so overwhelming that it totally drowned out everything else.

She was vaguely aware of his mouth moving, framing her name in a taut protest; she could feel the muscles in his throat moving against the palm of her hand, feel the tension in his body, but as she clung to him his reaction changed, the hands which had grasped her forearms as though he intended to push her away suddenly relaxing, their touch becoming caressing instead of constricting.

As she felt his fingertips smoothing over her skin, stroking the delicate flesh of her inner arms, following the blue line of her veins as it disappeared beneath the loose sleeves of her top, her whole body became engulfed in an open rigour of need so intense that her flesh shuddered in the aftershock of it, leaving her clinging helplessly to Adam's body, her breasts pressed flat against his chest, her arms wrapped tightly around him, her mouth soft and helpless with shock against his.

She said his name—in denial? A protest? A need? She had never known which, only that the helpless little sound of anguish she had made against his mouth had seemed to trigger off something within him which even he himself had no power to control.

To describe what had then happened as a kiss was probably like describing Niagara Falls as a tumbling brook. It was true that their mouths had met and merged, that their lips had caressed and clung, that their tongues had twisted against one another in the sinuous, sensual dance beloved of all lovers; but a kiss described merely the meeting of two mouths, two pairs of lips, two tongues.

What they shared was an embrace, so intimate, so intense, so consuming that its effect on her was as powerful as though they had actually been lovers in every physical sense.

And yet when Adam released her, slowly untangling his fingers from the silky thickness of her hair, whispering soft words of comfort and reassurance to her as he continued to caress her mouth with his, smoothing her hair back from her face, hot and flushed now, instead of coming back down to earth and recognising what she had done, she had clung to him, shamelessly winding her arms round him, pressing her body against his with a wantonness, a deliberateness she had not known herself capable of expressing. Her lips trembled and she moved them fiercely against his skin, tasting the sexual heat of him, feeling the rough abrasion of his jaw against the soft inside of her mouth, shivering openly with all that she was feeling as she begged him not to send her away... not to stop touching her now; not to deny her womanhood this need it had to experience fulfilment, to feel his hands on her body, his flesh deep within her own, driving away the emptiness Nick had left within her.

He had hesitated, tried to reason with her, tried to stop her, but she had overruled him, pleading, begging, and finally touching him with such a sure intimacy, knowledge and a desperation she had not known she possessed so that he had finally given way, holding her, touching her, stripping the clothes from their bodies with hands that trembled slightly, kissing the firm swell of her breasts, gently at first and then with such urgency that she had cried out in a thrilled shock of pleasure, her arousal so intense that tiny climactic quivers already ran through her.

She had thought of herself as a woman of negative sex drive, blaming herself, as she knew that Nick blamed her, for the lack of excitement or pleasure his touch engendered, resigning herself to the fact that for her the sexual side of their marriage was at best a sharing of intimacy and at worst a passage to be endured with guilt for her own inability to respond to Nick's carefully choreographed caresses.

She knew, because Nick himself had told her so, that his sexual expertise had given pleasure to other women, which made it all the more confusing and disarming that she should respond so much more intensely and overwhelmingly to Adam's touch than to Nick's, especially when her brain recognised that there was nothing calculated or planned about the way Adam was touching her; that, like her, he was far too caught up in the rolling surge of his own desire to lead her through a carefully planned arousal technique.

But it seemed she needed no technique, no skilled, carefully monitored sequence of caresses; her body was already trembling on the brink of orgasm, the sheer delight of feeling Adam's skin against her own, of breathing in the familiar and yet headily unfamiliar scent of him, spiked as it now was with the heat of his arousal and desire, of touching him hesitantly at first with just her fingertips and then voluptuously sliding the whole of her hand against his flesh, absorbing its texture, feeling the hardness of his bones, the power of his muscles, and knowing that magically, beneath her touch, all that strength and power became so weakened that she caused him to groan out loud; these were enough to bring her to a state of arousal so intense and so unfamiliar that she had no time to fight against it or to try to control it. It swamped her, engulfed her, delighted and terrified her as finally she was forced to abandon herself completely to it, pushing herself against Adam, lifting her hips against him, her body urgently seeking the union it needed as eagerly and voluptuously as though they had already been lovers a thousand times.

In the end though she had had to do more than arch her body against him in a sinuous instinctive movement of invitation and demand, and the hands he placed on her hips were there not to hold her against him while he slowly filled her with the longed-for hardness of his body, but instead to hold her away from him while he told her that they could not...must not...

But she was beyond listening to reason, beyond accepting as she would surely normally have done his rejection of her; now it was not just her body that screamed tensely for release but her senses, her emotions as well, and as he gently urged her away from him she did something she had never imagined herself doing, reaching out to touch him, closing her fingers round him, moaning his name, pressing hot, agonised kisses against his skin, begging him not to leave her, not to refuse her.

Beneath her hand he was hard and erect. She had never touched Nick like this, never imagined doing so, not wanted to, and yet now she was unable to withdraw her dizzy, fascinated gaze from Adam's body, a sense of wonder and power softening the urgency of her own desire as she absorbed the hot silky feel of his skin; the strength and need that pulsed against her fingertips, and, most tellingly of all, a wholly female and previously unknown awareness of how very vulnerable that strength and power was; how even the most male and indomitable man as Adam could be rendered vulnerable by a woman's touch.

Governed by an impulse that was more protective than sexual, she bent her head, gently touching her lips to him in a kiss, a caress aroused by love and not by passion.

Tears filmed her eyes as she lifted her head and started to move away from him, reluctantly releasing him from her touch.

He was right. They could not... must not. He did not love her as she now knew she loved him. He never had done; to be here with him like this was not just a betrayal of her marriage and Nick but in a way a betrayal of Adam as well. She had seen in his eyes the conflict between his sexual arousal and his desire to behave honourably, and yet as she lifted her head and looked at him, intending to tell him that she understood, something seemed to break apart inside her, releasing a need, a yearning so intense that before she could stop herself she was crying out to him to please not refuse her, to please, please ease the ache within her as only he had the power to do, to fill her with the silky heat and power of his flesh, to let her feel the movement of him within her and to know it echoed the movement of every vital force within the universe.

Which of them then moved first she wasn't sure, never being able to remember whether it was her hand that guided him into her body or his that touched her, soothed her as he made that first achingly slow and careful thrust into her body.

Oddly, the physical release of her desire, the actual moment of orgasm, climactic and consuming though it was, did not touch her as powerfully or intensely as the emotional completeness she had—the sense of being held, protected, wanted... loved, she had felt.

It had been then, afterwards, lying blissful and replete in his arms, her face still damp from the exalted tears of sexual release she had cried and which he had tenderly licked away, that she came abruptly to earth and realised what she had done, recognised the heaviness and unfairness of the burden she had placed on Adam's shoulders in overwhelming his scruples.

He didn't love her, he felt *sorry* for her. He was a compassionate, caring man who would feel endlessly guilty and responsible if he realised the truth and discovered that she loved him.

She could not face that happening, could not bear to watch Adam carefully and courteously distancing himself from her, hating having to hurt her and yet too honest to lie and pretend to feelings he did not have.

'What is it? What's wrong?' she heard him asking her as though he had felt the tension sharply invading her body.

It had to be now. She had to do it now while she had the strength...

She pushed herself away from him, turning her head so that he could not see her face as she told him dully, 'You were right. We shouldn't... I shouldn't... I'm Nick's wife and...'

'And you love him,' she heard Adam saying quietly behind her. 'I know that, Fern...'

Did he *really think* she loved Nick or was he simply trying to be tactful, trying not to hurt or humiliate her by letting her see that he knew how she felt about him?

She felt his hand touch her shoulder, brushing her hair off her skin. As he had made love he had whispered to her that he loved her hair; that he wanted to wrap it around his body, to...

'You mustn't blame yourself for what happened. It didn't mean anything, we both know that...it was simply a...a means of expressing your pain...a reaction against the way Nick hurt you.'

No, she had wanted to deny, no, you're wrong...This had nothing to do with Nick. Nothing at all.

'You mustn't worry about it. Or feel guilty,' Adam was still saying to her.

'How can I not feel guilty?' Fern had protested, shivering now, her face still averted from him, shock and despair taking the place of her earlier euphoric emotions.

'You have nothing to feel guilty for,' Adam insisted, adding quietly but firmly, 'Nothing happened, Fern, nothing at all...'

She did look at him then, her eyes registering her pain. What was he trying to tell her? That he wished it had not happened? That he preferred to pretend that it had not happened?

There was no need to remind herself that she had been the one to urge, to insist...to plead and beg...that *he* had been the one to call a halt, to try to stop.

'You're Nick's wife. You love him.'

'Yes,' she had agreed dully, her eyes hot and dry with the pressure of the tears she could not allow herself to cry.

She had started to dress then, her fingers trembling as, like Eve pushed out of the Garden of Eden, she suddenly became aware of her nakedness and ashamed of it.

Adam stopped her, gently pushing away her clumsy fingers and then dressing her with patient care and the kind of gentleness that brought fresh tears to her eyes.

'Don't. Don't cry, Fern,' he had told her as he brushed her tears away. 'Go back to Nick and forget this ever happened.'

Forget? How could she? And then the phone had rung and with a sob she had run as fast as she could from his house.

Tiredly she lifted her head. Beyond the window of Cressy's house the sky was lightening. Her body felt stiff and sore, her muscles tense and aching. She felt suddenly very old and drained. Wearily she focused on the greyness beyond the window.

What was there after all to look forward to? What purpose left in life? She had tried to make a go of her marriage, to fulfil her parents' expectations of her. She had tried to love Nick and up until last night she had believed that he had been genuine in his claim that he needed her; that he needed and wanted their marriage to succeed.

She closed her eyes briefly and was once again back in Adam's arms, feeling herself come to life, her senses, her body, her emotions suddenly so sensitive, so heightened that she had scarcely been able to endure their intensity. If she kept her eyes tightly closed and concentrated very hard she could almost feel the sensation of his mouth moving over hers, his hands touching her face, his tongue stroking her lips, his body...

Abruptly she opened her eyes, staring down at her clenched fists as though they were alien to her. Slowly she uncurled her fingers, watching the way they trembled, feeling the slow, inexorable tide of pain sweep through her.

This was reality. *This* was life. *This* was love... And somehow she would have to learn to live with it. One thing was sure: she could no longer go on pretending, hiding behind the barrier of her marriage, diverting all her energies and emotions into propping up its empty façade.

Everything Cressy had said to her had only underlined what she had already known in her heart. She had to leave Nick. Not because she loved Adam, but because she needed to regain her self-respect, to take charge of her own life and to be in control of it.

She needed to rediscover herself and she needed to learn to live with the person she discovered.

'So what will you do? You can't go back to him—not now.'

Fern smiled calmly at Cressy. They were walking along the beach that marked the boundary between Cressy's land and the sea, a long, curling ribbon of wet sand backed by marsh grass and the raised outline of the path along the dyke.

Once this land would all have been water; in its way it was a testament to what man could achieve, his determination, and his obduracy... his stubborn determination to conquer and control.

From locking out the sea and building the dykes, man had progressed to refusing to share his captured territory with its original owner, wanting it for his own use alone, jealously guarding his stolen prize. The skyline here had a haunting melancholy about it, the cries of the seabirds mingling with the soft soughing sound of the wind.

'No, I can't go back,' Fern agreed quietly. 'Our marriage is over.'

'So what will you do? You know you're welcome to stay here as long as you want...'

Fern laughed, amusement crinkling the corners of her eyes and curling her mouth. As she watched her, Cressy thought that she had never seen her looking more attractive, more mature... more of a woman.

'That's generous of you, but no, I shan't do that, Cressy,' she responded, touching her hand. 'Nick and I have to talk for one thing, and for another...' She turned to look out across the sea.

'What you need is a completely fresh start; somewhere new where you...'

Fern shook her head. 'No,' she told her friend quietly, adding, 'I have a few friends at home, a life...I've been a coward for long enough, Cressy. If I run away now... Nick won't like it, of course.'

'Will you be able to manage...financially?'

'It won't be easy,' Fern admitted. 'I shall have to find some sort of job, and of course I don't have any proper training, much less any real experience, but I am willing to learn.' She pulled a rueful face. 'There must be something I can do. Finding somewhere to live won't be quite as easy, but...'

'But surely Adam will be able to help you there? He must have contacts...know people...'

Automatically Fern stiffened, turning away so that Cressy couldn't see her expression.

'Adam is Nick's stepbrother. I don't want to involve him in this.'

'You might not be able to stop him from involving himself,' Cressy told her drily. 'Adam is that kind of person.'

'Adam is Nick's stepbrother,' she repeated. 'I don't want or need his help.'

As she turned round Fern saw the perplexed frown furrowing Cressy's forehead and knew she was over-reacting, but it was impossible for her to stop the panic and desperation from entering her voice.

'But Nick resents and envies Adam, Fern,' Cressy told her. 'He always has done. How on earth Adam has managed to tolerate him so patiently I'll never know. Look at the way Nick pushed Adam out of your life. What's wrong? Are you cold?' she asked in concern as Fern suddenly shivered.

'Yes. Yes, I am a little bit,' Fern fibbed as she hugged her arms around her body. She didn't want to talk about Adam like this...didn't want to risk making herself feel even more vulnerable than she already was.

Although she could not admit it to Cressy, it was her feelings—her love—for Adam that was likely to cause her to move away to a different area, rather than her separation from Nick.

'Are you sure you won't stay a little bit longer?' Cressy pressed her three days later when Fern announced that it was time for her to leave.

'I can't,' Fern told her, adding wryly, 'Besides, I have to face Nick some time.'

'Don't let him change your mind, will you, Fern?' Cressy cautioned her. 'Don't let him make you think you owe him anything. You don't.'

'You've made me see him in a completely different light,' Fern told her. 'Made me realise... I thought it was all my fault, that it was *my* responsibility...*my* duty to make our marriage work.'

'He manipulated you...used you,' Cressy told her grimly. 'You are the injured party, Fern, not him. *He's* the one who has been unfaithful. With a good divorce lawyer...'

Immediately Fern shook her head. 'No, I don't want that,' she told Cressy with uncharacteristic firmness. 'I don't want anything from our marriage, Cress. Somehow I feel as though it would be tainted, as though *I* would be tainted.'

'But you're entitled...'

Again Fern shook her head. 'No... Not really. I haven't contributed anything financial to our marriage.' She smiled gently as Cressy made an angry explosive sound. 'It's true. We don't have any children. There's no need for Nick to make any financial provision for me. I don't want him to.'

'But he should... You *have* worked, Fern. You've worked damned hard for him, far harder than anyone else would have. Far harder than he's ever worked for you. Don't be a fool...I know how you feel, but even if you're lucky it's going to take time for you to retrain. Jobs, even for qualified people, aren't that easy to come by.'

'I don't care. I want to do it alone. I want to do something for myself,' Fern told her. 'I can manage, Cress. I'll find work, cleaning, child-minding...anything. I don't care how hard it is, I'll do it. I *want* to do it,' she added with fierce energy. 'I *need* to do it.'

Cressy looked at her. 'Yes,' she agreed softly. 'Perhaps you do, but remember, I'm always here, and remember as well that I want you as my wedding attendant—and you still haven't met Graham. Are you sure you can't stay?'

'Positive,' Fern told her, hugging her, adding as they embraced, 'Thanks, Cress.'

'For what? Telling you the truth about Nick? It was my pleasure,' Cressy told her forcefully.

Fern laughed.

'Don't you dare change your mind,' Cressy warned her as she got into her car.

'I shan't,' Fern promised her. 'I shan't.'

CHAPTER NINETEEN

SOMEHOW, like hospitals, airports, wherever they were, all smelled the same, Eleanor reflected tiredly as she stepped out of the terminal at Marseille and came to an abrupt halt, dizzied not so much by the strong Provençal sunshine but by the unexpected intensity of the light, pure, brilliant, sharply clear, its intoxicating effect somehow heightened by the scent of the air, hot, dusty and yet underlain with a giddily hedonistic warmth and earthiness.

'I shall send someone to meet you,' Pierre Colbert had told her when she had telephoned to accept his invitation, and now, as her eyes adjusted to the brilliant clarity of the light, she looked hesitantly around her, searching for someone carrying a placard with her name.

There wasn't anyone. Momentarily her attention was diverted by the sight of the man getting out of an expensive open-top convertible car. Tall and dark, his looks were typically French, his clothes expensively casual. He was about her own age, perhaps slightly younger, and very good-looking... almost too much so.

She flushed slightly as he turned his head and caught her watching him. Before she could look away he smiled at her, and then started to walk towards her.

Cursing herself under her breath, Eleanor was just about to move away when he reached her, holding out a hand as he said her name and introduced himself.

'I'm André; my uncle asked me to come and meet you. He described you well,' he added, smiling at her. 'He told me,' he added, giving her a small sideways look, 'that you were extremely beautiful and extremely clever. And I, I'm afraid, am extremely susceptible to beautiful, clever women.'

He laughed as he said it, his expression winsomely rueful, inviting her to share his amusement and his carelessly insouciant flirtation.

To her own surprise Eleanor found herself laughing, and as she heard the sound of her own laughter she recognised how unfamiliar with it she was.

How long was it since she had last laughed like this, since she had felt so light-hearted... so light-headed almost?

It was a question which kept repeating itself to her over the next two days, forcing itself upon her whenever she was on her own, which was not very often, or for very long.

When she was not involved in discussions with his uncle, André insisted on filling her time with sightseeing trips into the countryside surrounding Arles.

247

Normally he would not have been her type; he was too egotistical, too flirtatious, too dangerous—and it made her all the more aware of the rift which seemed to have developed between herself and Marcus to recognise how surprisingly vulnerable she was allowing herself to be to André's outrageous compliments and flirtatiousness.

It was not that she was in any danger of taking him seriously, she recognised after he left her at her hotel late one afternoon, having failed to persuade her to spend the evening with him.

It was just that it felt so good to be paid that kind of attention; to feel desired and wanted; to feel feminine and valued. She could almost feel the pressure lifting from her, her self-confidence, her self-esteem flowing energetically back into her as she soaked up the heady combination of André's outrageous sexual flattery and Pierre Colbert's assertion that he wanted her to take on a large part of his translation work.

Boosted both professionally and personally, warmed by the sun, freed from the draining pressure of her problems at home, she not only felt but looked a different person, Eleanor recognised as she stared at her reflection in the mirror.

This evening she was having dinner with Monsieur Colbert while they haggled over final terms for their contract. In the morning she would fly home.

She paused as she recognised the feeling that knowledge brought, the reluctance and tension.

She had spoken to Marcus twice since her arrival and on both occasions he had sounded curt and distant.

Of course she wanted to be back home with him... with her sons. With Vanessa?

She looked in the mirror again. It was amazing to see how much just thinking about home and the problems waiting for her there changed her. She could see the tension tightening her face, drawing it into sharper, ageing lines... causing her mouth to turn down instead of up, her body to stiffen defensively, her posture to change.

By rights she ought to be looking forward to going home to Marcus, not... Not what? Not almost dreading it?

Guiltily, she turned away from the mirror and hurried into the bathroom to get ready for her meeting with Pierre Colbert.

In London Marcus stared at the file open on his desk. The air in his study smelled stale and claustrophobic. As he stood up to open the window he heard the front door open and a warm, laughing voice call out, 'Hi, Marcus, we're back.'

And then the three of them were crowding into his study, Vanessa, Sasha and Sondra.

The long, usually neatly groomed hair was flowing casually down over her shoulders, almost inviting a man to reach out and touch it, the scent of her skin, the upward laughing curl of her mouth and above all the invitation, the knowledge glowing so warmly in her eyes, encouraging him ... urging him ...

He turned away, and focused abruptly on the photograph of Eleanor standing on his desk. Eleanor ... She had been right to doubt that he would be able to cope with Vanessa and Sasha.

If Sondra hadn't happened to call round with those papers he needed ...

He grimaced to himself, remembering the scene she had interrupted: Vanessa's belligerent insistence that she was old enough to direct her own life.

'In your eyes, maybe,' Marcus had told her flatly. 'But not in the eyes of the law. I meant what I said, Vanessa. You're not old enough to go out alone to the kind of nightclubs you——'

'But I wouldn't be alone,' Vanessa had interrupted him hotly. 'Sasha will be with me.'

'No!' Marcus had said, and the force of that harsh denial was still reverberating in the air when Sondra walked in.

'I'm sorry about that,' he had apologised to her as he ushered her into his study.

'That's OK,' she had told him sunnily, adding, 'I've been there myself, you know. I had some pretty bad fights with my dad before I grew up enough to recognise that he wasn't trying to spoil my fun ... just see to it that I didn't get hurt.

'It makes things tougher when he's not there all the time, of course. Up until I reached puberty he'd been pretty easygoing, spoiling me rotten, I guess. It was Mom and my stepdad who laid down the law, but even so it came as pretty much of a shock once Dad started getting heavy with me, cross-questioning my dates and bringing in all kinds of rules and suchlike. Seemed like I only had to want to do something for him to tell me no. We said some pretty tough things to one another at times, but now there's no one whose opinion I value more. You'd get along real well with him, Marcus. You're pretty much two of a kind. Guess you'd better watch out, huh? They say a girl kinda tends to go for men like her dad when she's had a good relationship with him.'

She had laughed as she said it, but even so Marcus had been aware of the very real meaning beneath her comment and of his own *frisson* of response to it.

'Just as well I'm already married ... and too old,' he had laughed back, but he suspected she was not deceived and that she had recognised that small, very masculine surge of sexual excitement she had given him. She had come to collect some papers as well as deliver some, and since they weren't quite ready she had offered to go into the kitchen and make them both a cup of coffee.

Quite how and when the coffee had turned into full-blown 'afternoon tea' with Vanessa and Sasha coaxed downstairs to help her he wasn't sure.

Or how he had come to abandon his work and take the three of them out for 'proper' afternoon tea? Or how he had allowed Sondra to persuade him into allowing her to take the girls to the exclusive gym where she had a temporary membership, exclaiming when he had expressed doubts that he was always welcome to join them and keep a fatherly eye on them if he wished.

He hadn't done so, nor had he taken her up on the suggestion, when he had thanked her, that he could always repay her by taking her out to dinner.

It had been Vanessa who, when Sondra had commented that she was taking a couple of days off to do some sightseeing, had begged to go with her.

Marcus had pointed out to his daughter that Sondra was hardly likely to want her company, but the American girl had overruled him, claiming that there was nothing she would enjoy more.

She had arrived this morning, whisking both girls off with her, leaving him to get on with his work in the peace he had begun to think he might never experience again.

Only, instead of concentrating on his work . . . he looked at Eleanor's photograph. She was due back tomorrow only suddenly, urgently, betrayingly he wanted to be with her now, out of the way of this charming, dangerous girl-woman who had made her desire for him so plain. Because he didn't want her and wasn't tempted by her, or because he was?

He could see from her expression, when he explained his plan for her to ask her if she could stay with the girls for a couple of nights, that he had both surprised and annoyed her; that his reaction was not the one she either expected or wanted.

Even so, she agreed to stay, but not without first touching him lightly on the arm, and inclining her body just that little bit too close to his own, giving him a look from under her eyelashes which just fell short of being too openly sexual as she suggested that he delay his departure until first thing in the morning.

'Your wife will probably be having dinner with her business associates,' she pointed out to him, 'and won't be able to spend the evening with you. Why not have dinner here with us and then leave in the morning?'

'I've already checked,' Marcus lied. 'The only available flight is this evening. I was just waiting for you to get back to confirm my booking . . .'

'Your wife is a very lucky woman,' Sondra told him softly. 'I wish I had a man in my life who missed me so much.'

Although she was smiling at him, there was a speculative, feline look in her eyes which told Marcus what she was really thinking.

Normally her behaviour would have merely amused him; it wasn't a situation that was new to him, after all, and he was glad that she could not know, as he did, that beneath his awareness of his own male vulnerability to what she was offering ran the far more dangerous threat of his anger and resentment against Eleanor.

For what? Being too busy with her own problems, her own life to recognise what was happening to him? He was not a child now; Eleanor was not his mother; she was not responsible for his feelings and the way he reacted to them; *he* was.

Watching Vanessa before he left, he was aware of the way her body was changing, of the way she was changing, turning from a child into a woman.

He and Julia had not planned to have children, she because of her career and he because of his own ambivalent feelings towards his own childhood and the problems he felt he had still not resolved, but once Vanessa was born he had been determined to be as good a father to her as he could be.

He had never felt physically entirely at ease with her, though, had never shared the easy closeness he had witnessed and envied in other fathers.

Now, witnessing the way she had been behaving towards Eleanor, seeing her surly deliberate aggression and recognising her deliberate attempts to humiliate and upset his second wife, he wondered how much he himself was responsible for her behaviour.

Very few children could ever happily accept their parents' divorce, he knew and accepted that; teenagers were notoriously difficult to deal with even for their natural parents, and the anecdotal tales told of the horrors of stepmotherhood were legendary, but that didn't stop him from feeling guilty when he saw the way Eleanor was struggling to establish a better relationship with Vanessa. Nor did it help knowing that he found it easier to deal with Eleanor's sons than he did his own daughter. It was not that he didn't love Vanessa; he did, but at times he also resented her for the problems she was causing between Eleanor and himself. And Eleanor for letting her?

Well, she seemed to have taken well enough to Sondra, and the American girl was tough enough to be able to handle her. She, unlike Eleanor, would not be hurt if Vanessa chose to reject her. She was far too tough for that.

Eleanor dressed carefully for her dinner date with Pierre Colbert, putting on a silk jersey Donna Karan wrap dress which she had had for several years, but which was still one of her favourites. The rich colour suited her skin, the cut emphasising with subtle elegance the feminine slenderness of her body; it was a dress which made her feel confident of herself as a woman, without being too overtly sexual. It was also, she admitted, a dress which discreetly flattered the ego of the man accompanying any woman who wore it, because it said so eloquently that she wanted to look good for him.

Not that she wanted to look good for Monsieur Colbert in any sexual sense; but, meeting him now on his own home ground, she had quickly discovered that he was a man to whom the opinion of others was very important; his home, a small, almost starkly elegant villa in what she had learned was one of the most sought-after areas locally, bore out that opinion.

As did his wife, whom she had met the first time she had visited their home. A small, dark, extremely chic ex-Parisienne, she had been dressed in clothes which had undoubtedly come from one of the major couturiers; Jade would no doubt have been able to tell her exactly which one. The house, she had explained to Eleanor as she showed her around it, had been designed by a top French architect, the décor by an Italian interior designer, and although Eleanor had admired it she had admitted to herself that its cool starkness did not appeal to her anything like as much as the older, less elegant homes she had seen, with their sunlight-faded stuccoed walls, the open doors hinting invitingly at quiet, secluded patios filled with terracotta pots of tumbling geraniums, their shuttered windows concealing the cool dark rooms beyond them.

Arles itself and the surrounding countryside had entranced her, but Provence was a place for lovers, not for a solitary businesswoman.

Ideally too she would have much preferred to be staying at one of the small local hotels and not this luxurious but somehow unatmospheric place into which Monsieur Colbert had booked her.

Chiding herself for being ungrateful, she checked her make-up and hair. As André had subtly pointed out to her, it was the most expensive hotel in the area.

'My uncle must think very highly of you indeed,' he had told her, watching her. 'And I am beginning to understand why. There is something very sexually provocative about a beautiful, intelligent woman,' he had added softly.

There was also very definitely something provocative about a highly sophisticated and very good-looking flirtatious man, Eleanor had acknowledged wryly to herself, and if André had been merely a good-looking dilettante...

But he wasn't. As she had quickly discovered, he had all of his uncle's shrewdness and more, and she suspected that he was the one responsible for the carefully planned expansion of Monsieur Colbert's originally quite small business.

Initially it had come as quite a shock to her when he had casually mentioned graduating from Harvard Business School.

'My father is from a town on the French and Italian border,' he had told her with a smile. 'He has family in America. Where my uncle considers himself to be completely and solely French, I think of myself more as a citizen of the world.'

It was just as well that Monsieur Colbert had organised this final dinner to set the seal on their contract, Eleanor reflected as she picked up her bag. This afternoon, as she was walking with André, someone had backed into her, causing her to stumble slightly, and just for a moment, as André turned to steady her, just for a heartbeat of time while he looked down into her face and then very deliberately at her mouth . . .

She gave herself a small admonitory shake. Yes, it was perhaps just as well that she was not seeing André this evening.

Monsieur Colbert had told her that he would send a car and a driver to pick her up and take her to the restaurant, which was not situated in the town but in the hills beyond it, the favoured haunt of the very rich and famous who had made the area their home, he had informed her.

There was no doubt Monsieur Colbert considered that taking her to dinner there was a treat, but if Marcus were here with her he would have understood that she would much have preferred to dine somewhere less ostentatious, somewhere where both food and décor were simple and reflected the countryside.

As she walked into the foyer, the first person she saw was André. He came towards her, smiling lightly.

'A surprise, *non*? But I hope a pleasant one. I managed to persuade my uncle to invite me to join you, and I am now to act as your chauffeur.'

As he was talking to her, André was looking at her, and suddenly Eleanor wished that she had worn something other than the Donna Karan dress. Worn for a business meeting with a man who placed a good deal of importance on creating the right image, it was one thing; worn in the company of a man who had already made it subtly obvious that he was sexually interested in her, it was another.

Nothing was said, André was far too sophisticated and subtle for that, but the way he looked at her, the proximity of his body to hers as he escorted her out to his car, the way his touch lingered on her arm as he helped her into it, all carried a message that he was well aware of the discreet sensuality of her appearance and that he was responsive to it.

The restaurant was everything Eleanor had expected and a little bit more; surprisingly, the food *did* have a very local flavour, the chef Paris-trained but originally a local boy who had returned to his home to adapt the skills he had learned in Paris to reflect the best of the local cuisine.

The food, wine and the conversation subtly directed by André, all must have gone slightly to her head, Eleanor reflected later when it was time to leave and she realised that she was standing almost invitingly close to André as he came to her side.

Almost immediately she distanced herself from him, thanking Pierre Colbert for the evening and promising him that she would sign and return the contract to him just as soon as her solicitor approved it.

His terms, although stringent, were fair, the fees more generous than she had expected, although the time clauses he had wanted to insert had initially proved to be a small stumbling block. In the end Eleanor had got her way and he had agreed to modify them.

'There really is no need for you to drive me back,' she protested to André. 'I can get a taxi.'

'I *want* to drive you back,' he assured her, and the way he smiled at her sent an urgent warning homing into her brain, at the same time as her body responded to the smile he was giving her and the light pressure of his hand on her arm.

They were in the car when he turned to her and murmured, 'It's early yet; there is a small village close to here with a stone fountain built by the Romans. It is still in use today. You would like to see it...?'

'But it's dark,' Eleanor protested, laughing in spite of herself. How long was it since she had last felt like this, behaved like this, felt so free and unburdened, and, yes, perhaps a little silly as well? But it was fun being with André, being flattered and admired by him, even though she knew he was not the kind of man she would ever want to have a permanent relationship with... a serious relationship...

Was *that* part of what was wrong between her and Marcus... they had become *too* serious, forgotten what it was like to have fun together? Marcus seemed so distant and disapproving these days; where André made her feel almost giddy and girlish, Marcus made her feel increasingly aware of all her responsibilities, and her inability to deal properly with them.

He was impatient with her, irritated by her, she sometimes felt, shutting himself off from her, and not just when it came to Vanessa.

Caught up in her thoughts as she was, it was several seconds before she recognised that André had turned off the main road.

As she turned to look at him, he smiled at her and told her softly, 'The moon is almost full; it will give us enough light for you to see the fountain by.' And then he started to grin and added more prosaically, 'Besides, the square is floodlit at night so that tourists can admire the fountain and the church all the more easily.'

Eleanor had to laugh, but she still shook her head.

'No, André, I can't,' she told him regretfully. 'My flight leaves early in the morning and I still haven't packed. Please turn round and go back...'

'If you are sure that is what you want.'

Eleanor looked steadily at him. He was right about the moon; its light was strong enough for her to see the outline of his profile, strongly beautiful in a way that was entirely masculine. He had to have just about the most sensual mouth she had ever seen on a man, she admitted to herself, and that included Jade's Sam. And just for a second she allowed herself the indulgence of wondering what it would be like to be kissed by him...

Just for a second. As soon as her brain recognised what her emotions were doing, it caused her to sit more firmly upright in her seat and to turn her head away from him as she told him quietly, 'Yes, that's what I want.'

He didn't make any attempt to change her mind, although she noticed the way the car slowed down slightly as he passed a secluded shadowy lay-by.

When she made no response the car soon picked up speed again, and if he was seriously disappointed by her refusal he gave no sign of it, chatting easily to her about his uncle's business and his own part in it.

Any small feminine *frisson* of disappointment she might have felt that he had accepted her refusal so easily was soon squashed by her own acknowledgement of the dangers involved in even such a small indulgence of vanity.

A brief verbal flirtation, the odd languishing look, perhaps even the odd kiss, there was no harm in them in themselves, but as to where they might lead . . .

It was not the desire and admiration of another man she wanted, she admitted as they reached her hotel, it was the return of her relationship with Marcus to what it had once been.

André escorted her towards the hotel entrance, but once they reached the doors she turned round and smiled at him.

'There's no need for you to come any further,' she told him softly.

He paused for a moment, looking searchingly at her.

'If you're sure . . .'

'I'm sure,' she told him.

There had been a moment in the car when she had been tempted, not so much by André himself, she recognised now, as by what he represented, but that moment was gone now. What it had done more than anything else was to reinforce her awareness of how much Marcus meant to her. But how much did she mean to him? Their marriage, their relationship, which had once seemed so strong and sturdy, had seemed recently to have grown increasingly fragile, or was it just that the recent damage to her own self-confidence made her see things that way?

Suddenly she couldn't wait to reach her room and telephone home; suddenly it wasn't enough that she would be there herself tomorrow. She wanted and needed to speak to Marcus now.

She was halfway across the foyer when she saw him, shock, disbelief and then finally incredulous joy illuminating her face as she stood watching him walk towards her.

'*Marcus!* What are you doing here?'

'I wanted to be with you,' he told her simply and truthfully. It didn't matter why he had originally left London. Now he was here with her, seeing the way she reacted to him, seeing the emotion, the love in her eyes. All that seemed important was that he *was* here with her.

He could see the sheen of tears in her eyes and the way her mouth trembled, and suddenly he ached for her with an intensity it was hard to control.

'Oh, Marcus...Marcus...' he heard her whisper huskily as he took hold of her.

Later, curled up against him in the huge bed in the suite he had booked, Eleanor asked him sleepily, 'Tell me again who's looking after Vanessa.'

He told her briefly, nuzzling the soft, vulnerable skin of her neck as he did so.

'Sondra Cabot?' Eleanor repeated. 'Isn't that the American girl you said was over here on an exchange?'

'Mmm.'

He was working his way down the slope of her breast now, and already her nipple, her skin was quivering in delicious anticipation of his caress, but she still felt the slight change in his breathing, the hesitation...the tension almost, and the hand she had slid into his hair as she caressed the back of his skull stilled for a second as she looked down at him, puzzled slightly by his reaction.

'Marcus, wh——?'

'Forget Vanessa,' he told her thickly, brusquely she recognised, as a tiny chill of foreboding ran through her.

His daughter, it seemed, was still a dangerous subject between them, and she felt too vulnerable, too afraid of spoiling what they had just shared to raise it. Vanessa wasn't an issue that was going to go away, she reminded herself, but the thought was hazy, the issue one she did not really want to pursue. Not now...not when Marcus was slowly teasing the erect nub of her nipple with his tongue, its warm, moist lap providing an almost unbearable sensual contrast to the cool dryness of his breath.

She couldn't even manage to tug herself free of the sensual spell he was weaving around her for long enough to explain to him that it hadn't been Vanessa she had been about to mention, but the American. Dizzily she told herself that there would be time enough later to ask him how she came to be looking after Vanessa... For now... She gave a soft half-smothered murmur of pleasure as Marcus abandoned his delicate teasing to draw her nipple fully into his mouth, sucking slowly and lingeringly on it and then far more fiercely and with far less control as she moved urgently against him, her fingers clutching at his hair.

They had two blissful days together before Marcus announced that they had to return, and it was only on the flight home that Eleanor recognised that, while their time together had proved to her that Marcus still desired her, it had done nothing to resolve the other problems and fears.

She had wanted to talk to Marcus about them, and yet a part of her had almost been afraid to do so. Last night she had started to tell him how anxious she was about the house, but he had frowned immediately, exclaiming irritably, 'Do we have to discuss that now, Nell? Is it really so important?'

He had apologised almost immediately, but his attitude had left her feeling slightly edgy and wary.

When they got home the house was empty. It was an odd feeling to Eleanor to walk into its silence, and its neatness. She ought to have been pleased, relieved to have been spared a potential confrontation with Vanessa immediately on her return, she knew, and yet as she walked into the kitchen, saw its immaculate order, she could feel the tiny hairs on her arms and her nape starting to lift antagonistically.

The house even seemed to smell different, she recognised, although it wasn't until half an hour later, when Sondra returned with Vanessa and Sasha, that she recognised why.

The alien smell was the American girl's perfume, she realised with a sharp thrill of dislike.

Dislike? Why on earth should she dislike her? Or was it not dislike but jealousy she was suffering from? she wondered as she listened silently to the teasing comments exchanged with both teenage girls.

It had been Marcus who had gone to let them in and now the three of them and Marcus were standing to one side of the kitchen table while she remained on the other, feeling alien, an outsider in her own home.

'You look well,' she heard Sondra saying to Marcus. 'You've even got a tan. We made fudge brownies this morning,' she added, still smiling at him. 'Would you like to try one?'

It was almost three hours before she finally left. Eleanor knew because she had counted every minute of them; and most of the final sixty minutes upstairs alone in the bedroom, unable to endure any more of the scene being played out downstairs in *her* kitchen, *her* home, with *her* husband, without betraying what she was feeling.

She tensed as she heard Marcus come upstairs and walk into the bedroom.

'What's wrong?' he asked her. 'Aren't you feeling well?'

'I'm feeling fine,' she told him angrily. 'But I don't like being made to feel that I'm an outsider in my own home.'

Marcus was frowning at her, but he was an astute, experienced man, and he must have recognised what was going on as easily as she had done herself. The girl had hardly been subtle about her interest in him. Eleanor was not an overly jealous or possessive person, but to have to sit in her own kitchen and watch another woman not merely flirting with her husband but making it plain that she was very sexually interested in him was not something she was prepared to tolerate. And what made it worse was that Marcus had done nothing to stop her; even Sasha and Vanessa had recognised what was going on. Her stomach churned sickly as she recalled the triumphant gloating look Vanessa had given her. No wonder Vanessa had taken so well to the American. She would take well to anyone who she thought might displace her in Marcus's life, Eleanor thought bitterly. She turned away from Marcus and stared out of the window.

'Nell?'

She swung round. '*Why* did you let her stay here, Marcus?'

He frowned as though he did not understand her question and then, as he pushed his fingers into his hair in a gesture of irritation, he told her, 'You know why. So that she could look after Vanessa.'

'Having perhaps already looked after you...'

The sentence, the accusation was out before she could stop it, the look that crossed Marcus's face mirroring her own shock and distaste.

She wanted to stop herself but she couldn't; it was as though some alien and destructive force had taken her over as she heard herself demanding bitterly, 'Tell me again why you came to Provence, Marcus. To be with me, you said. Because you wanted me? Because you wanted me... or because you wanted to compare me with her? Well, there isn't any comparison, is there? Ask Vanessa.'

Marcus stared at her, caught between anger and guilt. He had done nothing... nothing to merit the accusations Eleanor was flinging at him. On the contrary, he had done everything any man could to resist the temptation offered.

And yet Eleanor was still accusing him... blaming him.

And if he had been tempted, was that his fault? Didn't Nell realise what she was doing to him, to their relationship with her obsession with that damned house? Didn't she realise how it made him feel to know how low down he came on her list of priorities? Even in Provence all she had really wanted to do was to talk about the house. Couldn't she see how he felt? Didn't she realise that he didn't even damn well want to move?

But he couldn't tell her that... it meant too much to her.

'I am not having an affair with her if that's what you're trying to imply. I haven't even thought of——'

'*She* has,' Eleanor interrupted him fiercely, 'and if you're going to tell me that you didn't know that, don't bother, Marcus. You must have. You should never have let her come here.'

She was close to tears now, her anger gone, to be replaced by shock and pain. Marcus might not have slept with the American, but he had not discouraged her from believing that he found her attractive. He couldn't have done. If he had...

If he had, she would not have been standing there in her kitchen, flirting with him, teasing him... behaving as though Eleanor herself simply did not exist.

When Marcus came to bed later, she pretended to be asleep.

CHAPTER TWENTY

'NELL... How are you?'

Eleanor sighed as she recognised her accountant's voice.

'I'm fine, Charles,' she told him. 'How are you?'

'Fine. Look, I'm having one or two problems with the finance for the house, which I need to discuss with you and Marcus. I've got a conference to attend this weekend, but I'll be back early next week and——'

'Marcus will be in The Hague then,' Eleanor interrupted him. 'He's got a case there. He's not sure how long it's likely to go on for.'

'Mmm. Well, we really do need to get this finance sorted out. I'm putting as much pressure on the lenders as I can. Perhaps you and I can get together, then. How would Tuesday morning suit you?'

'Fine,' Eleanor told him wearily.

As she replaced the receiver she could feel the beginnings of a tension headache cramping her neck and forehead, the pain a jarring discord to the music thumping from Vanessa's room.

The weeks had gone agonisingly slowly, but now it was only another couple of days until Julia returned. Sasha, thank goodness, had gone shortly after Eleanor's and Marcus's return from France, shrugging aside Eleanor's anxious questions about how she intended to travel back to school and whether her foster parents needed to be contacted.

'Sasha does her own thing. She doesn't let her foster parents, *or* anyone else tell her what to do,' had been Vanessa's contemptuous response when Eleanor had commented over dinner on her concern at the other girl's behaviour.

Things had not been easy since their return from Provence; the brief hiatus of happiness they had shared while they were there had been exactly that.

On the surface they might have appeared to make up their quarrel over Sondra. Marcus had admitted that he had been aware of the American girl's interest in him, but he had also insisted to Eleanor that she was wrong in suspecting him of returning it, and for her part Eleanor had admitted that she had perhaps over-reacted a little.

Today, after she had dropped the boys off at school, she was taking Vanessa shopping, a 'treat' she suspected neither of them was looking forward to.

Monsieur Colbert had rung her the previous evening asking if they could bring forward the commencement of their contract, as he had some urgent translation work for her to do.

Later, worrying about what she had taken on, she had tried to explain to Marcus her anxiety that she would not be able to cope with the amount of work he wanted done without the regulation of a proper office environment where she could shut herself away from all other interruptions. Working here at the house, where she was guiltily aware that she was, reluctantly at last, taking over Marcus's study, and where there were so many other distractions, was making it impossible for her to achieve her normal output. The work Pierre Colbert required was extremely complex and involved, requiring her full concentration, and how could she give that, she asked Marcus, when she had so many other worries on her mind?

What she had hoped to do was to delay the commencement of the contract until after their house move was settled, but now she was forced to acknowledge that it would be many months before she was able to even contemplate working at Broughton House and, moreover, supervising and overseeing all the work the house needed was going to mean she would be physically as well as mentally unable to give her full time and attention to her work.

And yet increasingly she was forced to acknowledge that the expense involved in buying the house and making it properly habitable was going to mean that they would need the extra income her new contract provided.

Vanessa had repeated her loathing of the idea; said that the last thing she wanted was to have to spend any time in some falling-down dump of a house in the country, and, far from being thrilled at the idea of having her own room and being given a free hand in its décor, all she could talk about was Sondra and how the American girl had never liked her own stepmother.

'Her father divorced her in the end, and Sondra said it was obvious why. He's married again now to someone much younger and she and Sondra get on really well together...'

Eleanor was trying not to lose her sense of humour, but the fear was there that, despite Marcus's assurances, he was not as indifferent to Sondra as he had said.

'You haven't forgotten that it's this weekend I'm going to The Hague, have you?' Marcus asked her as he came into the kitchen.

'No, I haven't.'

She kept her back to him, her voice registering tension. Despite the fact that they had made up their quarrel and that she believed him when he said there was nothing between him and Sondra, she still couldn't stop herself from feeling hurt.

'Look, Nell...'

She tensed as he came up behind her and placed his hands on her shoulders, turning her round to face him.

'Why don't you come with me?' he suggested gently. 'I know I won't be free to spend much time with you, but there are some wonderful galleries and museums in the area, and we'd have the evenings together. There's a reception being given by our ambassador one night; you'd enjoy that... it would give us——'

'Marcus, I can't,' she protested, her voice shaking a little as she acknowledged how much she would have liked to be able to go with him.

His hands lifted from her shoulders, his face hardening.

'I can't leave the boys,' she told him. 'And then there's the house... Charles phoned earlier and——'

'Forget the damned house,' Marcus interrupted her furiously. 'For God's sake, Nell, can't you think about anything else? All I ever hear is the house, the house. It's only a pile of bricks and mortar, for heaven's sake, and not even a particularly attractive or stable one at that. I know how much the place means to you, but the way you're carrying on about it... It's almost as though it's become the most important thing in your life.'

Eleanor stared at him, shocked by his explosion of anger. 'That's not fair, Marcus,' she told him. 'I want this house because I know how much better it will make things for all of us. I...'

'Will it?' Marcus asked her cynically. 'Or will it just make them better for you? I've seen plenty of instances where property can destroy a relationship, Nell, but none where it can mend one. What is it you're really hoping to achieve? A better relationship with Vanessa? She doesn't want to move, she's told you that, but you won't listen. More freedom and space for the boys? But at the same time you'll be removing them from schools where they've already established themselves, from friendships they've already made. They're only just beginning to adjust to our marriage... security doesn't come from living some story-book, romanticised idyll of childhood in the country; it comes from the people you live with; from knowing you're loved and valued by them.

'Right now the message you're giving off is that Broughton House is a lot more important to you than they are. Think hard, Nell. Do you want this house for them or do you want it for you...?'

Eleanor looked at him silently for a moment and then said shakily, 'You don't want to move there, do you? You never have.'

'No,' Marcus agreed quietly. 'I don't. It's too far away, for one thing, Nell—I'd spend more time than I want to commuting; for another, I don't think we can afford it. Ultimately, there'd come a time when perhaps both of us would resent the amount of time and money we'd need to spend on it.

'I'm not even sure it would provide the kind of environmental benefits you seem to think. And it isn't just the practical things. You're investing far too much hope and importance in the effect it will have on the rest of us. It's a house, Nell, not a magic formula for instant family happiness.'

He paused as he saw the way she was looking at him.

'All this time,' Eleanor told him huskily, her eyes almost blank with pain. 'All this time you haven't wanted it and yet you said nothing. What were you going to do, Marcus? Wait until we were on the point of exchanging contracts, or were you just going to let me go ahead and then turn round later and say, "I told you so" the minute anything went wrong?'

She was trembling now, pale with emotion and anger, her reaction causing Marcus to curse himself under his breath for his lack of timing.

'Well, look, I . . .'

He stopped as Tom and Gavin came noisily into the kitchen, arguing over the ownership of some pencils.

'We can't talk about this now,' he told Eleanor quietly. 'I have to go . . . This evening . . .'

Stiffly Eleanor turned away from him, ignoring him as she spoke to her sons.

He had hurt her and made her angry, Marcus acknowledged as he pulled on his jacket. He hadn't intended or wanted to, but, if she had been less engrossed in the house, surely she would have recognised for herself that *he* didn't share her enthusiasm for it? After all, he had given her enough hints.

As he walked out to his car he was uncomfortably aware that somewhere at the back of his mind, beneath his regret at hurting her, was a small, slyly sanctimonious voice that whispered egotistically that if she had not been so wrapped up in the needs of others she would have recognised his feelings long before now. Angrily he squashed it, refusing to acknowledge what its existence was telling him.

'What about this?' Eleanor suggested tiredly, holding up a pretty apple-green cotton seersucker shorts-suit.

'Yuck, it's gross,' Vanessa informed her. 'There isn't anything in here,' she added contemptuously. 'Can't we go somewhere else?'

Was there anywhere else left to go? Eleanor wondered as she obediently put the suit back and followed her stepdaughter towards the shop door. They must surely by now have been in every shop there was, without Vanessa being able to find a single item she liked—but no, apparently there were one or two places still left to try.

In one of them, full of racks of dull dusty-looking second-hand clothes, Eleanor tried not to wrinkle her nose in distaste as the fusty, ancient smell filled the air.

Fortunately it seemed that nothing here appealed to Vanessa either, although Eleanor wondered if she had congratulated herself too soon when the next shop Vanessa announced she wanted to try turned out to be the junior version of an upmarket and very expensive high-profile designer range.

'It's only Diffusion stuff,' Vanessa informed her with a bored shrug when she expressed her doubts. 'Much cheaper than his main designer line. Sondra said that everyone in New York wears his stuff.'

Ten minutes later, blinking a little at both the clothes and their prices, Eleanor decided wryly that if 'everyone in New York' did wear it they must possess extremely indulgent and wealthy parents.

While Vanessa disappeared in the direction of the showroom with a handful of outrageously priced Lycra, Eleanor stood silently staring out of the window. Not at the models, but thinking instead about Marcus's comments to her earlier.

Why had he left it until now to tell her that he didn't want to move to Broughton House? Was he right when he said that it was not for everyone else that she wanted the house but for herself, not because she hoped it would bind them all together as a family, but to fulfil her own childhood fantasies?

And in those few words he had given her an image of herself she didn't want to see: an image of a woman too determined to have her own way, too caught up in her own desires, too obsessed by her own needs to re-cognise the needs of others.

Was that really what she was like? Was that really how Marcus saw her...?

'I want to see what this looks like outside...' Vanessa had emerged from the changing-room wearing a dress that was surely far too tight and short for a girl of her age, but Eleanor could see from the mutinous expression on her face that it would not be wise to point this out to her.

Having been given permission by the salesgirl to go outside, they walked through the doorway, setting off the security tags with a noise that made Eleanor wince.

'No, I don't like it,' Vanessa announced, both to Eleanor's surprise and relief. 'Hold this for me, will you?' she commanded Eleanor, handing her the large, heavy shoulder-bag which seemed to go everywhere with her, adding as she turned round, 'There's no need for you to come back inside with me.' Silently Eleanor waited while Vanessa went back inside the changing-room and then reappeared in her own clothes, handing the dress to the salesgirl before coming to join her outside.

Despite the fact that she had not found anything she liked, there was an air of suppressed excitement and energy about her as they headed back to the car; Eleanor even caught her grinning at one point, and her spirits started to lift. Perhaps they could after all establish some sort of common ground... some sort of workable relationship...

'We could have lunch out if you like,' she suggested, but Vanessa im-mediately shook her head.

'I want to ring Sasha,' she told her, 'and then I'll have to pack. Did Ma say what time she would be picking me up?'

'No. She wasn't sure what time her flight would land,' Eleanor told her, trying to ignore the way she was beginning to scowl.

They had been back half an hour when she went upstairs to ask Vanessa what she wanted for lunch. Her bedroom door was open and Vanessa was lying on the bed, facing away from the door, speaking into the telephone.

'Yeah, it was a doddle...just like you said. She never knew a thing. I've got it with me now...'

As she spoke she rolled over and saw Eleanor standing inside the door. Immediately her expression changed.

'Look, Sasha, I've got to go,' she announced into the receiver, quickly replacing it before turning back to confront Eleanor. 'You don't have to spy on me...I'm not a prisoner,' she began belligerently, but Eleanor ignored her, demanding quietly instead,

'Where did that dress come from, Vanessa?'

Both of them knew the answer. It was identical to the one Vanessa had tried on in the designer shop, the label was still on it, and no doubt the security tag was still inside it, Eleanor recognised sickly.

'Vanessa?' she repeated.

Vanessa shrugged sulkily. 'All right, so I took it,' she admitted irritably. 'So what? Everyone does it. They even add the cost of it on to the clothes because they know it's going to happen. It doesn't mean anything.'

Eleanor stared at her in disbelief. 'You stole a dress and you don't think it means anything?'

'I didn't steal it. *I* just put it in my bag,' Vanessa told her smirking at her. 'You were the one who walked off with it...'

Eleanor stared at her, suddenly recalling with vivid intensity the moment Vanessa had asked her to carry her bag for her, and to wait outside the shop with it.

Too angry to dare to allow herself to express what she was feeling, she bent down and picked up the dress.

'What are you doing?' Vanessa demanded. 'That's mine.'

'No. It belongs to the shop and that's exactly where it's going,' Eleanor told her fiercely. 'Vanessa, how *could* you do such a thing?' she added in shaky bewilderment. 'Your father...'

'Oh, you have to bring him into it, don't you? I bet you just can't wait to go running to tell him all about it. Well, it's no big deal—everyone does it. It doesn't mean anything.'

'Vanessa, it's theft!' Eleanor protested. 'Don't you realise the consequences? And to just take something...' Eleanor's feelings overwhelmed her for a moment.

'Yeah, it's wrong for me to take something,' Vanessa shouted at her, 'but it's OK for people like you, isn't it? Only——'

'What do you mean?' Eleanor demanded. 'I've never taken any-thing...stolen anything...'

'You took my father,' Vanessa told her bitterly.

Eleanor sat down on the bed, half unable to comprehend what she was hearing.

'You... adults... grown-ups...' Vanessa sneered. 'You just do what you like, don't you... take what you like, and then you turn round and tell us that it's wrong? Well——'

'Vanessa! Is that really what you think; that I've taken Marcus away from you? Your parents were divorced long before he and I met...'

'Yes. But everything's different now. You want to change everything. I bet you wish I was dead really, don't you... dead or in prison? You pretend that you want me here but I know you don't really. I've seen it all before. Some of the girls at school... they've got stepmothers. At first they're all over them, giving them things, making a big fuss of them— that's before they get married, but once they are it's all different... then they start having babies and complaining about the noise teenagers make, about how disruptive they are... saying there isn't enough room for them...'

Numbly Eleanor remembered what Tom had said to her about her and Marcus having children; then she had simply thought Vanessa was being malicious.

'And Ma's just as bad. She can't wait to dump me on you and go to America...'

Eleanor watched her helplessly. Had she been her own child her instinctive reaction would have been to take her in her arms and hold her very tightly while she told her how much she loved her, how important she was to her and how she would always be a part of her life. But she *wasn't* her child, she was Marcus's, and it was his love and reassurance she wanted, not hers.

Besides, one look at her hostile, stiff body confirmed that the last thing Vanessa wanted was any display of physical affection or compassion from *her*.

Was all this emotion genuine or simply a means of deflecting her attention from the real issue? Either way, she couldn't afford to take any chances, she recognised.

'I'm going to have to take this dress back to the shop, Vanessa... When I have I——'

'You'll what?' Vanessa interrupted her aggressively. 'Report me to Dad? He doesn't want me here any more than you do. He never wanted me. I was an accident. They weren't supposed to be having any children...Ma told me that, not that you'd know it to listen to him now. It's always Tom this and Gavin that...'

Eleanor swallowed hard as she heard the frustrated anger and pain in her accusation.

'Lots of people have children they haven't deliberately planned, Vanessa. It doesn't mean that they don't want and love them. As a matter of fact I didn't plan to have Gavin——'

'Oh, come off it,' Vanessa interrupted her, saying rudely, 'Mrs Perfect, making a mistake like that? Well you might be perfect at everything else, but you'll never be a perfect stepmother. I'd rather Dad was married to someone like Sondra.'

Perfect? Was that really how Vanessa saw her? If only she knew the truth!

'I'm not a fool, you know,' Vanessa carried on aggressively. 'Ma pretends that there's nothing she wants more than to take me with her to LA, but I know better... and you don't want me here either.'

'That's not true,' Eleanor objected.

'Yes, it is. You can't wait for me to leave so that your precious sons can have my room.'

'Vanessa, you're wrong. We *are* short of space here, and that's the whole reason why we want to move, but...'

She stopped. It was Marcus she needed to talk to, not Vanessa... Marcus who could and must find a way of assuring his daughter that she was loved and valued.

Eleanor winced as the dress set off the shop's alarms when she walked inside it. She asked to see the manager, mentally rehearsing her prepared speech, but when she gave it, avoiding her eyes as she explained that the dress must have slipped into her bag by accident, she could see that the girl did not believe her.

'It happens all the time,' the girl told her as she took the dress from Eleanor. 'We do what we can to stop it, but it's impossible to get them all. It's a game to them, you see... a challenge. Most of them could easily afford to pay for what they take. Ask the police.'

Upstairs Vanessa was packing. She hadn't spoken to Eleanor since her return from the shop; Eleanor herself was supposed to be working but it was impossible for her to concentrate.

When the doorbell rang she got up tiredly to answer it.

'Jade!' she exclaimed in surprised pleasure as she saw her friend standing outside.

'The very same,' Jade agreed as she came in. 'I'd got a couple of hours to spare, so I thought I'd come round. I'm leaving for the States at the end of next week...'

'With Sam?' Eleanor asked her.

Jade shrugged. 'That's up to him. I'm getting too old and too tired to play games any more, Nell,' she confessed. 'Trust me to go and fall in love with a guy right at the very time when... What's wrong?' she demanded quietly.

Eleanor grimaced. Were her feelings really so obvious?

'It would be easier to tell you what's not,' she said feelingly.

'Tell me,' Jade invited...

'So, Marcus doesn't want the house,' she interrupted Eleanor several minutes later. 'So find another...'

'You don't understand... he didn't say anything to me, Jade. He just let me go on making plans, believing that it was something we shared when all the time... It's almost as though I don't really know him any more. He made me feel so... so self-centred. So unaware. He accused me of wanting the house to fulfil my own childhood fantasies... of using it as some kind of magic formula, when...'

'Weren't you?' Jade asked her with unusual gentleness. 'I'm not trying to criticise, Nell, I know how much you love Marcus... and I understand what you're trying to do, but Marcus *is* right, you know. A house can't miraculously bond you all together in some kind of perfect blissful family unit. To be perfectly truthful, I don't think that kind of unity actually does exist, outside the imaginations of advertising executives.'

'But Jade, all I wanted was for all of us to be happy, and now Marcus is making me feel as though... as though I'm deliberately ignoring everyone else's feelings and needs and concentrating purely on my own.

'When he talked about the house I could hear the resentment in his voice and I began to wonder if it was the house he actually resented or me.'

'Nell! Marcus loves you!'

'The worst thing about it all,' Eleanor told her quietly, 'is that all along everything that's happened has underlined the fact that the house isn't really for us and yet I've ignored it all, gone ahead... just as I've ignored what Marcus says he's been trying to tell me. What kind of woman am I, Jade? I can't tell when my own sons are unhappy... I don't know what my husband is really thinking or feeling... I don't recognise it when my partner wants to end our relationship... I apparently can't see that my stepdaughter thinks I've stolen her father from her... Women are supposed to know all these things... we're supposed to understand and empathise. We're supposed to be emotionally aware and sympathetic and yet here I am...'

'You're a human being, Nell, not God,' Jade told her drily. 'You can't know how everybody else will react or read their minds.'

'No, but I could be more receptive to what they're trying to tell me instead of apparently ignoring them. I wanted to make it all so good for us, Jade, and all I've done is make things worse.'

'It isn't just down to you to make things good,' Jade told her. 'That takes input and willingness from everyone. Stop worrying so much about other people's happiness and concentrate a little instead on your own.'

'According to Marcus I'm doing too much of that already,' Eleanor told her bitterly. 'And that isn't the worst of it,' she added, tiredly telling her about Vanessa and the dress.

'Let Marcus deal with it,' Jade advised her. 'That's probably half the reason she did it anyway.'

Eleanor looked at her.

'You mean a bid for his attention? But, Jade, Marcus does love her. He...'

'Does he?' Jade asked her quietly. 'How much did he actually see of her until you came on the scene, Nell? And now ask yourself how you'd feel in Vanessa's shoes, suspecting that your father tolerated you simply because your stepmother thought it was her duty to make sure he saw you. Look, I've got to go... I've got an appointment with my trainer in half an hour.' She gave a small shudder. 'He's brutal... but very effective... My thighs...'

Eleanor laughed. 'Your thighs are perfect,' she told her drily. 'Just like the rest of your body.'

'Talk to Marcus,' Jade urged her as Eleanor escorted her to the front door. 'And if you really want Vanessa to have a taste of what adult repression can be like, how about sending her over to me in New York for a few days?'

She had gone before Eleanor could say anything, or thank her.

For a while after Jade had gone Eleanor simply sat, assessing what she had said, and then she went and got the file containing all the papers relating to Broughton House.

Slowly she removed the sale brochure and studied it, tears filming her eyes.

Whoever it was who had said that the truth didn't hurt couldn't possibly have had a good understanding of the vulnerability of the human psyche, especially the female human psyche.

'Marcus...'

Marcus frowned. He had arrived home late and tired. It had been a bad day, made worse by his own awareness of his feelings of guilt over this morning's row. He knew that they needed to talk, but right now...

'Marcus...'

He turned round abruptly. 'Not now, Eleanor, please,' he protested. 'I've got a flight to catch and I'm already running late. Look,' he added bitterly, 'if the house means so much to you then go ahead and buy it. I've tried explaining to you how I feel, but you obviously don't consider my feelings to be important, so go ahead. Do what the hell you like. But I...' He broke off as he saw her face, suddenly sharply aware of what he was saying and doing. 'Nell...'

The doorbell rang. Ignoring him, Eleanor went to answer it. 'It's your taxi,' she told him quietly, coming back. Marcus cursed under his breath. There wasn't time now to explain, to tell her...

'Look, Nell, I've got to go. When I come back...'

Quietly, without responding to him, Eleanor walked past him.

He had been gone less than fifteen minutes when the icy calm of her anger splintered and the pain broke through.

Why hadn't she *told* him that it wasn't the house she wanted to discuss...why had she let him leave like that?

She glanced at the clock and snatched up her keys; there was still time to catch him before his flight left.

She was lucky and had a good run to the airport. At Heathrow the terminal itself was very busy and it took her several minutes to make her way towards the First Class check-in desk. As she pushed her way past the travellers and cases she could see Marcus standing with his back towards her. As she watched him, a small yearning ache began inside her.

She was just about to go to him, to call his name, when she saw the woman walking towards him.

It was as though a giant fist was squeezing her heart, the pain, the betrayal she was experiencing too intense to be borne.

Barely able to breathe, never mind move, she watched as the American joined Marcus, linking her arm through his, pressing her body close to his, leaning her face against him.

After the pain came sickness, a cold, sweating nausea similar to that which preceded a faint.

Dizzily Eleanor staggered back away from them, quickly turning on her heel before they looked round and saw her, completing her humiliation.

Despite the accusation she had flung at him before, she had never really believed that Marcus would be unfaithful to her.

'Come with me,' Marcus had urged her, and she had refused. *When* had he decided to take the American girl instead? Were they already having an affair, or was this trip to be the start of it?

Her tears blinded her as she pushed her way through the uncaring crowds in the busy airport.

CHAPTER TWENTY-ONE

THE telephone rang. Sleepily Zoe reached for the receiver, at the same time automatically moving over in the bed, searching for the heavy warmth of Ben's body to snuggle into, only remembering as she picked up the phone that Ben wasn't there.

'Zoe, darling, I'm sorry to ring so early but I wanted to catch you before you left for work. Could you possibly make lunch today?'

As she heard her mother's voice Zoe sat up in bed and then tensed as she felt the familiar onset of nausea.

Somehow she managed to hold it at bay, quickly agreeing to her mother's request so that she could end the phone call and rush to the bathroom.

After she had finished being sick she stood there for several minutes, tears of shock and self-pity rolling down her face.

This should not be happening to her; she should not be having to face this unexpected and unwanted trauma on her own.

Ben should be here with her, sharing it with her; Ben, who was equally responsible for what had happened . . . Ben, who seemed so oblivious to what she was feeling that he had not even noticed . . .

She shivered, suddenly icy cold and aware of a frightening and unfamiliar vulnerability, a fear almost.

Was it really only such a very short time ago that she had been so laughingly confident, secure in the belief that she was the central focus in the lives of those she loved: her parents, Ben . . . ? She loved them, of course, but they *needed* her, while she had always been free of such a restrictive and hampering vulnerability.

Fear and panic, both totally alien emotions to her, seemed to have taken over her life. Since she had discovered that she was pregnant she had felt as though she had somehow become trapped in an unknown and frightening world where no one seemed to recognise her terror and anxiety.

She could *not* have this baby, it was impossible, and yet, for some reason she could not even begin to understand, despite the anger that made her feel trapped like an animal in a cage, half demented by her own inability to do what she most wanted to do—which was to turn the clock back before that fatal conception, to wipe out that split-second of time which had resulted in the creation of the life which was now threatening her own—she could also feel within her an awareness, a shadow of a pain so intense and unbearable that it made her want to turn and run in fear, to be saved and protected from the enormity of it. And yet who was there in her life who could protect her?

Not Ben, whose attitude towards his sister's pregnancy had only underlined what she already knew about his rejection of the very concept of his own fatherhood. Not her parents, who had problems of their own she had never even guessed at.

Was it true that her mother, who had always seemed so content with her life, had secretly hankered after something else, resented her perhaps as she was already resenting her own child? Zoe wondered in sick panic.

She remembered how secretly a part of her had semi-despised her mother for her lack of ambition even while she had loved her.

At work several people commented on how pale she was looking; her job was demanding in both the physical and mental sense but today the pressure and competition which she normally found so challenging left her feeling drained and helpless.

At lunchtime, when she went to meet her mother, she had still not rung the clinic.

If her mother had been upset by the quarrel Zoe had overheard last night it did not show in her face, her daughter recognised. On the contrary, she looked younger, happier, more vibrant than Zoe could ever remember her looking before.

She was dressed differently as well, Zoe noticed, the elegant silk separates exchanged for a pair of soft, well-fitting jeans that showed off her slim figure, her hair carelessly tousled, a white T-shirt tucked into her jeans, the blazer she had been wearing over it casually discarded.

It was her mother and not she who was drawing the discreetly admiring glances not just of the waiters but of the male lunchers as well, Zoe saw as they sat down.

'Zoe, I'm so excited,' she announced as soon as they had ordered. 'I heard yesterday that I've been accepted. On that course I applied for! I tried to ring you to tell you but you weren't in...'

No, she had probably been on her way home, Zoe recognised, but she said nothing, trying to smile and share her mother's enthusiastic excitement, all the time a small inner voice asking why it was that her mother had not noticed how subdued she was, how pale...how different from her normal ebullient self.

'I'm afraid your father doesn't really approve.' Zoe watched as her mother made a slight face. 'But it's as I told him: I need to do something for myself...to achieve something for myself. I thought he'd understand that. After all, I've always understood how important his career is to him. I know *you'll* understand, of course. I've felt so envious of you these last few years, Zoe...you've made me aware of how little I've achieved in life.'

How little? Didn't her mother consider *her* to be an achievement, then? Didn't *she* matter? Wasn't *she* important?

'I had you, of course,' she heard her saying almost as though she had read her mind, 'but you're independent now. You don't need me any more.'

Yes, I do, Zoe wanted to protest, I need you more now than I've ever done, but the words refused to be spoken; how could she say them after all and betray her selfishness; her self-pity almost?

It was like being sucked down into a thick bog of cloying, destructive mud from which she couldn't fight free.

As she sat silently listening to her mother's excited chatter, witnessing the quick, almost girlish movements of her body, the interest she was attracting from people around them, Zoe was aware of feeling, not only fear, but anger as well, as though somehow her mother had stolen her role from her while committing her to the unfamiliar and unwanted passivity of merely being an onlooker on life.

Why had she felt that her mother, both her parents, were people who somehow had to be protected and indulged, people who lived only on the periphery of the real vitality of life that was hers?

This woman facing her now was not someone who needed to be protected from the fact that her daughter was pregnant and needed her help, her support; this woman did not need to lean on her, Zoe recognised, and with that knowledge came a small, slight lightening of her burden, a sharp, resuscitating sense of relief and hope.

She leaned forward across the table.

'Ma, there's something——'

'I can't tell you how much this means to me, Zoe,' her mother continued, not hearing her. 'I'd forgotten how good it feels to be valued as an independent person, to be able to make my own decisions, to be judged as a person, not someone's wife or mother. It will mean time spent away on various courses, of course, which your father won't like, but it will put something back into our marriage which I had begun to think was lost. Your father says he loves me, but he also takes me for granted; sometimes when he talks to me these days it's as though he feels he's talking to a child, not an adult.

'You've made your own life, which is just the way it should be; you're independent of us, of me, and, although I've only begun to realise and accept it very recently, selfishly I'm glad. If your life were still at the unsettled stage I'd be worrying too much about you to give the commitment I need to this course.

'I love you, Zoe, and although I never thought I'd say it I love you far more as an independent woman than I did as a dependent child...'

She was still smiling as she stood up, glowingly aware of the admiration she was attracting, a poised, self-confident, happy woman looking outwards towards life, and excited by the challenges it promised her.

Silently Zoe stood up as well. How could she tell her now? How could she claim her concern and support after what she had just heard?

Numbly she kissed her goodbye and wished her luck.

She was sick again during the afternoon at work, arousing the curiosity of one of the other girls who came into the cloakroom while she was there.

She couldn't go on like this, she acknowledged numbly as she stared at her pale face in the mirror. If she did, it wouldn't be long before someone guessed.

In her office she opened the telephone directory and then picked up her phone.

'You seem very sure that you want a termination.'

'Yes,' Zoe agreed wearily.

Her appointment had been at five o'clock but it had been closer to six before she had actually seen anyone. The woman seated opposite her was professionally detached and calm. She had already explained the various options open to her, but Zoe had not really listened. They both knew the reason she was here.

There was only one reason why people...women...came to these places, wasn't there?

'The child's father...what does he think or want?'

Zoe stared at her. 'Ben? He doesn't know,' she told her, caught off-guard by the question. 'I haven't told him.'

'Don't you think you should? It is, after all, *his* child as well as yours,' the kind, firm voice pointed out.

His child... Bitterness curled Zoe's mouth, hardening her eyes.

'Ben doesn't want children,' she told her flatly. 'Not ever...'

'A lot of men say that and then change their minds. Even these days men...boys grow up with the inbuilt male belief and fear that it's up to them to support their partners and their children, and this is often why they seem to fear and reject parenthood. Who can blame them? Having a child *is* a frightening emotional and material burden. Is that why you feel you should have a termination? Because you believe it's what Ben wants?'

'I don't believe it's what he wants. I know,' Zoe told her curtly, 'and I'm not just doing it for Ben's sake...I'm doing it for my own as well. We can't afford a child...not just financially but professionally as well...'

'For Ben's sake and for your own...but what about the child?' the woman pressed.

Zoe felt sick. She stared at her in mingled resentment and disbelief.

'I came here for an abortion, not a lecture on the sanctity of life,' she told her furiously.

The woman remained calmly unruffled.

'We provide a counselling service for pregnant women, offering them a variety of options, allowing them to make their own decisions. It is not my job to persuade you either to continue with the pregnancy or to terminate it, but it *is* my job and my responsibility to make you aware, not just in the short term, but in the long term as well, of the far-reaching consequences of whatever course of action you decide to take.

'What we can give you is a physical end to your pregnancy; what we cannot give you is emotional immunity to the consequences of such an action.'

She saw Zoe's bitter expression and sighed gently.

'Believe me, if I could promise you that a termination would resolve all your problems, that it would be guilt-free and that you could continue your life as though you had simply never conceived, I would. The only way we could do that would be if we had some way of wiping the mind, the memory clean of its knowledge.

'We may have invented a process which will remove the physical reality of what has happened from your body, but so far no one has produced one which will have the same effect on our minds and emotions, and, left up to the male sex, I doubt that we ever will,' she added sardonically.

'I know you think I'm trying to persuade you to go ahead with your pregnancy. I'm not. Just as much suffering can be caused by doing that as can by termination. All I'm trying to do is prepare you for the fact that you *will* suffer pain. Contrary to what the media appear to believe, I have yet to deal with a woman who has not done so...maybe not always immediately...

'Think about what I've said. Tell your partner. Let him make his own decision.'

'I can't do that,' Zoe protested. 'It wouldn't be fair to burden him.'

'And so you prefer to protect him at your own expense. That's a very dangerous course of action which can lead to a very deep and destructive sense of resentment, not just on your part but on his as well if he does ever discover the truth.'

'It doesn't matter what you say,' Zoe told her stubbornly, desperation lending a sharp edge to her voice. 'I've made up my mind that I want to go ahead with a termination.'

'Very well. I'll arrange for you to see our doctor. It will be at least two weeks, possibly closer to three before she...'

'What?' Zoe stared at her. 'But I wanted...I thought...' She stood up abruptly.

She had come here fully expecting, believing that the termination procedure could be carried out almost immediately. That was what these places were for, wasn't it?

'I'm sorry,' the counsellor was saying gently. 'But we always insist on giving women time to think things through properly before we operate. We've got your telephone number here, haven't we? I'll make an appointment for you to see the doctor as soon as possible and ring you. She'll discuss all the medical procedures with you then...'

* * *

Ben rang ten minutes after she got back to the flat. His voice sounded harsh and faraway.

'Where have you been?' he demanded. 'I've rung three times.'

'Er...I was...I had to work late,' she lied tersely. 'How's Sharon? When are you coming back?'

It was several seconds before he replied and when he did his voice sounded even more distant.

'That's why I rang,' he told her. 'I'll be back later this evening.'

'And Sharon?' she pressed.

Again he was silent.

'I can't talk about it now. I'll tell you everything when I get back.'

Miserably Zoe stared at the meal she had just made for herself and now no longer wanted. He would eat on the train, Ben had told her, because he didn't know what time he would be in.

She felt drained and depressed. When she had made that appointment at the clinic, she had thought...hoped...

She knew what she wanted to do, what she had to do, she thought angrily. She didn't need any more time to think; she had done enough of that already. Her head, her brain ached with the strain of it.

What had the woman been trying to do? Make it even worse for her than it already was? All right, so she would feel guilt...maybe even regret... Quickly she pushed that knowledge aside. *Why* was it that everyone got so damn sentimental over conception? And how many of them wanted to know once the child was born? You only had to look around you to see how many children suffered every kind of deprivation and cruelty, and not necessarily in the Third World and supposedly less aware countries.

Surely it was far better to end it now, when the only person to be affected was her? If she allowed the child to be born, would he or she thank her? Would Ben? Would her parents? All of those closest to her in their separate ways had betrayed their real feelings.

She got up, pacing the flat restlessly. Why couldn't she have got it all over and done with straight away? This waiting, this awareness and knowledge that with every day that passed her child tightened its hold on life, was a burden she was *not equipped* to carry.

Ben was back earlier than she had expected. He looked tense and tired when she let him into the flat.

'You're here, then,' he said flatly, almost as though he half hoped she might not be.

A tiny shiver of sensation brushed icily over her skin.

'Of course I'm here,' she agreed, forcing herself to ignore it. 'Where else would I be?'

'Working?' Ben suggested.

'What does that mean?' she demanded.

'You weren't working late. I rang the hotel.'

Her heart sank, panic and ice-cold churning sickness in her stomach.

'Yes, I was,' she insisted, but she couldn't look at him. 'I was probably in the loo or something when you rang. Tell me about Sharon.'

'She's fine,' he told her quietly. And then he turned his head and looked away from her. 'The baby isn't, though. She lost it.'

She was totally unprepared for the feeling roaring over her: the pain, the despair, the anger and anguish she felt.

'Well, what are you looking so miserable for?' she demanded cruelly, driven by what she was feeling to make him hurt and ache as she was doing. 'That's what you've wanted all along, isn't it? You should be pleased, not...'

'Zoe, for God's sake, that's not...'

She could hear the anguish in his voice, but she had gone too far to respond to it, her own feelings too emotive, too strong for her to give any recognition to his need.

'It's not what? Not what you wanted?' She looked mercilessly into his haunted face. 'Don't lie, Ben. Not to me. I know the truth. You never wanted Sharon to have her child.'

'No!' he denied thickly. 'What I never *wanted* was for her to get pregnant. To distort her life before she had had any chance to even think about what she really wanted. That was what I wanted. This...this senseless, pointless destruction of...this was never...never in my mind, Zoe.'

His voice thickened as he made a small imploring gesture, reached out towards her, and for a second she hesitated. This was Ben, whom she loved, wanting her, needing her, wanting her to recognise and share his pain...but he had not recognised hers. He would never have to suffer what she was suffering now; the very nature and structure of their relationship precluded her from burdening him with her problems.

'I'm tired,' she told him distantly. 'I'm going to bed.'

She still loved him, she acknowledged miserably half an hour later when he slid into bed beside her. It would have been easier if she didn't. But mingled with that love was also anger and resentment as well as a confused awareness that she was being unfair, that he could not be expected to read her mind, nor to understand that for her the very pivot of their relationship had changed and, from being the one on whom others leaned, there was now a need for support and protection within herself.

'Zoe.'

She heard him whisper her name as he moved towards her but she rolled over on to her side, keeping her back towards him, ignoring him.

Ben was not the type to force himself on her in any way; she had always been the one to take the lead...

It was no good. He couldn't sleep. Throwing back the covers, Ben carefully eased himself out of the bed. Zoe was asleep, genuinely so now.

Where had she been when he had telephoned her earlier? He knew she had lied to him. He had seen it in her eyes.

Had she found someone else; a man who could give her all the things he could not? He had thought that after what he had seen today he was numbed against pain, but he was wrong. He could feel it seeping slowly, with agonising thoroughness, through every sensitive emotion.

His feelings, his love for Zoe were so intense that he was sometimes afraid of admitting them even to himself. All his life he had struggled against this vulnerability within him, against loving too much. He had recognised it first as a child when he had rescued David Bernstein from his antagonists, had recognised it and resented it.

That kind of emotional vulnerability was a luxury someone like him could not afford. He could not allow himself to fall in love. He had other duties... other responsibilities, and until he met Zoe he had thought he had mastered his neediness.

Zoe... He looked across at the bed. In theory she was a product, a child of everything he most resented. Her self-assurance, her confidence, her belief in herself and others' willingness to please her sprang not from reality but from the protective security of an upbringing which had sheltered her from every kind of emotional and material harm. And yet, instead of resenting her, he had fallen in love with her, letting her bully and chivvy him, letting her take control of their lives and at the same time doing what he had always done for all those closest to him—watching over her with a protective anxiety he never allowed her to see.

He had often thought about what he would do if she left him, if he lost her, trying to do what he could to prepare and arm himself, knowing that if she ever wanted to go he would have to set her free. Ironically, over these last few months, he had actually begun to feel that perhaps after all he might have been wrong, that she might actually stay. But what he had never prepared himself for was the fact that she might lie to him.

It was just something he had not expected. A bald, defiant statement that she had met someone else, yes, but lies, deceit... no.

He glanced again at her sleeping figure. He had ached so much to hold her tonight, to let the pain spill out of him as he filled her with his body and felt her own quicken in response.

He couldn't tell her about what had happened, about how he had felt. It had never been easy for him to reveal his emotions, and besides, how could he tell her about those long hours spent waiting, hoping, and then knowing...? Standing with Sharon, holding her hand, trying to comfort the terrified girl who screamed out to him to help her and to stop the pain while her body purged itself of that poor, pathetic, lifeless little body.

You wanted it to happen, Zoe had accused him bitterly, but she had said it without knowing anything of the agony, the anguish, the anger and despair he had suffered in knowing that not all his love, not all his support, nothing he or anyone else could do could save his sister from her pain, nor her child from its death.

He looked back at the bed. His body ached, craved for sleep—he had been up all the previous night with Sharon—but his mind, his thoughts would not allow him any rest.

'Zoe?' they had told him at the hotel. 'No, I'm sorry, she left ages ago. She said she was going to see someone.'

It made him feel more guilty than he could bear to acknowledge that tonight, when all his thoughts should be with his sister, selfishly too many of them were of his own needs and his own fears.

This was what he had always dreaded: that in loving someone he would lose his awareness of his responsibility to others, replacing it with the selfishness of his own needs and desires.

In her sleep Zoe cried out sharply, a small, tortured, almost animal sound of fear and pain.

Ben walked over to the bed, smoothing the damp hair off her face, touching her gently.

'It's all right, Zoe,' he lied softly. 'Everything's all right.'

Bleakly he straightened up and walked over to the window.

CHAPTER TWENTY-TWO

'CLIVE wants to see us.'

Zoe looked listlessly at Ben. 'What for?'

He had been increasingly less affectionate with her recently, complaining that Aldo was making things difficult for him at work, and despite the fact that she could hear the anxiety he was trying to mask she had not, as she would normally have done, tried to calm and reassure him.

Somehow she just didn't seem to have the energy... for anything.

Life seemed to have taken on a blurred, out of focus quality—a dangerously protective numbness which isolated her not just from everyone around her but from reality as well.

'I'm not sure,' Ben responded, frowning slightly. 'He rang while you were out. I arranged that we'd see him tomorrow morning...'

He paused and looked at her. 'You won't be working late, will you?'

Zoe focused on him. There was something in his voice, in his expression, a hint of bitterness and sarcasm, that was alien to him.

'I don't think so...'

'It's time I was at work.' He got up and then, as he started to move past her, he stopped and looked hard at her.

'Oh, by the way, there was a phone call for you.'

Zoe felt the tension grip her stomach. It was almost a week since she had visited the clinic and she had still heard nothing. Remembering the counsellor and all that she had said to her, she had begun to wonder if the woman was deliberately making her wait... making...

Making her what? There was nothing to decide, she told herself firmly, clamping down on her panic. Nothing to say... nothing to think. Ben had hardly mentioned the hotel since his return from Manchester, but yesterday, when he was at work, she had been looking for an envelope and had come across some notes he had made, a small but ruthless analysis of his goals and hopes.

He might not be saying much about the hotel, but she already knew how much it meant to him. How could she not do, when for the last six months they had thought and spoken about very little else; when virtually from the moment they had met they had had this one common goal in mind?

She realised that he was still waiting for her to make some response to him.

There was a phone call for you, he had said casually, not knowing, not dreaming...

'Who? Who was it?' she asked him, her voice hesitant, stammering almost as her anxiety tightened its coiled grip on her nervous system.

As he watched her, Ben forced himself to harden his heart against the misery he could see in her eyes.

'A woman. She said she'd ring back.'

If she didn't care enough about him to at least be honest with him, then why should he help her, make it easier for her to tell him that there was someone else? Was it serious, or was it simply something casual? Casual—Zoe? He remembered her passionate commitment to all that she did, her sexual intensity... her way of giving herself so utterly and totally to all that she did, and he was almost tempted to take hold of her and demand that she tell him the truth. Instead he asked her quietly, 'You're still keen on going ahead with the hotel then, are you, Zoe? You're not having second thoughts or anything?'

Zoe stared at him. For a moment he looked different...older somehow and grimmer, a glimpse of how he would look in years to come when maturity and life had set its seal upon him. It suited him, Zoe recognised starkly, gave him added weight and authority, made him look the kind of man a woman—people could rely on and turn to. The kind of man who...

Who would what? Make a good father?

'No, I'm not having second thoughts,' she told him, and then added, 'I do know how much it means to you... how important it is. It's what you've always wanted.'

What *he* had always wanted? How much it meant to *him*? What about her? Ben wondered painfully.

'I shan't let you down.'

'Let me down! Zoe, what——?'

'I thought you said you had to go to work,' Zoe interrupted him quickly. She knew her face was flushing, betraying her nervous agitation.

Why on earth had she said that? She could see from his expression that her comment had disturbed him. If she wasn't careful he might start to query and question, to find out...

What good would it do if he did? she asked herself wearily once he had gone. What would it change? Not his feelings...his beliefs.

The day of his return from Manchester he had tried to tell her that she was being unfair in saying that privately he was pleased that Sharon had lost her baby.

But she had stopped listening to him.

Things had changed between them. There was an awareness, a tension, a distance which she would once have scornfully derided as an impossibility.

There was nothing they could not discuss...share...resolve, she would once have said. There was no subject they could not discuss...nothing which was taboo.

How wrong she had been.

Even sexually they were withdrawing from one another. The intimacy and closeness they had always shared taunted her now as she recognised how impossible it was for her to share her body with him when she could not share her thoughts and her fears.

And she *was* afraid, she acknowledged miserably... afraid and angry, sometimes hating the life growing within her for all the havoc it was wreaking, sometimes hating herself... sometimes even hating Ben... and yet at the same time she was still driven to protect him.

Because he needed that protection from her, or because she needed to give it to him? Who was she really protecting... Ben, or herself? What did she really fear? That he might not perhaps need her after all and that if he didn't he might not want her?

She remembered the way he had looked this morning; the unfamiliar maturity and hardness she had seen, the feeling she had had that somehow she was no longer necessary to him...

No. She was wrong. He did still need her. She had heard the tension and anxiety in his voice when he'd asked her if she was having second thoughts about the hotel.

The hotel... Even that had been spoiled now, her excitement and anticipation doused by the shock of discovering her pregnancy.

This baby... this *thing* which she had never planned, never wanted, was like a parasite, draining her, not just physically stealing her energy and clouding her brain, but stealing from her as well her happiness and her future... And Ben's love?

She shivered.

'I don't want you and I don't love you,' she told the child within her bitterly. 'What right have you to do this to me... to take over my body... my life? Can't you see? There *is* no place for you here... not with me and certainly not with Ben. We don't *want* you...'

She said the words out loud and could almost feel the force of her own emotions trembling on the air.

She could feel the angry tears pressing against her hot eyeballs and she squeezed her eyes tightly closed, willing them to disappear. What was the point of crying? What good would it do? She needed time to think things through properly, the counsellor had told her gently, but she had been wrong. There wasn't anything for her to think through.

Resolutely she picked up the phone.

Yes, she had telephoned her, the counsellor confirmed. Luckily the appointment with the doctor fell not only in her own off-duty time, but while Ben was at work.

'And once I've seen the doctor... how long... when...?' Zoe discovered that her mouth had gone almost too dry for her to speak.

'The doctor will discuss the arrangements for any termination with you,' the counsellor told her.

Was she imagining it, or had the woman's voice become slightly cooler? Despite the fact that she had claimed to be impartial, in Zoe's mind there had been no doubt which decision she had wanted her to make.

How did she think of her? As a murderer, destroying the life of her own child? But *she* didn't know what it was like. She didn't have Zoe's responsibilities.

Zoe could picture what *her* life was like: a nice, safe, comfortable marriage, two neat, clean, tidy children who were now doubtless married with children of their own, their marriage secure carbon-copies of their parents' marriage, in which parenthood would be a sacred, cherished commitment.

Angrily Zoe dashed the tears from her eyes and glanced down at her body.

Outwardly nothing had changed; if anything she was even slimmer, the sickness she was still suffering occasionally leaving her looking slightly paler than normal, slightly frailer perhaps; but so far there was nothing about her body that proclaimed that she was pregnant.

She touched her still flat stomach, closing her eyes, willing herself to reject the image she could see in the darkness.

'I can't help it. Can't you see that? Can't you understand? I don't have any choice. Damn you, stop doing this to me. It isn't my fault...I don't want you...'

As she said the words out loud, she felt physically sick, and then, as she opened her eyes and glanced down at her body a second time, she realised that her hands were pressed protectively across her stomach, almost as though she was trying to prevent the baby from hearing what she was saying about it. The baby... It wasn't a baby. There wasn't going to *be* any baby. There couldn't be any baby.

'Zoe, what is it...what's wrong?'

'Nothing,' Zoe responded tersely.

Next to her in bed she could feel the restless movement of Ben's body. She heard the faint sigh he expelled.

'I'm just a bit tired, that's all,' she told him shortly. 'Why should there be something wrong just because I don't want sex?'

Ben winced as he listened to her.

Sex—was that all it had become to her? Even though she had her back to him and was lying over a foot away from him, he could sense her tension.

He wanted to reach out to her and to hold her, to explain to her that it wasn't the fact that she was too tired to make love to him that bothered him, but the fact that he knew she was lying.

She had been too tired last night, and the night before, and yet he had known she was lying beside him awake, long after anyone who was genuinely tired would have been deeply asleep.

Miserably Zoe clenched her muscles. What was wrong with her? She still loved Ben, she knew that. Only this evening, watching him with his head bent, his shoulders hunched as he worked on the restaurant's weekly wages—just one of the extra and unpaid tasks Aldo had foisted on him— she had been overwhelmed by a tide of emotion so strong that she had had to blink away the tears it brought to her eyes. Yes, she still loved him; it was just that, sexually, something within her froze into a desire-obliterating block of resentment at the thought of making love with him.

It was a reaction she couldn't explain even to herself, and even now a part of her almost wished he would overrule her, take hold of her and love her, help her to obliterate even if momentarily the emotions she was trying to reject.

It amazed her sometimes that neither Ben nor anyone else had actually guessed. Some days she felt as though the full horror of the truth was written clearly in her face for everyone and anyone to see. And surely Ben, who purported to love her, must somehow sense ... must have some awareness of what she was suffering? Or was he merely concerned with his own emotions, his own needs?

No one seemed to care about her, not Ben, lying now with his back towards her, sulking no doubt because she had refused him sex; not her mother, who was so preoccupied with her own life that she barely had time to speak to Zoe on the phone any more, never mind listen to her.

'Ben, Zoe ... I'm glad you could both make it.'

Clive looked preoccupied as they were shown into his office and Zoe was aware of Ben's tension.

Irritably she glanced at him. What was there for him to be tense about? He was getting what he wanted, wasn't he? Why didn't he simply relax and enjoy it instead of permanently looking for problems? If he wasn't worrying about the hotel he was worrying about his present job. Only yesterday he had made some comment about Aldo being increasingly difficult.

'Well, it won't be for much longer, will it?' Zoe had responded unsympathetically.

'No,' Ben had agreed quietly. 'I don't suppose it will.' And after that he hadn't said anything else. Didn't he realise that sometimes she simply did not feel like reassuring and supporting him; that sometimes *she* was one who needed ... ?

'I thought it was time we got together so that I could update you on what's happening,' Clive was saying.

'There isn't a problem, is there?' Ben asked him quickly.

Zoe watched as Clive carefully realigned the papers on his desk with precise, controlled movements.

'Not a problem exactly,' he responded. 'It's just that things may not go ahead as quickly as we'd originally hoped. I'm seeing the architect next week and ...'

'Doesn't he think the house is suitable—is that it?' Ben pressed, while Zoe stared at him and frowned. Wasn't Ben listening to what Clive had said? He had just told them that nothing was wrong, and yet as she looked back at Clive again she saw in his eyes a flicker of both hesitation and respect as he studied Ben.

'No. It isn't that the house isn't suitable,' he said slowly. 'It's just that Adam Wheelwright, the architect, feels that it could be difficult getting planning permission—that it might take rather longer than we'd originally believed. I've got his plans here, as a matter of fact. He's done a fine job on them; there are two different sets, the first showing the conversion to the restaurant and the second showing the later stages of extending the house into a hotel complete with conference suite and leisure complex. He's drawn up the designs in such a way as to ensure that the basic layout of the grounds will hardly be altered at all. He feels that will be a plus point when it comes to applying for planning permission.'

Ben barely glanced at the plans. He was frowning, Zoe saw now in irritation, his face shuttered and slightly bleak.

'What on earth's wrong with you?' she demanded when they had left Clive's office. 'The house is ideal, you said so yourself. You've got what you've always wanted...'

She checked abruptly, hearing the sharp note of bitterness in her voice.

'*We* haven't got anything yet, Zoe,' Ben told her curtly. 'You heard what Clive said about the possibility of our not getting planning permission...'

Zoe made an exasperated noise. 'That wasn't what he said at all,' she argued. 'You weren't listening to him...'

'No,' Ben contradicted her. 'You're the one who wasn't listening. Look, I've got to get back to work,' he told her curtly.

Zoe stared at him. 'Work? But you're supposed to be having the whole day off...'

'Aldo changed his mind.'

Only another day, Zoe told herself tiredly, and then tensed as she felt the fine shiver that convulsed her.

Had she discussed things with her partner? the counsellor had asked her. But, even if she had wanted to, she couldn't. They didn't seem to be able to discuss anything these days without quarrelling.

She bit her lip, mentally acknowledging that she was more than half to blame for that, sometimes almost deliberately picking at Ben, goading him.

She knew he was worried about the hotel, but she sensed that there was something else bothering him as well. So often these days she felt torn between her desire to protect him and her resentment at having to do so, of always being the one who was the strong one. She had told him over and over again that he was worrying unnecessarily about the hotel,

looking for problems where none existed. How would he cope if he really
had something to worry about...if, like her...?

She shivered again. No, she was not going to think about that now.
After all, it would soon all be over...finished...terminated...

Everything was organised. She finished work at lunchtime. She would
come back here to the flat and then go on to the clinic for her appointment.

How long after that would it be before...? Her body trembled as the
feelings which had been growing within her and which she had been
fighting so desperately to suppress threatened to overwhelm her.

Why, when everything should have been so *easy*, so *logical*, was she
feeling like this? she wondered so despairingly. She could not have a
child, she didn't want a child, so why...why did the thought of what
lay ahead of her make her tense her stomach muscles so fiercely, so protectively? Why did it make her feel such a surge of anger and resentment
against Ben? Why did it weaken her so frighteningly, make her so vulnerable, when she so desperately needed to be strong, not just for her
own sake but more importantly for Ben's?

Ben needed her.

I love him, she whispered into the silence. I love him and there isn't
room in my life for both of you—can't you understand that?

Ben watched as Zoe got ready for work. Her hands trembled as she zipped
up her skirt. She looked so pale and withdrawn, and she was losing weight.
Who was she thinking about when she had that distant look in her eyes?
The man he was losing her to?

When was she going to tell him about it? Who was he? he wondered
jealously. Someone she worked with...a married man perhaps? Was *that*
the reason why she had said nothing—because he wasn't free to love her?
Immediately he felt a surge of angry protectiveness at the thought of
someone hurting her.

Zoe was so vulnerable, even if she herself did not know it.

He watched her broodingly for a few seconds. The hotel and their
future, which had been so important to her, no longer seemed to matter
to her. She couldn't even see, as he could, that Clive was seriously concerned that they might not get planning permission.

When he had tried to talk to her about it she had shrugged impatiently,
calling him a pessimist.

His throat ached with love for her. There was nothing he wanted to
do more than to reach out and take hold of her, but every time he'd tried
to touch her recently she had shrugged him off.

'What time will you be in?' he asked her quietly as she picked up her
coat.

'Uh...I'm not really sure. I might have to work late.' Bright colour
stung her face as she dipped her head forward, trying to conceal her
guilty blush with the tumble of her curls, but Ben had seen it.

'Again?' he asked her wryly.

'We're...we're very short-staffed...'

She hated lying to Ben, Zoe acknowledged miserably later as she left the hotel and made her way home, but wasn't it partly his fault that she was having to do so? She tensed as she felt the now familiar surge of mingled guilt, pain and love storm through her.

She had a shower and then dressed carefully in clean, easily removable clothes. The doctor would want to examine her, of course. Her body tensed.

She was just brushing her hair, trying not to think about what lay ahead, when Ben unlocked the door and walked into the flat.

Zoe stared at him in shock.

'Ben...what are you doing here?' she asked him weakly.

His eyes hardened and he looked at her.

'I could ask you the same question,' he told her evenly.

'What? Oh, they didn't need me after all...but I'm not staying. I...I have to go out...I...I'm seeing Ma,' she lied desperately.

'You don't normally have a shower just to see your mother.'

Zoe stared at him. The bathroom door was open, the steam still escaping, the damp towels on the floor at her feet.

'No, well...I felt hot and sticky. I... Why are you back so early?' she demanded, unable to continue lying.

'Primarily because I've been sacked.'

Ben cursed himself as he saw her expression. He hadn't meant to tell her like that, but coming home and finding her here, listening to her lying to him so obviously, had made him want to reach out and shock her into realising what she was doing.

'No! You can't have been!' Zoe protested. 'You said you weren't going to leave until the hotel was finalised.'

'I wasn't given any choice. It seems Aldo has a nephew who can cook ten times better than me and whom he can pay five times less. Oh, it's all right...I've been in touch with one of the agencies and they've got some temping work for me, and at better money than Aldo was paying me. It isn't as secure as having something permanent, of course, but it's better than nothing.'

'But, Ben...' Zoe protested.

'Hadn't you better go?' he asked her, giving her an unkind smile. 'You don't want to keep your *mother* waiting, do you?'

The doctor was pleasant but brisk, calmly outlining the procedures and explaining to Zoe just what would be involved.

'The optimum time for a termination is just around the twelve-week mark, the time nature normally chooses when she decides to terminate a pregnancy. That would mean...let me see...some time next week, yes?'

'Yes,' Zoe agreed.

When she left the clinic she felt sick and light-headed. With relief, she assured herself fiercely as she tried to breathe deeply and calmly.

She didn't return to the flat straight away. For one thing, Ben would be there, and she didn't feel she could face him without betraying what she was feeling.

Instead she wandered numbly around the shops. The window display of one of them caught her attention and she stood staring at it for a long time, until the reflection of the heavily pregnant woman standing next to her made her realise what she was doing.

Shakily she turned away. What was she doing, staring at a window dressed as a child's nursery? She had *made* her decision and she knew it was the right one. The *only* one...

Ben was changing for work when she got back to the flat. He looked at her silently for several minutes before asking calmly, 'Did you have a good time?'

A good time... If only he knew!

'Yes,' she lied, giving him a falsely bright smile.

'And your mother? How is she?'

'She's fine,' Zoe told him.

Ben turned his back on her. His hands had started to tremble. He knew she was lying to him. Her mother had rung ten minutes after Zoe had left and from her conversation it had been plain that Zoe had not gone to meet her. Which left only one plausible explanation.

He could feel the emotions building up inside him: the pain, the anger, the sense of betrayal and loss... and most of all the helpless, aching intensity of his love.

It was no good. He couldn't go on ignoring it, and perhaps after all this was what Zoe actually wanted—that *he* should take the burden of explanation and revelation off her shoulders and carry it for her.

He turned round to face her.

'Zoe... is there someone else?'

Someone else...? Zoe stared at him in shock, immediately opening her mouth to deny it, and then she closed it again, recognising on a suddenly sharply illuminating and painful burst of truth what she had previously refused to admit.

There *was* someone else... someone who, with each day that passed, came more firmly between them, driving them apart, tearing *her* apart, tormenting her with conflicting emotions and loyalties... It was a strong fighter, this new life inside her, using every emotional power at its disposal to protect its frail hold on life, but her commitment had already been made and given long before it had even existed.

I can't, she whispered silently in the shadows of her mind. I'm sorry, but I can't...

'Zoe...' Ben pressed. The look on her face hurt him with its pain and confusion.

She focused on him, staring blankly at him for a second before telling him huskily, 'No, Ben. No...there's no one else. There's no one else.' She repeated more fiercely, 'No one. There never has been and there never will be!'

CHAPTER TWENTY-THREE

'SO YOU'RE back, are you...?'

Calmly Fern ignored the aggressive hectoring tone of Nick's voice, carefully putting her case down on the kitchen floor, her mind absorbing the information that the kitchen sink was stacked full of unwashed things, the floor unswept and dusty, the table littered with the remains of not one but apparently several meals.

The air in the kitchen smelled stale and thick; she could smell the heavy unpleasant scent of Nick's body... his aftershave, or was it just that after several days in an exclusively female environment meant her nostrils were too sensitively attuned to the maleness Nick exuded?

It was odd how a certain male smell, the right male smell could be so strongly erotic, while the same mingling of heat and sweat and musk from another man could cause almost revulsion.

'Nothing to say for yourself? What the hell do you think you're playing at, Fern? What was this disappearing act of yours supposed to prove?'

'We need to talk, Nick, but first I want to unpack and get this mess cleaned up...' She wrinkled her nose fastidiously. 'Couldn't you even have managed to wash up?'

Fern watched as shock mingled with anger momentarily silenced him, but it was only momentarily. Fern could see from the tension coiling his body; any moment now he would start, and once he had... She took advantage of his brief silence to add quietly, 'Oh, by the way, I hope you've thanked Venice for returning your tie. It was very thoughtful of her.'

She looked him full in the face, refusing to let the rage she could see burning in his eyes bully her into looking away.

'What tie? What the *hell* are you talking about? Just what did you mean by your note?' he demanded, but the angry red tide of colour flushing his face had given him away.

Fern said nothing, simply turning away from him and picking up her case.

It was a new and very heady feeling, this sense of being in control, of having the advantage, of being the one to direct things...very, very heady.

She must be careful not to get too carried away, she warned herself as she opened the door and walked upstairs.

She was halfway up them when Nick came after her, bellowing her name.

She stopped and turned round, looking down at him, her expression mild and impassive.

'I don't know what the hell you think you're doing,' she heard him saying furiously. 'You disappear for damn near a week on some crazy whim of that bitch of a woman you call a friend...

'Do you realise I had to go out and buy myself a new shirt yesterday because I didn't have a clean one to wear? You're my wife, Fern. It's your duty to——'

'To what, Nick? To allow you to humiliate and manipulate me? To force myself to pretend that I'm happy? To pretend that this *thing* we call our marriage is anything other than a mockery and a farce... to stand quietly to one side while you have an affair with someone else?' She shook her head. '*You* think those things are my duty, Nick, but I don't. My real duty... my first duty is to myself, to maintaining my own self-respect, and I can't do that any longer while I remain married to you.'

Turning her back on him, she continued her way upstairs, ignoring the angry accusations which followed her.

She had made her decision and she was not going to change her mind no matter how much pressure Nick put on her to do so.

'But why should he want to stay married to me when he doesn't love me?' she had asked Cressy in bewilderment.

'Because Nick is one of those people who can't bear to let anything or anyone go,' Cressy had told her grimly. 'And because he enjoys his power over you, Fern.'

The picture Cressy had drawn of Nick had shocked her at first, but now she was beginning to recognise the truth of her friend's statements.

Carefully she unpacked her clothes, telling herself she was not going to be a coward and stay up here, too afraid to continue to confront Nick, but her hands were still shaking slightly when she had put the last item away and closed the case.

Nick was waiting for her in the kitchen, his mouth twisting into a bitter sneer as he told her, 'Don't think I don't know what you're up to, Fern, but it's no good going running to Adam. He doesn't want you any more now than he ever did. You never did have much sense of timing, did you?' he added goadingly. 'Didn't you know he'd gone away—with the Jameses and their daughter...? They've gone to Tuscany; the Jameses have a villa there... Trust dear old Adam to fall on his feet. Old man James is rolling in it. Still, Adam is going to need a rich father-in-law if his plans for Broughton House fall through—and they will, Anthony Quentin will see to that. He isn't too keen on the idea of a new super-market opening locally... What's wrong, Fern? Not having second thoughts, are you, now you know that dear Adam isn't around to let you crawl into his bed?'

'This has nothing to do with Adam,' Fern protested fiercely.

'Don't lie to me,' Nick contradicted her heatedly. 'This has *everything* to do with him. You've always wanted him... preferred him... but he's never wanted you, Fern, and he never will. We used to laugh about you together, about the way you used to follow him around, hanging on his every word. He warned me against marrying you...'

She must not say anything...must *not* betray what she was feeling, how much he was hurting her, Fern told herself. Thank God Cressy had opened her eyes to what he really was.

'I'm going out now,' Nick told her. 'But while I'm gone I want you to think about one or two things, Fern. Like how you're going to live without me to support you? You haven't got your parents to go running home to now, have you? No money...no home...no Adam. What *are* you going to do? One thing's damn sure, you couldn't earn a decent living on your back...'

He added something so crude and insulting that Fern winced. She thought herself shock-proof, armoured against everything he could say to her, but she was not, she acknowledged nauseously half an hour later as she slowly started to restore order to the chaotic kitchen.

Her face still burned from the final insults Nick had hurled at her. She had known that Nick would make things difficult for her but she had not realised until today just how much he must have always disliked and despised her.

Her hands started to shake. She felt weak...dizzy...sick...as the after-shock of their quarrel washed over her.

Her body ached as though it had been beaten, tension locking every muscle; all she wanted to do was to crawl away somewhere safe and protected. She found herself longing for Cressy, wishing that she had taken her friend's advice and stayed on with her for a few more days.

Cressy had counselled her not to confront Nick directly but to telephone or write to him.

'He'll bully you into staying with him if he can, just for the pleasure it will give him to punish you for wanting to leave him,' Cressy had warned her.

Fern had laughed then, telling Cressy that Nick was hardly as malevolent and destructive as she was painting him, but now, recalling the things he had said to her, Fern wondered if she had been wrong and Cressy right after all.

He had completely ignored her reference to his relationship with Venice. *Had* Adam discussed her with him...as he had said?

He must have done, even if Nick had exaggerated his comments.

Tears burned her eyes. She walked over to the sink, each step a physical effort.

She was not doing this for Nick's benefit, she told herself half an hour later as she washed the final item, but for her own, and when she had finished cleaning the kitchen she intended to walk into town and visit the local estate agents. Somewhere someone must have a room she could rent; her modest resources would allow her to do that. She could also call in at the employment agencies as well, although what kind of work she could find...

The phone rang just as she was about to leave. She picked up the receiver and said her number.

'Fern?' She recognised Venice's voice immediately, and was grimly amused to hear the surprise in it. Plainly Venice was not aware that she had returned.

'I need to speak to Nick,' Venice told her quickly. 'It's...it's very important...a business matter...'

'Nick isn't here, I'm afraid,' Fern told her quietly, adding wryly, 'and I'm sure you have a much better idea of how to get in touch with him than I do, Venice. Oh, it's all right,' she added when Venice was silent. 'I know about your affair—that tie you brought back gave it all away, but then you must have known it would.'

For a moment Fern thought Venice would simply hang up without saying anything, but then she heard her take a quick breath and say fiercely, 'He doesn't love you, Fern. It's me he wants, not you! He didn't even come to look for you when you left, did he? Shall I tell you what he was doing while you were away?' Her voice had softened to a silky, sensual purr now, a softness that barely concealed the razor-sharp claws of her malice.

'He was with me...he was in my bed, Fern, making love to me...wanting me... He never even gave you a thought. To tell the truth, I don't think he'd have given a damn if you'd never come back. Why *did* you come back, Fern? To try to patch up your marriage? You don't have a marriage any more...haven't you realised that yet? I want Nick and I intend to have him. If you've got any sense you'll go back to that friend of yours, but this time you'll stay there...

'Oh, and by the way, there's no need to tell Nick I rang. I'll be seeing him this evening anyway...'

She had hung up before Fern could speak.

It seemed she was not the only one to want to end their marriage, Fern acknowledged shakily as she reflected on Venice's comments. But if Nick had already decided to end their marriage himself, why had he simply not said so?

Because he wants to put the blame on you, an inner voice told her. Because Cressy was right in everything that she said about him. Because he enjoys hurting and humiliating you. Because... She tensed as she glanced out of the window and saw Nick's car pulling up outside.

As she watched, he climbed out and walked towards the house.

Even without being able to see his face she could tell that he was still angry. His movements betrayed both his anger and his aggression.

'Come to your senses yet, have you?' he demanded as he came in. 'You're a fool, Fern, you always have been and you always will be. My God, you're damn lucky that I'm prepared to let you come back. How many other men would take back a woman who'd slept with another man...and not just *any* other man but——?'

'You've slept with other women,' Fern interrupted him coolly. 'You still are doing.'

'And who the hell's fault is that?' Nick demanded savagely. 'I'm a man, Fern, not a bloody monk. What man wouldn't be tempted to turn to someone else married to a frigid bitch like you? Adam was right when he warned me not to get involved with you, not to let my pity for you blind me to reality. Even Adam, cold fish that he is, didn't want you in his bed, did he? *Did* he?'

'Unlike Venice, who does apparently want you in hers,' Fern cut across him.

As she saw the look that crossed his face she was both amazed and appalled at her own recklessness.

'She wants you to get in touch with her, by the way,' she added, refusing to be quelled by the look he was giving her. 'You might have told me that you intended leaving me for her, by the way, Nick,' she added quietly. 'It would have saved us both having to go through this pointless charade.'

'What the hell are you talking about?' Nick demanded furiously. 'I didn't say anything about leaving you.'

'No, you didn't, did you?' Fern agreed levelly. 'You let Venice say it for you... I'm going out now,' she added, heading for the door and pausing when she reached it to turn round and tell him pleasantly, 'Oh, and it's all right. Venice has already told me that you won't be in for dinner.'

She was shaking as she walked out of the house, but she was determined not to let Nick guess how vulnerable she felt.

Venice saw Nick arriving through her bedroom window. She had been standing there watching...waiting for the last half-hour, but she didn't hurry downstairs to let him in.

Instead she walked into the dressing-room attached to her bedroom—there was no way she was going to allow the carefully copied French empire style of the latter to be spoiled by the banks of wardrobes and cupboards, the floor-to-ceiling mirrors, the harshness of the lighting which came as near to natural daylight as was possible and which was essential for the careful and professional application of her make-up.

For Venice the outward appearance with which she faced the world was extremely important; she planned her public appearances with all the dedication and concentration of a master strategist...just as she had planned this meeting with Nick.

She smiled secretly to herself. He of course would never know exactly how much work had gone into this summons here to her house, her presence; how much energy and intensity she had poured into her re-

lationship with him... All the carefully timed strategies, the subtle shepherding and coaxing of him... the deliberate manipulation of his moods
and needs.

Now, as she checked her appearance in the mirrors, she permitted herself
a small, satisfied smile.

Her make-up gave her skin a soft luminescent glow which in the careful
lighting of her drawing-room and bedroom would easily pass for 'natu-
ralness'. She had left her hair soft and loose, its style almost demure.
She was wearing a navy printed chiffon dress with loose panels that floated
enticingly around her body and she had even changed her perfume, for-
going her preference for Schiaparelli's Shocking for something softer,
lighter...

It was time to go down and let Nick in and bring to a close the campaign she had embarked on. A successful close, of course. How could
there be any other?

She paused for a moment, reflecting pityingly on Nick's wife.

She had been no opponent at all, really. Some women had no idea
how to hold on to their men. She gave a small shrug. She would get over
it. She would have to.

She opened the door to Nick just as his irritation was mounting to the
point where he was about to walk away.

Originally, when he had first met Venice, Nick had been wary of her.
Wary of her and extremely excited by her. He knew all about her reputation; he had heard the story of her marriage to a much older and very
wealthy man, her openly uninhibited enjoyment of the wealth he had left
her and of her own sexuality... He had known then how dangerous it
would be for him to get involved with her, but ultimately he had been
unable to withstand his craving for the heady, drugging mixture of excitement, danger and jealousy she aroused within him.

It was a new experience for Nick to be involved in a sexual relationship
where he was not in control, where he was not in a position of mastery
and manipulation. But, although his sense of self-preservation had warned
him to pull back, he had become too deeply infatuated, too drunk on
the ego-boosting drug of sex and sympathy which Venice was feeding
him to allow himself to be weaned of his addiction.

Venice was clever enough to know just when to pull back to allow him
to think he had the edge over her, to bow to his 'male superiority', thus
soothing his pride and allaying, silencing that warning voice of inner
caution and self-protection.

Fern's unexpected rebellion had come at a bad time for him. His accountant had warned him that he would suffer heavy business losses if
he wasn't careful. Venice was not proving very easy to pin down to the
various proposals he had put to her, on which he had hoped to earn fat
commissions. In bed she was all compliance, all agreement with his carefully rehearsed post-coital advice on what she ought to do with her in-

herited millions, but then, later, when he tried to pin her down to making an actual commitment, she became irritatingly vague.

He scowled now as she opened the door to him, ready to demand an explanation from her.

What had got into her? Pulling that idiotic trick of returning his tie like that. Now the postscript at the bottom of Fern's note was beginning to make sense. She must have known that even someone as dim as Fern would put two and two together, and then telling Fern that she wanted to see him... He could feel the irritation bubbling up inside him. He couldn't afford to antagonise Venice now, not when he was so desperately in need of her business, nor was he ready yet to give up his place in her bed. She was an exciting lover, a little too demanding perhaps at times...a little too unfemininely aggressive in the insistence that he complete her pleasure. His ego did not take happily to the suggestion that what he had already given her might not be enough, that he had not totally satisfied her, but whenever he tried to correct this annoying habit, by subtly trying to shift the responsibility for her failure to reach her own preferred peak of orgasmic satisfaction on to her, she somehow or other always managed to turn the tables on him, refusing to accept, as Fern would have done, as other women had, his careful redirection of the 'blame' on to her shoulders, by implying that she was not perhaps sexual enough...not perhaps quite woman enough... She simply laughed at him, mocking him almost as she told him graphically and with an almost shocking bluntness just what it was about his own performance she had found lacking and just what it was she wanted him to do to correct this shortfall.

And in truth there was a part of him, an alien and previously unknown part, that was almost squirmingly and secretly excited by this kind of humiliation. In truth, on those occasions when Venice did complain about his performance, he always invariably found himself being driven, compelled, obsessed almost by the need to prove her wrong...to show her...to reinforce upon her *his* mastery, *his* control...*his* supremacy.

It was only afterwards, lying exhausted, drained, soaked with sweat, his muscles still trembling with effort, in her bed, the fog of almost manic intensity gone, that it struck him that he was far from being in control, from being her master, and that, in contrast, *she* was the one who was supreme, the one who manipulated and used him. But these thoughts seldom lasted very long.

Venice was a woman, and, like all women, she was weak and vulnerable, easily dominated by his sex.

He needed Venice in his life right now, he reminded himself as she let him in. He needed to keep her sweet, to give way a little to her...

But she had to realise that when it came to his marriage...

He was frowning as she led him into her drawing-room. He couldn't tell her, of course, why his marriage was so important to him; why it was so essential that Fern not be allowed to leave him for Adam...Adam, whom he had always loathed from the moment their parents had married and he had seen the way his mother had turned away from him, giving to Adam's father and to Adam the time and attention which had previously belonged exclusively to him . . . gently upholding Adam to him as a role-model.

'Darling, what kept you so long?' Venice was pouting teasingly at him, her manner all little-girl-lost, all soft and coaxing.

For a moment he was briefly soothed, and then he remembered his irritation.

'Do you realise what you've done?' he demanded, pulling away from her, turning his back on her as he walked over to the window. 'Fern recognised that tie and now she's starting to make a fuss about me seeing you.'

No need to tell her what Fern had actually said; and perhaps by threatening and hinting that he might have to curtail their meeting he could both subtly punish her for breaking one of the unwritten rules of their affair—rules which he had laid down in his head even if he had never discussed them with her—and experience the discreet pleasure of reminding her of who it was who actually controlled their relationship . . . and her.

He turned round, keeping his face impassive, waiting for the protests, the apologies, the tears which he knew would follow.

He would make her squirm for a while . . . draw out the punishment just a little before magnanimously forgiving her.

He could feel the pressure and tension aroused by Fern's unexpected rebellion and the row they had had starting to ease, the uplifting mental and emotional narcotic of knowing he was the one in control running swiftly through his veins.

'Darling, I'm sorry, but I had to do it.'

He could hear the remorse in Venice's voice. He turned round, starting to relax slightly.

She had been jealous, of course. Women were like that: jealous, possessive, vulnerable . . . Any minute now Venice would start telling him that it was her love for him that had driven her to it. He would have to point out to her of course that Fern was his wife . . . that . . .

'She had to know. And it seemed kinder, more tactful to do it that way than to wait until . . .'

Nick frowned. Something had gone wrong. That was not what Venice should have been saying. Where was the remorse and self-abasement now? All he could hear in her voice was smooth determination, and a certain dangerous coolness.

She was smiling at him now, but it wasn't an apologetic or pleading smile. His muscles tensed as he recognised the catlike quality of Venice's smile, the knowingness . . . the superiority of it.

Something was wrong . . .

'Darling, I've got the most wonderful news. I'm pregnant.'

Nick stared at her.

Watching him, registering his shock, Venice continued to smile beatifically and vacuously at him. It was a smile she had been practising in front of the mirror for weeks now. Long before she had actually conceived... It was a copy of a smile she had seen on one of the vacuous, innocently virginal faces of a stone madonna statue she had seen on the last holiday she had had with her late husband before his death. They had gone to Italy... it had been a kind of a pilgrimage. He had been stationed there during the Second World War. If he had returned seeking a miracle, he had not found one, because he had died shortly after their return.

She had spent her time shopping and planning. She had seen his will by having finally managed to coax the young junior partner at this legal firm to provide her with a copy. The boy, if not precisely a virgin, had been young and inexperienced enough to have a brief novelty value as a lover, and it had given her an extra *frisson* of excitement to know that she had outwitted Bill and had seen his will.

It had been a relief to discover that he was still besotted enough with her to leave her everything unconditionally, but she was always conscious of the resentment her inheritance had caused his family. There was always the threat that with a clever lawyer and enough stamina they might just be able, if not to get the will totally overset, then potentially to overturn her total control of Bill's estate.

Unless she did something about it... made her position so secure, her reputation so inviolate that she could not be touched. She had worked far too hard for Bill's wealth to let it go.

She had been pondering the problem when she had first met Nick. Then he had simply been another attractive and vain man who had intrigued and amused her, and who had excited her sexually, but then, as time had gone on, she had begun to perceive that he might just possibly be able to play a different role in her life.

As a mother, she had reasoned, she would surely be more secure, invite more sympathy during any potential court case than as a young widow with no dependants. A mother needed to be able to support her child... her children, and if she could be seen to be not just a mother, but also something of a modern madonna as well...

As she watched Nick and saw the panic, the fury, the powerlessness overwhelming him, she smiled secretly to herself.

'Pregnant?' Nick stared at her in disbelief. Had she gone mad? Didn't she realise what this meant? It would ruin him... and she was standing there with that stupid expression on her face, looking at him as though he should be pleased.

Babies... He had never particularly liked children, and certainly never wanted to father any of his own. To have done so, outside his marriage and with a woman like Venice who lived such a high-profile local lifestyle...

He closed his eyes for a moment, trying to fight down his panic.

'Isn't it wonderful?' he heard her saying. 'Darling, I'm so thrilled.'

Thrilled? He finally found his voice, making no attempt to disguise his shock. 'Are you mad?' he demanded jerkily. 'For God's sake, Venice, I'm a married man... You'll have to get rid of it.'

He was sweating now, his shirt clinging clammily to his skin, his heart racing. All the irritation he had felt earlier had returned, only this time it was hardened and intensified by resentment as well.

How could Venice do this to him? She would have to be made to see that the pregnancy could not be allowed to continue.

She would see it, of course... he would make sure that she did. He would make sure that she understood just what was at risk. Their relationship, for a start... He felt the pressure easing slightly as he remembered that *he* was the one in control, that, like all women, she would be manipulated into doing what he wanted, but for some reason this knowledge failed to have its normal restorative effect on him; instead the feeling of panic remained.

Venice was pouting now, her eyes filling with the tears he had expected to see earlier. Was it his imagination or behind those tears did her eyes really look as cold and hard as sharply cut glass?

It *must* be his imagination, surely, because Venice was coming towards him, her eyes widening with distress, her body trembling in that feminine, vulnerable way which so excited him in bed, underscoring as it did his male power over her.

'But, Nick, I thought you'd be so pleased...'

'Pleased? For God's sake, Venice, I'm married!'

She stared at him. 'But, darling, don't you see? My having this baby makes everything so much easier. After all, no matter how sympathetic people might feel towards Fern, they're bound to acknowledge that in divorcing her to marry me in order to protect your child, and of course his or her inheritance, you'd be doing the only honourable thing.'

She paused delicately, her eyes wide and innocent.

'Nick, I'm so afraid. Bill's family have never really accepted that he left everything to me. I'm afraid that once they know I'm having a child they'll try to get some kind of control over Bill's fortune through my baby...'

Venice waited, calmly sure of the effect this pronouncement would have on him. She knew Nick very well by now. Very well, and she knew just how badly his business had been hit by the recession.

It had amused her to listen to his carefully rehearsed speeches about the need for her to protect herself and the fortune she had inherited. He was quite right, of course. It did need protecting... especially from men like him. But she was more than a match for the Nicks of this world.

'Don't you see, darling?' she coaxed now. 'We need you... the baby and I... and it isn't just that...'

She turned away from him, each movement underlining her supplication, her need; each movement carefully choreographed and rehearsed.

'Nick, I've got such plans for us...'

Plans? What was she talking about? Nick was still trying to wrestle with the information she had just given him. His child, inheriting Bill's millions... His child perhaps coming under the influence, the control of others. His child. Bill's millions...

He was sweating again, but for a different reason this time.

Bill's millions... Why had he not thought...? But there was still Fern... Fern whom he would have to divorce if he was to marry Venice and safeguard his role in their child's life. Fern, who would be free, and Adam...

'Darling, I've had the most wonderful idea...' Venice was saying.

He frowned, not bothering to conceal his irritation. She was probably going to start telling him how she planned to decorate the nursery...

'You know that Jennifer Bowers has decided to retire from politics? Apparently her father isn't well, and she feels that she needs to be at home with her family. If you ask me it's probably far more likely that she's worried that Maurice might stray, but... Anyway, that means that the party will be looking for a new candidate to take her place as local MP. Think of it, darling. Think of the influence you'll have, the power...'

Nick was thinking of it... His head was dizzy with the magnitude of what she was suggesting. MP... MP... How small and unimportant that would make Adam and his place on the local council look... Adam who would have to acknowledge his political superiority, his wealth... his status... MP... It would be him that everyone looked up to... him and not Adam. He would be the one cited as a role model. He would be the one people spoke of in tones of awe and admiration.

'And it needn't end there,' Venice was telling him. 'You're young, Nick, and there's no limit to what we could achieve. A ministry... the cabinet... A title...'

She had him now, Venice recognised; she could see the bemusement, the bedazzlement, the bewitchment reflected in his eyes. She smiled triumphantly to herself. She had always known she could do it, of course, just as she had known within a very short time of their becoming lovers how ideally he could be moulded to become her ticket to the life she craved.

She could have done it herself, of course; she had the intelligence, the cunning... but the intensely sensuous and sexual side of her nature, the need to control and dominate, the love of secrecy that drove her—these would have been difficult to accommodate in any public role, especially that of a politician. The Press would have seen to that.

No, it was far better that *Nick* be the one on whom the public attention focused. She looked at him again. He was like a child, dazzled by the bright colours of a pile of cheap toys, not recognising how easily they could break and be worthless. He could not see, as she could, how tight-fitting and restrictive his role would be.

She need never fear that Nick would stray. He might be tempted...he *would* be tempted; but temptation was all he would experience, she would see to that...There would be no pretty, greedy, ambitious researchers for Nick... No doe-eyed, adoring secretaries...no late-night session with co-workers while she waited demurely at home for him.

The power of wealth was a wonderful thing. They would have a London base, and she would live there when the House was in session.

The child would of course be at boarding-school, it and any others they might have, and she intended to make sure that anyone and everyone who came into contact with Nick understood who actually controlled not just the purse-strings but *his* strings as well. Poor Nick. He thought he was the one in control, the one with power...

Dazed, Nick shook his head, excitement taking over from shock.

Venice was right. They could do it... *He* could do it...

'I know you don't want to hurt Fern,' Venice told him. 'But we have to get everything sorted out quickly, Nick, so that when your name goes forward as a candidate no one can start any kind of smear campaign against you. I don't know, but I wouldn't be surprised if Adam decided to try for the candidacy. Not that he could afford it, of course...'

Nick stared at her. He wasn't going to let Adam take this prize from him. He wasn't going to let Adam take from him the glory, the power, the prestige Venice had just shown him.

'Mmm.' Venice was snuggling up to him now, rubbing her breast against his side, sliding her hand down his body.

'Mmm. Just thinking about you becoming an important, powerful politician is making me feel so sexy. Let's go to bed...' She touched his body lightly but deliberately.

'That's something else you've got that Adam doesn't,' she told him softly as she kissed his mouth. 'Poor man, it must be dreadful to have so little sex appeal. Now you...' She kissed him again, flicking her tongue over his lips, rubbing her body against his, slowly starting to unfasten the buttons on his shirt and then drawing her tongue over his exposed flesh.

He smelled and tasted of sweat, reminding her of her first lover. It wasn't a pleasant association. Contrary to the impression she gave, Venice did not like her men to be openly sexual in that sense. She preferred them almost antiseptically clean and disempowered of their maleness. But she was not going to give Nick the opportunity to back out now. She was almost there...almost...

'Take me to bed,' she whispered against his skin, all pleading little girl, all vulnerable supplicant. She knew what Nick liked—what made him feel good and in control. Unlike him. For all his arrogant confidence in his sexuality, he really knew very little about pleasing a woman. Unlike his stepbrother. Now there was a man who...

Under her breath she sighed. What a pity it was that Adam was so impervious to her. But then, maybe perhaps not. It was better this way...

This way she would remain in control...in power.

As she manufactured one of the small, delicate shivers she knew Nick took as a sign of his superiority and her weakness, she smiled triumphantly to herself.

CHAPTER TWENTY-FOUR

'I'VE got to go.'

'No...' Venice pouted, reaching out to wind her arms around Nick's naked body. That was one thing he did have, a good body...lithe and firm without too many obvious muscles, his skin sleek and tanned from the sunbed he used at the country club. He really was incredibly vain...but she liked that in a man. It made him more vulnerable.

'No, stay here with me tonight,' she whispered. She felt his resistance even before his body tensed. But she was prepared for it.

'We still have so much to talk about...I want to sell this house, Nick, buy something else. We'll need to stay within the constituency, of course...somewhere impressive and large enough to entertain. There'll be people in London we'll want to invite down...'

'But what about Fern?' Nick protested, but he was already weakening, seduced and excited by the picture Venice was so cleverly drawing.

'Leave Fern to me,' Venice told him softly. 'She's a sensible woman. She won't be able to deny that your marriage has been in trouble long before you met me. You told me yourself how unhappy you were.' She paused suggestively. 'How unfulfilled...' She touched his face, trailing her fingertips along his jaw, kissing the base of his throat, mentally estimating whether she was going to need to arouse him again before he gave in. If she did she would do it orally. He loved that...loved watching her as she took him in her mouth. Why was it that men were so idiotically proud of that ridiculous few inches of flesh? Had they really no idea how vulnerable it was? It amused her the way he attempted to dominate her, to thrust himself into her mouth.

The first time he had gone too far she had stopped him with a sharp nip of her teeth. She had claimed it was an accident, of course, filling her eyes with tears and the air with abject sounds of remorse.

The trouble was that she had a very sensitive throat...very narrow. She was sorry if she had hurt him. She had never intended...

He had believed her, of course, and she had made sure that he now knew that when she performed fellatio on him she was doing him a very special favour which had to be paid for and with interest.

As always, though, he tended to forget this fact when he was caught in the grip of his own excitement and now, as she watched his face, assessing and judging, she leaned forward, pushing the sheet from her body, whispering breathily, 'Nicky, Nicky...I'm so hungry for you. Where's my big bad playmate? I want to give him a nice big kiss and...'

How predictable some men could be, she reflected—and how boring...
How infantile. Nick wasn't the first of her lovers to respond eagerly to
the kind of language which would have been disdained by any intelligent
three-year-old. There were others, of course, who preferred a different
kind of verbal foreplay, liberally sprinkled with plenty of four-letter words,
but Nick wasn't one of them.

'Don't worry about Fern,' she repeated soothingly. 'Once she knows
about the baby she'll have no option but to give you a divorce. We can
sweeten things for her, of course. She'll get the house and...'

'The house? No...'

Venice drew back and looked at him, lifting one eyebrow in surprised
amusement.

'Darling, you can't possibly want to keep the wretched place. And
besides, think how odd it would look if you didn't let her have it.
Remember, from now on you're going to have to think of your public
image.'

She smiled coaxingly at him, wrinkling her nose, adding, 'We can't
afford to have people suggesting that you're treating her badly, Nick. It's
unfortunate that she's managed to create such a public role of little helper
for herself. Of course, the fact that I'm having your baby is bound to
sway a lot of public opinion our way, and we can always help it along
by arranging for discreet hints to be dropped that she wasn't perhaps the
perfect wife that everyone believed.'

Nick tensed.

'What do you mean?' Despite the fact that he himself had threatened
Fern with it often enough, the last thing he wanted was for her fling with
Adam to become public knowledge.

Venice shrugged. 'Oh, nothing too over the top. Just the fact that
perhaps, although she was a wonderful housekeeper, she was not so wonderful in other departments. That should get the men on your side, and
some of the women, and let's face it, it would be the truth, wouldn't it?
You told me yourself that she was useless in bed. But, as I just said, I
don't think we'll have too much trouble getting public opinion on your
side, especially if we... *you've* been seen to behave generously financially
towards her. After all, divorce is no really big deal these days, not if it's
done discreetly and quietly.'

'That house is mine! I——'

'Nick, darling, *think*! You're going to be a politician... you'll have
power and prestige. What does the house matter? I... we could buy half
a dozen like it and scarcely notice the cost.'

She had his attention now. Greed was always a great motivator, as she
had good cause to know.

'Stop worrying about Fern,' she told him, smiling secretively to herself
as she lied. 'I know you don't want to hurt her, but we have to put our
baby, ourselves first, don't we? Just leave everything to me.'

He gave in, as she had known he would. After all, she had made a very thorough assessment of his personality before laying her plans.

As he slept beside her she looked at him. He really was perfect: vain and egotistical enough to be easily blinded by his own importance, charismatic enough, physically and outwardly at least, to appeal to voters. Greedy enough for all the material benefits she could give him to be compelled to stay within their marriage. She had no intention of marrying a man and turning him into a powerful political force only to be forced to abdicate from her chosen throne by some manipulative little vixen who wanted to take her place.

No, this marriage would be for life. Getting Nick to agree to it had been the easy part.

Getting the local electorate to accept him would be equally easy, and once that was done... Nick was young enough...

Nick would be a gift to the media, the political equivalent of the Royal Family's clever adoption of the Princess of Wales.

He was young, good-looking and, most important of all as far as she was concerned, so self-centred and wrapped up in himself that it would never dawn on him that she was controlling and manipulating him. Through Nick she would have what she had always wanted: power!

He wasn't particularly good in bed, of course, but then she had always felt that sex found its best and most exciting expression outside the marriage bond.

She had it all planned. Once the news of the break-up of his marriage became public they would, outwardly at least, adopt a repentant, guilty awareness of being the ones to blame. They would vocally and repeatedly announce how sorry they were for hurting Fern... how swept away they had been by their love, how compelled to do the best thing for everyone, but most especially for their child. Nick would later then be able to adopt that excellent and well-proven route to the voters' hearts of claiming to represent good old-fashioned family values, of putting the needs of the young and vulnerable before all else. At the same time she would make sure that there were people who knew that Fern had not been wholly blameless... that, even though it was not actively her fault, she was so sexually unresponsive, it had had a detrimental effect on their marriage, eventually and of course regrettably allowing, indeed encouraging Nick to look elsewhere for the sexual and emotional intimacy his marriage was denying him.

She would play her part, of course. Like a chameleon, she had the ability to adapt, to merge with her surroundings and circumstances.

As the new MP's wife she would be irreproachable and unimpeachable, a woman set apart from others. She would be envied, of course, and even resented by other members of her sex, but, since they would never even to themselves feel comfortable admitting the real cause of their resentment of her, they would work even harder at pretending that they did not.

Yes. She had dealt successfully with Nick. All she had to do now was deal equally successfully with Fern. Only, unlike Nick, she had not made the mistake of dismissing Fern as a totally unworthy opponent.

It was common knowledge how much Fern loved her husband. But then she would have to, to put up with the way he treated her, Venice reflected cynically. Poor Fern... one way or the other she was going to have to give him up, but Venice suspected it wouldn't be all that difficult. Once she knew about the baby...

Nick hadn't returned home. Fern had slept in the spare room, lying tensely in bed, ready for the argument she knew would begin the moment he came in, eventually falling asleep in the early hours of the morning.

She had no doubt that in his eyes by staying all night with Venice he was somehow punishing her, but in reality she simply felt relieved.

He would have to be faced sooner or later, of course, for she was not going to change her mind; not going to allow herself to be browbeaten into backing down.

It might not be as easy as she had first hoped to find somewhere to live, but somehow she would do so, she told herself firmly as she put on her coat.

She was going to visit the local library to borrow some careers books. She would have to get some kind of qualifications, of course, and find a job to support herself in the meantime.

It had been Cressy who had told her that since she already had a natural gift for listening to people without judging them she should consider training for some kind of counselling work—an echo of what Adam had once said to her...

Adam...

She shivered, switching her thoughts back to the present and to reality. She had protested at first that her friend was overestimating her abilities, but Cressy had been insistent and Fern acknowledged that her suggestions had appealed to her.

She had already brought home some leaflets from Relate and read through them, confirming what she had already suspected, which was that the training and standards involved in such work were extremely high, and that only a very small percentage of those who initially embarked on the training programme actually made it to the end and became fully accredited counsellors.

She could see why, of course, but the information she had read had been extremely daunting. Daunting and yet at the same time challenging.

She smiled wryly to herself as she walked into town.

For once there was no need to avoid Adam's office. Adam was in Italy with Lily James and her family, she reminded herself wryly as habit made her pause to check the square before hesitantly starting to cross it.

How ironic it was that this should cause her so much more pain than the ending of her marriage to Nick.

She lifted her head and looked boldly and directly towards Adam's office and then stiffened in shock as she saw Adam opening the door and walking out.

Adam was in Italy, Nick had told her tauntingly, but Adam wasn't in Italy, Adam was here, right here, only a handful of yards away from her, his back turned towards her as he closed his office door, mercifully oblivious of her presence.

Just for a few precious seconds Fern allowed herself to drink in the physical pleasure of seeing him, the familiar dangerous bumpy thud of her heartbeat, the acceleration of her pulse, the sweet, slow, destructive pleasure of loving him; a drug as fatal to her as the most lethal of poisons.

And then the exhilaration, the sharp quivering pleasure of seeing him was gone and in its place came the familiar pain of slow despair, spreading heavily through her, hurting her far more than any of Nick's viciously cruel words. Nick had told her that Adam didn't want her and she had known it was true, but somehow this . . . seeing him, loving him hurt even more.

He paused, turning to look back over his shoulder, and Fern wondered sickly if somehow he could have felt the ache of her own yearning, as to her horror she realised that he was crossing the square, coming towards her.

Pride kept her where she was, pride and the fear that in retreating she might somehow betray what she was feeling and in doing so embarrass him and humiliate herself.

'Fern.'

She closed her eyes against the soft warmth of his voice, immediately taking a step back from him, turning away from the small frown pleating his forehead.

'How are you?'

How did he manage to make the casual, impersonal question seem so tender and caring? But then that was Adam, his concern embracing everyone he knew. Even her. . .

'I'm fine . . . fine,' she lied. 'And you . . . Lily . . . ?'

'Lily?' His frown deepened.

'Yes . . .' Fern was stammering slightly now. 'I thought . . . I heard that you . . . that she . . . I thought you were in Italy with . . .'

His frown eased slightly. 'Yes, I was, but I had to come back . . . some business.'

Behind her a car entered the square. Adam reached out a hand as though to guide her closer to him, but Fern immediately stepped away from it, from him . . . out of reach. Her throat ached with pain and emotion, with the sickness of loving him.

'I must get back,' she was stammering again, her face flushing, her body tense.

'Yes...'

She could feel Adam looking at her, but she dared not look up at him. If she did...

She turned away from him quickly, hurrying in the opposite direction, willing herself not to give in to the temptation to look back.

Adam watched her sadly. He didn't try to deceive himself—he knew quite well that if she had been able to she would have disappeared without speaking to him. Could he blame her? In her shoes, wouldn't he have done the same thing?

He felt the pain and the guilt tighten around his heart in a familiar vice-like grip, its pressure relentless, remorseless.

Fern... If he stood still and closed his eyes and breathed in slowly without moving, without disturbing the air around him, it was still just...*just* possible for him to breathe in the elusive fragrance of her. Once that fragrance had been his, wrapped around him, engulfing him, clinging to his skin, so that even after she had gone he had felt as though he carried a part of her with him.

Fern... He swallowed hard past the lump in his throat while his gaze dimmed and glittered. Fern...

By the time she returned home Fern told herself that she was over the shock of seeing Adam and that she wasn't even going to think about it. What was the point? She was a woman, not a girl; she had other problems, other pressures.

She made herself a cup of coffee and sat down with her books, willing herself to concentrate on reality and not drift into pointless and impossible daydreams.

Determinedly she picked up one of the Relate leaflets she had already read and started to study it.

When she heard someone knocking on the front door she frowned and put the leaflet down. It couldn't be Nick, of course, he had a key...

She opened the door and stared at her unexpected visitor in surprise. 'Nick isn't here,' she told her quietly.

'No, I know he isn't.' Venice was inside before Fern could object.

'As a matter of fact,' she announced, 'he's in my bed; he spent the night with me last night.'

If Nick had spent the night with her, what was she doing here? Fern wondered.

'We need to talk,' Venice added. She grimaced openly as she glanced around her. God knew why Nick wanted to hang on to this place. It was badly decorated, and even more badly furnished.

Fern turned round, perplexed, unable to see the purpose of Venice's visit.

'Nick wants a divorce,' she heard Venice telling her, and then, before she could say anything, never mind attempt to point out that Nick already knew that as far as she was concerned their marriage was already over, Venice dropped her bombshell.

'I'm pregnant...it's Nick's baby.'

Fern stared at her. She wasn't sure what stunned her most, the fact that a woman like Venice could prove vulnerable enough to conceive by accident, or the fact that Nick was prepared to publicly accept responsibility for the conception.

What she did not feel, she realised with relief, was any sense of envy or anguish, and as that knowledge flowed gently through her she recognised how very badly she needed to be free of her marriage; how intensely damaging it had been...how destructive.

'I know how you must feel,' Venice was saying to her. 'But Nick and I... Well, we tried to fight what was happening... Neither of us wanted to hurt you.' She looked directly at Fern, tears standing out brilliantly in her eyes.

Fern blinked, wondering if Venice actually expected her to believe her.

'But now for the sake of our baby...'

Venice was enjoying herself, Fern recognised. Relishing the role she had cast for herself.

But what of *her* role... the role of deserted, abandoned wife left alone to face the humiliation of seeing another woman carrying her husband's child... another woman bearing his name...? If she had in actual fact loved Nick...

But she didn't love him, and Nick knew that. He also knew that she was no barrier to his relationship with Venice. So why hadn't he told her that?

A cold finger of apprehension stroked down her spine. Nick had left the house last night claiming that there would be no divorce...that there was no reason for them to divorce.

Fern thought quickly. Just now, sitting daydreaming about the future she could potentially have, the independence, the satisfaction of working to help others, she had known how strongly she wanted to be free. And if that meant aligning herself to Venice... allowing herself to adopt the role Venice had cast for her...if it meant suffering public speculation and pity, well, she had the strength to endure it.

Besides... It had occurred to her just now, rereading the leaflets, that instead of staying here in Avondale she should consider moving to Bristol. There she would have a better chance of finding non-skilled work; she could also hopefully enrol on a postgraduate course of study.

Why the hell didn't the stupid bitch say something instead of staring dumbly at her? Venice wondered impatiently. It had surprised her that her announcement of her pregnancy had not provoked the intensely emotional reaction she had anticipated. Venice considered herself to be a shrewd judge of character. She had had to be. Fern was the self-sacrificing type, the humble, irritating, walk-all-over-me-and-then-turn-round-and-kick-me type that Venice acutely despised.

At the very least Venice had anticipated that the announcement would provoke shocked tears, perhaps a denial followed by the acknowledgement that no, she could not stand in their way, could not rob an innocent child of its father.

'I know how you must be feeling,' she prompted, concealing her irritated impatience. She had other things to do. She didn't want to leave Nick on his own for too long at this stage. She didn't want him getting cold feet, changing his mind. Not that he could afford to. She had seen to that.

'If it weren't for my baby...' She lowered her head mock modestly. 'You can see, can't you, that I...we have to put him first.'

'Yes, I can see that,' Fern agreed calmly.

If they did, it would probably be for the one and only time in Nick's or her life, she reflected ironically, as she watched Venice fight to control the triumph gleaming in her eyes. It was plain that she felt she was on safer ground now. Her head came up, her body tensing almost like that of a fighter.

'There will have to be a divorce, of course...and quickly. Nick will accept full responsibility...admit adultery. He'll make the house over to you, of course...' Venice paused delicately. 'And provided there aren't any problems...any *delays*...' She stressed the word, looking directly at Fern for the first time. 'I'm sure he'll want to make proper financial arrangements for you...'

First the threat and then the bribe, Fern reflected. What kind of woman was Venice? Did she honestly think that, if Fern had actually really loved Nick, she would have wanted to put him through the misery of a long-drawn-out and acrimonious divorce? Love meant putting the other person's needs first, not one's own. And as for that comment about the house and the money, Nick must be besotted with Venice if he had agreed to that.

For the first time she allowed something of her own feelings to enter her voice as she told Venice coolly and very drily, 'That's very generous of Nick, but quite unnecessary.' It was on the tip of her tongue to tell Venice that the last thing she wanted was any kind of reminder of the misery her marriage had been, much less this house which Nick had always so determinedly claimed was his and his alone.

Venice looked nonplussed. 'You mean you'll agree to the divorce?' she questioned.

Fern permitted herself a small inner smile. 'How can I not?' she responded sorrowfully. 'For the baby's sake.'

She could see that her capitulation coupled with her rejection of the money had confused Venice, who now did not seem to know exactly what to do.

'Nick's clothes...' she suggested. 'You'll want... If you'd like to wait I could pack them... or...'

Venice stared at her. Could this woman be real? Her contempt for her grew. How could she be so submissive, so... so accepting?

Fern could see the look Venice was giving her, but of course what the other woman did not know was that the last thing she wanted now was for Nick to come round, change his mind. The last thing she wanted was any further contact with him.

It didn't take her long to pack; she literally threw everything into the suitcases, reflecting with savage satisfaction that it would no longer be her job to keep his pure cotton shirts flawlessly uncreased, his wool suits immaculately pressed, his shoes cleaned.

Not that she could see Venice performing any of those tasks for him.

As she heaved the final case downstairs, Venice came out of the sitting-room. She was holding a small booklet in her hand.

'I was just reading this. I hadn't realised that the Broughton House gardens had been designed by Gertrude Jekyll.'

'Yes, they were,' Fern agreed. 'Mrs Broughton showed me the actual plans.'

'Do you know where they are now?' Venice demanded. Fern looked at her. 'The plans?' Venice prompted excitedly. 'Do you know where they are?'

'Well, I presume they're with the rest of her papers, with her solicitor,' Fern responded.

What on earth had prompted Venice's excited interest in Broughton House's gardens? Fern wondered curiously.

'So it's agreed, then?' Venice announced, after Fern had carried the final case out to the car for her. 'You won't contest the divorce and, in return, Nick will sign the house over to you and make you an allowance?'

'I shan't contest the divorce,' Fern told her quietly, and she certainly didn't intend to accept any money for her compliance.

Her compliance... Why hadn't Nick told Venice that she, Fern, had already announced that she wanted a divorce?

With that kind of deceit between them, how *could* their relationship—their marriage succeed? But then that was their worry and not hers...

Thank goodness.

She glanced at the phone. She would ring Cressy, tell her what had happened, ask her what she thought of her moving to Bristol.

She couldn't believe how good she felt... how relaxed... relieved... how happy... how *free*...

Venice got out of the car, almost running into the house. Nick was seated at the table in the breakfast-room dressed in a towelling robe, glowering moodily into a cup of coffee.

'Where the hell have you been?' he demanded as she walked in. 'And where are my car keys?'

'I don't know...have you lost them?' She gave him a wide-eyed look of innocence. The car keys were safely locked away in her bureau, and the key was on her keyring. There had been no way she had been going to allow him to leave until she had seen Fern.

'I've seen Fern. She accepts that we have to put the baby first and she's agreed not to contest the divorce. I had to promise her the house, of course, and a small allowance, but it will be better that way. People will soon stop feeling sorry for her and blaming you once they see how generous we've been.

'I want to arrange a dinner party. Just ourselves, the local agent and another couple. It won't do any harm to put things in motion...register your interest and, of course, let people see us as a couple. I'll have to ring my solicitor and get him working on the divorce. Oh, and by the way, Nick, I've had the most marvellous idea. It was while I was waiting for Fern to pack up your things. I saw this article on Broughton House. Did you know the gardens had been designed by Gertrude Jekyll?'

'So what?'

'So, my precious, wonderful darling, now you can kill two birds with one stone. Stop dear Adam from getting his planning permission and become recognised, not just locally but hopefully nationally, as an alert environmentalist, ready to protect Britain's heritage...

'The gardens, Nick,' she told him when he scowled sulkily at her. 'If we can prove they *were* designed by Jekyll, and according to Fern there are actually plans in existence, then we can mount a campaign...get a preservation order on them. Don't you see...it will be the *perfect* cause for you? It's local, environmental...just the kind of thing that has mass sentimental appeal. You'll become known as someone who cares...someone who gets things done. Look at how it's worked for Adam; but he's only got limited local appeal, whereas this...

'It will need careful handling, of course, and the right kind of publicity...the right kind of team behind you. We don't want anyone else taking over and getting the glory.'

Nick thought quickly. When he had woken up alone in Venice's bed this morning and remembered what had happened the previous night, his first thought had been to tell her that he had changed his mind, but now, subtly, she was drawing him back under the spell she had cast the previous night once again, reminding him of the glittering future she had drawn for him.

Greed had momentarily pushed Adam and his destructive resentment of him into second place... Gloatingly he reflected on how he would make Adam squirm when he was MP...on how he would humiliate and punish him. He would be the one that everyone looked up to then, not Adam.

Venice was right, he did need a cause. Broughton House...

'What would happen if the house had already been sold before we could do anything?' he asked Venice.

She looked at him. 'Nothing. Whoever bought it would probably lose their money, because one thing's for certain, there's no way the heritage people would allow them to destroy those gardens, much less give planning permission on them . . .'

As she watched the satisfied smile hardening his eyes, Venice congratulated herself. He was so easy to read, so vainly oblivious to his own vulnerability, so perfect for the role she intended him to play.

From the first moment she had realised the power over certain men her sexuality gave her, Venice had decided to hone and use it. That had been when she was fourteen, and she had seen the way her stepfather was watching her.

For the two years until she was sixteen she had skilfully kept him at bay, alternating between subtle promises and fierce rejection, taking the increased pocket money he gave her, the clothes, the treats and then holding him off with virtuous indignation and feigned innocence whenever he tried to demand payment.

Venice had quickly learned that weak men, sexually hungry men were the easiest to manipulate and control. Her own father had been a successful businessman, but when he'd left her mother to marry his secretary and father a second family there had been an abrupt decrease in Venice and her mother's standard of living, and a change of school from the small private school Venice had previously attended to a large inner-city comprehensive.

She had seen then the difference that money, wealth could make, and she had determined that one day she would possess the kind of wealth that no one could ever take away from her. And, being Venice, she had also very quickly decided that the easiest and quickest way for her to get it was via her sexuality.

There had been a couple of discreet liaisons with wealthy, married men before she had met Bill, but once she had met him she had quickly discarded her then lover, recognising that in Bill she would have not merely access to his bank account in the form of expensive presents, and 'rewards' for the use of her body, but control over it in the form of marriage.

Bill had been a very lonely man, a man who had worked hard all his life for very little personal happiness. Venice had promised that she would change all that, but, as she had quickly discovered once she was Bill's wife, wealth was one thing, but there were other forms of power, even more of an aphrodisiac, and her hunger for power, complete, absolute and total, was a hunger that had not ceased growing with marriage to Bill—far from it.

Bill had had no social or political ambitions and Venice had quickly recognised that it was pointless trying to urge him towards them.

With his death, though, things had changed. Venice was astute enough to recognise that the very sexuality within her which had enabled her to achieve her original ambitions would be counter-effective with her new ones. Those who guarded the social barriers she longed to penetrate would recognise what she was at one glance and debar her, and as for the political ones... Her mouth curled in a cynical smile. Perhaps if her sex had never been given the vote she might have stood a chance...

As it was... She glanced at Nick. He would serve her purpose admirably. He was neither rich enough nor well-connected enough ever to be able to defy or ditch her; she would always have absolute and complete control over him.

She glanced complacently down at her body. She would go to Valentino for the dress she would wear for the ball they would give to celebrate Nick's acceptance as MP. It was a pity Lord Stanton was still alive; the hall was bound to go for a knock-down price once he had died, and the ballroom there would be a perfect venue for such an event.

She would have to make sure that things were timed so that Nick didn't formally take over from Jennifer Bowers until after she had had the baby.

It would be a boy, of course. She wasn't going to have daughters who would one day grow up to compete with her!

Yes, everything was working out exactly the way she had planned.

CHAPTER TWENTY-FIVE

'SHALL we head for Passport Control?'

'Yes,' Marcus agreed tersely, pulling away slightly as Sondra leaned closer to him. He could feel the warmth of her body through the thickness of his suit, smell her perfume. He paused for a moment, looking back over his shoulder, hesitating, but Sondra was urging him forward, telling him how excited she was about the trip and how much she was looking forward to seeing something of The Hague.

Marcus said nothing. These consultations with his Dutch and fellow European peers were commonplace affairs: hours spent in dark, crowded rooms while some fine point of international law was thrashed out.

The International Court of Justice had no power to enforce its decisions, but its judgments nevertheless carried considerable weight. Once, Marcus acknowledged, he had treated these consultations with as much enthusiasm as Sondra, but these days they were just something else to be crammed into an already overstretched schedule.

He was now approaching that point in his career when he had to decide whether to continue into the higher echelons of taking on only the cream of the work he was offered, or whether to put aside litigation work and opt instead for another role within the judiciary. He had already received tentative approaches to sound out how he would feel if he were invited to become a judge.

There was of course another option; he could always move permanently to Brussels and accept one of the many lucrative offers he regularly received to act as a consultant for one of the huge multinational companies.

Part of the problem was that, at this stage in his life, he wasn't sure if he was ready to give up the adrenalin-activation of litigation work, and yet at the same time he acknowledged that he could not continue to take on the amount of work he was doing at present.

Couldn't Nell see how impossible it would be for him to work as he was doing at the moment and to commute from Wiltshire?

'You will be able to work at home sometimes,' she had burbled happily.

Couldn't she see—didn't she realise...? He moved uncomfortably in his seat as the jet prepared to take off.

Beneath the anger he still felt, the belief that Eleanor wasn't listening to him, wasn't aware of the problems he was facing, was more concerned with other issues, other people than she was with him, lurked other emotions... Emotions he was too cowardly to confront?

He wished Eleanor could find a way to make peace with Vanessa, despite the girl's bad behaviour, which seemed to be designed to shock Eleanor.

He had been shocked too, but what was he supposed to do? Vanessa was almost an adult, old enough to know right from wrong; far too strong-willed to be disciplined by anything he could say or do.

After the break-up of his first marriage, everyone had said how sensible he was being in allowing Vanessa to remain almost permanently with her mother. Much better, especially for a girl, all his friends had said. How could he, a single man, working the hours he did, have taken charge of a young child?

It would have been impossible. Financially he had made sure that she never lacked for anything, and yet recently, listening to Eleanor, he had felt almost as though she were somehow accusing him...blaming him...

He remembered the first time he had discussed Vanessa with Nell and the surprise she had quickly hidden when he had admitted that he didn't see very much of his daughter.

Was it his fault that he simply wasn't a particularly paternal man? Was Eleanor blaming him...rejecting him because she considered that he had somehow failed Vanessa?

Just how important was *he* to his wife? he wondered tiredly as he opened his briefcase and removed some papers. How far down the list did he come? Well beneath her sons? Beneath his own daughter? And certainly well below that damned house.

If Nell hadn't been so wrapped up in that, he might have had a chance to talk to her about his own problems, to explain to her that, while he realised they needed more space, he simply did not have the time at the moment to get involved in the kind of domestic disruption she was planning.

As he checked through his diary, his frown deepened. He had a meeting which would take up most of tomorrow morning. There were some facts he wanted to check up on in the library, and then at six there was a reception at the British Embassy he would have to attend.

Beside him Sondra moved slightly, so that the soft, full weight of her breast pressed against his arm.

It has been a surprise to discover that she was accompanying him on this trip. She had thought it would be a wonderful opportunity to see the European Court system in action, she had told him. He had known two days ago that she would be going with him, but he had said nothing to Nell.

But then, why should he? It wasn't as though he was doing anything wrong...or even contemplating doing anything wrong. All right, so Sondra had made it plain how she felt about him, but that didn't mean that he was going to respond.

He frowned as he remembered Eleanor's earlier reaction to Sondra and the argument they had had.

Arguments were all they *did* seem to have these days, and he was beginning to feel almost as though he hardly knew Nell at all. At times he felt almost as though she was deliberately distancing herself from him, withholding herself . . . rejecting him. As his mother had done?

Angrily he made a small, sharp sound.

'Hey, what's that for?'

Sondra smiled at him as she touched him on the arm. She was a stunningly attractive young woman, Marcus admitted, and one who quite obviously knew how to use that attractiveness.

'I've been doing some reading up,' she told him. 'The Hague has some wonderful museums and galleries . . .'

'Yes, you'll enjoy seeing them,' Marcus agreed.

Immediately she pouted slightly. 'I was rather hoping that you would come with me, or would that be too boring for you?'

In spite of himself, Marcus laughed.

'You should have chosen politics, not law,' he told her drily.

'What makes you think I won't?' she riposted back. 'In the US the law can often be a stepping stone to Capitol Hill. What are *your* ambitions, Marcus?'

His eyebrows lifted. 'At my age one is supposed to have achieved them,' he pointed out, ignoring the small warning voice that told him of the danger he was courting. She was more than intelligent enough to recognise such a subtle counter-flirtation, and he was not really surprised when she pounced with delicate, catlike dexterity and relish on the small morsel of encouragement he had given her, demanding softly,

'What age . . . ? No real man even starts to become interesting until he's approaching forty, and I know for a fact that the decade between forty and fifty can be not just one of the most professionally fufilling but also one of the most sexually fulfilling of a man's life. There's something very, very attractive to a woman about an adult man who knows what he wants from life and how to get it . . . something so potently sexually attractive that very few women can resist it . . .'

How long was it since Nell had flirted with him like this . . . made him feel like this . . . boosted both his ego and his libido . . . ?

He was comparing two very different women, he reminded himself, and not very fairly. Nell had never had the kind of sexual self-confidence and aggression that would allow her to come on to a man the way that Sondra was doing.

In bed . . . in private, she had *told* him, *shown* him how much she desired and wanted him.

Had *shown* him? Guiltily he remembered the way they had made love in Provence; the eagerness with which she had come to him.

Long ago, in old-fashioned, traditional marriages, women had bartered sex for possessions and security. Nell was not that kind of woman, she never could be, but in her way, if one looked beneath the surface, Sondra was exactly that kind of woman, using her sexuality, her youth as a lure, a bribe... relishing the power they gave her. He knew that, Marcus acknowledged, so why did he still find her sexually exciting?

What was it he really wanted? To lose himself and forget his anxieties and problems in the lush sexuality of her body? Or to punish Nell for not recognising and meeting all his needs by betraying her, betraying their marriage? Was he really that selfish—that weak? That male?

That was the trouble with being a lawyer, he recognised as the captain announced they would soon be landing; one always felt bound to assess both sides of the story.

Since both of them had brought only carry-on hand luggage with them, Marcus noticed wryly as they left the plane—Sondra's bearing the unmistakable Gucci signature, unlike his own—there was nothing to delay their departure from the airport.

In the taxi taking them to their hotel, Sondra sat close to him, slipping her arm familiarly through his as she told him, 'Well, at least we'll have this evening free. What shall we do? I know... you can show me The Hague by night. The canals may not be as romantic as those in Venice, but the smell will probably be a lot better.' She laughed as she wrinkled her nose.

As he listened to her, Marcus immediately registered his danger and his own foolhardiness. Those key words 'we' and 'romantic' had made her intentions plain enough. If he agreed to what she was suggesting, he had no doubts where the evening would end. And he wasn't sure yet if that was really what he wanted. Nor really whether he actually liked being treated as the more passive partner.

'I'm sorry, but I can't,' he told her. 'I've already arranged to spend the evening with an old friend...'

It wasn't true, of course. What he *had* intended to spend the evening doing was getting up to date with some of his paperwork.

As soon as they had checked into their rooms, he picked up the phone, mentally keeping his fingers crossed.

Half an hour later he left the hotel, summoning a taxi and giving the driver his instructions. He had rung though to Sondra's room and told her that he was going out. He could tell from her voice that she wasn't pleased, and, remembering the soft, warm weight of her breast pressed against his body, he wasn't sure if he really was doing the right thing himself.

The Hague was not a flamboyant city like Amsterdam; on the contrary, its buildings spoke of solid, respectable, middle-class wealth and lack of showiness, sedately prosperous, its streets immaculately clean, its very mien extraordinarily consistent with its role as the home of international justice; it had a sober, responsible, almost Scottish dour air about it which somehow made it somewhere totally unsuited for adulterous sex— or was that simply his own conscience prodding him? he wondered, as the taxi set him down outside one of a street of classically restrained canal houses.

The door opened almost immediately to his knock, the solid-fleshed, broad-shouldered man welcoming him giving off the same air of solid respectability as his home.

'Marcus, it is good to see you,' he greeted the Englishman, clapping him warmly on the shoulder. 'Come in...'

'It's good to see you too, Piet. Sorry to land myself on you at such short notice.'

'Not at all...I am only too glad to have your company. Elise is away with the children visiting her parents in Friesland and the house feels very empty without them. Have you eaten yet, or...?'

'We were offered something on the plane, but I'm certainly more than ready to eat again,' Marcus told him, pausing as he saw the question in his friend's face.

'We? You are not alone, then?' Piet peered round the door as though looking for someone else.

'No...a colleague. An American lawyer who is spending some time with us studying the European judiciary system. She thought this trip would be of benefit to her.'

'She?' The thick, reddish-brown eyebrows rose a second time, and Marcus grimaced slightly to himself.

The legal community in The Hague, like that in London, was close-knit, sometimes almost incestuously so. He doubted it would be very long before Piet knew all about Sondra Cabot.

And thereby guessed what had brought him here to his door tonight?

A man couldn't be convicted for being tempted, Marcus told himself wryly, as Piet led the way to his study.

He had first met Piet when they had both been studying law, and he had attended a course in The Hague. It had been this which had first given him a taste for international law and he and Piet had remained friends over the years.

Piet and Elise had been guests at his marriage to Eleanor. Piet was also Vanessa's godfather, although he and Julia had never liked one another. In contrast, Eleanor and Elise had got on very well together, although on the surface they did not have much in common, since Elise did not work, devoting herself full-time to their four children and the various charity committees on which she worked.

In Piet's study, the desk was littered with papers, a large bulky file open.

'A very complex and tragic case,' Piet announced as he saw Marcus glance at his desk. 'I am to defend a man accused of murdering his twin granddaughters. Yes, it's very shocking,' Piet agreed when Marcus made a small sound of distaste. 'Elise did not want me to take the case.'

'He'll be convicted?'

'Oh, yes, without doubt. Naturally we had initially intended to plead diminished responsibility, but the psychiatrist's reports and the man's own statements...' He shrugged.

'They have him under heavy guard. He has already tried twice to take his own life, and I am not sure whether it would simply be kinder to allow him... However, that is a very dangerous line of thought for men such as us. We are here simply to plead the fact of the case as best we can, and to thank God that this primitive male jealousy which can so often be the curse of our sex does not affect us.

'The true tragedy of the case is that he actually loved his grand-daughters, loved them but believed that his wife loved them more than she did him. A familiar story...' He glanced at Marcus. 'We have all heard it before.'

'Yes,' Marcus agreed heavily, frowning to himself. Piet was right; male jealousy could be a destructive, dangerous thing. How many men had he heard say that they had killed their wives, their lovers rather than lose them? How many men had he heard speak enviously and resentfully of women's relationships, friendships, closeness to their friends and family, feeling that that closeness excluded them and threatened their relationship?

As he himself had felt about his mother's relationship with his grand-mother? And Eleanor's desire to draw Vanessa closer to her?

'And you,' Piet was saying. 'What brings you to The Hague?'

'Oh, the usual thing,' Marcus told him absently. 'One of my clients has a case before the International Court—just a preliminary hearing this time—a formality really.'

'And Vanessa, my goddaughter. How is she?'

Marcus gave him a wry look.

'Ah, like that, is it?' Piet commiserated. 'These teenagers; they suffer so, poor things, and us with them. Our eldest is fourteen now; his voice has not yet quite broken but he insists that he is a man; an adult. One minute he is telling me I have no right to interfere in his life, the next he is running to his mother, hiding behind her skirts.

'She is too soft with him.' He shook his head and then paused. 'There, you see, it is just as I was telling you before. Elise accuses me of being jealous of him and, although I do not admit it to her, sometimes I think there is perhaps a grain of truth in what she says, although it is not so much him I resent but all that he represents. And he seems to sense it and play on it. I tell you, Marcus, sometimes he would try the patience of a saint, but then, when I swear I could quite easily murder him, I look at him and remember that he is my son, my child, and I feel myself melt with love for him.

'It will be harder for you, of course, and for Eleanor; to be the mother of a teenage stepdaughter is not an enviable task.'

'I've tried to tell Eleanor that, but she takes it all so personally... blames me, I think sometimes... believes that I'm encouraging Vanessa in her antagonism towards her. Nell has this idiotic idea that by moving to a huge barn of a house in the middle of the country she will somehow be able to weld us all into one big, happy family...'

'And you don't agree?'

'Not really. The house is isolated, in need of a complete renovation and redecoration. None of the children is used to living in the country. Eleanor herself... She thinks I'm deliberately being awkward. She can't see that all I want to do is to protect her from being hurt...'

He saw the look Piet was giving him and grimaced. 'All right, so I'm not particularly keen on the move myself, but I honestly *don't* think it would be right for any of us, including Nell; but she can't see that. She thinks...'

He broke off and gave a small, exasperated sigh. 'I'm sorry, Piet. I shouldn't be burdening you with my problems.'

Piet spread his hands in a gesture of acceptance.

'What else are friends for? I think, my friend, that there is far more here than just a move of house. You say that Vanessa and Eleanor do not get on. Could that not make Eleanor feel vulnerable, and Vanessa as well...? They are, after all, two women loving one man, hmm...?'

'*Vanessa*, vulnerable!' Marcus shook his head. 'If you could see her... hear her. Sometimes I wish...' He paused, not wanting to admit even to one of his oldest and closest of friends how resentful he sometimes felt about the strain Vanessa's presence placed on his marriage.

Resentful of whom? Vanessa for being there? Or Eleanor for not being able to find a way of dealing with her? Or was his resentment fuelled by both of them; by their femaleness... their difference... and his inability to find a logical male answer to the emotional trauma of their relationship?

'Come on, let's go out and eat,' Piet suggested.

Half an hour later, seated in a small, comfortable restaurant, Marcus glanced round at his fellow diners. Men in the main; sober-faced and equally sober-suited; an echo of the town itself; the décor, the food, the people, all of them were respectable and conservative, outwardly at least. Who knew what emotions, what turmoil, what trauma they might feel inwardly? 'And now,' Piet announced when their meal had been served, 'I think you should tell me all about this young American who brings you scurrying to my door for sanctuary.' He added slyly, grinning at Marcus, 'It is a very sad thing to be a middle-aged man, my friend. One is never more aware of one's vulnerability and the passage of time. Is she very beautiful?'

'She is very attractive, and very determined,' Marcus told him wryly. 'But not beautiful; Eleanor is beautiful.'

As he said it he realised that it was the truth, and suddenly he felt as though a weight had started to lift from his shoulders.

It was late when he eventually returned to his hotel room. He was just getting undressed when the phone started to ring. He stared at it, quickly envisaging Sondra in her own room, lying on the bed, her body naked, sensually relaxed and her skin burnished with that glow of health a certain class of American woman seemed to exude so effortlessly.

His mouth had gone dry, his body tensing; and not just with apprehension, he recognised as he reached automatically for his robe to conceal his growing erection.

The fierce sound of the shower drowned out the ring of the telephone. It was better this way... saner... safer... and besides, he had things to think about.

Remembering listening to Piet telling him about his case made him frown; but he was not a murderer—he would never hurt anyone... would he? Hadn't he hurt Nell... destroyed their love? Hurt Vanessa too perhaps, by the way he had distanced himself from her, unable to admit even to himself the conflicting emotions she caused in him? He had an illuminating mental memory of Vanessa as a small child, clinging nervously to Julia while she tried to coax her to go to him. Vanessa had been almost two at the time; he had been away for a month in Brussels and at that age it was hardly surprising that she had been a little afraid of him. Given the hours he had been working, he had after all virtually been a stranger to her.

He closed his eyes, standing motionless under the hammer of the shower, remembering another incident. Vanessa... six years old... three years after the divorce...

It had been her school sports day, something he had reluctantly attended, chivvied into it by the woman he had been seeing at the time. She had mistakenly thought that by encouraging his paternal sense of duty she would bring him a step closer to marriage. As far as Marcus was concerned, however, their relationship had already run its course; but he had given in to her demands that they attend Vanessa's sports day.

They had arrived late... just in time to see Vanessa win her race. She had seen him, her face lighting up as she came over to him, flinging herself into his arms... only he had stepped back from her, fending her off.

Why had he done that to her? Beneath his closed eyelids he could see two different images, two different children... himself and Vanessa... both of them young, helpless, wanting... aching to be acknowledged and loved... both of them rejected by the person whose love they needed the most.

'Oh, my God...'

In the close confines of the shower the words seemed to echo as loudly as though he had shouted them.

His client had been jealous, Piet had said... Jealous of the love his wife had shown their daughter and their grandchildren... Just as *he* had been jealous of the love Nell had for Vanessa—not her sons; no, he hadn't been jealous of them, they were boys... male—but Vanessa! He had even been jealous of the house, resenting it not just because of the time it consumed, the attention it took away from him, but because Nell had wanted it for Vanessa... Every time Nell had exhorted him to spend more time with his daughter, every time she had worried about her or shown concern for her, the jealousy he had refused to acknowledge had been driven a little deeper...festered a little more poisonously. But, unable to accept or understand this, he had blamed not himself for what he was feeling, but Nell.

In London Eleanor sat up in bed, her stomach ice-cold with fear and despair. She stared at the receiver she had just replaced. Marcus wasn't in his room... Where was he? Did she really need to ask?

She remembered the way she had seen Sondra leaning into him; the intimacy of their bodies, their total lack of awareness of her presence.

'That damned house is more important to you than me,' Marcus had accused her. 'If the house means so much to you then go ahead and buy it...but I...'

'But I won't be living there with you.' Was that what he had been going to say?

What had happened to them? Where had it all started to go wrong? She had tried so hard... Too hard. 'You're trying too hard,' he had told her when she had expressed her concern over Vanessa's attitude towards her, and she had sensed then the criticism and irritation in his voice, had felt then the beginnings of her sense of somehow having failed him or fallen short of certain standards by not being able to get on with Vanessa.

How little it took to erode one's self-confidence: an antagonistic teenager, the betrayal of a business partner, the feeling of a life going slowly out of control, the awareness of personal needs that were not being met, the need to reach out for something to hold on to, the almost childish need for some kind of comforter... For some women it was food, for others it might be sex; for her it had been a house. No, not a house but a home, the home she had never had as a child; the home which as a child she had believed would magically make her world safe and secure and would bring her her parents' love and attention.

Was that what she had been looking for with Broughton House—not, as she had believed, as somewhere for their children to experience the kind of childhood she had wanted, but for herself, a consolation for not achieving the 'perfection' she was supposed to achieve...perfection not just as a wife, but as an independent career woman, a devoted, caring mother, an understanding, wise stepmother, a good friend, someone to whom others turned and leaned on, someone secure in herself?

But she was none of those things. So what was she, then? Just another tired, stressed woman who was fed up with trying to match impossible standards, who was afraid of admitting she couldn't achieve the goals others seemed to reach so easily, who was so afraid of not reaching those goals that she would rather crawl into the sanctuary she had found for herself and hide away than confront the reality of her life.

What was it she really wanted? Not the perfection she had once believed she must attain; just thinking about the effort it would require, the ceaseless battle to be so many things she was not, exhausted and drained her.

No, what she wanted was simple acceptance of what and who she really was. What she wanted was to be allowed to fail sometimes; to be allowed to be human and vulnerable, to be allowed to forget that her sons needed new football boots and to be allowed to feel angry and helpless when she was confronted by her stepdaughter's antagonism.

And to be allowed to be jealous and to show it when another woman made a play for her husband.

To be allowed to be hurt and afraid at the thought of him having an affair with her.

Irritably Marcus glanced at his watch. The reception was dragging on longer than he had expected. He had been hoping to catch an early flight home. There were things he needed to do, to say.

As he looked up he was aware of Sondra trying to catch his eye, smiling at him under her lashes as she flirted with the bemused young aide she was talking to.

He smiled back. How could he ever have imagined he was attracted to her? She was attractive, yes—sexually aware of herself, intelligent too...but she was not Eleanor.

As soon as he could, he walked over to her.

'Look, I want to get back to London as quickly as I can,' he told her, adding before she could say anything, 'There's no need for you to cut short your visit, though. You've still got all those art galleries and museums to see, and by the looks of it you seem to have found someone far better equipped than me to show them to you,' he added with a brief glance in the direction of the jealously watching aide.

She tried to dissuade him, pouting a little, protesting that he surely could stay on a little longer, but Marcus shook his head firmly, disengaging her hand from his arm as he stepped back from her.

'Well, if you have to go...'

'It isn't a matter of having to,' he told her softly.

He left her and went to find the ambassador, explaining that he had to leave to catch an early flight. They had met before on several occasions and Marcus chatted with him for a few minutes before finally taking his leave. He was asked if he intended to become a permanent feature in Brussels or The Hague and Marcus replied, 'I doubt it. It would mean spending too much time away from my family and that's a sacrifice I'm not prepared to make.'

'Can't say I blame you,' the diplomat agreed.

There was still a long way to go, Marcus reminded himself as he boarded his plane; a hell of a long way and most of it over some very tricky ground indeed, but at least he had made a start; at least he could now acknowledge that the journey needed to be made, and in which direction.

And Nell? Would she be prepared to make it with him, to help him over the rough patches, guide him when necessary? He winced as he remembered the things he had said to her. If the house really meant that much to her, surely they could find some way of reaching a compromise...a small flat in London for him during the week perhaps, until such time as he could make the transition from Q.C. to the Bench.

As a circuit judge he would still have to spend time away from home, and it would be dishonest of him not to admit that he would miss the cut and thrust of pleading a case, but there were other things he needed to do now...other people he had to consider. Was it already too late to stop Vanessa from repeating his own mistakes, to show her the love, give her the security he now acknowledged he had subconsciously withheld, help her perhaps to become the parent he himself had not possessed the strength to be?

Nell would show him the way...help him, support him...

Nell...

'So what are you going to do?'

Eleanor shook her head as she looked across at Jade. 'I don't know. If he is having an affair...'

'You don't know that for sure,' Jade reminded her.

'No,' Eleanor agreed tiredly. 'I do know one thing, though, and that is that it's pointless going ahead with the house now. I'll have to tell the agents.'

Her eyes filled with tears, which she shook away. 'I feel so stupid, Jade. How could I not have known what he was feeling? Why didn't he say something to me? Why did he just let me go on believing that...? Why couldn't I see...?'

'You're not God,' Jade told her drily. 'You can't be expected to second-guess everything, although sometimes you'd think that's exactly what is expected of us. You'll never guess what Sam said to me the other night. He claimed that I was using this job in New York as a means of getting out of making a commitment to him! There I am bending over backwards not to make him feel pressured or trapped, not to let him know how important he is to me, dammit, and he accuses me of not caring, when the truth is that I care far too damn much. Perhaps that's why Marcus said nothing, Nell...perhaps he was afraid that, if he did, he might find out that the house was more important to you than him...'

'What?' Eleanor stared at her. 'That's ridiculous... Marcus knows how important to me he is... how much I love him. I only wanted the house because... No, you're wrong, Jade. To tell the truth, I don't think Marcus cares what I feel for him any longer. These days, when he looks at me, I get the impression that all he sees is a woman who's a failure... in her career, with her children... with his daughter and with him... Look, I've taken up enough of your time. I know how busy you are,' she added as she stood up. 'Thanks for listening...'

'You know what your main trouble is, don't you?' Jade told her, as she too got to her feet and they made their way through the crowded restaurant. 'You put yourself down too much. OK, so I listened... once. What's that compared with all the times you've listened to me? Talk to Marcus, Nell,' she urged her. 'Tell him how you feel... what you think....'

Eleanor gave her a tired smile. 'I'll try, but what's the point if he doesn't want to listen?' And she went outside.

There was one thing she had to do before she saw the agent... before Marcus came back from The Hague.

This time she was firmly direct with Mrs Garvey when she told her that she wanted her to stay when the boys returned from school.

'Well, I suppose I could stay on... just this once,' the older woman agreed grudgingly.

Eleanor picked up her keys, and the letter she had written to Louise telling her not just how upset she had been by the fact that her partner had not informed her that Monsieur Colbert had been trying to get in touch with her, but pointing out as well that, since they had been equal partners in the business, it was only fair that Louise take on equal responsibility for ending it.

What she was doing, what she should have done weeks ago, she acknowledged, was taking charge of her life again, trying to master her own inner fears of inadequacy and failure. After all, if she and Marcus were to separate, to divorce, she would need to be strong, to...

Tears blinded her as she got into her car and started the engine.

It was a still, hazily hot day, the temperature just on the right side of mugginess even though it was now September, the stillness of the air enhancing the silence of the garden.

In the borders, daisylike asters looked to the tumble of clambering roses for support; poppies, run to seed, grew everywhere, pushing their way up through huge clumps of catmint and geraniums.

Eleanor took her time; after all there was no reason to hurry. Not now she had the whole afternoon ahead of her.

In the iris dell, the flowers were over, all that remained the dying, untidy stalks and browned flower heads.

Overhead, the late summer leaves provided a cool canopy, the path shadowed and sheltered.

She didn't allow herself to cry until she reached the pool. Now for the first time she allowed herself to acknowledge what she had really known for some time. Even if Marcus had wanted the house, the problems they would have faced in turning it into the home of her dreams would have been virtually insurmountable. Her accountant had tried to tell her this, and so had the architect, but she had been too afraid to let go of her dream, too afraid of facing up to what letting go of it actually meant, too afraid of relinquishing its displacement value, using it as a shield to protect her from reality and her very real problems.

'Marcus loves you,' Jade had said, adding drily, 'Come on, Nell, be realistic. How many men aren't tempted to stray occasionally, and how many women have to learn to live with that fact, to accept and ignore it ... ?'

Eleanor had shaken her head. 'I know what you're trying to say, Jade, but I can't. It's not so much the physical act of infidelity, it's the slow destructiveness of never knowing if it's me he really wants, or if he simply stays with me because it's so much easier than going through another divorce. I can't live like that, no matter how much I love him. I need his respect as well as his love,' she had told her friend simply, 'and I need my own self-respect as well. Loving him on its own isn't enough ...'

She was standing staring out across the pool when Marcus found her. He didn't walk right up to her, stopping several yards away instead and saying her name quietly.

He watched as her face lost its colour and her body tensed warily.

'Marcus! You're back ... I ...'

'I got an earlier flight,' he told her brusquely.

She was frowning now, withdrawing from him physically as well as emotionally, as she stepped back into the shadows.

'How did you know I would be all the way down here? I didn't tell anyone I was coming ...'

'When you weren't at home I knew where I would find you.'

'Yes, I suppose I am predictable.'

'I hope so,' Marcus agreed.

There was no emotion either in his voice or on his face, but something, some sixth sense alerted her to his tension.

'We need to talk, Nell,' he told her quietly. 'But first ... just one question. Do you still love me?'

Eleanor looked at him for a long time. Why was he asking? Out of guilt, perhaps. What was he hoping she would say? What was his reason for asking? She hesitated, anxious and fearful, before acknowledging that there was only one answer she could give; that honesty, no matter how painful, was the only course open to her.

She took a deep breath and then told him shakily, 'Yes. Yes, I do.'

She wasn't sure what she had expected, but it certainly wasn't that he would cover the space between them so quickly, nor that he would take her in his arms, holding her as though she were the most precious, fragile thing he had ever held, slowly running his hands over her, tracing the shape of her face with his fingertips, his own face unfamiliarly flushed, his fingertips trembling slightly as he touched her with an absorbed, almost blind concentration on what he was doing.

As she watched him, registering his intensity, Eleanor had the feeling that somehow he was showing himself to her, revealing a part of himself she had not previously known even existed, and yet instead of feeling hurt or angered by this knowledge she felt a quick springing up of joy and recognition, an awareness that went far beyond the physical and emotional. It was as though he was somehow showing to her the most private and spiritual part of himself, the pure undiluted essence of all that he was.

Instinctively she responded to it, moving closer to him, touching him, silently acknowledging her inner awareness of all that he was showing to her.

When they kissed, it was not with passion, but with a slow, gradual acknowledgement of one another, a true binding together of their differentness into one perfect whole.

'I love you too,' Marcus whispered shakily. 'And if this house really is what you want...'

Eleanor shook her head. 'It isn't the house,' she told him. 'What I really wanted was what it represented to me. You were right, anyway, buying it isn't a practical proposition. Why didn't you say something, though, Marcus? Why didn't you tell me you didn't want it?'

'I couldn't,' he told her starkly. 'I couldn't admit to you that I was jealous of it.' He took hold of her arm. 'Let's walk,' he told her. 'There's a lot I need to tell you.'

Eleanor listened to him in silence.

'You were jealous of Vanessa...! But I thought...' She shook her head. 'I thought you were irritated because I couldn't cope with her. I felt you blamed me for her aggression. I felt you were comparing me with another woman who might have been able to reach her and establish a real bond with her. I felt such a failure, Marcus. And not just with Vanessa but with the boys as well. They were so unhappy, and I hadn't even realised it.'

As she looked at him, Eleanor recognised how hard it must have been for him to examine his own feelings, to exhume the painful memories of his own childhood and face up to his deep-rooted fear of being displaced in her affections for his own child. Now, having heard him talk about his own suffering and his real feelings about it, she could understand him so much more clearly; understand why he had felt it necessary to withhold this part of himself from her.

'When I was listening to Piet, I recognised what I'd been trying to conceal from myself, and that was my own fear of being rejected, of being found wanting for being the wrong sex.

'It sounds so simple, doesn't it? So obvious,' he added ruefully.

'People's emotions are never simple,' Eleanor comforted him. 'It can be very hard to accept certain aspects of ourselves; we've both been guilty of not having enough faith in each other or in ourselves to admit to our vulnerabilities. I was afraid of losing you ... of ...'

'You could never lose me,' Marcus told her gently, turning her round to face him.

Eleanor searched his face slowly and then told him quietly, 'I saw you at the airport with Sondra. I came to tell you I was sorry... about our argument. I rang you at your hotel that first night. There was no answer.'

'No, I was in the shower...I'd just got back from seeing Piet. I thought you might be Sondra,' Marcus admitted wryly. 'It seemed safer not to answer...'

She wasn't going to ask him any more, Eleanor acknowledged; not now, and maybe not ever. Not because she was afraid of the answer, but simply because it was no longer of any importance.

'Are you sure you don't mind...about the house, I mean?' Marcus asked her later that night.

'No,' Eleanor assured him. 'It's served its purpose; helped me to see...to understand ... to face up to what I am and what I can never be. I wanted to be so perfect for you, Marcus.'

'You are,' he assured her. 'You always have been. Even more so now,' he murmured, as he bent his head to kiss her.

It was unfamiliar and very precious, this feeling of absolute freedom and light-headedness it gave him, knowing that she knew all there was to know about him; that he had revealed to her all the dark places within him and that she had acknowledged and accepted them ... That she loved him with them.

Contentedly, Eleanor leaned her head against him. He was so precious to her, even more so now that he had told her what he really felt, allowed her to see the pain he had suffered; a pain Vanessa must not be allowed to endure, they were both agreed about that.

'What can I do?' Marcus had asked her, when he had explained to her his own ambivalent feelings towards his daughter.

'Just love her, Marcus,' Eleanor had told him gently. 'Love her and show her that you love her. She needs that more than anything else.'

It wasn't going to be easy, but somehow they would find a way. Jade had offered her the use of her flat as somewhere to work; she didn't want to let it until she was sure she was going to stay permanently in New York, she had told Eleanor.

They would still have to move, but this time, this time *they* would be searching for a house, instead of merely her frantically trying to fulfil a dream.

What would happen to Broughton House? she wondered. She hoped it would find someone who loved it, someone who would cherish it and bring it back to life. It needed and deserved that. She smiled faintly to herself, her mind busily engaged on all that she had to do, and then she looked at Marcus and firmly banished them.

'Let's go to bed,' she whispered to him.

He looked startled. 'It's only just gone nine o'clock...' And then, when he saw the look she was giving him, he too started to smile.

'Why not?' he agreed. 'I could do with an early night. All that travel weariness.'

'Mmm...you poor thing,' Eleanor murmured against his mouth. 'You must be totally exhausted.'

'Totally,' Marcus agreed, laughing, as he started to kiss her.

CHAPTER TWENTY-SIX

TODAY was her day off and Zoe had the flat to herself. There was so much constraint between Ben and herself these days that she was actually glad he had already left for work, she admitted miserably.

She had made all her arrangements and her decisions. It had been a piece of good luck that both her mother and father happened to be away. Ben had given her one of those quick, sharp, assessing looks she was getting from him increasingly these days when she had made her announcement.

'Ma's been feeling a bit down lately,' she had told him, striving to appear casual and relaxed. 'So I thought I'd spend a bit of time with her, go and see her on my day off and stay overnight.'

'If that's what you want.'

Ben's voice had been edged with an unfamiliar hardness that made her ache inside.

Things had been different between them since he had asked her if she was seeing someone else. Part of her had wanted to laugh hysterically at what he was implying, and another part was so filled with anger and hurt that he should be so blind to what was really happening to her that she had almost been tempted, goaded into telling him that there was. Did he really believe she was capable of that kind of deceit? Didn't he know how much she loved him? How much she needed him?

Tears flooded her eyes now as she got out of bed. She felt sick and shaky; the relief she had anticipated would follow the final making of her decision had not come; instead...

Instead she was filled with a nerve-grinding mixture of panic, fear and despair.

As hard as she fought to suppress the growing demands of the new life inside her and tried to cling to the reality of just how devastating an effect having a baby would have on not just her life but on Ben's as well, the baby fought just as hard, mustering some kind of deceitful hormonal trickery into making her vulnerable to its presence, its claims on her.

Sometimes she even found herself talking to it, trying to reason with it, to explain that it wasn't simply a matter of Ben's claims on her over its own.

Even if she left Ben, ignored her love for him, made it easy for him to walk away from them to a life without them, she would still be guilty of damaging Ben's future. Without her, it would be impossible for him to go ahead with the new venture; he needed her to work alongside him and to shoulder the day-to-day administration of the business, leaving him free to concentrate on providing the food which would bring people flocking to the restaurant. How could she let him down?

'You must understand,' she had told it fiercely. 'I cannot let myself love you. There isn't any point. Ben needs me...I owe it to him not to let him down.'

And yet all the time, at the back of her mind, a tiny, bitter voice asked why it was that Ben did not seem to recognise *her* need...why it was that *she* was always the one who had to do the giving, the supporting.

She made her way slowly to the bathroom. There was after all no need to rush. Her appointment wasn't until late morning.

In the mirror, she tried to avoid looking at her naked body. Not that there was anything to see; if anything she had lost weight rather than gained it...all that sickness, all that tension.

'You're getting too thin,' Ben had told her abruptly only the other day.

At first, naïvely, she had assumed that it would all be over quickly and that she would be able to go straight home, but the doctor had shaken her head, explaining that they would want to keep her in overnight, as she had told them that she had no one at home to keep an eye on her. 'Just to be on the safe side.'

Zoe's stomach had churned and knotted ferociously as she had added quietly, 'It's a very safe procedure medically, but an extremely traumatic one emotionally and physically.'

Zoe put her hand on her stomach, shivering frantically. This was perhaps the last time she would do this...the last chance she would have of talking to her baby, of trying to explain...

She removed her hand, curling her fingers into tight fists, tears burning her eyes. How could you explain why you had to end a life, to destroy it before it had even properly begun? How could you explain to a child that its father did not want it, that there was no place in your life for it, that it wasn't wanted or loved?

Her body started to shake violently, every instinct screaming rejection of what she was thinking, the intensity and passion of her instinctive and immediate denial overwhelming her with pain.

'No! No!' she muttered savagely under her breath. 'You can't do this to me...I won't let you.'

It was just her mind playing tricks on her, she told herself fiercely. What she had to do was concentrate on reality, write down all the reasons why it was impossible for her to have this child.

In her mind she visualised the list; it would be long and logical, the facts plain and inescapable, the weight of them heavily outweighing the pitiful, single emotional claim that was all there was to put in the opposing column.

It was too late to change her mind now. The decision was made, everything organised...arranged...

*   *   *

The receptionist was calmly efficient, greeting Zoe with a professional smile as she gave her name.

A firmly competent nurse came to take her through to her room, her fingers lightly cool and soothing on Zoe's arm.

'You haven't had anything to eat or drink, have you?' she asked.

Zoe shook her head.

'Good. If you'd just like to undress, I'll come back in a few minutes to give you your pre-med.'

Slowly, Zoe took off her clothes, her movements automatic, her eyes and mind deliberately blank.

The paper gown she had been left flapped loosely round her as she pulled it on, her skin icy cold to the touch. A welcome numbness seemed to have engulfed her, even the tormenting little voice which had haunted her so much silenced now, as though it knew that the battle was finally over.

The nurse came back. 'All right?' she asked her, as she took hold of Zoe's arm and dabbed her inner elbow with a piece of antiseptic wet cotton wool.

The light from the window flashed momentarily on the needle.

Zoe stared at it as the nurse lifted her hand, focusing on it . . .

The flat smelled hot and stuffy . . . airless and alien somehow.

It was probably just the contrast between its shuttered, sunstroked windows and the clinical coldness of the air-conditioned clinic, Zoe told herself emptily, as she sat down.

The doctor had been reluctant to let her come home alone, but she had insisted, and eventually they had given way, although they had insisted on a nurse seeing her into her taxi.

Her legs still felt oddly weak and shaky, her body lethargic, heavy and tired. All she wanted to do was to crawl into bed and sleep forever. It was as though all the emotional turmoil and misery of the last few weeks had finally caught up with her, her mind and body too exhausted and drained now to go on fighting against them, craving only sleep and escape.

She was too exhausted even to bother undressing, never mind wipe away the tears which coursed silently down her face.

She had started crying in the taxi, a silent slow flow of tears that ran as ceaselessly and steadily as blood, and which were just as impossible to stem.

Ben unlocked the door and walked into the flat, checking as he saw Zoe's bag on the table.

A sharp, cold thrill of fear pulled his body as taut as a bow. He stood silently tense, his senses alert, like an animal checking for danger.

He had known that Zoe was lying to him about staying over with her mother. Deceit wasn't something that came easily to her, and he had been sorely tempted to end the misery for both of them by telling her that he knew the truth.

Lying awake at night, wondering who he was, this other man who had taken her from him, he had asked himself bitterly whether it was because he loved her too much that he couldn't bring himself to do so, or whether it was because he didn't love her enough.

Loving someone, really loving them and not merely being in love with them, surely meant putting them first, before and beyond one's own needs and desires, and yet *he* wasn't doing that... wasn't perhaps even capable of doing it. Because, if he was, surely he would have put an end to what was happening between them.

He told himself that with all that he knew of life and people he shouldn't have been so shocked at how quickly the corrosive acid of mistrust on his side and the death of love on Zoe's was destroying a relationship he would once have sworn was as secure as any human relationship ever could be.

It had taken him a long time to acknowledge his love for Zoe, and even longer to accept hers for him, but, once he had done so, his commitment to her and his belief in her commitment to him had been total.

One day when the time was right, when Zoe was ready, they would marry, he had hoped. He recognised rather ruefully that there was that need within him for a legalised commitment that Zoe's stronger sense of security and self-worth did not as yet share.

Zoe was the whole focus of his life, although he had striven not to overburden her with the intensity of his feelings, careful not to suffocate her with his love. Naïvely, perhaps, he had feared losing her through his own intensity rather than to another man.

As he focused on her handbag, he frowned, wondering what it was that had brought her home when she had so obviously planned to be with her lover.

He heard a sound from the bedroom and froze, nausea a burning acid bile inside him as he thought the unthinkable. She couldn't surely have brought *him* back here, to *their* home... *their* bed...

He stared at the half-closed bedroom door, torn by two equally powerful conflicting male emotions: the first to go in there and take hold of his rival with his bare hands; the second to protect Zoe from the unexpectedness of his return, from the embarrassment and shock she would suffer and even from his disruption of her privacy with her lover; but in the end the deeper, more atavistic feeling won and he strode towards the door, thrusting it open.

Zoe was lying fully dressed on the bed, and she was alone... alone but not happy, Ben recognised, as he saw the tear-tracks on her face and the bleakness in her eyes. She looked, he thought, caught up in a wave of mingled resentment and tenderness, like a bereft, unhappy child.

What had happened? Had the man, whoever he was, let her down? Was *that* why she had come back here to cry all alone in their bed?

'Zoe...'

He saw the shocked darkening, the blackness in her eyes as she turned and stared at him, struggling to sit up, one hand resting against her stomach in that odd mannerism he had noticed her adopting so frequently recently.

'Ben...I...'

'I finished work early,' he told her, and then heard himself saying curtly, 'I thought you were going to see your mother.'

Her face changed, her skin flushing, her eyes flooding with hot tears. He had to fight not to go over to her and take her in his arms, to tell her that it was all right...that he would make it all right...that whoever had hurt her, made her cry, would be punished for it... He wanted, he recognised grittily, to tell her that he loved her, and that *he* would never hurt her, unlike this other man.

Instead, he sat down on the bed, facing away from her, keeping his voice as steady as he could as he told her quietly, 'Zoe, we can't go on like this. I can see how unhappy you are now. What is it? What's wrong?'

Still struggling with the shock of seeing him, with the trauma of all that happened, Zoe had no resistance left. She had fought hard to protect him, to protect their love, but now her strength was gone and in its place all that was left was a terrible enervating weakness, both physical and emotional.

She focused on his back, so broad, so strong, so powerfully male, his shoulders broad, firmly muscled. Physically he looked so strong...so dependable...but appearances could be so deceptive.

Closing her eyes, she turned her head away from him and took a deep breath.

'I'm pregnant.'

She had no sense of tension or anxiety, no thrill of shock at having at last told him, no sharp nervous questioning of whether or not she had done the right thing, of wondering how he would feel...how he would react. She had gone far, far beyond all that now.

Earlier, in the clinic, watching the downward descent of the nurse's arm, knowing what was going to happen, she had suddenly known that she couldn't go through with it, and had known it so compellingly, so strongly, that it had been as though she had been anaesthetised against some gigantic pain and that anaesthetic had suddenly worn off.

They had all been kind to her...kind and concerned, and, she suspected, although they were all far too professional to show it, pleased by her decision.

And although she had known it was still far too early for anything like that yet, she could have sworn she felt a sensation within her, as though the baby had somersaulted with joy and relief at her decision.

It's all right for you, she had told it silently. You will live, but Ben's love for me will die.

After that initial surge of emotion, she had felt no euphoria, no relief, no sharp, clear awareness of having made the right decision, of having a burden removed from her shoulders; only a slow, pervading numbness... a distancing of herself from her decision and what it would mean to her life.

She hadn't thought even as far ahead as what she was going to say to Ben...

'Pregnant?' Ben turned round and stared at her, his body stiff with shock—and rejection?

'When... how long... what...?'

'Nearly twelve weeks,' Zoe told him emotionlessly. 'I won't have an abortion, Ben,' she added more firmly. 'I'm sorry, but I just can't do it... I've tried...'

'*What?*'

She could hear the horror, the loathing almost, in his voice, and it was like the first scalpel incision in her heart, the pain so hard and tight that it cut off her breath and made her body jerk in reaction against its agony.

'I'm sorry,' she told him brokenly. 'It's no use trying to persuade me. I... there's still time for you to find someone else to take over my role in the new business... I hate letting you down, Ben, but...'

Ben wasn't listening to her disjointed words. He had stopped listening. His face stern and bleak, he demanded, 'Why didn't you say something—you tell me you're three months pregnant with our child and you've said nothing... Why?'

Zoe shrugged tiredly. 'What was the point? I already knew what you'd feel... what you'd say. You've always made it clear you didn't want children.'

'Neither of us did,' Ben interrupted her sharply.

'No,' Zoe agreed. How could she explain to him what had happened to her? He couldn't share her emotions or her inner conflict. He couldn't feel, as she had done, the fiercely demanding tug of that new life and its claims upon her.

'Zoe, you should have told me...'

She could hear the emotion in his voice. 'I hadn't planned for this to happen,' she told him bleakly. 'At first all I wanted to do was to stop what was happening... but I couldn't. I'd never really thought about the emotional aspects of having an abortion. I'd only seen it in practical terms. I thought it would be easy... that we could just go back to being the way things were before. I didn't want it to be like this, Ben,' she told him, her eyes filling with tears as she looked at him for the first time. 'I didn't tell you because I didn't want to worry you... to burden you. And anyway, I knew what you would say... and... and it had to be my decision...'

'*Your* decision?' Ben asked her in a hard voice. '*Your* decision about *our* child, *our* lives?'

Zoe focused on him, her body tensing. 'I'm not changing my mind, Ben,' she warned him. 'You're not going to force an abortion on me the way you wanted to on Sharon.'

For a moment they stared at one another, not lovers any more but antagonists, Zoe recognised achingly.

It was Ben who spoke first, his voice raw with anger, overloud in the confines of the small, cramped room. 'You thought I would do *that*? That I would force that kind of decision on you...?'

'You would have forced it on Sharon,' Zoe reminded him.

'Sharon is sixteen years old...a child still, carrying the child of an equally irresponsible boy, neither of them fit or ready to become parents...to give that child the love and security it deserved and needed.

'*They* are children...we're adults. Do you honestly think...?' He took a deep breath. 'Zoe, for God's sake, I love you and, all right, I admit that having children, a child, isn't something I'd wanted or planned; but your pregnancy, our child is a joint responsibility...something we should both have shared...'

'It was for your sake that I didn't tell you,' Zoe repeated, but the look Ben was giving her said that he didn't totally believe her. Her heart missed a small beat, but stubbornly she ignored its message.

'I didn't tell you because I love you...' she insisted doggedly.

'I love you as well, Zoe, but perhaps you don't think my love is as strong as yours...perhaps you don't think I'm as strong as you are...as capable of shouldering life's burdens. I hadn't realised you saw me as someone so pathetic and weak that I needed to be shielded from life's harsh realities.' His mouth twisted bitterly. 'Have you told anyone else...your mother...?'

Zoe shook her head.

'She's going to get quite a surprise then when she discovers that she's going to be a grandmother in six months' time. So will my mother.'

Zoe gave him a wary, uncertain look, watching as he stood up and then leaned over the bed.

'I can't pretend that I wanted a child, Zoe...I'm not going to lie about that. But now that you *are* pregnant...' He gave a small, tired shrug. 'It's happened, and we're both responsible. It doesn't change my feelings for you...my commitment to you. I just wish...' He gave her a brooding look. 'I just wish that you'd trusted me enough to tell me about it, Zoe...that you'd felt you could rely on me to give you whatever support you needed, regardless of my own feelings.'

As he straightened up, Zoe recognised how much she had hurt him. A sharp quiver of pain went through her. Could she have damaged their relationship more by not telling him than by trying to protect him? She had seen the bitterness in his face when he had contrasted their love for one another, and the worst of it was that she hadn't been able to deny what he was saying, to reassure him that she *did* believe in his strength and his ability to support her.

'Zoe, darling, I know being pregnant isn't always very easy or comfortable, but...'

As Zoe looked up at her mother, the reproach died from her voice and her expression changed. 'What is it, Zoe, aren't you feeling well?'

'No, Ma, I'm fine,' Zoe reassured her mother. She knew how tired and tense she looked and she knew why. It wasn't so much the growing bulk of her baby that exhausted her, but the constant feelings of guilt and misery that tormented her.

Not once since she had announced her pregnancy had Ben done or said anything to indicate that he was angry or resentful about what had happened.

The strength and support she had ached and yearned for in the early weeks of her pregnancy, alternately railing against the fate which had decreed that she should conceive and Ben's lack of awareness of what she was going through, were constantly in evidence now, and yet, instead of feeling relaxed and reassured, she found that her tension and anxiety had only increased.

Ben might say that he loved her, he might claim that, while he might never have deliberately wanted them to have a child, the fact that she had accidentally conceived changed everything—he might on the surface appear to have accepted things—but what was he *really* thinking... what was he feeling inwardly?

He might have been able to adjust to her pregnancy, but how would he feel once the baby was a reality? Would he reject it, hurt it with his lack of love for it? Would he reject her?

'You and Ben don't seem to get much time to spend together these days,' she heard her mother saying quietly.

Zoe looked at her, a small frown touching her forehead.

'I don't want to interfere, darling, but you must be careful not to shut Ben out. I know how easy it is to get wrapped up in what's happening to you, to become absorbed in it almost to the exclusion of everything else. I suppose that's nature's way of protecting its new life. I know you don't mean to do so, but you do seem to be pushing Ben to one side a little bit.'

Zoe stood up irritably. 'For heaven's sake, Ma, stop lecturing me. The next thing you'll be saying is that I should be grateful to Ben for standing by me. We...'

'Zoe, I wasn't going to say any such thing,' her mother protested quietly. 'I know how independent you are, but independence can sometimes be seen as a form of rejection. Don't let yourself become so wrapped up in the baby that Ben begins to feel you don't want or need him any more. I must go...' Her mother got up too. 'I'm meeting your father at Covent

Garden at eight. He's taking me out to dinner to celebrate my being about to begin my course.' She gave a rueful smile. 'Your poor father; I'm not sure which has been hardest for him to adjust to: the prospect of having a working wife, or the thought of becoming a grandfather. How are things with the hotel, by the way? You haven't mentioned it for a while.'

Zoe gave a small shrug. 'I don't really know,' she told Heather, but her voice suggested that she not only didn't know but didn't really care either. 'Ben's had more meetings with Clive and everything seems to be going ahead without any problems. I'll have to have a word with Clive and see if we can't arrange to have a small part of the garden fenced off for the baby...' She was frowning again, fretting slightly at the prospect of her child having to spend its time shut in an airless suite of rooms. Babies, children, needed fresh clean air. They needed love and security, two parents who loved them, not one who did and one who did not. It was unfair of her mother to accuse her of neglecting Ben, she decided after she had gone. For one thing, her mother didn't know all the facts; she didn't know, for instance, how guilty Zoe herself felt about the way she had initially not just rejected her child, but almost actively hated it, selfishly resenting its existence, blaming it for something that was not, after all, its fault.

She would make it up to him or her, of course. Already she knew how fiercely she would love it. Already she felt intensely protective of it, ready to shield it from any sign that Ben might reject it.

She still loved Ben, of course, but things between them were not the same. How could they be? Along with the burden of guilt and remorse she carried for her initial rejection of her baby, she was miserably aware that, unlike her, Ben had not chosen parenthood freely; that she had made the decision for both of them.

It didn't matter how often he told her that it was not anger he felt that she had not chosen to discuss her plans with him, but unhappiness be-cause she had not trusted him enough to confide in him—and she sensed that, no matter how often she reiterated that she had wanted to protect him, he did not fully believe her—increasingly she was tense and irritable with him, anxiously watching for every small sign that he regretted his decision to stay with her... with them.

He might not say it, but inwardly she was sure that he blamed her for making the wrong decision; that he wished she had gone ahead with the termination.

Three nights ago, when he had not returned home until the early hours of the morning, having been gone since five the previous morning, she had accused him of wanting to avoid being with her, regretting his com-mitment to her.

'Zoe, I'm working extra hours because we need the money,' he had told her wearily. 'When the baby comes...'

'When the baby comes we'll be in the hotel,' she had snapped at him. 'There's no need to turn yourself into a martyr, you know, Ben,' she had added bitingly.

'No,' he had agreed quietly. 'One of us doing that is more than enough.'

He had apologised later when he'd found her crying in the bathroom, urging her not to get upset, but to think of the baby...

She had laughed then with half-hysterical bitterness, tempted to say what must be in both their minds: that from his point of view it would be a merciful release if something did go wrong and, like Sharon, she lost her child; but somehow she had bitten the words back, not for Ben's sake, but for the baby's, not wanting to tempt fate even in the smallest way.

Was it true that babies experienced some kind of awareness of their mother's emotions while they were in the womb? Would hers know that initially she hadn't wanted it?

It amazed and appalled her now that she could ever have felt like that. Looking back, it was like looking at another Zoe...another life.

She had changed, her mother had told her, and she had sounded as though she regretted that change, but Zoe didn't. She had been too selfish...too light-hearted, too prone to skim the surface of life. Now she felt different.

Every day she exercised, gently, not for her sake but for the baby's. Books, articles, features on pregnancy and childbirth absorbed her; she was determined only to eat and do those things which most benefited her child...she was determined to make it up to it for the irreparable harm she had so nearly done it.

Since their quarrel the other night, Ben had seemed to become very quiet and withdrawn, but stubbornly Zoe was refusing to respond to the way he was behaving. She had to put her baby first now. Ben was an adult...it was ridiculous of him to claim that he needed to work all these extra hours when they both knew that, once they were in the hotel, they would be much better off financially. Since they would be living in it, it shouldn't be too difficult for her to combine her work with looking after the baby, although Ben would have to find someone else to front the restaurant, since she would not be able to leave the baby alone in the evenings.

She frowned, remembering an article she had been halfway through the previous evening before her mother had telephoned to ask if she could call round.

Irritably she started to hunt for the magazine. Her mother had amazed her with her casual approach to the baby's arrival. Of course, if she hadn't been so taken up with this new career of hers... No wonder her father was feeling a little bit left out and resentful—and her mother had the gall to accuse her of neglecting Ben!

She made a small sound of satisfaction as she saw the magazine under a pile of junk mail on top of the cupboard.

As she reached up for it, she dislodged the whole pile and had to kneel down on the floor to pick up the flood of papers.

Most of it was for throwing out anyway, she acknowledged, as she retrieved the magazine and then set about picking up everything else.

There was a letter in among the brochures, and she frowned as she realised it was from Clive.

Ben hadn't said anything about his writing to them. She gave a tiny shrug and was just about to pick it up and put it back on the cupboard when something made her stop and read it.

She did so quickly, and then more slowly, the pins and needles in her legs ignored as the contents of the letter sank in.

They were not going to be able to go ahead with the hotel after all, Clive had written. The problems with the planning permission could not be overcome and, as he had explained to Ben at their last meeting, he was also having second thoughts about the wisdom of getting involved in such a costly enterprise when it was becoming increasingly obvious that many similar ventures were not succeeding.

Zoe sat back on her heels and stared blankly at the wall, a terrible surge of anger and fear engulfing her.

How dared Ben not tell her about this? There was not going to be any hotel...there was not going to be any secure income...any healthy country garden ... there was not going to be any anything.

How dared Ben not tell her about this? How dared he simply push the letter to one side and ignore it?

It was gone two o'clock in the morning when he finally came home. He was working in a restaurant that specialised in entertaining parties and which consequently stayed open late. The tips were good, he had told her wearily when she had complained that he was working too late.

Zoe watched him walk into the bedroom, hardening her heart as she saw the weary way he moved, throwing off his jacket and running his hand through his hair; he looked older tonight, his shoulders hunched and rounded.

'Zoe!' She heard the tension in his voice when he realised that she was still awake.

'Why didn't you tell me about Clive's letter?' she challenged him before he could say anything else.

A small grimace touched his mouth. 'Dare I say it was because I wanted to protect you? Because I didn't want you to worry...? But no, of course, I'm not strong enough to do that, am I? I'm the weak, dependent one; you're the strong decision-maker.'

As she heard the bitterness in his voice, Zoe flinched. He was never going to stop blaming her, was he? No matter what he might claim outwardly, inwardly he resented what she had done.

'You don't have to stay, you know,' she told him fiercely. 'I can manage without you.'

Even as she said the words, she knew suddenly and painfully how false they were. As he stared at her in the silence, she could feel the panic and fear building up inside her. She longed to reach out to him and to beg him to hold her, to wrap his arms around her and tell her that she was safe...that he loved her...that he would always love her and that nothing else mattered.

But it wasn't love she could see in his eyes, it was anger, and she shrank back from it as he leaned across the bed and told her savagely, 'Can you? Well, I'm damn sure that I can't manage without you, and if that makes me weak and dependent, another burden for you to carry, then I'm sorry, but...'

He saw her face, saw the tears pouring down her cheeks and made a small fierce sound in his throat before reaching out for her and holding her.

'Zoe, Zoe...what's happening to us? I love you so much and I don't want to lose you.'

As she clung to him, Zoe heard herself saying something she had once believed it would be impossible for her ever to say.

'I'm afraid, Ben,' she told him, shivering intensely. 'I'm so afraid. What are we going to do...what will happen?'

She tensed as Ben started to kiss her. They had made love since she had told him about her pregnancy, but not with the abandonment and intensity she could sense in him now.

'Don't shut me out, Zoe,' she could hear him telling her as he held her, smoothing his hands over her stomach, bringing her closer to him. 'Don't shut me out.'

Later, exhausted and serenely, almost snugly content, she lay in his arms, sleepily aware of the weight of his hand where it lay possessively against her stomach.

Tonight, for the first time since she had become aware of her pregnancy, they had shared their old intimacy and closeness; tonight she had been fiercely conscious of her love for him, and his for her, sharply aware of all that she would lose if she lost him. But it wasn't just herself and her own needs she had to think of now.

Bleakly she wondered how long it would be before Ben started to betray the resentment he must feel. Tonight the shock of losing the hotel had brought them close together, but that closeness wouldn't last long; it couldn't...

In the darkness Ben touched her gently.

'Don't worry,' he told her softly. 'Everything's going to be fine.'

Don't worry? How could she do anything else? How could they bring a baby up in this small, cramped flat? Ben didn't even have a proper job...just this temporary work. It was all very well for Ben to say that he could understand Clive's decision...

It was only later the next day at work that Zoe realised that she had said nothing to Ben about *his* disappointment. She had known how much this venture had meant to him, how anxious he had been about it right from the start, how reluctant to believe in it. She had laughed at him then, teasing him for his pessimism.

Her shift finished at four and she was home for just after six. Ben opened the front door for her, and the sight of him standing there formally dressed in his suit and white shirt, a shirt he must have had to iron for himself, sent a small shock of fear icing through her.

'Ben...?'

She said his name questioningly, suddenly so afraid that her breath was a sharp pain in her lungs, suddenly seeing him with a new clarity. Last night they had truly been lovers, but now, today...

She looked at his suit again and then glanced nervously into his face, half afraid of what she might see there.

'I've been to see Clive,' he told her quietly.

Clive... Hope rose inside her.

'What's happened? Has he changed his mind about the hotel? Has he——?'

Immediately Ben shook his head. 'No, it was nothing like that. You weren't listening to me properly, Zoe. I said that *I* went to see him, not that Clive asked to see me.

'I've been doing a lot of thinking recently. It's obvious that things can't continue as they are.'

A sickness invaded her stomach which had nothing to do with her pregnancy.

Here it was...what she had feared all along. He was going to tell her that he couldn't stay; that he resented the burden of the fatherhood she had forced upon him.

Her face must have given her away, because he suddenly frowned, his mouth hardening not with anger, she recognised, but with pain.

'Zoe, Zoe, when will you learn to trust me? To have a little faith in me? Have you any idea how it makes me feel, knowing that you believed *you* had to protect *me* from reality...knowing that you weren't able to share something as important as *this* with me?' He touched her stomach lightly as he spoke. 'Deep in the psyche of every man there's a part of him that has an atavistic need to be the archetypal male strong guy with the broad shoulder to lean on. No matter how much of a wimp the rest of the world might think him, deep inside every man is a certain something that tells him that it's his duty, his responsibility, his role to be leaned on; to be the one who gives support rather than receives it.

'I may not be Mr Macho...I may not ever want to be, but before God I want you to feel that I'm there for you, and not that I have to be protected and lied to because I don't have the strength to accept the realities of life.

'When you first told me about the baby and about concealing the truth from me, I felt hurt and angry because, by believing that deceit was necessary, you made me feel so much less of a man; and then I recognised that it wasn't *you* who was making me feel like that. All *you* were doing was simply reacting to the subconscious message I was giving you. *I* was the one who was responsible for the fact that you felt you couldn't trust me...couldn't rely on me.'

He made a small, helpless gesture as he saw the tears filling her eyes.

'Zoe, all my life I've been used to people leaning on me, all my life. I...'

'I know...that was why. I didn't want to be like them, Ben,' she told him passionately. 'I wanted us to be equals...to share everything...Remember how you told me that if Sharon had her baby it would ruin her life? All I could think was that if I had our baby it would ruin yours. I tried so hard to do the right thing, but I couldn't, and even if it means that I lose you...

'No, it isn't that,' she told him fiercely when she saw the sadness in his eyes. 'I don't love it...him or her, more than I do you. Just in a different way. Who does the baby have to love and protect it if it doesn't have me, Ben?'

'It's my baby too,' he told her gently. 'Although recently I've been wondering if you wished it weren't, wished it didn't have a father, but were yours exclusively, you've been shutting me out so much.

'I'm sorry I didn't realise what was happening, Zoe. I wish I had done...I wish I'd been more sensitive...more aware. I wish I'd never said what I did about Sharon's baby. The guilt I feel for having said it, for her having lost it, is something I shall have to live with all my life; and if you...I love you,' he told her thickly. 'I love both of you. *That's* why I've always said I don't want children. Not because I've been afraid I won't love them, but because I know that I will.

'Look around this flat and then tell me honestly that this is the kind of environment where you want our child...our children to grow up...I grew up in poverty, Zoe. I know just what it means...just what it does.'

'Ben, I'm so sorry,' Zoe wept, and she was. Sorry not just about the baby, but for all the ways in which she could now see that she had hurt him, punished him even if only subconsciously by refusing to allow him to share what was happening with her, by refusing almost to allow him to take any responsibility.

When she had told herself that she had been protecting him, she had also, she recognised now, been punishing him a little as well, motivated not by any lack of love for him, but by her own fear and unexpected insecurity.

He looked tired, older, and yet despite his slumped shoulders she suddenly had the impression that they were also broader...stronger...

She opened her mouth to reassure him, to tell him that somehow they would find a way, and then she remembered what he had just said and, instead of telling him anything, she *asked* him hesitantly, 'Ben, what are we going to do?'

He smiled at her then, a broad, almost boyish grin of pride and satisfaction.

'What we are going to do is find ourselves a small, easily manageable and reasonably priced restaurant which I, with my skill and flair, will quickly turn into *the* place to eat. We'll be so busy that we'll be turning people away, and I shouldn't be surprised if Princess Di herself doesn't start ringing up and asking us to keep her a special table for lunch. Oh, and yes, I nearly forgot; what we're also going to do is make sure that this restaurant comes with some good-sized living accommodation and a nice private back garden. Babies need gardens,' he told her gruffly, 'and so do kids. Clive agrees that it's a viable proposition and he promised that he'll back us...I called in at a couple of agents on the way back and collected some stuff. Most of it will be rubbish, of course...'

'Ben, Ben...why didn't you say something? Why didn't you tell me what you were planning? You didn't just do this on the spur of the moment...not you...'

'No,' he agreed, quieter now. 'No. When you told me about the baby, I knew that he or she was going to need a proper home. I knew that, while you might be happy somewhere like this while it was just us, you'd want more, much more for our child.' He touched his fingertip to her lips as she started to protest and told her softly, 'That wasn't a criticism, Zoe, not a dig at your parents and the way you were brought up. Of course you want the best for our baby...so do I. We wouldn't be human if we didn't.'

A feeling, a sensation began to bubble up inside her. It was joy...it was love...it was relief and gratitude, Zoe recognised dizzily, half holding her breath in case it went away again; but most of all it was love. Not just hers for Ben, not just his for her, but theirs for each other and for their child.

'I know this isn't what you wanted, Ben,' she whispered against his lips. 'It isn't what we planned, but it is going to be all right, isn't it?'

'Everything's going to be fine,' Ben assured her as he held her and kissed her slowly with lingering pleasure. 'Everything's going to be fine.'

Behind his back his fingers were crossed. He wasn't sure how yet, but somehow he would make sure that it was. For Zoe's sake.

And for their child's? He closed his eyes momentarily.

He wasn't going to spoil things now by allowing himself to remember the bitterness, the resentment, the jealousy and sense of being shut out and unwanted that he had felt these last few weeks.

He loved Zoe and he would learn to love their child. Somehow.

CHAPTER TWENTY-SEVEN

'FERN, my dear, how are you?'

'Fine,' Fern responded bracingly, stepping back into the shadow of the shop window awning to allow another shopper to skirt past her and Roberta.

Everybody knew about the pending divorce now, of course, and very probably about Venice's pregnancy. Nick was living openly with her, after all. Fern had seen them both the previous day as they drove through town in the expensive new Rover saloon car Venice had bought him.

'We preferred the safety features on the German models,' she had overheard Venice confiding to someone as she passed her in the street yesterday. 'But we both feel that we have a duty to support British industry and the British working man.'

The pity she could see in her friend's eyes irked her a little; was it silly of her to feel increasingly annoyed by the show Venice was putting on of publicly and repeatedly acknowledging her guilt and responsibility for the unhappiness she had caused 'poor Fern'; cleverly making something of a virtue out of a vice by adding with modestly lowered head and soft, whispery, half-ashamed voice that there was of course the baby to consider?

She was feeling decidedly tired of being miscast in her unwanted role of grieving martyr, Fern reflected to herself as she prepared to try for the umpteenth time to convince Roberta that she was neither suicidally depressed nor emotionally devastated by Nick's defection.

The trouble was that it wasn't really possible for her to announce the truth... and besides, who would believe her if she did?

Perhaps if, when the news had first broken, she had not taken refuge with Cressy... But at the time it had seemed a sensible thing to do... for one thing she had then still been half afraid that Nick might change his mind and come back, still been half afraid of believing in her good luck.

And then, when she *had* come back, she had had to spend a lot of time in Bristol checking up on courses, accommodation and part-time jobs.

At Cressy's insistence, she had plucked up the courage to approach Relate and had been surprised and delighted by their positive response to her and the helpful advice they had given her on the kind of qualifications and training she would need if they were to consider enrolling her, with a view to her eventually practising with them as a counsellor.

She remembered from her previous reading of their literature how arduous and demanding the training course was, given the kind of work involved, but what *had* surprised her had been the fact that the extent and intensity of the commitment and work involved had only hardened her determination to go ahead.

The realisation that she could be so determined and motivated had not just increased her self-confidence, but had also brought with it a sense of excitement and anticipation she could not remember experiencing for years.

She had come home late the previous evening after a brief return visit to Cressy to inform her of her progress and to meet Graham.

Seeing them together had firmly convinced her that the two of them were ideally suited for one another. Their obvious happiness and completeness together had saddened her a little but she had very quickly controlled the small tendrils of envy which had tugged at her emotions.

She had come into town today intending to put the house on the market for sale, and despite what Venice had said to her she had no intention of letting her patronise her by making her accept Nick's share of the profit.

There was, after all, nothing to keep her here now. She had already been accepted on the Relate training course starting in October, and she had narrowed down her choice of accommodation to three definite possibilities. The course would be run in the evenings with some weekends also given over to training, so she would have the opportunity to find some work during the day to support her.

The thought of leaving the familiarity of the town and her own safe domestic routine, which would have once filled her with apprehension and insecurity, was now, instead of something to be dreaded, something to be eagerly anticipated.

It had hurt her a little at first to realise how many of those she had considered to be, if not friends, then at least acquaintances now seemed anxious to avoid her.

There were exceptions, of course, and Roberta was one of them, but even in *her* manner towards her Fern could detect a change...a hesitation...an avoidance of the subject of Nick's apparent desertion of her and his relationship with Venice.

Fern tried not to mind. After all, if Roberta had raised the subject, what could she have said? That she had already decided to end the marriage herself before Nick had left? Would Roberta believe her?

Probably not, but it still made her pride sting that she should be the object of so much curiosity and well-meant pity.

'Are you going to the meeting tonight at the Town Hall about Broughton House?' Roberta asked her.

Fern frowned, her thoughts momentarily diverted from her own problem. 'What meeting?'

'It was in the paper last week...you must have seen it,' Roberta insisted. 'Oh, of course, you were away, I'd forgotten. It was very interesting, and extremely well informed. It pointed out what the town would stand to lose if planning permission was granted on Broughton House. I must admit *I* hadn't realised until I read it that the gardens had been designed by Gertrude Jekyll, nor that there's a society especially devoted to the preservation of her work ... I ...'

'Only part of the gardens were designed by her,' Fern interrupted her friend quietly. A tiny niggle of something she couldn't quite put her finger on was beginning to stir in her brain.

'Really? Oh, well ... The point is, Fern, that towns like ours are being eroded and damaged all the time. Plans are passed, buildings, places of historical value are destroyed under our very noses, and by the time most of us realise it it's too late. Sometimes the very people we think are there to protect our heritage for us can be the ones ...' She broke off. 'Local councillors are not always able completely to separate their public responsibilities from their private needs, especially in a time of recession. It's easy to understand how someone might feel tempted by the thought of a large profitable contract into ignoring his moral responsibility to the people he represents ...'

She was talking quickly now, her voice and manner almost defensive, and as Fern listened to her she suddenly realised what Roberta was trying to say.

'You're talking about Adam, aren't you?' she interrupted her. 'Adam and that supermarket consortium he's involved with.'

'Well, you've got to admit it is all a bit suspect,' Roberta told her defensively. 'Adam must know what people are saying, but he's done nothing to contradict or deny that he is involved in plans to acquire Broughton House as a potential development site.

'Personally, I think whoever wrote that article does have a point. It was very intriguing, really ... Its being anonymous, I mean. At the end of it there was a paragraph inviting everyone who was interested in opposing the granting of any kind of planning permission and preserving the house and gardens as they are as part of the town's history to attend a meeting tonight at the Town Hall. You've always loved the house, Fern. Why don't you come along?'

'Perhaps,' Fern told her non-committally. She wasn't ready yet to make public the fact that she would soon no longer be part of the town, and if the meeting had been about anywhere other than Broughton House she knew she would not even have considered going.

But it *was* true ... she did love the house and its gardens. Given that, surely she should be as enthusiastic and pleased that something was going to be done to protect them as Roberta appeared to be. So why wasn't she? It couldn't be because of Adam's involvement, could it?

She was frowning as she said goodbye to Roberta and hurried towards the estate agents, pausing briefly as a leaflet in a shop window announcing the meeting she and Roberta had just been discussing caught her eye.

'Good idea, that,' a woman standing next to her also reading it commented to her. 'It's about time someone looked into what these councillors and the like get up to... if you ask me there's far too many of them more interested in lining their own pockets than in doing what's right by the likes of us.' She sniffed disparagingly, turning to tell the child at her side to stop scuffing his new shoes on the pavement, before taking hold of him and disappearing inside the shop.

Still frowning, Fern walked on. What was happening? Adam had always been one of the most popular and well-liked of all the local councillors, and certainly one of the most trustworthy and honest, and yet now it seemed even people who knew him well, like Roberta, were beginning to question that honesty.

And all because of one anonymous article which had appeared in the local paper.

Perhaps she *would* go to this evening's meeting after all, she decided thoughtfully.

The estate agent was helpful and efficient. They would send someone round in the morning to measure up and take photographs, he promised, although, given the present state of the market, he could not say quite how long the house might take to sell.

Thanking him, Fern turned to leave, and then froze as, directly opposite her and just about to cross the street, she saw Adam.

Time, movement seemed to slow down, accompanied by an icy mind-numbing tide of shocked anguish that flowed as pitilessly as poison through her veins. She saw him pause to check the traffic, his face and body in profile to her, his skin still tanned from his holiday with Lily and her parents, and still she stayed there, her body as tautly defensive as that of a crouched petrified animal, unable to speak, move, or do anything to avoid the inevitable moment when he turned and saw her.

Only when it actually happened, when he looked at her, focused on her, changed the direction of his path to come towards her, was she sprung from the trap of paralysis and shock.

Panic filled her, making her over-react wildly, rushing, running almost in the opposite direction, head down, muscles bunched and tense, heart pumping so fast that she could feel its fierceness shaking the cavity of her chest.

Where she had been icy cold, now she was sickly hot, her body bathed in a flood of nervous perspiration, her legs shaking, her eyes almost blinded by the rush of angry tears which stung them.

Behind her she heard Adam call her name; she was aware of people pausing to watch her, aware too of her own idiocy and folly, but these were distant awarenesses, numbed by the intensity of her need to escape, to get away.

Ahead of her, a tall middle-aged dark-suited man stepped to one side out of the way of her flight, and as he did so she heard him exclaiming, 'Adam! I was just on my way to your office...'

Weakly, sickly she leaned against the door of her car.

There was no need for her to run any further; Adam was not pursuing her any longer...

It was only now, as her brain started to clear, and her overstrained body tried to deal with the effects of her shocked, terrified surge of adrenalin, that she fully appreciated how stupid she had been.

It was one thing for *her* to know how afraid she was of seeing Adam, of listening to his inevitable expressions of sympathy and having to will herself into accepting that they were simply the same polite, concerned emotions he would have shown to any acquaintance in the same situation, that they had no personal significance or meaning; it was quite another to have behaved publicly in such a way that other people might question what had caused her stupid behaviour. Other people—and Adam himself.

The sensible, the only reaction she should have shown ought simply to have been a calm and distancing acceptance of his sympathy.

She felt the pain wrenching at her body as she tried to stifle the impact seeing him had had on her. How was it possible for her literally to ache with so much need and desire simply at the mere sight of him?

She smiled grimly to herself. Who needed to see him? Just thinking about him could have that effect on her. Just thinking about him and remembering...

That was over, finished, she reminded herself fiercely. She had a new life to live now...to look forward to.

Fern was late for the meeting at the Town Hall, primarily because she had been in two minds as to whether or not to go.

In the end it had been that same niggle of doubt she had experienced earlier in the day which had finally motivated her; that and curiosity to know the identity of the writer of the article in the local rag which had sparked off so much interest, expressing, so it seemed, the hitherto unexpressed views of the majority of local people, that those who were supposed to serve their interests might not always do so.

Whoever had written it had been very clever, she acknowledged, tapping into a vein of doubt and suspicion which seemed to run counter to the views people expressed publicly. It had been someone clever enough not merely to understand the darker side of human nature, but also to make use of it. Fern frowned. Why was it that she had the feeling that there was far more involved in tonight's meeting than the apparently excellent cause of protecting Broughton House...a cause which after all she ought to be fully applauding...?

The Town Hall was packed when she arrived, with standing room only at the back: further evidence of the skilful way public opinion and curiosity had been manipulated. Manipulated...?

An hour later Fern knew exactly why she had felt that small niggle of doubt.

It had been a shock to see Nick taking the platform to address the meeting and even more of one to hear the speech he gave.

Knowing him as she did, she knew that the sentiments he was expressing, the passionate desire to preserve a place of local heritage and importance, the calm, skilful questioning of how far they could trust local officials who had unadmitted interests that ran counter to their duty to protect the local environment, were totally alien to Nick's conception of life.

Someone else had put those words in his mouth, those ideals...those morals. But who, and why?

Nick's motivation Fern already understood. She had recognised it immediately she saw him taking the stage. Although Adam had never actually been mentioned by name, no one in the hall, least of all herself, had any doubt that it was Adam whose morals and honesty were under discussion.

Nick was very careful, of course...no one would be able to lay any charges against him, any accusations, either legal or moral. Whoever had written his speech for him had seen to that, and as she listened...and watched, Fern could see that what he was saying was finding a positive response with far more people than she would have expected.

And it was partially her fault. *She* had been the one who had supplied Venice with the information about Gertrude Jekyll's plans for the gardens, even if only accidentally, and she had also been guilty of doubting Adam herself; but standing here tonight listening to Nick, watching the faces of those around her, she knew she had been wrong to do so. Whatever Adam's involvement with Broughton House, whatever his motivation, there could be nothing dishonest or underhand about them.

Sick at heart, she slipped out of the hall before the meeting had ended, acknowledging that if *she* could so easily have doubted Adam initially, then how could she blame others for also doing so?

Tonight Nick had been a powerful and convincing orator, and even if she had got up on the stage herself and revealed to everyone listening how much Nick hated his stepbrother, how much ill will and malice he bore him, she knew that very few of them would have believed her.

Standing in the darkness a few feet away from the door, Adam watched her go. Like Fern, he had been late in arriving at the meeting, primarily because of the meeting he had had with Clive earlier in the day.

He frowned. It had been unfortunate that Clive had arrived early and prevented him from catching up with Fern.

It has been a shock to come back from a business trip up to Gloucestershire to hear the gossip about the break-up of her marriage. He knew how she must be feeling...how much she loved Nick. Did she still love him as intensely, as protectively now that he had left her to go and live openly with another woman, publicly humiliating her? Of course she did. She was that kind of woman.

He wondered if she herself had heard what people were saying...about the way Nick was claiming to have struggled to make the marriage work for some time, but that Fern had been uninterested and unresponsive... 'More interested in being a housekeeper than a wife...a woman,' had been one of the criticisms Adam had overheard.

Had Venice been responsible for that, just as she most undoubtedly had been responsible for this evening's metamorphosis of Nick into a caring, concerned environmentalist, passionately protective of local heritage?

Nick's less than subtle attack on himself had not escaped Adam's attention, but he was not overly concerned about it. If people wanted him to step down from the local council then he was quite prepared to do so. He had never seen his role there as some kind of perk-laden privilege to be abused for his own advantage, but rather a form of public duty and responsibility, and with the growth of his architectural practice he was finding it increasingly difficult to find time for everything he wanted to do. He was not going to be drawn into having a public quarrel with Nick, as he knew his stepbrother would have liked. He knew Nick far too well to allow him to goad him into lowering himself to match Nick's standards. He would have to do something, of course, take some kind of action to ensure that Nick and everyone else realised that he wasn't going to allow Nick to get away with attempting to damage his reputation and question his honesty, but that would have to wait; right now he had far more important and more personal matters on his mind.

This last month's holiday with the Jameses had been time he had ill been able to afford to spare, but Lily's father had wanted to consult him about building a second villa on the plot of land he owned in Italy, and if it came to fruition it would be an interesting commission.

Just as Clive's proposals for the conversion of Broughton House would have been, but as Adam had warned Clive right from the start, he did not think he could morally advise Clive to go ahead when he himself felt that it would spoil the ambience and character of Broughton House to extend it as he wished.

It had been a difficult decision to reach. The house would ultimately be sold, perhaps to some speculative builder who would hold on to it, hoping ultimately to get planning permission for its wholesale destruction. At least Clive had intended to maintain the existing house and the gardens. And of course there had been the added issue of the extra business the proposed hotel and restaurant would bring in to the area.

Business and jobs. But in the end Adam had had to inform Clive that he felt he could not justify supporting any plans which would change the character of the house, and that even if as a councillor he abstained from voting on such planning permission, he still could not recommend to Clive as a client that he go ahead with costly plans making a bid for a property which he might then find had become useless to him when he was unable to get the necessary planning permission.

Clive had thanked him for his honesty, telling him ruefully that he had begun to have his own doubts about the project.

'Without any clear end to the recession, I'm not sure it would be wise to go in for such an ambitious scheme just at the moment.'

'Mmm...' Adam had agreed. 'Quite a lot of recently opened country house hotels appear to be in financial difficulties, some to the extent of having to call in the receivers...'

They had parted amicably, but too late for Adam to make the beginning of the meeting.

And now, as he listened to Nick bringing his speech to an end, his mind was not on his stepbrother but on Fern.

She had looked very distressed as she left the hall...very distressed and very alone, and no one had thought to go with her. She shouldn't be alone at a time like this...he knew how vulnerable she was, how hurt and alone she must feel. She would not want *his* comfort, of course...she would probably be afraid that he might...of a repeat of...

Even so he could not bear to think of her on her own, in that house she had shared with his wretched stepbrother, believing even in the face of all the evidence to the contrary that Nick loved her.

Or had she perhaps known the truth but decided to ignore it, hoping...praying that her love for him would be enough to carry the marriage?

Silently he walked out into the night. His car wasn't parked very far away...

When Fern heard the knock on the door she went to answer it automatically, too stunned by the sight of Adam standing there on the doorstep to do anything to stop him when he walked in past her.

'Adam...'

If he had caught the note of despair and rejection in her voice he had chosen to ignore it.

'I saw you leaving the meeting and I came to see if you were all right. You shouldn't be here on your own like this.'

He spoke the words under his breath, frowning as he glanced round the dim shadowiness of the hallway. 'I know how you must be feeling, how much you must be hurt, but going to that meeting tonight... Fern, can't you see that Nick doesn't...?'

Suddenly Fern had enough. She didn't want Adam's pity, his compassion...his belief, like everyone else's, that she was stupid enough actually to regret Nick's going...to want him back...

'That Nick doesn't what?' she demanded fiercely. 'That he doesn't want me, that he doesn't love me, that he prefers Venice's bed and her undoubted skill in it to mine and my equally undoubted lack of it?'

She turned on him, her eyes blazing. 'Of course I can *see* those things, Adam. All of them and a lot more as well. Like the fact that Nick is weak, vain and manipulative...like the fact that he married me without loving me, lying to me even then. That he and Venice between them have made me not just an object of public curiosity and pity but of public amusement as well. The woman who would rather be a housekeeper than a wife...a woman. Oh, yes, I've heard the gossip, but it doesn't matter any more, Adam, none of it. Just as Nick doesn't matter any more either.'

'Are you trying to tell me that you don't love him any more?'

His disbelief was obvious. Obvious and humiliating.

'Do you honestly think that I could? That *any* woman could? Do you really think me so lacking in intelligence, Adam...so devoid of self-respect? I *never* loved Nick.'

Suddenly it was a relief to say the words, to discard the burden of loathing and guilt that knowing that fact and yet being unable to express or admit it had caused her. There was relief also in being able to free herself of the label of a woman too emotionally vulnerable and intimidated to face up to the reality of what her marriage actually was.

Adam was staring at her as though he had never seen her before, she recognised, pain twisting savagely in her heart as she acknowledged that this would be the final meeting between them and that they would part not as lovers, not even as friends, but as two people forever destined to be unknown to one another.

'You don't mean that...'

His voice was hoarse...harsh...filled with rejection and anger, and Fern tensed in shock as he reached out and took hold of her, the fierceness of his grip threatening to bruise the soft flesh of her upper arm.

'You don't mean that, Fern,' he repeated tersely.

Fern refused to be quelled. Why, after all, should it matter to Adam what she felt or didn't feel for Nick? She would be gone out of both their lives very soon now. There was no need for her to hold on to the protection of the deceit she had lived with so long.

Her head lifted...as she looked at him, tensing her body away from his, the angle of her head proud and defiant, she told him fiercely, 'I *do* mean it. I *never* loved him. Not before our marriage, not during it...not ever.'

As she spoke, the defiance left her voice and flatness took its place. She found after all that she could not continue to look at Adam.

'I married him because *he* wanted me to. Because he said he needed me... loved me... and I stayed married to him for those same reasons. Those and the fact that I believed it was my duty to do so. My duty and my responsibility towards my parents and the way they had brought me up. I forgot, or perhaps I never knew, that my first duty should have been to myself. Perhaps if I *had* remembered or known that, both Nick and I would have saved ourselves a lot of misery.

'And for the record...' She took a deep breath and before she could lose her courage told him quietly, 'I had already told Nick our marriage was over before he left me for Venice. Not that I expect you to believe me. Why should you?' she asked tiredly. 'After all, we both know that in your heart of hearts you must prefer to believe that I did love Nick.'

Silently she started to pull away from him, exhausted now, not just by the emotional intensity of what had just happened, but by all the strain and pressure of the preceding weeks as well.

'Yes, you're right. I would prefer to believe that,' Adam agreed heavily.

She had known it all along, of course, but somehow hearing Adam actually say the words hurt more devastatingly than she had believed possible. She had thought herself inured to pain, anaesthetised to it, somehow safely beyond it, but now she was discovering that she was wrong, and the agonised low-voiced moan she couldn't control broke through the exhausted silence of the tired air of the hallway, replacing it with a tension so intense and stifling that to Fern it felt almost as though she could hardly breathe in the density of the emotion-congested atmosphere surrounding her.

She took a step back into the open sitting-room doorway, grasping weakly for the door for support as she stumbled.

'Fern...'

She froze as Adam grabbed hold of her. He was holding her far too tightly, far too close to his own body. She could feel the panicky thud of her own heartbeat as she closed her eyes and tried to stifle behind their darkness the sharp image of his face.

The scent of him surrounded her, male, musky, shockingly familiar; she hardly dared breathe because of the effect it was having on her.

From somewhere she found the will-power to grit her teeth and demand feverishly, 'Let me go!'

To her astonishment, instead of complying with her demand, she heard Adam saying thickly, 'No... I've let you go twice already, Fern, let you go and watched as you walked out of my arms and into Nick's. There isn't going to be a third time.'

She opened her eyes and looked at him. The expression on his face made her body tremble. She started to say his name, but his hands were already cupping her face, his mouth, his head descending... his lips feathering gently, questioning, against her own.

It couldn't really be happening, of course. Adam couldn't possibly have looked at her with so much love, so much need, so much anguished regret . . . just as he couldn't possibly be holding her now, kissing her, whispering against her lips how much he loved her, wanted her, ached for her.

Hazily she reached out to touch him, the warmth of his skin, the pulse beating beneath it, the thick, clean crispness of his hair; these were things, sensations, she could surely not be imagining.

Against her body she felt him tremble and harden and a wild whirlwind of response raced through her.

'Adam . . . Adam . . .' Without knowing she was doing so she was repeating his name in a soft, anguished litany of love.

He was saying something to her, telling her how much he had longed for this . . . for her. His mouth caressed her jaw, her ears, and her body arched instinctively into his embrace, seeking more than just the intimacy of his clothed flesh against hers.

'Why . . . why didn't you tell me any of this before?' he demanded between kisses. 'You know how I felt about you . . . how much I loved you.'

Fern tensed and pulled back from him, looking into his face and seeing there the truth of what he was saying.

'No. No,' she told him shakily. 'I didn't know . . . I thought you just felt sorry for me. Nick had once told me that you . . . that you thought I was too sexually naïve to be desirable . . .'

'And you believed him? For God's sake, Fern! Didn't you guess? Didn't I show you that time . . . ?'

'I thought it was just . . . just male lust. I thought you felt sorry for me . . .'

'And I thought you were just turning to me for comfort because of Nick's betrayal. You let me think that you loved him even then!'

'Because I didn't want you to feel responsibility . . . or that you owed me anything. I was going to leave him, but . . . but he wouldn't let me . . . and I was afraid that if I did you'd think . . .' She shook her head, too emotionally overwhelmed to continue. 'I thought you must have known how I felt,' she said helplessly at last. 'After the way I . . .' Her hands balled into two small anguished fists as she looked away from him, bringing out into the open for the first time the thing which had tormented her for so long. 'I was the one who insisted . . . who demanded . . . who forced you to . . .'

'Is that what you really believe?' Adam demanded, so incredulously that she was forced to look at him.

'Fern, Fern . . . I wanted you so much, loved you so much that . . . Even if you hadn't touched me when you did, it wouldn't have made any difference. I would still have made love to you. Have you any idea how much remembering what happened between us has tortured me? Not just with guilt and remorse, but with need and wanting, too; with love, lust and anger and a thousand other emotions I can't even begin to describe.'

'Make love to me now, Adam,' Fern whispered, shivering as she said the words.

She felt his tension and looked up at him.

'Not here,' he told her unevenly. 'Never here. Come home with me.'

As he held out his hand to her, she put her own into it.

'We're going to go back to the beginning,' Adam told her softly as he led her upstairs to his bedroom. 'To the loving we should have shared... would have shared, if Nick hadn't come between us. He told me that you didn't want me, you know. He said you were too embarrassed to tell me so yourself...that you found me too old and boring...'

He paused to push open the bedroom door and then take her in his arms and gently kiss her as he heard the small anguished sound she made.

'Oh, Adam, it was never like that. I loved you even then, but I was too shy, too immature...too unknowing. I thought you were just being kind to me. I never...'

'Shush,' Adam told her gently. 'It doesn't matter now. None of the bad things that happened are important...they don't even exist any more. I just want you to think of this, Fern, that the time, the hours I spent with you are the most precious hours of my life, and it's been the memory of them that's held me back whenever I've been tempted to settle for second-best.'

'Oh, Adam.'

She wept as he kissed her, drawing her with him into the room and towards the bed.

The room was soft with shadowy light, the furniture large and comfortable, well-polished, sturdy antique oak, the bed deeply mattressed, its linen starkly white, the scent of Adam's skin still clinging to it, mingling subtly with its crisp freshness.

As she lay there watching him, savouring the intimacy of their togetherness, the unbelievable delight of it, the still almost uncertain joy of knowing that he loved her, Fern touched him gently, wordlessly, communicating her need to him.

He understood at once, lifting her hand in his, holding it and then pressing a kiss to its palm before stepping back from her and quickly undressing.

Fern watched him, mesmerised, not just by her own desire but by a dazed feeling that this still might not be real...that it could still be wrenched away from her...*he* could still be wrenched away from her.

She had thought she had remembered every aspect of their previous lovemaking, every angle of his body, every muscle and sinew, every shadow and hollow of its maleness, and yet now the reality of him was somehow much more sharply male, much more intensely masculine. She could feel her body tensing in sensual awareness of his sexuality and her response to it.

Suddenly she longed to be free of her own clothes and her fingers were already reaching eagerly for the buttons on her shirt when Adam leaned over her and gently took them away.

'No,' he told her softly. 'We're going right back to the very beginning ... remember?'

Later, leaning against him, her whole body trembling with unfamiliar pleasure as his mouth gently caressed the curve of her breast, and then opened over her nipple in slowly careful exploration, she rested her head against the thick darkness of his downbent head, stifling her small moan of pleasure as his deliberately gentle kisses gave way to a deeper rhythmic sucking that caused her spine to arch and her body to shake beneath the onslaught of the intense tremor of sensation that spread downwards from his mouth, tightening her body into a sharply spiralling coil of desire.

Each time he touched her it was as though he sensed her need ... knew exactly what she felt ... what she craved.

Lying naked next to him, she was aware of emotions, sensations she had never experienced before. Slowly she recognised what they were ...

For the first time in her life she was aware of how it felt to be loved.

As Adam leaned over her, slowly kissing his way over her body, his hand rested lightly over her sex. Protecting her modesty? No need for that now perhaps, but if she had still been the girl she was when they first met ...

'Oh, Adam.' She reached out, gently touching his head, overwhelmed by the intensity not just of her arousal but of her emotions as well. She felt him lift his hand, his mouth slowly caressing the inside of her thigh.

Her body trembled ... a woman's body not a girl's, with a woman's strongly powerful sexuality and arousal.

She could feel tears begin to sting her eyes as, beneath the surge of pleasure that swamped her, she recognised the care, the tenderness, the reverence almost of his touch.

She could feel his control as well as his need, his care and cherishing of her as well as his masculine desire to take her and hold her, to fill her with his body and fulfil the primitive biological programming of his sex towards the re-creation of himself within her.

'Adam,' she cried out his name in anguished pleasure as she felt the heat of his mouth on her body and gave in to its demand that she abandon herself to its promise of pleasure.

'Now, Adam. Please, please now,' she begged him huskily, her fingers tightening in his hair, her voice sharpening with need—need and anticipation.

'N ... no ... not that,' she told him fiercely as she felt his mouth begin to move more possessively, more passionately on her sex. '*You* ... I want you, Adam. Inside me. Now.'

She shuddered, torn between impatience and arousal, stiffening her body against the shock of losing the sensuous contact of his mouth as he moved to obey her.

Later she would show him the same pleasure he had just shown her, caressing his body with her mouth, arousing it with the deliberate and intimate loving touch of her tongue; give to him the same special expression of her love, her desire to know him completely as he had just given her. Later, not now. Now her impatient, urgent body craved the full possession of him; her senses, her emotions demanded, commanded that she give herself up completely, abandon herself totally to woman's most deeply held and atavistic need to experience the total possession of her lover.

Just as strong as the need she could sense within him ran her own complementary need, to feel him so deep within her, to be so totally possessed by him, to feel that he was so absolutely and utterly hers that for those few brief seconds of time they were actually one complete whole, with no barriers, no difference, every thought, every feeling, every breath and every heartbeat completely shared.

So this, then, was the mystical, elevating, almost divine quality that really loving someone and being loved by them could sometimes bring to mortal physical union, Fern reflected dizzily as she cried out to him and reached out for him, comprehension, reality, all of them arrested and then completely overturned as she felt him move within her and was swamped by the exquisite, unbearable intensity of the feeling exploding inside her.

Later, calmer, saner, she flushed a little with self-conscious awareness of her abandonment, not just of her physical self-control but of her mind and emotions as well.

Had she really cried out to Adam that she would die for the feeling of him inside her? That the touch, the heat, the feel ... the scent of him aroused her to the point where she wanted to scream his name to the skies?

Had she really not been able to control the building urgency to respond to his thrust within her by scoring the smooth flesh of his back with her nails? As she glanced down at his body she saw that his buttocks still bore the crescent-shaped marks she had inflicted there when ...

Beside her she saw Adam reaching for her, smoothing the damp hair back off her face as he kissed her with lingering tenderness and then searched her face anxiously.

'Are you all right? Did I hurt you? You ...'

She shook her head, reaching out to touch his mouth with her fingertip, tracing the shape of it, pushing aside the last of her self-consciousness, sloughing it off like the unwanted skin it now was as she told him frankly, 'No. I wanted it to be like that ... needed it to be like that; it was so cleansing somehow, so ... so necessary.'

Adam's passion and her own, Adam's possession and her aban-donment of herself to it had swept away the sad poverty of her memories of Nick's touch... what had passed for Nick's lovemaking. It no longer existed, no longer had any place in her memory... no power to hurt or damage her.

'I love you, Fern,' Adam told her emotionally. 'And just as soon as we can legally do so, I'd like us to marry.

'I want to be your husband, Fern... your lover... your friend... the father of your children. I want to share with you all the things we should have shared years ago if I hadn't been a fool and let Nick——'

'Shush.' Fern shook her head. 'It doesn't matter now. I was just as much to blame... it took Cressy to show me the truth. She's getting married soon... I was with them the other day. I felt so envious... I told myself I should be content with my freedom and my plans for the future, that wanting you, loving you... Oh, Adam, I still feel as though I daren't let myself believe that this has happened...'

'Believe it,' Adam told her, adding huskily, 'And believe this as well, Fern. Now that I've finally got you, I'm never going to let you go. There's no way I'm going to risk losing you again.'

'Nick won't like it,' Fern told him with a small shiver. Not for herself, but for him. Had he any idea of what Nick really was... of how much he resented him... of how dangerous he could be? As she looked up at him she saw that there was no need for her to put her thoughts into words.

'Why?' she asked unsteadily instead. 'Why is he like that?'

'I don't know. I used to think the answer might lie buried somewhere in his early childhood. The loss of his father, perhaps... but then, some people are just born that way.'

'He wants to destroy you, Adam. All this business about him being concerned about the environment and Broughton House...'

'Broughton House isn't in any danger from me,' Adam told her. 'The supposed consortium I'm part of to flatten it and turn the ground into a supermarket exists more in Nick's imagination than in reality.'

'I wish someone would buy it and turn it into a proper family home... the kind it must have been originally...'

'It's too large for most modern families,' Adam told her with a smile. 'Although...'

'Although what?' Fern asked him, half sitting up to look down into his eyes as she heard the speculation in his voice.

'You've just given me an idea,' he told her.

And then he looked down at her naked body, her breasts still slightly damp with sweat, the soft swell of her belly silky, gleaming, the tangle of her pubic curls damp and inviting.

'Mmm... Come to think of it, you're giving me far more than just ideas,' he told her sexily.

Fern laughed. She felt as comfortable with him as though this intimacy was something they had shared for years, and yet at the same time she was as quickly and erotically aroused as though she were a girl, still newly and passionately in love.

'Tell me about Broughton House first,' she demanded.

In between kisses, he did...

'You mean get the council to buy it and turn it into a kind of reform school for young offenders?'

'Not exactly... what I had in mind was more of a halfway house, somewhere they could be given the time and encouragement to take another look at the options open to them.'

'It's a wonderful idea,' she told him enthusiastically later, lying contentedly in his arms.

She suspected that he had been surprised, almost hesitant at first when she had turned to caress him as he had earlier caressed her, but, once he had realised that her desire to do so was genuine and not merely caused by any feeling that she had to repay the pleasure he had given her, he had abandoned himself totally to her loving, eager touch; and in doing so, she acknowledged mentally now, he had brought her fully and completely into fulfilled awareness of the strength of her own womanhood... her own sexuality, precious gifts indeed... as precious in their way as his love. Gifts she intended to cherish and treasure for ever.

'It won't be easy,' she warned him. 'Nick wants to get you off the council and...'

'The council doesn't matter,' Adam told her fiercely. 'I've got all I want from life right here in my arms. All I've ever wanted and all I ever will want. You, Fern. You are all that matters to me. You, your happiness and our life together!'

EPILOGUE

'So we can close the file on the Broughton House property now, can we?'

'Yes, I think so. We've had confirmation from the Revenue that the sale is going through. It should have fetched more, of course, but with the property market the way it is...'

'And the problems with planning permission for change of use...'

'Mmm... Well, the purchaser seems confident that he'll get that, although I'm surprised he isn't getting more opposition from the local residents. I don't think I'd be too keen on living in close proximity to a——'

'Sorry to interrupt you, Max, but Michael King is on the phone for you...'

'Right. I'll be right there. Yes, I think you can go ahead and close the file now.'

'So where's my granddaughter, then?'

Zoe laughed at the disappointed expression on her mother's face as she looked round the small sunny sitting-room.

'She's out with Ben. He's taken her to the park. It's the new chef's first solo attempt at lunches today, and I suspect he was glad to get Ben out of the way.'

'Yes. I saw how busy the restaurant was as I came past.'

'We've been lucky,' Zoe told her. 'Ben's found just the right niche in the market. It's the restaurants which are catering for the expensive business account lunchers which are really suffering. Out here, out of the city centre where most of our customers are local, we're still managing to keep pretty busy.

'We've had to prune our costs, of course, and take into account the fact that people are much more concerned about value for money these days. Clive's backing has been a tremendous help. Without him we'd never have been able to afford to buy either this house or the restaurant; not having to pay any rent saves a fortune on overheads. I just feel a bit guilty that I'm not contributing more to things...'

'You designed the décor and did all the costings...'

'Mmm... and I'm managing to go back to work at least part-time, even if it is only to work on the reception desk and do the cashiering. I didn't want Ben to feel that now we'd had Katie he wasn't important to

361

me any more.' Zoe laughed ruefully. 'Now if anyone has had their nose put out of joint I suppose it's me.'

'I warned you what would happen,' her mother told her, smiling at her. 'Men are notorious for becoming doting, adoring, possessive daddies when they have daughters. I've never gone along with this thing they're supposed to have about wanting sons. Some do, of course, but if they're honest most men will admit that there's something very special about having a daughter. I can still remember how thrilled your father was when you were born.'

Zoe was bending down to retrieve a soft felt rabbit half sticking out beneath the sofa.

'A flat over the restaurant?' she had suggested cautiously when they had first talked about moving.

He had shaken his head.

'You can't bring a baby up properly in a flat,' he had told her. 'No, I've got a better idea. There's a small house up for sale a few houses down from here. It's got a good-sized back garden, and we're just across the road from the park.'

'Can we afford it?' she had protested. Deep down inside she still felt guilty about the baby; worried that, although on the surface Ben had adapted surprisingly well to her pregnancy, inwardly his feelings were very different.

She wouldn't have blamed him if he *had* felt resentful, if, despite all he had said to her, he had perhaps really wished that she had simply gone ahead with the termination without burdening him with the knowledge of how she felt or what was happening. She had been, she acknowledged, still disturbed and disquieted by her own awareness that when she had really needed to be strong and independent, when it had really mattered, she had been no such thing.

All through the last months of pregnancy, while Ben busied himself with preparations for opening the restaurant and chivvied the workmen to complete their work on the house and the restaurant conversion, she had worried that despite what he had said, despite the love and concern he showed her, despite the protective way he behaved towards her, it was all really a sham and that he was hiding his real feelings.

Sometimes, overwhelmed by guilt and misery when Ben was out, she had curled up alone on their bed, her eyes blurring with tears as she whispered to the growing bulge that was the new life inside her that it wasn't to worry... that *she* loved it...

And yet as the birth drew nearer she had become more and more afraid, worrying about how Ben would react to the reality of the baby.

To accept her pregnancy was one thing; to say he loved her, to make plans for their future together... But what if, in reality, when the baby arrived, he found that he could not love it, that he *did* resent it? How could she let him go, knowing how much she loved and needed him, and yet how could she let him stay, let herself stay, knowing that he could not love their child?

Children needed love in the same way that they needed air to breathe and food to nourish them, and, if Ben could not love their child, by staying with him she would be forcing him or her to grow up under the burden of knowing of that lack of love.

She knew that her quietness during the last months of her pregnancy had concerned Ben, but she had not been able to explain to him how she felt. She had placed enough burdens on him already.

She had felt it would be disloyal to confide in anyone else, even her parents, and so she had kept her anxiety to herself, brooding on it. As the baby inside her grew, so too did her fear of what its birth might bring. And so too did her guilt for what she had done—to Ben and to her child...

'I'll never forget the night you were born,' her mother was saying reminiscently now. 'Nor the night Katie was born either. What on earth prompted you to go off to Manchester like that?'

'I don't really know,' Zoe admitted. 'I didn't really think there was any possibility of Katie arriving early. Ben was busy down here sorting things out and I just...'

She shook her head, unable to explain the need that had overwhelmed her that morning, the feeling that the only way she could resolve the guilt and anxiety inside her would be for her to talk to Ben's mother.

Now she was forced to admit that it had been a foolishly impulsive thing to do. At eight and a half months pregnant, she had tired easily and been very large. The train had been delayed by repairs to the lines and it had been over four hours before she had eventually arrived in Manchester. She hadn't wanted to trust herself or her aged Mini to such a long journey on the road, so the train was her best option.

She had put the beginnings of pain in her back down to the discomfort of travelling.

The taxi driver had grimaced slightly when she gave Ben's mother's address, and she understood why, because the utilitarian block of flats was in a rundown part of the city.

Ben's mother had been astonished to see her, but had welcomed her warmly, hugging her, exclaiming over her tired face and then taking charge with a speed and efficiency which Ben later admitted had surprised him when Zoe had dropped her mug of tea with a sharp cry of pain.

Ben had made it just in time for the birth, driven north by Zoe's father, who had taken the phone call from Ben's mother to alert them to what had happened.

When Ben had burst into the labour suite, his face white with anxiety and tension, Zoe hadn't realised at first that he was remembering, reliving the despair of the hours he had spent in the same hospital holding his sister's hand while she struggled to give birth to her stillborn child, nor of the fears which had kept him awake at night throughout Zoe's own pregnancy, fears of retribution in the form of the loss of his own child, and of Zoe herself.

That knowledge had come later, when all three of them were back at home, the baby safely asleep in her cradle, Zoe tucked in bed, protesting that she was perfectly healthy and that there was no need for Ben to treat her like an invalid and that no, she did not want a bowl of chicken soup.

They had both laughed then as Ben mimicked Sarah Bernstein's warning from his childhood, that no child could grow strong and healthy without it. 'I'd like Sarah to be one of the godparents,' he had told her. And then he had bent down and lifted Katie very gently from her cradle, holding her in his arms.

It was then that Zoe had known, had seen the depth and intensity of the love illuminating his face.

When Ben had turned round and seen her crying, he had put the baby down and come straight over to her, anxiety creasing his face.

'Zoe, what is it, what's wrong?' he had asked her, and with new maturity she had recognised behind his tension not only his love for her, but all his years of taking as his own burden the responsibility for the comfort and happiness of those closest to him.

'Nothing's wrong,' she had told him. 'It's just that I love you so much...'

As she said it she recognised how true it was and how much she had misjudged him in thinking, fearing that beneath his apparent acceptance of her pregnancy might lie a resentment not so much of her, but of their child; and that that resentment could turn to outright jealousy of their baby, a demand to be constantly told that he came first in her life.

She couldn't have been further from the truth, she acknowledged ruefully to herself now. If anyone was inclined to feel jealous, it was her; not that she really minded the mutual adoration society which had sprung up between Ben and Katie.

She had also discovered that, deep though her sense of mother love was, she also appreciated the time she had to herself when Ben took over. She enjoyed the hours she put in at the restaurant, the sense of self that came from being a working part of their business, and she enjoyed it all the more because that enjoyment was free of any sense of guilt that she was somehow depriving Katie.

Her dread that she would have to take on the role of loving her not just as a mother but in lieu of a father as well had gone, well and truly banished by Ben's relationship with their daughter.

'Are you all ready for your exams?' Zoe asked her mother now.

'I am. Your father's a nervous wreck,' her mother laughed.

'How do you like having him at home so much now that he's semi-retired?' Zoe asked her.

'I'm getting used to it now. At first I wasn't so sure it was going to work,' her mother admitted. 'After all the years of silently feeling slightly martyred because he was away so much and so wrapped up in his work, it was very difficult coming to terms with the fact that, once he did what I thought I'd always wanted and cut down on his work so that we could spend more time together, there *were* times when I almost resented his being there and felt quite stifled by his presence.'

'He's terrifically proud of you, you know,' Zoe told her mother. 'When he came round the other week he was boasting to Ben and me about how well you're doing on this course.'

Her mother laughed. 'Yes, I know. He keeps telling people that he's going to retire completely and send me out to work. I'm glad you're keeping your own work, Zoe. I hadn't realised how much I'd started to resent being so totally dependent on your father, not *just* financially, but emotionally... every way. Nor that he felt a similar resentment towards me. A healthy relationship needs a good helping of mutual respect. Your father might not have liked it at first when I announced what I was going to do, but now...

'Do you know, we actually stay up late at night now, *talking* to each other...'

They both laughed and then her mother added thoughtfully, 'It's strange, but there comes a point in a long-term relationship when to find it exciting and stimulating to talk to one another is actually more erotic than sex...'

'Oh, yes?' Zoe laughed. 'That's not the impression I got the other Sunday when I rang and caught the pair of you still in bed together. And don't tell me you were just reading the papers...'

Her mother laughed and blushed slightly.

'Here's Ben now,' Zoe told her as she heard the front door open.

Through the open sitting-room door, Zoe could hear her daughter gurgling contentedly.

'Hi... we're back.'

As Ben walked into the sitting-room, Katie in his arms, Zoe wondered if she would ever quite lose the grateful feeling of wonderment and joy, of somehow being singled out especially by fate to receive some of her most precious and extravagant gifts, she felt whenever she saw Ben and Katie together.

As her mother lifted Katie from Ben's arms, cooing dotingly over her, Ben smiled softly at Zoe.

'Missed me?' he asked her.

'Missed you? You've only been gone half an hour,' Zoe scoffed, but her eyes told him a different story as she lifted her face for his kiss.

'Your mother rang,' she told him. 'Sharon has passed her exams and she's got really good grades. They're hoping to come down to London for a couple of days to celebrate...'

'Mmm...and so she should have done, the cost of that crammer we sent her to,' Ben complained.

But Zoe knew him better now. She wasn't the girl who had skimmed so carelessly over the surface of life any more, too caught up in her own needs to look beneath it. She knew how pleased he was, just as she had known, despite his bluster and complaints when she had first tentatively suggested it, how much it meant to him that she had shared his desire to help Sharon repair her sense of self-worth and to take a fresh interest in life.

No one could ever wipe away the pain of losing her baby; no one knew that better than Zoe. One day, if she was lucky, Sharon would find someone as caring as Ben, and when she did she hoped that, unlike her, Sharon would have the maturity to recognise his true worth.

She turned to look at her mother, who was still cooing over Katie, her heart melting with love, and then trembling slightly as she remembered how close she had come to turning her back on the wonderful gift she and Ben had been given.

Katie, whose conception she had first resented and then feared, Katie who she had believed would never know the love and care of her father. Katie...

She looked at Ben and saw the way he was already anxious to have the baby back in his arms, and smiled wryly to herself as she murmured to him, 'Just think what you're going to be like when she's seventeen.'

Ben grinned back at her.

'I'm trying not to,' he admitted ruefully.

'Well, it probably won't be so bad when you've three or four of them to worry about instead of just one,' Zoe told him straight-faced.

'Three or *four*?'

'Yes, I think you're right,' Zoe agreed, deliberately misunderstanding. 'Four would be better. Two of each... Of course, they might all be girls, but I don't think I could stand that much competition.'

'Four...' Ben repeated, looking slightly dazed. 'Four...'

'Mmm...or perhaps six,' Zoe murmured, sliding her arm through his and laughing up at him, and putting her head to one side while she studied him for a minute before teasing, 'Yes, I definitely think you look like a father of six.'

'Oh, you do, do you? Well, we'll just have to see what we can do about that, won't we?'

'What are your mummy and daddy whispering about, I wonder?' Heather asked her grandchild.

Katie didn't know, she only knew that she liked it very much indeed, here in her nice, safe, warm world surrounded by people who loved her and cherished her. Very much indeed.

As Jennifer Bowers stepped up on the podium and waited for the applause to die down, Nick surreptitiously checked his reflection in the half-open glass door into the hall.

The suit was a new one—Armani—no dull, staid Savile Row tailoring for him; he was young enough, handsome enough to be able to carry off a sophisticated, modern image without alienating the voters, the PR firm Venice had hired had assured him.

'You look perfect,' Venice had purred when she had been called in to inspect him. 'Perfect.'

It had irked him that others should apparently deem it necessary that Venice's approval was needed, but he had learned to be wary about what he said to his wife.

There had been some medical concern over Venice's health during her pregnancy, although Nick had never been able to establish what it was; certainly it did not prevent her from taking a controlling interest in everything that he did, from selecting his clothes to negotiating the purchase of the elegant London house which was to be their base once he was elected.

Nothing was to upset her, she had told Nick; there were to be no arguments, no unexplained absences from her side.

She had smiled at him as she said that, just as she had smiled at him when she had explained that Lucy Ferrars, the pretty little brunette who worked for the PR firm and who had soothed his battered ego with her obvious adoration, had lost her job.

'Peter didn't feel she was the right type and I must say I had to agree with him. From now on Peter himself will take charge of your public relations, Nick.'

It baffled Nick sometimes how Venice, who during the last weeks of her pregnancy never seemed to stir from the house, complaining that she felt too ill and looked too awful, nevertheless seemed to be aware of exactly how he spent every single second of his day.

His business had been sold; he wouldn't have time for it any more, Venice had told him, adding with one of those dangerous, calculating smiles he had come to loathe so much that it had hardly been the type of thing that would do anything to add to his prestige.

'It's not as though you had any proper qualifications, a proper profession, like Adam for instance, is it?' Venice had purred.

She gave him a generous allowance, very generous, but he had seen the look in Peter Villiers' eyes when it had been discussed; the amusement and contempt that had made him seethe with resentment and rage.

When he had tried to express his feelings to Venice, she had simply shrugged her shoulders.

'What does it matter what he thinks?' she had asked him carelessly, ignoring Nick's complaint that there had been no reason for the man to be in on a discussion which should have been limited to Venice, Nick and her accountant.

There had been some delay over the party's accepting Nick as a prospective candidate. Nick wasn't sure, but he suspected that it came from Jennifer Bowers herself. In the end, though, Venice had got her way.

What did a small delay matter? she had told Nick when he had fumed and protested. 'Much better to get the birth of the baby out of the way first anyway.'

He was the one who was going to be elected, not her, Nick had wanted to say, but for some reason he had not been able to.

It wasn't that he was afraid of her, of course. How could he be? She was only a woman...his wife, sitting decorously beside him now, dressed, like him, in the subtle elegance of one of Italy's premier designers, her hair newly styled, casually elegant, the scarlet nail polish banished and replaced by demurely natural buffed nails.

'You should take a leaf out of Venice's book,' Peter had told him, his voice warm with approval as he added, 'She knows exactly what to do...exactly how to present herself. You're a very lucky man,' he had added.

Lucky? *Was* he? Nick wondered sourly. Sometimes he felt that Venice treated him like a toy she had bought in a shop, something akin to one of those expensive clockwork things she had bought for Guy.

Guy...he hadn't even been allowed to choose his own son's name. Not that either he or Venice had very much to do with the baby, other than pose for carefully arranged 'casual' photographs.

'The fact that you've got a baby, that Venice can be seen to be part of the new movement towards women combining motherhood and a career, can only be—is bound to be—an added advantage,' Peter had enthused.

Nick had noticed the way Peter had flushed slightly beneath his tan as Venice looked at him and smiled slowly.

On the podium Jennifer Bowers was saying, 'And I should now like you to welcome our new MP, Nicholas Wheelwright.' The clapping was polite and controlled.

Nick stood up, paused for a second to take a last final glance in the glass before walking towards the podium.

'It should have been you, you know,' Jennifer Bowers told Adam regretfully as they watched Nick circulating, Venice at his side, smiling prettily as they accepted people's congratulations.

Adam turned his head, his arm still round Fern's waist, a greatly expanded waist at the moment, Fern reflected ruefully as she felt one of the twins kicking energetically inside her.

She had laughed when Dr Riley told her she was expecting twins. There was a lot of laughter in Fern's life these days; a lot of laughter and a lot of love.

She leaned slightly into Adam's warmth, watching him as he listened to Jennifer Bowers.

'You would have made a far better MP than Nick, Adam, you must know that.'

'It wasn't what I wanted,' Adam told her. 'It would have meant making far too many sacrifices. I have all I want here,' he added, turning to smile down at Fern.

'Yes, I can see that,' Jennifer agreed softly.

'Venice wasn't too pleased when the party refused to give her a free hand and let her organise this "do" herself.'

She made a rueful face. 'Apparently she had hoped to persuade Lord Stanton to let her put a marquee up in the hall grounds. She wanted to bring in top London caterers and of course make sure the media knew what was going on.'

'Is it true that Nick only got in by a very small majority?' Fern asked quietly.

'Yes, I'm afraid so. This is considered a very safe seat for the party, otherwise I'd never have risked stepping down mid-term. Of course there's always a smaller turnout for a by-election, but in view of all the rallying Venice and Nick did... and to listen to the speech Nick gave tonight, you'd have thought he was celebrating a landslide victory.'

She made a slight face. 'Sorry... I'm letting my prejudices show. I'm sorry, Adam, but I can't help wishing that it had been you, even though I understand why you felt you couldn't stand.'

A little later on, when they were on their own, Fern watched Adam's face as he watched Nick. 'Have you really no regrets?' she asked him quietly.

He turned towards her and touched her cheek lightly. 'Do you really need to ask me that? What I said to Jennifer is true. I have all I want here, Fern. All I want and more than I ever dreamed I might have. I'm not a politically ambitious man, I make no apology for that...'

'Not wanting gain for yourself,' agreed Fern, interrupting him, 'but for others. The Broughton House project, for instance...'

She broke off as she saw Jennifer Bowers making her way quietly back towards the podium, her stomach muscles tensing slightly. She knew what was coming, and how much it meant to Adam.

She had been worried at first when they had married that her past relationship with Nick, and the fact that he and Adam were stepbrothers, might have an alienating effect on others, but Adam had swiftly told her that he did not care what anyone else thought; that if anyone, anyone at all dared to make her feel uncomfortable in even the smallest way, then they would leave, move somewhere else and make a completely fresh start. But to Fern's relief she had discovered that their marriage was received far better than she had anticipated, and that Nick was not the popular figure he had always claimed; that in fact she, to her surprise, was better liked than her first husband.

Of course initially there had been some curiosity and speculation, but that had soon faded.

Adam had insisted on their marrying as soon as they possibly could, and when Fern had suggested tentatively that he might prefer to wait until after the council re-election, he had taken her in his arms and told her firmly that the council and everyone on it could go to hell as far as he was concerned, and that if she thought that being a member of it came anyway near to mattering one jot to him, then she understood him and the nature of his love for her far less well than he had believed.

Even so, the fact that he had been re-elected, almost triumphally so, had been a tremendous relief to her.

To discover less than a month later that she was pregnant had almost been more happiness than she felt she had any right to have.

She and Adam were now looking for a new house, somewhere large enough for themselves and the twins. They already thought they had found somewhere, a large, early Victorian villa on the outskirts of town, set in a very good-sized private garden and yet close enough to its neighbours not to be too isolated.

The present owner, a widower, was selling up because he wanted to move closer to his married daughter. Fern had already spent a blissful week with Adam planning the new nursery.

'What is it...what's wrong?' he had asked her anxiously the previous evening, when he had discovered her curled up on the sofa, slow tears running silently down her face.

'I just can't believe it,' she had told him. 'I feel sometimes that I don't deserve to be so happy, Adam.'

'Rubbish,' he had contradicted her as he smoothed the hair back off her face and kissed her. 'You deserve to be happy more than anyone else I know. You make me happier than I ever knew or hoped I could be, Fern...'

Jennifer had reached the podium now. People were breaking off their conversations to turn towards her.

She picked up the gavel and rapped it on the desk.

'Ladies and gentlemen. While officially I may no longer have any right to command your attention, before I finally step down from public office there is one more task I have to perform. I shan't say a duty because it is very far from that. I know the reason we are all here tonight is to welcome and congratulate our new member of parliament, but I'm sure that Nick won't mind if I use this occasion to thank and congratulate someone else.

'None of you here will not be aware of the work that Adam Wheelwright has done for our local community. I know Adam himself would be the last person to want to receive praise and thanks for what I know he considers to be his civic responsibility for something—a project—which reflects with shining credit not just on Adam himself but on the whole community as well. I am referring of course to the Broughton House project.

'As you may know, there was a good deal of serious opposition to the proposal when it was first mooted. People, quite understandably, were concerned that by turning Broughton House into a residential learning centre for young male offenders they would be putting their own property and peace of mind at risk.

'Why should we, a small, quiet, peaceful middle-class market town, take on the responsibility and all the potential problems that would go with having within our community these young people who had already proved that they had scant respect for the law?

'What sane community would actually welcome into its midst what amounted to an open prison?

'It is to Adam's credit that he managed, quietly and calmly, to re-educate us all; to show us that we had a duty to help these young people; that by establishing Broughton House as a place where they could serve out their sentence and at the same time learn not just the physical skills which will help them to earn a living, but also the social and emotional skills which will help them to integrate fully into society, we would hopefully benefit not only them but ourselves as well.

'It is by example that we can help them and, in doing so, ourselves, not by rejection, Adam told us. I know there are still those who are doubtful, those who will be watching what happens when Broughton House has its first intake of young offenders, those who will secretly be hoping that Adam is proved wrong, but thankfully their number grows smaller and smaller every day, and I suspect that it is not just his erring boys that Adam secretly hopes to convert, but all our Doubting Thomases as well.

'For a crusader and innovator, Adam is a man of extreme modesty, preferring what our media moguls refer to as a "low profile", but no one having seen him in action these last few months can doubt that he is a man of very serious determination and intent, ready to move mountains to achieve his goals if he perceives it necessary.

'I am not going to ask Adam to make a speech—not here this evening, though I am sure he will have plenty to say to us at the official opening of Broughton House next month; but what I would like to do is to thank him on behalf of all of us for opening our eyes to the needs of others, and for teaching us that it is our fear of our fellow man and his potential power against us which is more destructive, more dangerous than our hatred.

'Adam...'

Smiling at him, Fern disentangled herself from her husband's side, watching him walk towards the podium. Where were they now, his detractors, those who had scoffed that he was out of his mind even to suggest such a plan, that he was deliberately trying to destroy the community to advance his own half-baked ideas?

Well, one of them was here.

Fern's smile died as she looked across at Nick.

Despite his Armani suit, despite all the expensive hype that surrounded him, despite all the money Venice had poured into publicising and promoting him, despite the fact that he now surely had all that he wanted, his face, his expression had an unhappy, pinched bitterness about it. Poor Nick. She almost felt sorry for him.

'He can't do this!' Nick exploded as he watched Adam take the podium. 'I'm not letting him or that bitch Jennifer Bowers get away with this. I'm the MP, not him. He's nothing... nothing... just a small-town councillor. I'm going to...'

'You aren't doing anything,' Venice corrected Nick coldly, taking hold of his arm. 'Don't make even more of a fool of yourself than you need, Nick. Peter and I have worked hard on you, on your image; don't go and wreck it all by having one of your tantrums. Let him enjoy his petty moment of triumph. What does it matter? Once the place is open and his precious delinquents start making their presence felt...'

'You told me he wasn't going to be re-elected to the council,' Nick interrupted her bitterly. 'You said he had no chance of getting permission to use Broughton House as a rehabilitation centre. You...'

'When I said he wouldn't be re-elected, we still thought he was after planning permission to convert the house into a shopping centre. Now that he's taken on this saintly mantle of public do-gooder, there's nothing we can do to shift him. Not yet, anyway.

'Stop worrying about him, Nick, for God's sake. What is he, after all? Just some small-town councillor, as you said. You've got far more important things to worry about. Like convincing the party stronghold that you've got what it takes to play a far more high-profile role than that of mere MP.

'I've had a word with Peter and we're going to organise a dinner in town next month, not too early in the dinner-party season—the timing will be very important. Peter knows a few names he can get to come; a couple of titles and there's an ancient ex-PM he can drag out of moth-balls. The old boy's practically gaga, but it looks good, creates the right impression. Oh, and that reminds me, I'm going to have to go up to town for a couple of days next week to check on how the work's going on the new house. There's no need for you to come. You can't anyway, you've got that dinner to attend, haven't you?

'Peter will drive me up and bring me back...'

Venice smiled sensuously to herself as she listened to Nick's petulant protests. She had been lucky; she had got her figure back completely from the baby now. Peter had remarked on how smooth her skin was, how supple her flesh. Her smile widened. He was an adoring lover, amusing for the moment, but not for much longer. Ending their affair would also give her an excuse for changing PR agencies. She needed someone more upmarket now, someone with more political clout.

She glanced at Nick, contempt curling her mouth. It had been even easier to get him to toe the line than she had expected. She looked to-wards the podium where Adam was now stepping back down, immedi-ately reaching out to draw Fern close to him.

Ridiculous for a man like him to be so obviously and so intensely in love, and with dull, stupid Fern of all women.

Adam was completely wasted on her, and it was a pity that her plans precluded her from teaching Adam that fact.

She looked back at Nick. He was looking edgy and irritable, his face slightly flushed with petulance and frustration.

She would have to let him back into her bed tonight; she had seen the way he had looked at Peter's secretary this morning. She smiled cynically to herself. It wasn't very difficult to keep him to heel. Sex to Nick was like sweets to a child.

'Ready to go home?'

Fern looked up at Adam. 'We can't leave yet,' she protested. 'No one else has.'

'Someone has to be the first; besides, I'm tired of looking at you and not being able to touch you, not being able to show you how much I love you...'

'You show me all the time,' she told him, softly smiling at him—and knew that it was true.

'Are you sure I look all right?'

Marcus tugged uncomfortably at his tie as though he felt it was too tight.

'You look fine,' Eleanor assured him.

'Are you sure this is the right thing? I mean, won't she be expecting all of us...?'

'You're doing the right thing, Marcus. She'll be thrilled...'

'I'm not even sure I'll be able to recognise her,' Marcus groaned. 'Not after six weeks in New York with Jade.'

Eleanor laughed. 'Hurry up, otherwise you'll be late for her flight.'

She kissed him briefly and then more lingeringly, looking into his eyes, her own soft and tender with emotion.

'It will be all right, Marcus,' she told him softly.

'You say that, but...'

'It will be all right,' Eleanor repeated.

'Why couldn't we go with Marcus to meet Vanessa?' Gavin complained once Marcus had gone. 'I wanted to see the plane come in and——'

'You know why we couldn't go,' Tom told his brother before Eleanor could respond. 'It's a surprise for Vanessa.'

'Well, I want to tell her about the pond and the fish and...'

'She already knows about them, stupid,' Tom told his younger brother dampeningly. 'She saw the house before she went to New York.'

'Yes, but she didn't see the fish, did she?'

'No, but she knows about them because you wrote to her about them, didn't you?'

'Stop it, both of you,' Eleanor interrupted them firmly. 'You'll both see Vanessa soon enough, and no, Gavin, you can't take her out to show her the goldfish this evening, and remember, this is Vanessa's home as well as yours and she might want to discover some things for herself.'

She would never have believed what a difference a few months could make, Eleanor admitted as her sons reluctantly settled down with their homework. With hindsight, she felt it was probably the news from Julia that she intended to stay in America which had brought the first crack in the wall Vanessa had erected against them.

It had been Marcus who had told his daughter that her permanent home was going to be with them. Marcus, who had held her stiff, angry body when she had told him that she didn't want their charity, that she knew they didn't really want her; Marcus who had told her that she was wrong. But it had been Tom, of all people, who had really made the first breakthrough, funny, emotional, over-sensitive Tom, who out of his own spending money and entirely of his own volition had bought and made the cheap pegboard noticeboard which he had independently and un-known to Eleanor hung up crookedly in the bedroom he and Gavin had vacated.

'Tom, you've forgotten something,' Vanessa had announced tersely, after her silent arrival and even more silent walk up to her bedroom.

'No, it's for you,' Tom had told her stoically. 'Me and Gavin have one. Grandad and me made that one for you. It's for your photographs and things. Me and Gavin have one of Dad and Karen on ours and——'

'Yes, and we're getting a new one of baby Hannah, only she isn't a baby any more because it's her birthday next week, and she'll be having a birthday party, but not until half-term so that we can be there.'

Nothing else had been said, and, despite the contempt and bitterness Eleanor had been sure she had seen in Vanessa's eyes, the board had remained where it was.

There was no point in her changing schools, Vanessa had informed them. She could board, and besides, she knew really they would be glad to have her out of the way, but she had still asked for a camera for her birthday, and the photos she had taken of the boys, ostensibly to test the quality of the camera and film, had been removed from the board when she went off to school, only to return with her at Christmas.

It hadn't been easy; she had *still* been openly hostile towards Eleanor, but now that Eleanor no longer felt that Vanessa threatened her relationship with Marcus she was able to deal with it better, even to the point of firmly dealing with Vanessa's bad behaviour with the sort of punishment she would have given her *had* she been her own daughter.

'Treat her as you would if she was your child,' Jade had advised her. 'She won't love you for it, but she will respect you.'

And Jade, it had seemed, was right.

But, surprisingly, the one single thing which had altered their relationship most of all was the correspondence Jade had instigated between herself and Vanessa.

When Jade had said casually that Vanessa was going to write to her, Eleanor had been stunned; she had been even more surprised when the correspondence turned out to be a regular exchange of letters, culminating in Jade's inviting Vanessa out to New York to spend almost the entire school summer holiday with her.

Vanessa had wanted to go, a final fling before she settled down to work towards her GCSEs, and, uncertainly, Marcus had agreed.

Before she had left, almost twelve months since they had first made the decision to move, Eleanor and Marcus found their home.

It wasn't in the country, not unless you classified Wimbledon as such; it didn't have as large a garden as Broughton House, nor as many rooms, but Eleanor found it surprisingly appealing, and, much to her astonishment, so, it seemed, did Vanessa.

Admittedly she had shrugged and appeared uninterested when they all viewed it, but later she had said she supposed it was a good idea, even adding that it was time Tom had a room of his own and that he must be sick of Gavin's sports stuff filling the room they shared.

Completion had taken place just before Vanessa flew to New York.

She would have to choose the furnishings and décor for her room before she left, Eleanor had told her.

'What's the point?' Vanessa had responded. 'I don't spend that much time in it. I'm away at school and...'

She and Eleanor had been alone at the time; Eleanor had taken a deep breath and warned herself not to get excited; keeping her voice as neutral and casual as she could she had responded, 'You could always change schools, Vanessa. In fact, your father has already made tentative enquiries; there's an excellent one locally. Of course, I know you're at a very important stage with your exam courses...'

'*Dad* wants me to come and live here with him...?'

Vanessa's face had been slightly flushed, her eyes sparkling.

'Well, yes, of course he does,' Eleanor assured her gently. 'You're his daughter, Vanessa, and to be honest, I sometimes think he feels rather left out of it here with me and the boys...'

It wasn't true, of course; her sons, confident now of the love of their father and stepmother and their grandparents, as well as their mother, had formed a very good relationship with Marcus.

'I suspect he feels he rather needs an ally at times,' Eleanor added slyly, watching silently as Vanessa digested her comment.

Nothing more was said, no response made by Vanessa. Not then. But the new bedroom and bathroom furniture had been duly chosen and before she left for New York she had mentioned casually that it seemed a pity for Marcus to waste so much money paying for her to board at school when she could just as easily live with them.

And now she was coming home. And Marcus was going alone to meet her and welcome her back.

Eleanor nibbled anxiously at her bottom lip. It wasn't just for Marcus that she wanted things to go well, or for herself, it was for all of them. Vanessa's resentment and unhappiness of her merely reflected her inner unhappiness with herself.

Perhaps she was too sentimental, too idealistic, but she wished no child to grow up with that kind of burden, Eleanor reflected—no child, but especially not one close to her.

She walked into the hall and looked nervously at the clock. Vanessa's flight should be in by now.

Marcus almost missed her; she had grown taller, developed the beginnings of curves, changed her hairstyle; she looked, alarmingly, more young woman than child—and then she saw him, and hesitated, anxiety, longing, hesitation and vulnerability flitting across her face, making her once again a child... his child.

'Vanessa...'

He moved quickly towards her, not waiting for her to come to him, taking hold of her and hugging her, surprising himself by his reaction to the slender, fragile feel of her in his arms.

His child... his daughter, his flesh.

'Dad...'

There was a small husky choke in the girl's voice as she buried her head against him, and her voice shook a little as she told him, 'So uncool... Jade would have a fit. Where are the others?' she asked him, lifting her hair from his shoulder.

'Waiting at the house. I wanted to come and meet you on my own.'

It was the truth, he recognised, even if he hadn't known it until Eleanor told him, suggested it.

'I'll bet Gavin was pleased,' Vanessa commented. 'I thought he'd probably bring his precious fish with him.'

Marcus laughed. 'Oh, you've heard all about them, have you? I like the hairstyle, by the way. It suits you.'

He watched as she flushed with pleasure, acknowledging that the old Marcus, the Marcus who couldn't allow himself to express even to himself how much he loved her, would never have said as much.

'Do you really like it?' Vanessa asked him eagerly, and when he nodded she giggled and told him, 'It was Jade's idea. She said that Nell would have forty fits and that she'd probably prefer me to have my hair in nice neat braids like an old-fashioned schoolgirl.'

As he listened to her, noting the way she clung naturally to his arm, pressing close against him as they battled their way through the bustle, he recorded that easy, unselfconscious 'Nell', and the lack of malice which had accompanied her comment, and mentally thanked Jade.

'Has Jade decided to stay on in New York, did she say?'

'She said that Sam wanted to marry her, but that she's not sure. She will marry him, though,' Vanessa told him with new wisdom. 'She loves him really.'

'How's the new house? Are you all settled in? Is Nell making you work hard in the garden?'

'Fine, yes, and no,' Marcus told her teasingly, adding with a grin, 'I think Nell's saving the heavy digging for you. She thinks you've been spoiled enough. I ought to warn you, by the way, that Tom has bought himself a metal detector and he seems to have got hold of the strange idea that you'll be as thrilled with the potential of it as he is, so prepare yourself...'

'Well, it's a fairly old house... Victorian, Nell said, so there might be something...' Vanessa told him enthusiastically, a child once more, the emergent woman disappearing.

'Yes, probably a lot of rusting nails and rubbish,' Marcus agreed.

'Well, I suppose so, but it wouldn't be fair to put him off, would it?' Vanessa asked him seriously. 'Not if Tom's spent all his pocket money on it.'

Marcus glanced at her, his heart suddenly filled with an almost bitter-sweet pang of love.

She was growing so fast, maturing so quickly, giving him in one second a terrifying glimpse of the woman she would soon become and with it his awareness of how soon she would leave him to begin her own life, and at the same time the equally heartrending knowledge of how young she still was, how vulnerable...how precious.

He felt as tongue-tied, as shy and inarticulate as a boy, and just as unable to tell her how he felt about her; how much she meant to him.

As he collected her luggage and they headed for his car, he thought inwardly, Oh, Nell, how right you were to warn me not to let myself have regrets, not to turn my back on the pleasure of loving her.

'It's good to have you home,' he told her gruffly as he unlocked the car. And then as she looked at him he put down her case and went to-wards her, giving her a fiercely protective hug.

Ignoring the lump of emotion aching in his throat, he added teasingly, 'Jade was right, though, I'm not sure what Nell is going to make of your hair. It makes you look terrifyingly grown-up.'

When she flushed pink with pleasure, he knew he had said the right thing and knew as well that fierce dizzying surge of triumph that every father experienced when his teenage daughter, that beautiful, wayward, illogical and terrifying creature who had taken the place of his adoring little girl, smiled on him with approval.

'I can hear them. I can hear the car!' Tom announced excitedly, running downstairs and rushing towards the front door, flinging it open just as Marcus stopped the car outside.

As she watched the boy race towards them with uninhibited en-thusiasm, Eleanor felt her tension ease slightly.

The passenger door of the car opened and she discovered she was holding her breath slightly.

The girl standing watching her was not the same one who had gone away, she recognised, as she searched Vanessa's eyes for the old anta-gonism and saw instead only hesitation and a slight wariness.

It was up to her now. 'Treat her as you would your own daughter,' Jade had said.

Suppressing the flutter of anxiety tensing her stomach, Eleanor smiled and hurried forward, pausing when Vanessa turned her head to say some-thing to Tom.

The protest, 'Oh, Vanessa, your lovely hair!' couldn't quite be stilled, but to her relief all her stepdaughter did was laugh and look at Marcus.

'Jade said you wouldn't like it,' she told Eleanor as she came towards her.

'It's not that I don't *like* it,' Eleanor told her. 'It looks lovely and it suits you... It's just that it... it makes you look so grown-up.'

'She's just saying that because she's a mother,' Gavin told Vanessa. 'Mothers always say things like that. She wouldn't let me have a new pair of trainers...'

Mothers always say things like that...

Across the three bent male heads, Vanessa and Eleanor looked at one another.

'Your room's all finished,' Eleanor said quietly. 'You were right about the furniture—the aqua finish looks much better than the peach. Do you...?'

'I want you to come and see the fish,' Gavin announced firmly.

'What, before you've seen your present?' Vanessa teased him.

Half an hour later they were all sitting in the small sitting-room which was officially Nell's office, but to which all the family seemed to gravitate, despite the fact that she had banned a television set from it.

'This is for you,' Vanessa told Eleanor almost hesitantly, handing her a flat, beautifully gift-wrapped package. 'Jade helped me choose it. We got it in SoHo... from a craft shop.'

She looked so nervous that Eleanor longed to put her arm round her and tell her that no matter what it was she would love it because it came from her; but she didn't. Instead she started to open it, slowly, ignoring the boys' exhortations to hurry up.

They had already had their presents: a baseball jacket and cap for Gavin, and a beautiful leather-covered photograph album for Tom, who had recently taken up photography as a hobby, another piece of news Vanessa must have learned via one of Tom's letters, Eleanor reflected as she carefully smoothed the wrapping back from her own gift.

Her breath caught in her throat as she stared down at it, tears blurring her eyes.

'What is it... what have you got?' Gavin was demanding noisily at her side.

'Do you like it? I thought... Well, I know you like things like that. Jade thought it was too sentimental. There were others...'

Eleanor shook her head. 'Vanessa, it's perfect... I love it.' Too sentimental! Her mouth quivered slightly as she looked down at the pretty antique sampler in its cherrywood frame.

Long, long ago some young female fingers had stitched that slightly crooked 'Home is where the heart is', but the mother who had received it from her daughter could not have taken more pleasure and emotion in it than she was doing.

'It will be just right for over the fireplace,' Eleanor said quietly. 'Thank you, Vanessa.'

She didn't attempt to touch or kiss her. To have done so at this stage would have jarred, struck a false note, but neither did she attempt to hide from her stepdaughter the tears which shone in her eyes.

'Oh, and I've brought you two both back a poster as well,' Vanessa was telling her stepbrothers.

As she watched her handing them to them, Eleanor wondered if Vanessa was remembering as she was the ones she had torn up.

'And to think I was actually looking forward to coming home,' Vanessa protested ten minutes later as Tom and Gavin quarrelled over who was going to show her all the work which had been done on the house.

Registering that very natural and heartwarming use of the word 'home', Eleanor turned to them and told them equally, 'I'm sure Vanessa would prefer her father to show her, not you two. Haven't you both got homework to do anyway?'

'No, it's OK,' Vanessa interrupted easily. 'They can show me to-morrow. I mean, Dad might forget about the fish, mightn't he?'

'I can't believe how much she's changed,' Marcus said quietly to Eleanor later.

'She's growing up. She's not really a little girl any more.'

'No, she isn't,' Marcus agreed sombrely.

'She still needs you, though, Marcus...'

He reached out for her, drawing her gently to his side and wrapping her tenderly in his arms, dropping a kiss on the end of her nose before telling her softly, 'She still needs *us*, Nell.

'*You* are my home, just as you're Tom and Gavin's—and Vanessa's as well...and I think she knows it.

'One day when she's older I hope she'll recognise as I do how lucky we've both been to find someone whose heart is big enough for both of us.'

Upstairs in her room, Vanessa unpacked her things. The first thing to come out of her suitcase, the last thing she had put in in New York, was her photograph wallet. She scanned her new bedroom quickly for a moment and then smiled as she found what she wanted.

Eleanor had protested when she had insisted on bringing it with her, but she had stood firm, and now, as she walked over to the noticeboard Tom had made for her, she tossed her hair back off her face, concentrating as she extracted the photographs from the wallet one by one and pinned them in place.

Her father; her mother all made up and dressed for her film role; the boys; a group of friends from school; some new ones of Jade and finally the last one...one she had filched from Eleanor's photograph album five minutes before she had left for the airport.

Carefully she pinned it up in the middle of the board. In it, Eleanor was standing next to her father, looking up at him, her love for him shining in her eyes.

'Who's this, then?' one of the boys she had met in New York had asked her, studying the photograph.

'It's my father and——' she had begun, but he had cut her short, giving her a would-be louche leer and exclaiming,

'Yeah, your mom's a good-looking woman. You look a lot like her.'

It hadn't seemed necessary or important to tell him that Eleanor wasn't her mother; instead she had treated him to the very female and old-fashioned look she had just perfected.

There was no need for him to think *she* was taken in by his flattery. She bet he said that kind of thing to every girl he met.

She might tell Nell about him later, she decided, when they were on their own.

Humming under her breath, she opened her bedroom door and ran downstairs.

'Nell, I'm hungry,' she complained as she opened the kitchen door. 'Is there anything to eat...?'

Grown-up! Not really. Not yet, Eleanor reflected as she informed her that she could eat whatever she could find in the fridge, pointing out that she wasn't running a twenty-four-hour canteen service.

It wasn't too late. There was still time for them to get to know one another, to learn to love one another. After all, they already had the best start they could have: they already shared their love for Marcus.

For better or for worse; they were a family and somehow she had a very, very strong and hopeful feeling that it was going to be for better.